IT'S YOUR MOVE, WORDFREAK!

FALGUNI KOTHARI

eBook ISBN: 978-1-944048-05-1
Paperback ISBN: 978-1-944048-06-8

Cover design by Ebook Launch
Formatting by Kate Tilton's Author Services, LLC

Previously published in India by Rupa Publications and Co. (2012)

To Saroj and Narendra, who gave me the world.
To Ajay, Jay and Anya, who enhance my world daily.

This first book is for you.

I...*N*...*S*...*A*...*N*...*I*...*T*...*Y*...

"Now there's a perfect bingo, *kutty!*" Alisha Menon admonished her towel-clad reflection in the full-length mirror adorning one buttercup yellow wall of her bedroom. The narcissistic contraption was encased in a broad wooden filigree frame inset with citrine stones. It was bold and beautiful.

The exact opposite of the image it outlined.

Alisha took stock of her reflection. Brown eyes rimmed with fatigue and dark circles. Pallid complexion. Ugh. She should make an effort to cover up the corpse-like skintone. Gaunt shoulders, courtesy of genetics and nature. She was definitely not one of the fairest in Mumbai—not that she wanted to be. She only ever aspired to be one of the smartest.

Ergo, how was it that everyone was suddenly doubting her intelligence?

"Stop it! You will not let them psych you. You've thought this through. You have a plan. Stick to it." With a final narrow-eyed nod at herself, Alisha turned away from the mirror before she chickened out.

Plucking a bottle of moisturizer from the dresser, she walked to the bed and sat down to replenish her skin. It was late February, and the sliding windows in her room were open to the balmy evening air. Faint sounds of traffic from below and a louder *I'd like to move it, move it* wafted in like a rhythmic breeze. Little Chucky from next door was watching *Madagascar* yet again, she thought, grinning.

Looks didn't matter. Only smarts did.

"And I'd like to prove it, prove it," she rapped in time with the music.

She'd been feeling sluggish and out of sorts all day. Understandable, as she was still recovering from a bout of flu from last week. And if her hands trembled as they massaged cream into her pores, she put it down to a bonus from the mini epidemic. She refused to credit her nervousness to the Big Date she was getting all dolled up for.

Alisha's stomach dropped at the thought of the dinner date. She pressed a hand against her belly as if to hold it in place. Was she "off her rocker" to have agreed to meet Word-freak as her best friend, Diya, so eloquently put it last night? Granted, she didn't know him well—not at all in reality. She only knew him by way of their intensely competitive, online Scrabble games, and fun and flirty chats. That he could very well be Jack the Ripper snaring his next hapless victim had been pointed out to her. But it did not feel like that. *He* did not feel like that.

Damn it. She wasn't going to second-guess her decision. She was going on the bloody date.

Arguably, how could a blind date be any less or more risky than a random meeting between two people on a dating App, or at a club or a party, or, for that matter, inside a book shop? Really, even a family-arranged match had to...

Her iPhone jingled a merry marimba tune, cutting off her thoughts and quickening her pulse. He'd changed his mind.

He was calling to cancel, or—*Get a grip, Alisha. He doesn't have your phone number, remember?*

Alisha rolled her eyes at herself, then at the phone which displayed MOM in bold on the caller ID. She set the instrument aside without answering it, deciding that Savitri Menon could wait until morning to voice her angst—again—at her daughter's aberrant and imprudent behaviour. By tomorrow, Alisha figured that either she would be proved right and Wordfreak would be all that she hoped he would be—picture a taller, copiously younger version of Shah Rukh Khan. Or they—her mother, brother, best friend, neighbor and neighbor's dog—would be right and Alisha would have allowed her not-usually-impulsive-self to be mugged, raped, kidnapped, brutally murdered, or a combination thereof. They could all come and gloat while picking up her pieces.

Stop the insanity and just move it, move it! She was going to meet him, and that was that.

Stripping off the towel, Alisha donned the flowy blue dress she'd borrowed from her fashionista BFF. She turned this way and that, critiquing herself from every angle until she caught her own eyes again and grimaced. Diya would be so amused to see her like this—expectant, flustered. She wondered if she was going on the date just to prove a point. No, it wasn't. It was the promise of the man she'd met online. She needed to see if she'd been right.

Makeup application took two minutes flat. Practiced strokes of powdered foundation over her face, slashes of blush on her cheeks, colorless mascara curling her lashes, and a swipe of shiny sweet gloss on her lips.

Heels? Nope. What if he wasn't tall? Better stick with the flat silver Roman sandals as she stood five feet eight inches in her bare feet.

With one last critical look in the mirror, Alisha picked up

her purse and stumbled out of her South Mumbai apartment with butterflies in her stomach and two possibilities.

THE UBER ROLLED to a stop outside the pre-selected destination. Alisha paid the fare in cash, directed the tobacco-chewing Uber driver to keep the change, and climbed out of the incense-filled cab to take a long breath of fresh air. Although, Mumbai's air quality wasn't much of an improvement.

She checked her watch. She was a half-hour early. Perfect.

Red-brick walls flanked a pair of thick, wooden doors, making up the outer façade of the rustic-looking, yet trendy, little café on Juhu Road. A tiny sign on the right wall displayed its name: Mirch Masala Café. Giving her a lazy salute, a uniformed *chowkidaar* opened the doors, and Alisha walked into what was essentially a rain forest. The place had been designed in a plethora of earth tones—taupe, brown and green mingled with swirls of red, black and orange. Accent lighting added atmosphere to the lush paradise. A wet bar curved along the right side of the entrance, and every single bar stool was occupied. So were most of the tables. Not a surprise as the café was one of Mumbai's current hotspots.

To her left, a waterfall trickled into a rocky pool filled with fat orange fish. Flowers and foliage abounded—mini palm trees, orchids, daylilies and birds of paradise, all creatively arranged in gigantic ceramic planters and placed randomly around the café. Servers in crisp red and black uniforms were rushing to and fro from the kitchen at the back with practiced efficiency.

The restaurant's host smiled in welcome. "Good evening, Madam. Do you have a reservation?"

"Yes, it's under Wordfreak." Goodness, that sounded

weird. She cleared her throat. "I'm early. I don't think he... um, my friend is here yet. But I wouldn't mind being seated now." By the time she finished speaking, her heart and stomach were doing summersaults. Seriously, why was she putting herself through this?

The host ran a finger across the reservation book in front of him. "Here's your reservation. Ah! Your party's here already. You won't have to wait, Madam." He smiled, looking pleased.

Alisha gaped at him. She could not have heard right. Did he say her party was here already? *Ohmygodohmygodohmygod!* Her organs were no longer flipping summersaults; they were trying to leap out of her body. She was going to pass out, surely.

"This way, Madam." The man spun on his heel and led her into the restaurant.

She followed like a robot, horrorstruck by the turn of events. *She* was supposed to have been the early one. It had been *her* plan to wait and observe and scram if Wordfreak looked even the least bit fishy. Now what was she supposed to do?

There she was!

Aryan Rajaram Chawla stared at the tall, striking woman in blue coming his way. He gulped water once, twice and then for a third time, hoping to ease his nerves. He was positive the woman was Worddiva. There she was, the phrase had leaped into his mind like an epiphany as soon as he'd seen her.

He stood up as she neared. Her eyes—irises a delicious dark chocolate brown—grew round and wide when she saw him. She looked surprised—no, she seemed as stunned as he was feeling.

"Madam." The restaurant host held her chair as she took her seat. Actually, Worddiva plopped down awkwardly because her eyes were glued to his.

Aryan sank into his own chair, drinking in the wonder of Worddiva. He hadn't expected her to be tall. They would look good together. Aryan felt an absurd urge to laugh at his good fortune. He cleared his throat, preparing to launch into the greeting he'd memorized. Her gaze sharpened on his face, and her lips—fuck. Her pink tongue snuck out and swiped over her luscious lips. He was going to embarrass himself before he even said hello, he thought, as heat shot through his body.

He managed a watery "Hi!" without croaking, drooling or sliding into a brainless puddle.

Her answer was to close her eyes and mumble wordlessly. *Was she praying?* She also seemed to be having trouble breathing; her breaths were coming out in puffs.

"Isn't this amaz..." he began, but was abruptly cut off when she bolted. There was no other word for it. She shot out of her chair and dashed to the other side of the room, dodging several waiters along the way, leaving him and everyone else gawking after her.

What just happened? Aryan snapped his mouth shut. Had she taken one look at him, decided she hated him and run straight home? But...*why?* Not to seem conceited, but he was considered a good catch. He was good-looking, mannerly, a charmer even. He'd never repelled a woman before.

Confused, Aryan looked down at her empty seat, and whooshed out a breath of relief when he spied a silver evening bag on the Wenge wood table. She hadn't run if she'd left her bag. She'd simply needed to use the bathroom. But why hadn't she just said so instead of scaring him half to death with her hit-and-run act? Women, Aryan shook his head philosophically, were from Venus. A man wasn't meant to understand them.

She was lovely. Whatever he'd imagined Worddiva to look like, she surpassed all his expectations. She had a dusky rose complexion that looked amazing in the strappy blue dress. Her features were delicate, almost waif-like, for such a statuesque woman. And her eyes—those gorgeous chocolate eyes—had nearly swallowed her face as she'd stared at him.

The head server approached the table and Aryan returned his smile. "Sir, we have something new on the wine list. It will be to your taste," said Baban.

Being a regular patron at the restaurant, Baban knew Aryan's preferences well. The café was one of his go-to restaurants with an innovative farm-to-table menu, and when Worddiva had suggested they meet there, Aryan had thought it was serendipity. He wondered if she lived in the vicinity, or close by in Bandra, like him.

"Give me a few minutes. I don't know what the lady wants yet," Aryan replied.

"Take your time, Sir." Baban left the menus on the table and vanished like a genie into a bottle. The service at the café was impeccable.

Aryan waited for Worddiva, drumming his fingers on the table whilst waiting. When that didn't help, he began passing his finger across the flame of the tea light in the middle of the table. Baban strolled in Aryan's direction again, but spun around and marched away when Aryan glowered.

He wondered if he should look in on her, ask if everything was okay. But no, if he knew anything at all, he knew she would not appreciate being fussed over. Worddiva was a fiercely independent lady.

When she eventually emerged from the bathroom, she looked refreshed and composed. Aryan felt his lips twitch in amusement. Serenity emanated from Worddiva's bearing.

Gone were the shocked expression and uneven gait from before, she looked ready to take on the world.

"Sorry to keep you waiting," she said, not looking apologetic in the least. She took her seat again, drawing the length of her gorgeous hair over one shoulder. "I wasn't well last week and…everything was just too much." She gulped down half a glass of water, primly wiping her mouth with a napkin, then finally, she looked him dead in the eye.

"You…are…Wordfreak, right?" she asked, clearly needing a verbal confirmation.

He was having a hard time believing his luck too, but he'd pinched himself already.

"I am. And no need to apologize. We all have our moments," he said, turning up the charm.

Worddiva's eyes flicked to his face, then she rolled them up to the ceiling, mocking herself or him or both of them. And just like that, she bowled him over.

This was the woman he had come to meet. *This* was the woman who had haunted his days, plagued his nights, for the last five months. The impish, politically incorrect yet socially driven, spectacularly funny female who had argued and debated and called him a fool so many times he'd lost count.

Their online chats were enchanting; their Scrabble competitions, exhilarating. She'd captivated him even before he'd laid eyes on her. And now? Now, she'd knocked him flat out.

"What's your name?" he demanded. He wanted to know. He *had* to know.

She leaned back in her chair, worrying her fleshy bottom lip as she considered his question. Had he sounded too harsh? Too aggressive?

"Let's leave it at Wordfreak and Worddiva for now. Just until it's a little less embarrassing?" she said.

"There's nothing to be embarrassed about." He wanted to

kiss her. Didn't she understand? How could he ask to kiss her if he didn't even know her name?

"We are complete strangers. Of course it's embarrassing." Her cheeks pinkened.

Now he really wanted to haul her into his lap and kiss her senseless, their real names be damned. Jesus. Where had his inner Neanderthal been hiding? He'd always considered himself a gentleman.

"We're hardly strangers after all the things we've chatted about in the last few months. I think we understand each other rather well."

"That's oversimplifying things. Chatting through the buffer of a computer doesn't count. The reality…the physical reality of meeting you is a little overwhelming. For me, at least." The chocolate pools of her eyes begged him to let it go.

"Fine. Have it your way. For now."

Aryan squashed down his impatience because she was right. They were virtual strangers, even if they'd been chatting almost every night for the last few months. The anonymity that type of communication afforded had given them a false sense of security, an illusory level of comfort. They'd exchanged no names, no information, no personal baggage of any sort. It had been wonderfully freeing.

But now that he'd seen her, he couldn't imagine going back to the…faceless, nameless dance they'd been performing.

"What will you have to drink?" Since Baban was hovering close enough to listen, he sprang to attention when Aryan spoke.

"I'll start with a mushroom soup followed by the *paneer tikka* panini." She'd given her order without bothering to open the menu, confirming his suspicion that she did indeed frequent the café.

"Nothing to drink? How about a white to go with the panini? Or would you prefer a cocktail?"

She shook her head. "Water's fine. I...ah...rarely drink alcohol."

Aryan blinked. Wow. He didn't think he knew anyone who didn't drink at least wine. "Got it," he said, and proceeded to order a glass of Louis Jadot, Beaujolais '07, at Baban's recommendation, for himself, and his dinner choices —a garden vegetable soup and the chicken casserole.

"Is it a religious thing?" he asked as soon as Baban left. She completely fascinated him.

"It's a my-body-cannot-tolerate-alcohol sort of thing," she drawled, mischief lighting up her face.

The cheeky woman had imitated his faint but discernable Harry Potter accent, although very badly. "Well, that's a shame, innit?" he teased back, winking at her.

She laughed outright, then shrugged. "I drink on occasion. It just doesn't suit me. I get weird."

"Ah." Getting weird sounded like a lawsuit waiting to happen.

"I'm also a vegetarian." She flicked the non sequitur at him like the stub of a finished cigarette.

God did have the strangest sense of humor. The perfect woman was sitting right in front of him, telling him that she wasn't only imperfect but may be his polar opposite.

"Will you have a problem with the chicken at the table?"

"Not at all. Just thought I'd mention it." Suddenly, her eyes narrowed on his face. "How old are you?"

Aryan clenched his jaw tight to keep from laughing. He knew where this was going. He already knew that Worddiva was twenty-eight, but he'd never disclosed his age to her. Very early in their games, she'd snidely remarked how stupid and childish men were in their twenties. Incapable of mature decisions and serious conversation, she'd said. So, he'd purposely hidden his own pitifully puerile age from her.

"Nearly twenty-six. Why?" A small white lie. He'd turned twenty-five only a month ago.

Now, she looked appalled. Aryan burst out laughing, thoroughly enjoying her dismay.

"Are you serious?" She looked ready to bolt again.

But he wasn't going to let her escape. It had taken him two months to get her to meet him in person. She had better stay for the full date or he'd have to call fowl.

"It's not a big deal."

"Maybe not for you," she retorted. "It is to me."

"So I'm two years younger than you. So bloody what?" He arched his eyebrows.

"Three years. Goodness! You're a baby!"

More like three and a half years, but he wasn't admitting that, yet.

"Do you want to see how completely un-babyish I am?" The double entendre was crude, but he couldn't help it. He was annoyed.

"Don't be an ass. And you just proved my point with your infantile high school humor." She raised an imperious eyebrow of her own as if to put him in his place.

Aryan threw up his hands. "What has age got to do with anything? Besides, you didn't seem to mind my high school humor before. If I recall correctly, you happily participated in it."

Their soups arrived, putting a welcome dent in the debate.

ALISHA HAD NEVER BEEN MORE DUMBFOUNDED in her life. Wordfreak had sounded so wise and perceptive online, not at all like a twenty-five year old…boy. Her imagination had also failed her because she definitely hadn't imagined him as dropdead gorgeous. He was as tall as her brother—taller. Over six feet, she'd bet. The striped shirt and dark pants were incredibly flattering to his broad, masculine physique, and rather grown up. And everytime she looked at his face…

Alisha shivered involuntarily. Goodness! What was wrong with her? It couldn't be because of him. It was a reaction to the influenza, surely. Her usual composure had been thrown for a toss in her weakened state. Yes, that was it.

She took a bite of the buttered bread and washed it down with hot, creamy soup as steam rose in fragrant invitation from the bowl. The food steadied her a little, warming the frozen wasteland of her brain.

She could not get over what was happening. Her head could not wrap itself around two blazing facts: Wordfreak was movie-star handsome, and he was only twenty-five years old. So not what she'd imagined. Okay now, everyone knew that her stupid fantasies about SRK were just that—stupid fantasies. In truth, she had expected Wordfreak to be a smart, glib man of average looks; a nerd whose attractiveness would be his quick brain and conversational skills. What she'd got was all of that in a package that was better suited for an action movie.

Alisha ate more soup. It seemed like the safest option.

Diya would probably laugh at her, reproach her for looking a gift horse in the mouth. Alisha supposed it was true. Who would not appreciate the fabulous turn of events? Here she was, sitting in front of the man she had clicked with so brilliantly on the World Wide Web, on a first date that was going surprisingly well despite certain revelations, and he looked like some kind of X-rated fantasy come to life. Yet, was she focusing on those stellar points? No. She, Alisha Menon, was focusing on the one drawback in this karmic extravaganza—his age. Or a lack thereof.

She shot him a glance from beneath her lashes. He was busy eating too. She ran her tongue over her teeth for any wayward basil, found none, and cleared her throat. When he looked up, she smiled.

"How is it?"

"Great, as always," he answered after swallowing eagerly.

"You've been here before." Of course he had. It was a popular place.

"I come here once a week or get takeout. It's one of my favorite eateries."

They had similar taste in restaurants too, it would seem. "Oh, so you live around here?" She slipped the personal question right in like croutons in her soup.

"Close enough," he answered cryptically, then spoiled it by grinning. Delightful dimples winked inside his cheeks.

Alisha fought to keep her jaw from dropping into her soup. The man had dimples. Like SRK. Like John Abraham. Goodness gracious! Had God not made him beautiful enough—chiselled cheekbones, a defined jawline, a mop of jet black hair—that he'd been granted sexy little dimples too?

"Why do you have a British accent?" That's the way, *kutty*. Impress him with dumb questions.

He'd demolished his soup, so he pushed the bowl aside and picked up his wine glass. "I lived in London until I was thirteen, and went back there for university."

His laser-sharp eyes bored into hers and Alisha suppressed a shiver. "What did you study?"

"Civil engineering and architecture." Even his fingers were beautiful, wrapped around the wine glass as he swirled it around and around hypnotically.

"How fascinating," she murmured, feeling rather hypnotized. "What made you...what? Why are you shaking your head?"

"My turn to ask questions," he said, taking a long swallow of his wine.

That was only fair. Alisha ceded the floor to him.

"I know you work long hours." He squinted at her as if trying to guess her vocation.

"I'm a lawyer. A divorce lawyer," she clarified before he asked what kind, and started laughing at his bemused expression. His presumptions about her clearly hadn't taken him towards divorce law.

"Do you like what you do? I mean…Jesus. Can I even ask that?" He looked uncomfortable, so Alisha took pity on him.

"It's not about liking or not liking what I do. I'm good at it." Being a successful divorce lawyer wasn't something to brag about even if she was proud of her accomplishments. Five divorce cases on average every month for five years, that's how good she was. "I specialize in out-of-court mediation. I don't believe long drawn out, finger pointing battles in family court serve any purpose."

Most couples seeking a divorce agreed that settling their grievances across a conference room table was easier and healthier for all concerned parties, especially if children were involved. But every once in awhile, a case came along that became needlessly complicated because of an idiot's ego. The Kumar case was such a travesty, and Mr. Kumar was a boorish, stubborn ass.

"I draw up wills and contracts too, some estates and trusts. But it's mostly divorce."

"Why divorce law?" Wordfreak had aimed straight for the bull's eye and hit the mark. Bravo.

Alisha pushed her own empty soup bowl away and sat back in her chair. She'd agreed to meet him. She liked him. She wanted—needed him to know her boundaries before they went any further.

"My parents separated when I was eleven. It left an

impression. My father got everything, including custody of two small children who needed their mother and whom my father could not possibly care for because that's not what fathers do. It's not their job."

Bile flooded her mouth at the bitter memories. Her father had pulled strings to get the divorce to work in his favor and to punish his wife, to make her life unbearable because she'd dared to leave him.

"He died before the divorce became final. He was an alcoholic. That's why my mother left him. My mother had a wonderful advocate. She inspired me towards law." Alisha wondered why she was telling Wordfreak about her parents before she'd even told him her name.

"I don't suppose you believe in happily-ever-afters, do you, love?" he asked softly.

She turned cold at his astuteness. He'd gotten to the crux of her fear in one conversation. How did he do it? How could a virtual stranger understand her so well?

Alisha wanted to say something flippant and snarky but Wordfreak deserved to hear the truth.

"I suppose not."

DURING THE BRIEF EXCHANGE, Aryan saw Worddiva rebuild a fortress around herself, brick by brick, adding a steel panic room around her heart for good measure. She'd never be vulnerable again, she was telling him. No wonder she'd felt familiar to him even across the darkness of the Web. They were exactly the same.

Aryan wanted to gather her up in his arms. He wanted be her hero and slay her demons—not that she'd allow him. He wanted her father to resurrect so he could punch the crap out of the asshole.

Another thing they had in common—buggering bastards

for fathers.

"I lost my mum when I was thirteen," he confessed without preamble. He didn't want her to suffer alone, but when Baban arrived with their meals, Aryan was relieved for the reprieve.

"I'm sorry," she said softly while Baban prepared the table, refilled their glasses.

Aryan dipped his head in acknowledgement, wondering if he could stop there. If it was enough. But it wasn't, was it?

"She found out that my father was having an affair, then she…" Fuck. Even this much was hard to get out without choking after all these years. His fortress wasn't nearly as formidable as he'd thought. Maybe he needed a panic room too. He squeezed the butt of his fork hard enough that his knuckles turned white. "After her death, I was shipped off to Mumbai to live with my grandmother."

Aryan dropped the fork he was strangling with a jerk when Worddiva's hand covered his knuckles. Reluctantly, he looked at her. The empathy shining on her face as she reached across the table to comfort him made the tightness in his chest ease a bit. He turned his hand over, lacing their fingers together. He'd dreamed of touching her, holding her, and he couldn't believe it was happening. Her hand was soft, her grip strong. A solid foundation despite the leak in the roof.

He forced himself to shake off the morbid and bring some sunshine into their conversation. It was a date, for God's sake, not a grief counseling session. He rubbed a thumb over her knuckle suggestively. She narrowed her eyes. He winked with just a hint of a leer. She gave a droll look, and tried to pull her hand away. He wouldn't let her go, lawsuit be damned.

"Let go," she ordered, struggling to free her right hand from his grip.

"I feel so sad." He made a sad face. "I need sympathy and coddling."

"I'll give you coddling. Let go!"

"Don't be mean." He held on.

"Our dinner is getting cold. We should eat." She changed tack, cajoled like a lawyer.

"Eat with your other hand. It's only a sandwich," he suggested, digging into his casserole. Did she think he'd fold so easily? "*Hmm. Spicy and crusty and so good.*" He smacked his lips.

"Quit being cute, Wordfrrrr…" she shut her mouth, startled by what she'd been about to call him.

"Ready to exchange names, yet?" he cooed.

Her blush raced across her cheeks and neck, and still the stubborn woman wouldn't give in.

"Don't be a child. Let me go." She dug her nails into his skin. Not hard, but he let go.

Mission accomplished. Ms. Sunshine with the sharp tongue was back, albeit a tad frazzled.

The rest of the dinner passed by in quick-witted banter and some suggestive talk—mostly on his part. Boys would be boys, after all. But he knew how to toe the line. The highlight of the evening was the look on her face—awestruck and impressed—when John Abraham stopped by their table to say hello. Her eyes nearly popped out of their sockets when she realized that, not only did he know John well—they'd shaken hands and given each other manly backslaps over recent individual accomplishments—but he was also building a weekend house for the movie star in Alibaug. And then, John called him by his bloody given name and bloody outed him.

Worddiva refused to reveal hers even then.

CHAPTER 2

*A*lisha Menon, divorce lawyer and happily-ever-after skeptic, stared out of her office's sliding windows, a dreamy smile pasted on her face. She couldn't stop smiling. She hadn't stopped since the date last night.

His name was Aryan.

Humming a romantic tune while smiling, Alisha swivelled her faded blue executive chair back around to her desk, and tried to get her brain to focus on the work she'd been shamefully neglecting for the last two hours, ever since she'd waltzed into her office at her usual time at 9:00 a.m. sharp. She started reading the statement given by Jyoti Kumar's sister, Sheela, a few days ago, reinforcing Jyoti's statement of the repeated marital abuse she'd suffered over the years. And as it had been happening all morning, the words on the page blurred, merged, and Aryan's obsidian eyes—magnetic and enigmatic—floated on the paper. Alisha swivelled back to the window. It was useless trying to work until she stopped obsessing. It was insanity, what she was feeling.

She leaned forward, resting her hands and chin on the

windowsill, and gazed idly at the daily seen panorama outside. Waves of stone buildings clustered together like uneven teeth, lining the grid-fulls of narrow streets that bulged with humanity. Bridges rose and fell and curved towards the Queen's Necklace and the Arabian Sea beyond. Fearless foot vendors wove in and out of traffic jams, selling their wares at signals—books, incense, flowers, fruits—uncaring of the danger. The city clamored around them, filling the air with the sounds of temple bells, car horns, wheel squeaks, the pigeons on the roofs. Oh, she loved it all—the energy, the chaos, the vitality of Mumbai.

Alisha rested her forehead against the window, willing away the ennui her infatuation had created. Was it infatuation? Yes, it was. She wouldn't lie to herself. She was greatly attracted to him. She had been drawn to him even before she'd met him. Their chats had often stimulated her into a similar state of euphoria. She had laughingly called their chats "a virtual aphrodisiac," an online "lust-a-fest." But the reality of Wordfreak—of Aryan was so much more compelling.

Her mobile phone rang, saving her from madness. She twisted around, picked it up. "Hello!"

"You answered on the first ring, which means you're not in a meeting. Or dead, proving Wordfreak wasn't a dastardly or dangerous character. Tell me, tell me, tell me everything about your date, Leesha!" Diya Mathur was nothing except exuberance on legs.

Oh, Wordfreak wasn't dastardly, but he was definitely dangerous.

"Tell me! Or is there nothing to tell? I knew it. I know how these Internet hookups work. All talk and no show. Didn't I tell you? Would you listen? What happened? Say something. How awful was it?" Diya blathered on without pause.

Alisha shook her head. "If you shut up and let me speak, I'll tell you."

"Zipping it now." Diya didn't say anything for a couple of seconds and Alisha took that to mean it was her turn. She opened her mouth to speak, but Diya beat her to it. "And don't leave anything out. Give me all the juicy details. Or should I say the un-juicy details of the flop date? He was horrible, wasn't he? Ugly, short, nasty body odor, warts all over his face, oozing creepy Jack-the-Ripper vibes, right?"

Alisha ignored Diya's outburst. "How come you didn't call me last night? I was expecting to spill my guts to you."

"Had a thing that went on till late. Then the troupe went to an after-party. Yada yada. Stop avoiding the convo, Leesha. Tell me everything."

"Not avoiding anything except your big ugly nose," Alisha said with a grin.

"Hey!" Diya's outrage was immediate and loud. She was touchy about her nose, especially since she'd taken up modeling full-time.

"Fine. Are you sitting down? He's..." Alisha built up the suspense to nail-biting levels before adding, "Great!"

There was an anticlimactic "Huh?" from Diya, followed by an explosion of questions. "Great? What does that even mean? What was so great about him? Be specific. Wait! Are you saying you actually *liked* him?"

It was shocking, Alisha had to admit. It was hard to meet a decent guy these days. Harder still to like him. And trusting a guy? *Pfft.* Forget it.

"The question, dear friend, is not what was so great about Wordfreak/Jack/Aryan, but what wasn't great about him." The ridiculous statement earned another nasal "Huh?"

"Never mind." Alisha flapped her hand in the air, cutting off the ridiculous conversation before it deteriorated further. "Wordfreak, a.k.a Aryan, is gorgeous, stupendous, amazing and… He's only twenty-five years old." Her excitement deflated slightly then.

"What?" Diya screeched.

"Yup." Alisha was torn between hopping up on her desk and gyrating for all she was worth—and she didn't even like to dance—or, feeling bummed about the age factor.

"OMJeez, you're not kidding. How? Why? I mean… Wow!"

"Don't know. Don't care. Well, I do care about his age, but let's set that aside for a minute and rejoice in the fact that not all men are douchebags. What this proves, Ms. Skeptic-about-all-things-web-based, is that Wordfreak is more than what I expected, and the total opposite of what you expected and he… Did I mention he's only twenty-five?"

There wasn't even a squeak out of Diya. Apparently, she'd been rendered speechless. Taking full advantage of the minor miracle, Alisha launched into a delicious breakdown of her date, sparing nothing—words, moments or details.

"No way! He knows John Abraham?" Diya whispered in a suitably awestruck tone.

"Yup."

"Wow! Leesha, you've hit the jackpot."

"Well, I don't know about that. He *is* only twenty-five…"

"Will you shut up about his age?"

"That's easy for you to say since he's not going to be *your* boy—" Alisha shut her mouth. Goodness. She'd almost called him her boyfriend after just one date.

Diya had no such time restraints. "Boyfriend? Boy toy? Potential lover? Significant other? Marriage prospect? All of the above?"

"Control yourself, Dee." If hearts could dance, hers was breakdancing inside her chest. It was supposed to have been a dud date, Alisha thought. He could still turn out to be a douche.

She sighed. Who was she trying to convince? She'd always been attracted to him, even before she'd laid eyes on him.

"Wait a minute. What did you say his name was?" Diya asked.

"Aryan." Of the obsidian eyes and dimpled cheeks. Alisha pressed a hand to her cheek, remembering the warmth of his large hand against hers. She'd tingled all over with that simple touch.

"Aryan Chawla, the architect. You said he was designing a vacation home for Johnny boy, so it has to be Aryan Chawla of Prithvi Homes. OMJeez! Leesha, do you even know who he is? He's that wonder-kid that designs green homes," Diya trilled.

"Who?" Alisha grimaced. "And how do you expect me to go out with him if you call him a kid?"

"Wonder-kid. There's a difference. Anyway, you can be so clueless. Wake up and smell Page 3, darling."

"What?" The Page 3 section of the newspaper wasn't something Alisha read. She secretly thought all the humans who graced that page belonged on some far away planet completely alien to her. Aryan was one of those glitzy society people? Hadn't she known he was too good to be true?

"You have no idea what I'm talking about, do you?" asked Diya.

"Nope, and seriously don't care to. How you can read that rubbish, and deal with those snobs, I'll never understand."

"Forget all that. Does he look as good in person? He's absolutely hunky in print." Diya sounded like she was having a cardiac arrest. She was panting very hard.

"What's wrong with you? Did I give you my flu?"

"No, no," Diya huffed out. "I'm running back up to my flat. Want to check if I've got it right."

"It's not urgent, Dee. Wait. Why are you running up six flights of stairs? Is the building elevator not working again?"

Diya wheezed like Darth Vader. "No. Exer…cise. Mah mor…ning exer…cise."

Oh brother. "Then, for heaven's sake stop talking. At least until you can breathe again."

Diya worshipped at the altar of the fitness gods. To be fair, her profession depended on looking good, and she took that to heart and worked her pores out. The beauty gods had seen fit to grace her with abundant gorgeousness—fair, supple skin, a rosebud mouth, straight, shiny hair, and a long and elegant, though slightly snooty, neck. Giving weight to all of that was Diya's innate sense of style.

Alisha put the phone on speaker and stood up to stretch, her bones making soft popping sounds as they eased. Twisting left then right, she let out a groan as her lower back rotated, lengthened and rearranged itself into a much more comfortable position.

If Diya was right, and Alisha rather thought she was, then Wordfreak was some hotshot Page 3 dude. So, the question was, what could she possibly do with a twenty-five-year-old hotshot? A slew of naughty possibilities rolled through her mind, burning her cheeks.

Truthfully, she'd never been this strongly attracted to a man before. They'd hit it off right from their first Scrabble game where she'd beat him with a tile-thumping two hundred and sixty points. That had put Wordfreak's— Aryan's, she had to start thinking of him as Aryan—back up and he had promptly challenged her to another game. She won the second one too. And a third and fourth, and then her luck had turned. He'd won the next couple of games.

Playing one match after another had opened the doors to chatting. Initially about online word games, and the books they'd read, and would recommend the other read. One thing had led to another, and soon they found that they could chat for hours, and they honestly enjoyed the repartee.

Alisha didn't have many friends. It wasn't that she was unduly shy or an introvert. She was simply cautious about who she let into her life. With Wordfreak, trust hadn't been an issue. Her natural reticence hadn't reared up because he wasn't real, or so her mind kept rationalizing. Their friendship had bloomed quickly within the confines of hidden identities. Until two months ago, they hadn't even known they both lived in Mumbai.

"I'm back!" Diya's voice oozed through the speaker, minus the huffing. "Googling him as we speak. I know I'm right. I just want to make sure. Did you look him up?"

"I don't use my office computer for personal business." The truth was she didn't want to know anything more about him. She didn't want to wake up from her dream. She wanted him to remain anonymous. It was safer that way. And foolish, she thought, sighing.

"Hang on. It's loading…slowly. Ah, here we go. Annd… I was right!" Diya exulted in the corroborated evidence.

"So what?" Alisha shrugged. "I already knew he was an architect."

"So what? Honey, you are so far out of your league with this guy you might as well speak Russian. Look him up, for heaven's sake!" Diya tsk-tsked, then added, "Okay, here's our new plan. Fairy Godmother Diya to the rescue. We must go shopping. Can you finish early? I'll pick you up from your office."

"Were you possessed by a Dementor in the last twenty-four hours?" The question was purely academic. Wordfreak would have sent her a high-five emoji for her clever Potter reference.

"He's a regular on Page 3!"

And that was supposed to induce her to ditch work and go shopping? "I'm not at all sure that's a good thing, gracing Page 3 regularly."

"Says you, Ms. Bookworm who hates to partay!" Diya said the word party like a gangster on Netflix. "Seriously, which self-respecting single woman in her twenties refuses to paint the town pink? All you do is work, Leesha. You work beyond your billable hours most days, and you still take work home to finish. You're surrounded by stacks and stacks of papers, and you still spend most nights all alone reading for pleasure. And you're asking me if I'm demented? Would you let your hair down for once and just enjoy doing something spontaneous and outrageous, something that cannot be bound and printed? I promise it will not lead to the next mass extinction of brain cells."

It was an old argument between them, and more or less true. Though, she wasn't as big a party pooper as Diya let on. She knew how to have fun. And if she ever forgot, her best friend had her covered.

"Dee Dee," Alisha began but was rudely cut off.

"For some unfathomable reason, Providence has decided to drop that super scrumptious man into your lap and, you being you, will focus on two silly points, sweeping the other ninety-eight salient ones under the carpet. You make me so mad sometimes. I want to come there and smack some sense into you. I'll bet you didn't even kiss him."

"Um, Diya?" Alisha began when it seemed safe to do so. Diya grunted, but otherwise kept quiet, so Alisha said her piece. "Can I point out one tiny, really insignificant thing? My lifestyle, or a lack thereof, did, in fact, help me land Mr. Super Scrumptious though, didn't it?"

There was a noticeable gasp at the other end of the phone, then peals of laughter filled the fiber optic lines spanning between them.

"Oh, how I envy that quick wit of yours. I'm sorry, Leesh. I'm so sorry that I dissed your choices. I deserve a swift kick. Your lifestyle doesn't suck. Really. In fact—"

Uh-oh! Feeling another rant coming on, Alisha nipped it in the bud. "Got to go, Dee. Expecting a client soon. Talk to you later."

"Hey! Not so fast. When are you meeting him again? When am I meeting him?"

Crap! "Soon. Bye." Alisha disconnected the line cutting Diya's "Hey!" in half.

Sometimes rudeness could be excused, especially in defense of self-preservation.

"AND, what are you so cheerful about this afternoon? Well, evening now," Sameer Vaidya, co-owner and founder of Prithvi Homes, asked his nephew.

The nephew in question was bent at the waist over an angled drafting table slashing lines across a large sheet of graph paper, whistling while he worked. Aryan shot his *mamu* a wicked grin, prompting the older man to look at him even more curiously.

"I met someone," he confessed. Not that a grinning, whistling Aryan was such a rarity, still, today he felt deliriously happy. Because of her.

He would climb mountains for her. Swim across oceans. He would leap into the cloudless sky just to see her sweet face, and bask in its glory. Suddenly, he couldn't think about life in anything but hyperboles. Aryan threw back his head and laughed at his foolishness. The sudden burst of sound startled his uncle, resulting in coffee sloshing on his uncle's khakhis and the newspaper he'd been reading.

"What the hell!" His uncle sprang up from the office armchair with a curse.

"Shit. Sorry, Mamu." Aryan grabbed a handful of tissues and shoved them in his uncle's hands, who dunked the thick wad into a glass of water and began wiping at the stains on his pants.

Aryan bent back to preparing the preliminary designs for a two-thousand square foot apartment in South Mumbai. They would start work on the site within the month. The apartment was on the twentieth floor with an east-west layout, good light and crosswind. Best of all, he'd been given carte blanche on the budget so he could design it exactly as he envisioned it.

"Must have been some date."

Aryan slanted a grin at his *mamu*, who'd taken his seat again, minus the ruined newspaper which had been dumped along with the tissues. They'd just finished a meeting with a prospective client, and had decided to hang around the conference room to bounce off ideas for the new project.

"It was amazing." She was amazing. He couldn't believe his bloody luck in finding her.

"Anyone we know?"

Aryan's mouth kicked up in a cocky grin. "No one you know, Uncle Sam."

His uncle scowled at the *phirangi* moniker Aryan had bestowed upon him as a joke. Sameer Vaidya had become a diehard *desh bhakt* of late, voting at every election, expressing his liberal political opinions to anyone who cared to listen. Not many did, Aryan admitted, but did that stop Uncle Sam or his patriotism? Absolutely not. Only his sense of style— more GQ and no *khadi* whatsoever—kept his uncle from being tagged as a true "Gandhian."

Aryan's personal politics encompassed two nations since he'd spent the first half his life in the UK and the recent half in India. He retained a British citizenship, but had an Indian resident card. Loyalty was important, sure. But, if one was affiliated to two countries, Aryan figured he had enough loyalty for both, and some to spare. And if a conflict of interest arose, seek the universal truth.

She held some of the same convictions as Uncle Sam. And he was positive they'd get along like a house on fire. The thought of her meeting his family—Mamu, Nanu, everyone —had his heart pounding like a jungle drum.

He straightened from the desk and rolled his shoulders to ease the stiffness along his spine. Drawing floor plans by hand was stimulating, but also a pain in his shoulders.

Was he jumping the gun here? He didn't even know her name. If she didn't reveal her name tonight, he wasn't sure what he'd do. What could he do, really? It wasn't as if he had her phone number or knew where she lived. Frowning at his limited options, Aryan looked up to find his uncle watching him with some amusement.

"I haven't seen you this spaced out since…never. What the hell is going on, son?"

Aryan propped his hip on the edge of the table, crossing his arms across his chest. "I told you. I met someone. Someone rather special, it seems." He looked away, feeling as embarrassed as a groom on his wedding night.

It was happening too fast, whatever this was, and there seemed to be little he could do to control it. He wasn't sure he liked feeling so powerless. Yet, what could he do?

An eagle flew across the wall of windows, drawing his attention to the vast expanse of cloudless pink and purple sky. The eagle turned, gliding in a large circle, enhancing the beauty of a Mumbai sunset.

A loud whistle pierced the air. Aryan jerked back to attention.

"What is wrong with you? Have you suddenly developed ADHD?" Uncle Sam asked.

"Ha-ha. Funny, Mamu, really funny."

"What is the matter? Talk to me, Aryan." His uncle came to stand beside him.

"I like her. Too much. It's exciting. Yet, oddly daunting." He couldn't figure out if he was afraid of what she triggered in him or exhilarated as both of those emotions generated the same reaction—a high-speed race going on in his arteries and goose bumps popping up across his body. "She triggers something in me that no other woman has."

Aryan turned to the man who'd helped raise him, and shrugged. With only a decade separating them, they were more like brothers or buddies than uncle and nephew. There was nothing he couldn't tell Sameer Vaidya.

"Intense feelings can be terrifying," Uncle Sam said with a half smile.

"It's not lust." Aryan set his jaw. That is not what he felt for Worddiva. Not only.

His uncle blinked, clearly incredulous. "Are you saying it's love?"

Aryan's body went taut and the denial was immediate. "Of course not!" Not yet, anyway. He shook his head, more confused than ever. "How was it between you and Neeta Mami when you met? I remember you telling me that sometimes all it took was a look."

"Are you comparing your date to the moment I met my wife?" A speculative gleam appeared in Uncle Sam's eyes.

"Just answer, please. And leave the analysis for another day."

"Fine. It did take us only one look. And, of course, I was terrified. Sometimes I still am.'

Uncle Sam afraid? It was crazy. "Why?"

"Because marriage doesn't automatically take the fear away. Sometimes, it increases your fear because you have more to lose. Can it work? Will it work? Is it working? Is it enough? Is it worth it? You're constantly questioning the state of your relationship, and you have to work at surmounting the fears. Or ignoring them—although, ignoring doesn't necessarily work. It's hard to maintain a relationship, any relationship, and it takes time, dedication and commitment by all involved to sustain it. The ups and downs, the fights and make ups, it's as invigorating as it's frightening."

"Life is a roller coaster," Aryan murmured before the older man could.

"Absolutely. And, what a ride it takes you on!" Uncle Sam was a *bindaas* soul, a thrill seeker. He'd mellowed since his young and reckless days, but he still liked to get his kicks where he found them. "How did you meet her? Does Ma know?" he asked.

"You're the first to know. I'm not putting the cart before the horse by bringing Nanu into it, or Neeta Mami. By the way, I don't think Nanu is fine. She's been 'resting' a lot this visit. She tires easily, and you'll not believe this, she didn't want to cook the other day." That was not only shocking but worrisome. His grandmother lived to cook, and for her to not want to, that wasn't good.

"She's getting on in years, it's natural she's slow down," Uncle Sam replied.

"Are you sure that's all it is? She seems frail all of a sudden." Aryan hoped it was what his uncle said and not an onset of some old age-related medical problem.

His grandmother stayed with him for a week every month "to feed her sweet boy wholesome, home-cooked meals," even though she'd trained his household staff, including the cook, herself. It was an excuse to keep an eye on him, and everyone knew it.

Nanu hated the idea of Aryan rattling about alone in his flat. To tell the truth, he missed living at his uncle's too. There was something inherently cozy about being in a full house. But, it had been time for him to move out, especially after Lara and Riana were born—his little cousins were four and two, respectively. Space had become an issue since their births, privacy another. Not that Uncle Sam or Neeta Mami had made him feel like an extra—the opposite in fact—but, it had been time to spread his wings.

"If you're worried, I'll talk to her doctor and set up an appointment. Is that what this is about? Did she," Uncle Sam paused, his hand circled the air between them as if he was a DJ spinning a record at a nightclub, "set this up?"

"No. She hasn't brought any 'nice girls from good families' to my attention in a while. She's been behaving since the last time we both asked her to respectfully butt out of my life. It's nothing to do with Nanu." Aryan forked his hand through his hair, sliding it down to rub the back of his neck. In for a penny, in for a pound, he thought, and confessed it all. "It was sort of a blind date. Last night being the first one. Uh-uh. Let me finish before you start bombarding me with questions. While I've only met this girl in person once, we have been communicating for several months now."

"Did you swipe right on some dating app? Is that where you met her?"

"Not a dating app. A game app."

Uncle Sam groaned. "Is that wise in today's socio-political climate? Everything boils down to he said/ she said, son. It's not a safe time to meet anyone, much less a stranger online. Are you absolutely sure she doesn't know who you are?"

Aryan was sure. He'd run through the gamut of questions four months ago. "I'm not a complete moron, Mamu. She didn't know who I was until last night. And not everything is political. Look, I know apps and chatrooms must seem shady to a man of your age—"

"Watch it, son. I'm only a decade older. Hardly a fuddy duddy."

Aryan grinned, gesturing his uncle to take a seat as he took one next to it.

"Then hear me out," he said and proceeded to explain in vivid detail how he'd been matched with a super smart and snarky woman by the Scrabbulous app. How they'd been playing and chatting with each other for months before realizing they both lived in Mumbai. How he'd finally persuaded Worddiva to meet him. He didn't have to try hard. She'd wanted to meet him just as badly.

"You're not serious." Uncle Sam's eyebrows had shot up at the beginning of the saga and were glued there. Clearly, he had doubts about Aryan's sanity. No surprise there. Aryan had questioned it himself, many times, in the past few months.

"I'm as serious as a heart attack about her. It started out as fun and games. I mean, who the hell takes those chats seriously, right? I don't know when it changed. I don't know when it all started to mean something. No, I think it was that first time itself. We chatted all night long. Neither of us wanted to disconnect." Aryan still couldn't believe his good fortune. "To tell you the truth, I expected the bubble to burst last night. I went to meet her to put an end to the online idiocy. I was sure the real Worddiva would never match up to the woman my mind had conjured up."

"But, she did," Uncle Sam sighed.

"She's bloody wonderful, Mamu." Tara? Minal? Vandana? *What was her name?*

Aryan knew he was asking for the moon. She wasn't from their community, their circle of friends and family. She was a stranger—a lawyer. If he was wrong, it wasn't only his reputation on the line here.

"Fine," Uncle Sam said at last. "If you're sure about her, then I'm going to respect your decision."

Tension drained from Aryan's body. "Just like that?"

"Just like that." Uncle Sam broke into a boyish grin.

Bawling would be sissy-like, but Aryan felt his eyes sting nonetheless. "Thank you, Mamu. Do you know how completely great you are?"

"Of course, I do. But it doesn't hurt to keep hearing it. So, keep sucking up and I'll even make you a partner in Prithvi Homes some day."

As Aryan had already been promoted to partner the previous year, the winky joke only triggered hilarity between the men. Laughing, they stood up and embraced, slapping each other on the back. Aryan hugged his uncle hard as love squeezed his heart.

"So, when do we get to meet your Worddiva? What's her real name, by the way?" Mamu asked when they finally stepped back from each other.

"A rose is a rose, call it by any name," Aryan drawled since life was good. "I don't know her real name. She never told me."

He doubled over and laughed until his jaw hurt because Uncle Sam's slack-jawed expression was priceless.

*L*ater that night, as had been her routine since her first match with Wordfreak, Alisha got into bed, all snugly and warm, switched on her laptop and logged into the Scrabbulous app. When she saw that he wasn't online, the butterflies came raging back.

Damn that Wordfreak! He was playing havoc with her mind, her stomach lining and her professionalism. MT, a.k.a. Madhuri Tandon—Alisha's boss, mentor and honorary aunt —had caught Alisha daydreaming that afternoon, right in the middle of an important deposition. Alisha had blushed, stammered and tried desperately to get her aplomb back.

Wordfreak was holding her hostage in woo-woo land, and it just wouldn't do.

She rolled her shoulders to relieve the tension in her neck and spine. She spent too many hours hunched over a desk at work, and now she was hunched over her laptop, waiting for a guy. Pathetic.

Pushing back her mauve blanket, she got out of bed to pace around the room, shooting murderous looks at the laptop. What would she do if he never logged in to the game again? What if he was put off by her? By her profession or the fact that she came from a broken family. Had her candor put him off?

"What the hell is wrong with you?" She slapped herself, one slap on each cheek. "Are you truly getting worked up over a man? A mere man? A beauty queen from Page 3, no less?"

She grabbed a hairband from a basket on the shiny white dresser and pushed her oily mane off her face. Then she stomped over to her bed and checked his status. Drat it! Still offline. Why hadn't he logged on? He always, always, always logged on before her, waiting for her like a besotted, lovesick fool. She glared at the little red dot on the screen, willing it to flash green. Then suddenly it did. Alisha reeled back, blinking at it as if her eyes were playing tricks on her.

"Oh! Whew. Game on," she muttered, feeling mildly embarrassed by her tantrum.

Good evening, Worddiva.

Alisha quirked an eyebrow at the formal tone of his greeting. She flexed her fingers and typed back.

Good evening to you too, Wordfreak.

Go on, it's your move.

Her brows slammed together in the middle of her forehead as her fingers flew.

No, it isn't. Look at the board. It's your move.

Gotcha! Yes, I believe it's my move on the board. But since you insisted on keeping the ball in your court last night, it's your move with respect to our IRL game.

The man was too slick for his own good.

So, this is just a game to you?

**Shaking my head* I should have shut up while I was ahead.*

Alisha laughed out loud. He really should have. But then, who would she tease?

So, are you going to make a move anytime soon?

Do you want me to? ;)

Alisha bit her lip to keep from smiling. She had walked right into that one.

Yes, I would dearly love to finish THIS GAME tonight. With respect to the other game...the slower the better. She literally patted her back for the wicked comeback.

**Cough* Whatever you say, Sunshine. Your wish is my command.*

He'd started calling her Sunshine sometime over the past few months. She'd ignored it at first, but now she liked the nickname. A little too much perhaps.

He put down OUR on the board. A weak word. Had he put it down because he didn't have better tiles or was he getting some point across? She wouldn't put it past him to use the board as some kind of subliminal messaging system. Wordfreak was a sneaky bastard. Witness how he'd snuck into her brain and taken up residence. Sneaky. Too bad she didn't have the tiles to spell it and send her own covert messages.

She put down TRAY, making TRAY and YOUR and scored double the points he had.

How was your day? He wrote in the chatbox instead of making his next move.

Productive.

Good for you.

Then the wily bastard put down SNOOZIER and scored a zillion points.

Alisha mentally rolled up her sleeves, and settled in to annihilate him. She would not let him distract her with questions and sweet nothings tonight. Her TZARS brought her close to Aryan's score.

Nice! So, how many marriages did you break up today?

That wasn't very nice of you, she typed in response. Oh yes, he was feeling the pinch.

Just making conversation, but I'll shut up if you want me to.

You're trying to distract me, SneakFreak. I'm on to you.

You wound me, Sunshine. Would I ever play unfairly with you just to win a game?

You would and have before.

LOL! You've fallen for it before. What makes you think you won't tonight? He put down SPICES.

I've wised up. I'm not falling for you any longer.

Alisha froze as soon as she pressed enter. Shit. She splayed her fingers across the keyboard as if to grab the words back, making it blip madly. How had she made such a blunder? It was too much to hope that Aryan had overlooked it. Still…

That's a very intriguing statement you made there, Sunshine.

Yup, it had been too much to hope.

Oops. Lose the you *and replace it with an* it. Please God, let him leave it at that.

Not on your life.

Alisha sighed. It figured. When had God ever fulfilled any of her requests? She kicked off the blanket. She was starting to sweat despite the air-conditioning in her bedroom, despite only wearing flimsy pajamas and a faded grey tank top.

She put down HIM on the virtual board. He countered that with FE. Major bonus points to him as he wasn't mocking her about her faux pas. They shot off words like bullets for the next several minutes; her MEWED was followed by his OOF, and her JIN scored a lot more than his QI.

So, what did you mean exactly?

It was a typo. Get over it.

Didn't read as a typo.

You read far more into my statements, or non-statements, than is strictly normal. And, a gentleman would drop it.

Who says I'm a gentleman?

Obviously, I was mistaken.

LOL! You're a sourpuss today. Did you have a difficult day at work? Give me your phone number. I have a joke that'll cheer you up.

Alisha sucked in a mouthful of air and promptly started coughing. There it was, the Demand. Last night, he'd given in to her reticence over exchanging names or numbers, but no longer. She either moved forward or...?

And if I don't? She asked, playing YOW.

Yow indeed. How had she managed to squeeze herself between a rock and a hard place with Wordfreak standing right in front of her? Her mother was right. Where was her common sense?

Then we finish the game tonight. A short, succinct and not-so-sweet ultimatum.

He played PELT, and once more the ball was in her court.

Why was she yoyo-ing about taking their association further? She'd already jumped the first hurdle and met him, and it had been painless and promising. Shouldn't the next step be easier?

She put down ALONG. He made his move, YOB, but remained silent. His silence had the quality of a time bomb. She had until the end of the game, it said. She played BEER.

Do you like it? She made up her mind.

*What? Beer? *scratching head in confusion**

Alisha loved how he backed up his statements with picture painting words. She could almost visualize him scratching his head in confusion, his dark eyes opaque and leery.

Yes. Do you drink beer?

I do. What about you?

Come over for a drink.

*Now? Awesome! *flipping ecstatic summersaults in the air**

Alisha laughed at his goofiness. Well, that had been astonishingly simple.

No, silly man, tomorrow. Or...sometime. Call me, and we'll set it up.

Alisha bit the final bullet, and gave Aryan her cell number. Her hands went stiff after she pressed enter. She felt as if she'd just bungee jumped off a cliff. Oh God. Oh Goodness. Had she done the right thing? Could she trust him?

She really, really hoped so.

ARYAN STARED at the ten digit number that popped up in the chatbox in fascination.

"Yaaas!" His hands shot up in the air as if he'd just won a match against Mohammed Ali in the boxing ring. Then he quickly stored Worddiva's number on his phone under *My Darling Sunshine.*

She'd decided to trust him. After months of hesitation, deliberation and diffidence, she'd finally succumbed to this thing between them.

Before he even thought it through, his thumb pressed the green circle. But he quickly disconnected the call when his heart began to ba-boom in warning. He rubbed a hand back and forth across his chest, trying to sooth his nerves.

Shit. Should he call right away? What if she didn't pick up? What if she picked up and got pissed off for calling in the middle of the night? What if she got put off by his eagerness? He could picture her irritated face so clearly now that they'd met. Her fleshy bottom lip would curl in disgust, and—fuck, he was doing it again. Living inside his head.

The bold black numbers on his phone screen beguiled him. Ten little beacons of hope, luring a sailor to shore. *Call me now. Come to me now,* they said.

Aryan snorted at his foolishness. Like the cosmos had

nothing better to do than ship his little Scrabbulous romance.

She'd probably switched off her phone for the night. Or, it could be on Do-Not-Disturb until morning. And what if she freaked, seeing an unknown number in her display? *Bloody hell, if you want to call her, just call her!*

He called her. Her phone rang and rang, but Sunshine didn't pick up. Aryan squinted at the iMac screen on his desk. She'd typed a *brb*—be right back—in the chat box. A polite indication of a pee break. So, she hadn't ignored his call. Or had she? Was she playing mind games with him?

Spinning his phone between his thumb and middle finger like a fidget, he contemplated his next moves—on the board and with Worddiva. He leaned back in the office chair, and moaned as the back molded itself against his spine. The supple dark brown leather chair was a prototype by an up and coming Italian designer. It was rigged with numerous back support and spine lengthening settings—the ultimate, next gen, office chair. He'd used it for some time, and could vouch for its effectiveness. Prithvi Homes had bought a stake in the chair company, and it was turning out to be a pretty sweet and sound investment.

The chair had arrived a month or so after the word games had become a nightly ritual. A good thing too as his old chair, though aesthetically a better fit for the Scandinavian style den, wouldn't have been quite so supportive of his back. He'd even fallen asleep in the prototype a few times, with his house staff shaking him awake in the early hours of the morning when they came in to clean the room, with nary a back twinge. They must be wondering what was going on with him, sitting in the den, night after night, talking out loud to the computer screen like a crazy person. His friends would definitely think he'd lost his mind if they realized he was blowing them off for this. For her. They wouldn't let him hear the end of it, but he didn't care. All he cared about was this woman who always managed to light him up inside on moody and dark nights. Sunshine was his own eco-friendly spotlight.

Yawning, Aryan put down GRAIN and checked the score. He was still ahead, though she wasn't far behind, and wouldn't be for long if he didn't pay attention. Worddiva had a strong competitive streak.

He stood up to stretch his legs, shaking off some of his nervous energy. The chair didn't go with the space at all. He swept his gaze across the shadowy room. The desk was like a grand piano, central to the space he'd designed in taupes, whites and dashes of Scandinavian blue. An armoire, book shelves, a trunk that served as a coffee table, and two armchairs completed the den. It was an efficient room, cozy, and a hundred percent biodegradable.

That was his stand in life—environment-friendly design. He'd do what he could to save the planet, the only planet that seemed to have spawned life in the entire universe. He didn't get people who didn't get that.

The den was just off the main foyer of the flat. Aryan loved the flat's layout. The front door opened to a rectangular foyer that narrowed to a long passage, branching into rooms along the way. At the bottom of the corridor were the living and dining rooms, almost like an exclamation point to the flat—or so he'd thought when he'd first seen the place. The end of a journey the front door had begun.

He could picture Worddiva in his house. In his arms. Easily.

He hit call on his phone again. He'd leave a voicemail if she didn't pick up. He put the phone on speaker while it rang, and poured himself a glass of water. Suddenly, the ringing stopped and a brisk, low-pitched "Hello?" drifted out of the speaker.

Aryan gaped at the phone in shock, but only for a second. He dove forward, grabbing it with both hands, and ended up jostling the water jug and glass with his frantic movements. Water splattered onto the desk and keyboard. He swore, grabbing for tissues, and ended up making a bigger mess as his hand smacked against the water glass. It fell and shattered around his bare feet. He jumped out of the way, but it was too late. His right foot found itself right on top of some sharp, nasty pieces of glass and began to bleed. He swore colorfully, hopping about on his good left foot.

"Aryan, are you alright?" Worddiva's disembodied voice drifted out of the phone in his hand.

"I'm fine. Bugger it! Would you…just hold on, yeah? Hold on a second."

Hopping to an armchair, Aryan collapsed on it, bringing his bloody right foot up to rest on his left knee so he could see the damage. He focused the phone's flashlight on it. Fuck. It was completely red. How badly was he hurt? He hoped he wouldn't need stitches. He hated getting stitched up. He'd been stitched up twice before and knew exactly what it entailed—PAIN in capital letters.

He called Jaggu on the house intercom, and told him what had happened. Jaggu was the head honcho of the posse of household help, and general miracle worker. If anything could be fixed, Jaggu would fix it, or would know who to call to fix it. Within minutes, the door flew open and in ran Jaggu and Shyamu, his second-in-command, carrying a ridiculously large tray full of first aid medicine.

"*Yeh kaise hua, bhaiya?*" Jaggu asked anxiously while Shyamu switched on the room lights.

Blinking at the sudden influx of light, Aryan gestured to the chaos on the floor, and held his leg up for inspection. In short order, Aryan's foot was washed, the offending shards of glass tweezed out, and since the cuts were too puny to need stitches, a turmeric paste was applied to them and a bandage wrapped around the foot. Somewhere along the way, the Shoemaker's elves had also managed to mop up the floor. The elves left, shutting the door behind them, leaving him bloody foot free once again.

Aryan gingerly put his foot on the floor. It didn't hurt. Well, just a tiny bit.

He whooshed out a breath, letting his heartrate glide back to normal, now that the excitement was over. He should go to bed. He was exhausted, and he had a long day coming up with too many things on his plate. He also needed to finish the game.

The game! Bloody hell! Aryan jerked upright, frantically looking about for his iPhone. It was on the coffee table. He'd all but forgotten she was on the other end, waiting, listening.

"Hey! Are you still there?" he asked. She must think he was a complete lunatic. She'd called him that last night when he'd refused to let go of her hand. He blamed her for his substandard mental faculties. She made him do crazy things.

"Uh-huh." She was unquestionably amused.

"Brilliant! You're still on." He was beyond embarrassed.

She chuckled. It was a sensational musical sound that slipped into his heart, his very soul.

"I didn't take you for a klutz," she said, not sounding musical in the least.

Ouch. Male pride and dignity wounded, Aryan hissed out, "I'm not ham-fisted, not generally. I'm actually quite lithe and jungle cat-like. Sleek, sinewy and… What the hell is so funny?" he asked as she roared with laughter.

"Oooh! My stomach hurts. You're funny, but stop joking, or—" She hiccupped. "Sorry…*hic.* It happens…*hic*…when I laugh…*hic*…too much. Oh, goodness. *Hic.*"

Smart and beautiful and a quirky hiccup problem? Sunshine was definitely his kind of girl.

A huge grin split Aryan's face. "You sound cute with hiccups. Shall I tell you a joke so you can keep at it?"

"Please…*hic*…don't. Or I'll…*hic*…have to hang up."

Oh no, she wasn't. "No jokes for you then, Sunshine. Or laughter. Only grimness and solemnity from now on. Take a deep breath. Have some water. Just not together. Water plus deep breath—not a good combination. It could go down the wrong passage, and you could end up choking. Huh. On second thought, at least the choking might stop the hiccups, eh?"

His comedy set her off again, and they both enjoyed a few moments of mutual hilarity.

"You are my Sunshine, did you know that?" Aryan said, suddenly serious. He propped his feet on the antique sailor's trunk that served as the coffee table. He'd stripped, refinished and waxed it himself.

The hiccups had abated, and Sunshine hummed the song he'd inadvertently asked as a question. *You are my sunshine, my only sunshine.* A sweet childhood melody that parents sang to children. A tune that rang of happy moments and summery days. His mother had sung it to him, he recalled with a start.

"Am I really? Do I make you happy when skies are grey?"

Aryan closed his eyes and banished his mother from his mind. "You do, Sunshine. Every night."

Silence bloomed and stretched between them. Then out of the blue, she blurted, "My name is Alisha. Alisha Menon."

Aryan's eyes snapped open and a visceral exhilaration swept through him. She was letting him in.

"Alisha," he whispered reverently. *Alisha Menon.*

But she wasn't done. "My mother's name is Savitri. She is the principal of a boarding school in Pune. I have an older brother, Krish. He's an ass, and lives in Dallas. I live on the tenth floor of Poonam Mahal at Breach Candy. My office is at Church Gate. You know I'm a lawyer. What else do you want to know?"

"Why now?' he asked, savoring this moment of surrender, of trust. The only thing that would top this moment was if she'd said it in person, sitting on the trunk in front of him wearing a—nah, better leave her unclothed. It was his fantasy, after all.

"It was time to move forward. By the way, it's your move on the board. Let's finish the game fast. I have an early morning meeting, and I need to sleep."

"First, set a date." She'd opened the door, he wasn't going to let her shut it without a definite plan.

"Didn't I invite you over for a beer?"

So she had. "Now?"

"No, idiot. Tomorrow. Whenever." He would swear on his dead mother that she growled at him while saying this.

"What are you wearing?" He didn't want this night to end.

"Right now, or when I meet you next?" she shot back instantly.

Aryan sighed. Nothing fazed her, but it had been worth a try. "Fine. Let's finish the game, and I'll see you at your place tomorrow after work. Does that work? Or would you rather meet for dinner somewhere else?" He gave her an out, a safe zone. He refused to impose.

"I'm sure. My place. Eight o'clock."

Apparently, she didn't want a safe zone. While Aryan was amazed at his abrupt reversal of fortune, he was also slightly befuddled by it. He'd prepared for a night of cajoling, begging, demanding, charming. What had just happened? Why was she being bizarrely cooperative?

"What's the catch?" He narrowed his eyes at the game board.

"What do you mean?"

"What's the catch, Sunshine? Why are you being so accommodating all of a sudden?"

There was a soft intake of breath through the speakers, then she tsk-tsked at him. "I thought I was the one with the trust issues here. Anyway, I have no ulterior motives. Just taking our…um…friendship forward."

Aryan thought about that for a second. "Understood. I believe it's your move, Sunshine."

It only took seven minutes for Alisha to destroy him. She won the match, just barely, and rather obnoxiously criticized his word plays before she wished him goodnight and hung up the phone. He had to admit, his moves had been abysmal. He'd been distracted, was his excuse, and he was sticking to it. Besides, Little Miss Sunshine could win all the Scrabble games she wished, as long as he won the other game they were playing simultaneously.

Naturally, he didn't voice the thought aloud. He did prefer his balls attached to his body.

CHAPTER 4

"*W*ho is she, huh?"

Aryan folded the newspaper he was perusing and took the plate of chili cheese omelettes from his grandmother's hands. Jaggu brought in the rest of the breakfast on a tray—coffee, water, a basket of toasts, butter and jam.

"Thank you, Nanu," he said, attacking the perfectly golden, flecked with green chilies, omelette with gusto. "*Hmm.* Delicious."

Nanu took the seat next to him, adjusting her pink and green embroidered kaftan out of the way of her feet as she sat. She beamed at his obvious pleasure in her food even though her plump, wrinkled face was already alight in the glory of the morning sun streaming in from the windows.

"You look ravishing this morning." He slanted her a smile, his mouth full. That's when she gave him The Look. The look that said she had his number.

"I know you too well, *baba.* You cannot pretend with me. I know you heard my question. And I know when something is going on with you. Don't forget, I raised you."

It was her profound explanation for everything and anything remotely related to him—that she'd raised him, and therefore knew him better than even he knew himself. Aryan secretly believed it to be the absolute truth, but he'd never admit it to her. Bharati Vaidya was insufferable enough in her smugness as it was. He used to wonder how she'd always known when he'd been up to no good. He'd pondered over its mystery at length—especially in his teenage years when secrecy and stealth were a priceless commodity. Eventually, he'd concluded that it was a combination of a tiny amount of spying, some excellent observational skills, and a healthy measure of intuition.

"Tell me," his grandmother commanded. She crossed her arms on the table, leaning forward, and peered at him like a policeman preparing to interrogate a criminal.

"I have no idea what you're talking about." Aryan ducked his head and blew on the coffee to cool it. He knew he'd spill all eventually, but it didn't mean he couldn't have some fun with it first. He picked up the black and white coffee mug and took a slow slurp. One sip, that's all it took, to shake the cobwebs from his brain and send caffeinated energy sweeping through his veins. He made appreciative hums of approval in his throat, letting the cook hovering outside the kitchen door know that the coffee was ambrosia itself.

Narrowing her eyes, Nanu looked back at the happy cook and dismissed him with a nod. She was the de facto boss of the house, all right. One look from her and the staff scurried away like rats in sunlight.

"Now, we are alone. Talk." Her tone forbade further prevarication.

"My hand hit the glass, it toppled off the desk, shattered, spewing water and shards everywhere. Very clumsy of me, I know, but I stepped in it and got hurt. Nothing serious. Jaggu and Shyamu fixed me up. See?" Aryan pushed back his chair and lifted his leg up for inspection. He almost developed a stitch in his side from shaking with silent laughter as the wrinkles on Nanu's face crinkled into a frown.

"You need to cut your toenails. *Chee!* They've grown so long."

"Really? My foot might be infected with gangrene and you admonish my toenails?"

She poked at the yellowed bandage none too gently, and managed to make him squirm like a two-year-old. "There. I have checked your boo boo. And I did not ask about it because I know all about it. Jaggu reported to me last night. He said it was nothing. A mere scratch."

Aryan stiffened. Jaggu had disturbed her in the middle of the night? Nanu didn't sleep well as it was. Jaggu was a dead man. He would've stood up and stormed into the kitchen if not for Nanu's hand on his arm.

"Sit down, *baba*. There is no need to get upset. I was awake anyway. You know how my sleep is, comes and goes at will. When I heard the shouting, it was I who called Jaggu. I would have come to check on you myself, but Jaggu said there was no need, and that you were talking to a girl. Anyway, my knees were paining, so I stayed in bed.'

"What's wrong with your knees?" He'd known something was the matter with her health. Hadn't he said as much to Mamu? "I'm calling Dr. Mona to come by and check on you."

"It is not necessary, Aryan. It's just old age. Your body realizes before your mind does that its getting old, and stops working so hard. Don't worry, *beta*. I'm fine." She smiled and patted his cheek, "You're a good boy, my sweet boy. Now all you need is a wife, and everything will be fine." Stating that random life hack, she began to sip her chai.

Aryan quirked a sardonic brow. "Did you hear that sage little adage on one of your Hindi soaps? *Ek wife lao, saare dukh bhagao.* Hey! That's quite catchy, actually."

"You joke around all the time, but you will see that I am right," Nanu scoffed.

"If you truly believe marriage is an answer to all problems, what do you think happened to my parents?" he groused without thinking. His mother had been on his mind a lot, lately.

"We are not talking about your parents." Nanu set her chai cup back on its saucer with a click.

Suddenly irritated, Aryan set his coffee mug on a coaster. "That's right. Close the discussion. Leave the table. Don't talk about her. Never mention her. Nobody and nothing should taint your precious Sandhya's sainted memory."

Aryan snapped his mouth shut, appalled at what he'd said. Where had that come from? He never spoke to his grandmother in disrespect. He'd learned to keep his mouth shut and bury his questions along with his feelings about the senselessness that had destroyed his childhood.

Nanu refused to meet his eyes or respond to him. She should slap him for his outburst. Even the unflappable Uncle Sam wouldn't have let him get away with snarling at Nanu.

Uncle Sam was the only one in the family who didn't shy away from speaking about Sandhya Chawla. He talked of her off and on, keeping her alive in Aryan's mind. But Mamu had been ten years younger than his sister, so his memories were that of a teenager, and shaky and clouded by conjecture.

His mother had just turned eighteen when his grandfathers—best friends—had arranged a marriage between their children. Barely eighteen and hitched to a man who was barely twenty-three. Aryan cringed at the thought. His parents had been children when they'd married. Soon after their wedding, his parents had emigrated to England and started a new business venture—a boutique hotel in the heart of London—and their new life. They'd lived in London proper for fifteen years, flourishing and prospering, and somewhere along the way, they had him.

Then, the incident happened. Uncle Sam had just graduated from the JJ School of Arts and Architecture in Mumbai, and had begun interning with a top interior design firm. When things had gone wrong in London, he couldn't go, and so he only knew what Nanu had told him. And since no one could convince his grandmother to shed more light on the sorry state of affairs, it remained buried and locked up in a freaking Pandora's Box of Death and Disease.

Aryan touched the back of his grandmother's hand where her blue veins had popped up. "I'm sorry. I shouldn't have yelled. Don't be mad at me." He'd hurt her. He deserved a swift kick.

"I'm not angry, *beta*. I'm just heartsick." She sighed deeply, her shoulders drooping as if tired of holding the weight of the world on them. He hated to see her worry over the past, over him.

"You're right, Nanu. The past is the past. I should forget about it. Move on." He bent and kissed her soft, veiny hands. She slid one out from under his cheek and ran it over his head.

"No. You don't understand. And I'm sorry, *beta*, so sorry I haven't been able to talk about it.'

Aryan felt his throat tighten. His mother always made them cry, one way or another. "It doesn't matter."

"Oh, my sweet boy, it matters. Now keep quiet, and let me talk," she said. "It was my fault."

Aryan straightened up and waited for his grandmother to explain. Elaborate.

"Close your mouth or a cockroach will get in." She tapped his chin closed, but it dropped open again immediately.

"What the hell does that mean? What was your fault?"

"*Tcha-tcha!* Mind your tongue, Aryan. You are not that old that I cannot punish you."

"For Pete's sake, no lectures and no threats, please. And by the way, have you ever checked your son's tongue? It's black and blue from cursing. But, that's irrelevant. What exactly do you mean, Nanu?"

"Sameer's wife can take care of his black and blue tongue. But since you don't have a wife, yet," she paused, shaking her head at him. "The duty to raise a good, decent and well-spoken boy, so he can attract a good wife, still falls on this tired old woman. See? If you get married, your troubles will end."

Sunshine's tongue was possibly, however improbable it seemed, even more profane than his. Some of the words she knew and typed, could shame the devil himself. And, why the hell had he thought of Alisha Menon when his grandmother had mentioned a wife?

"That doesn't make sense," he said, rubbing a hand over his black T-shirt, right over his heart.

"Okay. Enough jokes." The humorous twinkle in Nanu's eyes faded. "You were born when Sandhya was only twenty. Your father wanted to wait to start a family. He wanted her to finish her studies before they had children. But I advised her not to wait. Why wait, I said? You're married. You should have children. He was…is a sensible man, your father. He always thought of her first, and of you." She shook her head, looking miserable. "Don't make that face, *beta*. I know you have problems with Raj, but if you give him a chance, you will see I'm right."

"Forget my father. Our relationship is beyond salvation. Explain how it's your fault."

"I was her mother, don't you see? I should have realized something was wrong. Sandhya was so upset after your grandfather passed away. Then all those miscarriages after you were born. That was my fault too. I kept telling her to try. I told her you should have siblings. She began to get moody. One day, angry and screaming, then another day of silence. She did not call me for days, would not talk when I called her. That should have warned me. I should have paid more attention. I should have known she needed my help. I should have known. How could I have not known my own child's suffering?" she asked, wretchedly. She was looking down at her hands as if she had something to be ashamed of.

Aryan went to his knees at her feet. He forced her to look at him by the simple expedience of thumbing her chin up.

"You're not to blame, you hear me? My mother was weak of mind and character, and so is my father. You did nothing wrong." He hugged her hard. He wouldn't let her do this to herself. Is this what she'd been holding back for the last dozen years?

"No, *beta*. I was wrong to interfere in her marriage. I was wrong to tell her when to have children, or how many. And that isn't all." She cupped his cheek with a clammy hand. "I took you away from Raj. That's what I regret the most."

"You didn't take me away from anyone," Aryan refuted immediately. "I wanted to be here with you. He didn't want me underfoot, either. So, it wasn't your fault. None of it is your fault, okay?" He refused to waste a single minute thinking about his father.

"That's what you believe, I know. I could have stopped this rift from forming between you and Raj. I should have stopped it years ago. In the beginning, all I wanted was for you to be with me, away from London, away from that place. I was distraught, you see. It had only been two years since we'd lost your grandfather, and then we lost Sandhya. I wanted you to be safe. So, I took you away from your father. And now you blame them both, blame them for abandoning you, when the truth is that your father never abandoned you.

He wanted you. He wanted to keep you in London. But, I was stubborn and insistent, and your father gave in to an old woman's grief."

Aryan got to his feet, his world spinning so fast that he was dizzy. What was she saying? That his father had wanted him? That he hadn't pawned off his son to start a new family with his girlfriend? No, no, even if it was true, what his father had done to his mother was unforgivable.

"I'm sorry, *beta*. Please forgive him, for my sake. Forgive them."

Aryan locked his jaw tight to keep from cursing again. Nanu meant the world to him, he'd do anything for her. He would bleed for her. But he couldn't do what she asked right now. He couldn't forget the past, and he would not forgive his father. Some things were too much to bear, even for her sake.

Disappointment clouded her face when she realized he wasn't going to give in. "Help me up, will you. This silly gown might be pretty, but it's long and I've tripped over it enough."

He helped her to her feet. "We should think about hiring a chaperone for you."

After a sharp intake of breath, she cuffed him on the head.

"Ow! What the…*Ow!* Nanu!" Aryan yelped, receiving two additional raps on the head.

"The first one is for thinking I am so old and feeble that I need a nursemaid, and the second one is for using bad language."

"What bad language? I never said anything," he growled in affront.

"You were going to," she said, smug once more.

"You're impossible. How can you hit me about something I might have said? That's so not fair. Not to mention, I'm no longer a child. You can't smack a grown man."

"If I can prevent you from the sin of bad language, then I will. And, Aryan, you will never grow so old or so tall that I cannot smack you." Her eyes twinkled as she looked him over, all six feet two inches of him. "Just ask your Uncle Sam." She began laughing, easing the tension around them.

Aryan laughed in relief too. He could handle his parents in small doses, anything more and his stomach revolted.

"Do you smack Mamu with Neeta Mami around? Do you smack them together?" He kept teasing her right up to her room where she'd rest for a bit, then shower, then head out to the temple, and then meet a bunch of old ladies for lunch. Was it possible his grandmother had a busier schedule than he did?

Nanu paused at the threshold of her room. "You did not tell me her name. *Shee baba!* We got distracted and I could not grill you about your friend. Invite her home to dinner. I want to meet her."

Why oh why was his grandmother's memory still sharp as a blade? Weren't old people supposed to suffer from Alzheimer's?

"Her name is Alisha, and I'll invite her to dinner soon. But you have to promise to behave and not scare her off with your…*ahem*…overzealousness. Okay?"

Clearly offended that he'd turned the table and scolded her, Nanu harrumphed at him and shut the door in his face. Aryan's shoulders shook as he strolled off to get started on his own daily ablutions.

CHAPTER 5

The doorbell rang at eight o'clock sharp.

"I'll get it." Alisha strode out of her bedroom only to have her forward motion blocked by her old nanny and current housekeeper. "Vallima, move out of my way," she hissed, trying to slip past the old woman.

Vallima was muttering in Malayalam, Alisha's mother tongue, about the dangers of entertaining strange men at home and good girl conduct—which she clearly thought Alisha was lacking right now.

"Your mother and I taught you better, *kutty*," Vallima said in a last ditch effort that Alisha ignored.

The doorbell buzzed again, and this time Alisha forced her way past, shooting Vallima a warning glance as she crossed the living room. "Please get over your attitude, Vallima. It's not the middle ages. And please set the table."

Apart from that little skirmish, Alisha was calm, cool and collected. She'd deliberately not fussed with her appearance, changing into a simple white cotton *salwar kurta* with a peach *dupatta* when she'd come home from work. She exuded comfort and nonchalance. Her thick, wavy hair was clipped off her face, and she wore no make up.

Alisha checked who it was through the peephole, took a fortifying breath and opened her home, and her life, to Mr. Gorgeous-in-tight-jeans, Aryan Chawla. A six pack of Kingfisher Blue hung from the fingers of his left hand, and he offered her a box of Patchi chocolates—her favorite—with his right.

"Hello, Sunshine." His dimples winked as he gave her a slow, thorough inspection, fracturing her tightly controlled nerves.

And because he'd flustered her so effortlessly, she raised her chin and smacked him down. "Did you think you were going to a frat party by bringing your own beverage?"

Aryan's grin didn't lose any wattage. In fact, it turned audacious. "Sorry, my mistake." He looked anything but repentant as he sauntered into her house.

She took the box and cans from his hands and set them on the side buffet by the dining table.

"I like your place, Sunshine. It suits you," he said, looking all around her living room.

The benign compliment relaxed her. Her home did suit her. It was bright and roomy. Hundreds of books and bric-a-brac were strewn all over, covering tables, book shelves, and in some places, stacked on the floor like pillars. Botanical prints covered one sunny yellow wall, and the niches and shelves along the other walls were filled with colorful pottery, framed photographs and a variety of personal mementos.

She took him on a grand tour of her flat.

"Of course, yellow is Sunshine's favorite color," Aryan commented with a laugh, after poking his head into her buttercup yellow bedroom and the guest bedroom painted a golden yellow.

"Does that mean Mr. Aryan Chawla of Prithvi Homes approves of my humble abode?" she asked over her shoulder while heading into the kitchen to prepare their drinks. She pulled out a can of chilled Kingfisher Blue from the fridge, and poured it out for him.

"He approves," he said.

She got the feeling he wasn't only talking about her apartment. She handed him the glass. He took it with a "Thanks," and a quizzical, "How did you know what I liked?"

Alisha poured a glass of lemonade for herself. "My friend googled you. Your Instagram bio mentions the brand of beer you prefer. You're pretty famous for your innovative home designs and have a bazillion followers, apparently."

Aryan's nose reddened charmingly. She led him back into the living room and they settled into opposite ends of her green and white sofa with their drinks and a bowl of nuts to share.

"You're pretty infamous too," she couldn't help teasing. "There are pages and pages of information about you online, in print. Most of it on Page 3."

The red spread to his cheeks. He took a long swallow of his beer, giving her a tantalizing glimpse of his bobbing Adam's apple, and the chest hairs peeking out of the open V of his dark blue Polo. Completely without her permission, her eyes swept over the rest of him. Wide shoulders, thick thighs, strong arms dusted with dark hair. Alisha took a sip of her drink to cool herself down, wondering who was teasing whom here.

"Right, since you know all about me, let's talk about you." His British accent was suddenly strong, his voice dipping low and deep.

Alisha forced herself to hold his gaze, even though she wanted to run into her room and do a Hubba Hubba dance. Goodness, he was beautiful. Straight-backed, muscular, and he had the world's most intense pair of black eyes that drew her own like a magnet.

"What do you want to know about me?"

"Everything."

So, she tried to tell him everything. It wasn't easy. Chatting with him online had been a piece of cake compared to talking to him for real. The conversation lagged in places, and seemed forced in others. They were skittish around each other, and there was no word game to keep them engaged or distracted. She should've set up the Scrabble board. They were both desperate to make an impression, and it was working against them.

During one such pocket of awkwardness, when the silence had stretched on for too long, Aryan went abruptly stiff. He'd propped an arm on the back of the sofa when he'd angled his body to face hers, and now only his fingers moved as he crooked them at her in a come hither motion.

The chauvinistic gesture should have repulsed her. At the very least, it should've put her own back up, but it didn't. It sent a shiver through her instead. Worse, she wanted to obey his command and scoot closer. Stunned by her mind's betrayal of all her values, it took her awhile to understand what he was asking her.

"What?" She stared. How had one long, blunt finger unhinged her feminist pride so easily?

He scooted closer when she wouldn't. "Your housekeeper is glaring at me."

Alisha looked over at the dining table where Vallima was setting the table for dinner and groaned. Vallima had her *I'll-boil-you-in-hot-oil-if-you-touch-my-baby* face on. "I'm so sorry she's making you uncomfortable. She's raised me from birth, and takes her role as my keeper and personal watchdog very seriously," she explained, since Vallima wasn't going to cease and desist the vigilance.

"Don't apologize. I'm impressed she takes her role seriously. And she's right to be suspicious of me. I'm a virtual stranger to both of you for all that we've known each other for months now. Until I prove myself, I'm no better than a big, bad wolf or a serial killer for her."

Alisha burst out laughing. She'd been jittery to begin with, then she'd been knocked sideways by a powerful punch of lust due to their close proximity, and now Aryan was echoing the very things her entire family had been saying for weeks. She laughed so hard that she got the hiccups.

"Do you always do that?" he asked, while she wiped tears from her eyes.

She nodded, still giggling. "Laughter hiccups. It's very annoying."

"I think it's adorable," he said huskily. He was sitting close enough to her to reach up and twirl a lock of her hair, dislodged from the ponytail, around the come-hither finger.

Her heart flipped over slowly. Enigmatic black eyes bored into hers. He felt it too. She could see it in his eyes. Whatever it was she was feeling, he felt it too. She'd stake her law degree on it.

ARYAN SAUNTERED around Sunshine's shabby chic-style living room, nursing his second can of Kingfisher Blue. He stopped by a wall of bulging bookshelves and what seemed like a collection of carefully curated books. *The Memorable Thoughts of Socrates*; *The Law*; *The Wheel of Law*; *India Unbound*. Sunshine had a one track mind, he mused. Though, mixed in with the legal tomes were titles by Dan Brown, classics like *To Kill a Mockingbird* and...

"Sex, Lust and Legalities," Aryan read the title scrawled on a spine. Now that seemed like a good discussion-worthy book. He shot a grin at the closed door of Sunshine's bedroom, behind which she was ensconced, talking to a client. Her phone had buzzed incessantly since his arrival—all work related messages and calls. The last one had come in halfway through their dinner. She'd picked up her phone with a frown, her face going poker blank as she listened to whoever it was on the other end. Then, she'd said she needed to handle something, apologized and left him to finish his meal alone.

Eating alone wasn't an issue, but doing it in Sunshine's house with the dragon-eyed Vallima breathing down his neck wasn't an experience he wished to repeat. He wasn't too fond of South Indian food as everything seemed to be rice-based, but he'd done justice to the meal, if only to pass time. He'd consumed two *dosas*, several *idlis* and *vadas*, and he'd actually liked the way the sweet and spicy *sambhar* had been prepared. When he'd complimented Vallima on her fine cooking skills, accompanied by his best suck-up smile, she'd flicked a hand in the air as if swatting at a fly and had marched off into the kitchen without a backward glance, muttering in some incomprehensible language. The woman perplexed him even more than her charge did.

Sunshine's bedroom door opened and she hurried out. "Sorry again. I couldn't avoid the call."

"No need to apologize. Sometimes work comes home with us. Anyway, it's good you were out of the picture for awhile. Vallima and I were bonding," he said with a straight face.

Alisha did a double take. "What?"

"Oh yes. She's almost like putty in my hands."

Her chocolate-brown eyes lit up with mischief. "My hero, vanquishing all obstacles."

Alisha collapsed on the sofa, and with a long sigh, curled up on it and tucked her legs under her. Then she patted the seat next to her.

But he kept standing. "You didn't finish dinner. Want me to ask Vallima to reheat your food?"

He'd clearly surprised her because she blinked at him, then squinted at him as if she couldn't quite believe what to make of him. That made two of them.

"You're very easygoing. Most men, at least the ones I've come across, are not so understanding. They wouldn't have waited. Not without complaining or making it into a huge favor I owed them."

"You're hanging out with the wrong men," he said.

But he got what she was implying. There were a lot of entitled assholes in the world. However, he'd been raised to be solicitous and respectful of his position, and he knew such values were uncommon. And it wasn't only Nanu's or Uncle Sam's influence, Aryan had never seen his father treat his mother as anything other than his equal, nevermind that he'd ultimately disrespected her by being unfaithful to her.

"I was under the impression the world was changing." Slower than was needed, but it was changing. The boundaries between the sexes were fading in almost every strata of society. There was nothing like women's work or a man's job anymore. If one thought himself—or herself—capable of doing something, one went out and did it. With varying degrees of success perhaps, but people were stepping out of their gender slots. Even in India.

The world was changing. *His* world was spinning out of orbit because of her.

"It is," she agreed with a half smile. "Thanks for thinking about my stomach, but I'm not hungry anymore. Sit. It's fine." She patted the seat again.

He sank down on the sofa, leaving a courteous distance between them, though he really wanted to haul her into his lap and kiss her senseless. Hug her. Comfort her. The phone call had bothered her. "Something wrong at work? Do you want to talk about it?"

Alisha sighed again. "It's a new case. I'm letting it get to me when I know better. But I can't seem to help it. Or help *her*. My client. It's… Never mind, it's not your problem."

"Tell me anyway," he encouraged.

She gave him another perplexed frown, but gave in to the need to vent. "The client was physically abused by her husband for years before she finally listened to her sister and filed for divorce. It's turned ugly. The husband is a brute, and he's smarting, and he simply won't let her go without destroying them both. He won't listen to his lawyers. And he's particularly pissed off at the sister, maybe even at me. He's using the children to bully her now. My client is a timid woman, so..." She stopped talking, and clasped her hands together on her lap, tightly.

"So, she calls you late at night, and you leave your dinner and reassure her for an hour." The better he knew Alisha, the more she blew his mind.

She flicked a hand, dismissing his words. "I'm only doing my job. The thing is—" she paused, bit her lip hesitantly. He watched as she wrestled with whatever it was that was bugging her. "I can't understand her. I can't understand how an educated, worldly woman could let herself be beaten for ten years. It's vile. Not her," she corrected instantly. "Him. The situation. Her helplessness. I can't understand why she even had children, or stayed after having children, and so I can't sympathize. I don't know what she wants."

His Sunshine was a strong, self-assured woman. A ball buster. Of course she wouldn't understand. "Doesn't matter if you understand or not. You're there for her, and she knows that and trusts you, or she wouldn't be calling, would she?"

"She cries all the time. I feel… I don't know what I feel,

Aryan." She shuddered, hugging herself. "Please, let's talk about something else. Something fun."

"Then I suggest we go out for ice cream and kill two birds with one stone. You haven't had dinner, I won't allow you to skimp on dessert."

They stood up together, and it felt natural to take her hand in his. But the second he touched her, all suggestions and/ or intentions fled from his brain. He was hyperaware of their proximity. His entire focus shifted to where his large hand seemed to swallow up her soft one. Her hand was cold. Without even being aware of it, he drew it up and blew hot breath on her knuckles until she warmed. She swayed towards him, and he snaked his free hand around her waist, bringing her flush against him. Her chocolate eyes went round and huge in her heart-shaped face. She had a button nose, and a stubborn chin. Her plush lips trembled in invitation, and with a groan, he bent his head to her.

The doorbell rang, the sound going off like a gong inside Alisha's head. With a squeak, she jumped back from Aryan, her heart thundering. *Oh, my goodness. He'd almost kissed her.* She blinked rapidly to clear the fog from her brain. The operative word was *almost,* and yet, she was trembling as if standing in the middle of an earthquake.

The doorbell rang again, and this time her semi-fried brain registered a still grumpy Vallima marching out of the kitchen to answer the door. *Oh, my goodness. If she'd seen them…*

"Vallima, my darling. Where's Leesha?" Diya flounced into the house much like a supermodel would flounce down a runway, then froze mid-flounce as if she'd just made a showstopping faux pas halfway down the ramp. She goggled at Aryan, pretty much looking like runway roadkill in a faded T-shirt, shapeless orange sweatpants, and with copious amounts of oil gleaming in her waist-length plait.

Diya's eyes ping-ponged between Aryan and Alisha, and as things began to dawn on her, they grew wider and wider with horror.

Then Diya Mathur, a natural-born Drama Queen, screeched at the top of her lungs and dove behind the sofa to hide.

Aryan displayed perfectly good manners even then—bonus points in his favor. He didn't seem shocked by Diya's outrageous behavior. He didn't laugh or so much as twitch his lips.

Ignoring Diya's murderous look from her crouched position, Alisha introduced her crazy best friend to her marvelous new man.

CLOSE TO MIDNIGHT, Aryan took his leave. Alisha could feel his reluctance as he stood up, mumbling about it getting late. He didn't want to go. She didn't want him to go. But Diya had installed herself as their unsolicited chaperone—more like a *kabab mein haddi*—for the evening and no amount of prompting had budged her size-two ass from the sofa.

She walked him to the door in a charged silence. Diya waved goodbye from the sofa, finally deigning to give them privacy for the two minutes it took for the elevator to ride up to the tenth floor. Several times that evening, Alisha had wanted to strangle her best friend who'd clearly been up to no good with her pointed questions to Aryan about his lifestyle, family, intentions—*Intentions!* As if they were the cast in a Jane Austen novel. As if Alisha was an impressionable young ingenue being led astray by the wicked rake. Alisha had never been innocent.

She closed the door of her flat and leaned against it, boldly staring at Aryan. He didn't look particularly rakish in the yellow light of the landing. He looked yummy. He smelled even more delish.

She wanted to say something meaningful to him. She wanted to reach out and run her fingers through his thick, glossy hair. She wanted to cup his face and lick his lips. She wanted it so badly that she gripped the door handle nudging against her back with both hands so she wouldn't launch herself at him. How embarrassing would that be?

He didn't utter a word either or step any closer. He stood four feet away, black eyes patient and penetrating, waiting for her to initiate their first kiss. He'd wanted to kiss her last night while they waited for her Uber to arrive. She'd held him off, saying she'd let him know when *she* was ready to kiss *him*.

She was so, so ready now, but her courage was taking its own sweet time to help her. She licked her lips. Just thinking about kissing him was making her tremble. She'd been imagining it all night and all day. She'd been dreaming of kissing him for months. Why had she refused him last night?

His eyes dropped to her lips. "I really want to kiss you," he said, his voice a rough whisper.

"Me too."

Alisha pushed off the door just as the elevator pinged open and Aryan stepped closer. Thank goodness the liftman wasn't inside. His head bent to hers, slowly. He was giving her time to change her mind, but she was done second-guessing this thing between them. She stretched up, touched her mouth to his and—*Oh*. An exquisite tingle danced up her spine. She leaned into his chest which rose and fell and shuddered beneath her palms. So warm to touch. He pressed into their kiss just a little harder at her urging. The tingle burst across her nervous system like fire-crackers.

Then he stepped back, leaving her frozen in place,

gasping for air. Her last glimpse of him as the elevator doors shut was of his dazzling, dimple-marked smile.

Alisha floated back into her flat on a magic carpet.

"That good, huh? And why didn't I know he was coming for dinner?" Diya pounced as soon as Alisha crossed the threshold. Then she screeched. Then she broke into a silly, bouncy happy dance on two-feet high sneakers.

Normally, Alisha would've rolled her eyes at the infantile display of glee, but she was still basking in Aryan Chawla's afterglow and nothing seemed over the top right then.

Vallima had begun clearing the dessert plates and macchiato cups from the coffee table, her face still swollen and grumpy because of their guest. Aryan had once mentioned that his favorite dessert was warm apple pie, remembering it, Alisha had ordered one from a neighbor who ran a home bakery business. He'd consumed three-quarters of it, rapturously praising its crispy tartness. Now she also knew Aryan preferred ice cream to whipped cream on his pie.

"I'm spending the night," Diya announced, still bouncing. "We have much to discuss."

Alisha requested Vallima to turn down the bed in the guestroom for Diya, before heading into her own room. She was still tingling. It was…weird. Grabbing a pair of pajamas from her cupboard, she went into the bathroom to change and brush her teeth.

When she came back into the room, Diya was stretched out on the bed, her face covered by her hands. "I look hideous. What must he think of me?"

Alisha rolled her eyes. In reality, her BFF looked normal instead of stunning. And Aryan had been great with her, managing to put Diya at ease within minutes of her crashing their second date.

"If you're fishing for compliments, you've hooked the

wrong bait. And desist rubbing your oil-saturated head on my bed, please. If you get stains on my brand new bedsheets, I will kill you." Alisha crawled into bed and reached for the TV remote.

Diya sat up to save the sheets. "Aryan means noble and illustrious in Sanskrit. I looked it up."

"How nice for him." Alisha began to flip channels.

"He's great, Leesha!"

"Uh-huh."

"He's fabulous!"

Didn't Diya's face hurt from all that grinning? "Glad you think so."

"He's sooooo dreamy."

With a sigh, Alisha stashed the remote back inside the nightstand. Diya wasn't going to let her watch the news in peace.

"You better not dream about him," Alisha warned, despite her best intentions not to engage in a debate.

Diya's shapely shoulders lifted and dropped. "I don't think it's in my control."

"You better bloody be in control. He's off limits to you, even in dreams." Whoa! Where had that come from?

"Oh ho! Somebody's getting possessive."

Alisha waited for the teasing to chafe. It didn't. "Possession is nine tenths of the law, my dear."

"You should have told me you were having your "possession" over for dinner. I wouldn't have dropped in then." When Alisha scoffed in disbelief, Diya pinched the skin on her swan-like neck. "Swear on my Jimmy Choos."

"I don't believe you." Alisha shook her head. "Especially, since you refused to leave us alone all evening. You still would've pranced in, had you known. Only, you would have been better dressed."

"I'm never going to live that down! What must he think of

me?" Diya face-planted on the bed this time, and her thick rope of oily, stinky hair flopped into Alisha's lap.

"Ick! What is that in your hair? It smells like a dead animal."

She'd been joking, but Diya nodded. "I think the oil has the ashes of one in it. It was specially brewed in Banaras, and Parina swears by it. She says if I apply it every night, my hair will grow longer, thicker and more lustrous, despite the damage it incurs with the countless blow-outs and hair treatments."

"That's if you survive the toxic fumes. What good will it do if you die from the stench? Ugh, stay away from me." Alisha cringed.

"Ha-ha. You're so not funny." Diya rolled on her side and propped her head on her hand. "He's seriously wonderful, Leesha. Don't freak out and mess things up, okay?"

"Let's not get ahead of ourselves. It was only a second date," she said, though the tingling told her different.

"I'm serious. You judge every guy in terms of your father. Then you flick them off like dead fleas on a dog when they won't live up to your impossible standards. Give Aryan a fair chance, Leesha. Please don't ruin things by analyzing him to death. He's a guy. None of them are perfect."

Alisha had no ready comeback for Diya. It was true she was wary of men and romantic entanglements that brought on nothing but headaches in the long run. She usually avoided both like the plague. She loved her independence. Valued it. Needed it. She wanted to be and do and live however she wished without having to explain herself or her choices to anyone. She hated it when people interfered in her life.

Interference made her cranky. Opposition made her furious.

In relationships—of any kind—there were bound to be

discussions, opposing views and the inevitable compromises. Even then there was bickering and negotiating, recriminations and finger pointing. Not to forget, the vocal battles and nasty words that echoed in your mind for years after the fight. And in her experience, men usually wanted to have the last word.

"I am giving him a chance, Dee. And how have we jumped from a random blind date into a full relationship? Weren't you the one trying to stop me from meeting him in the first place? Didn't you call me a gullible, Scrabble-crazy twit?"

Diya wagged her finger. "That was before we knew him."

"We still don't know him, Dee. We know his name, and we know his job info is legit only because he's famous—infamous. But what do I know about him? Who is he as a person? For all I know, he's doing this for a lark. Because he's bored. What if he's a playboy simply seeking a different sort of thrill?" No, that can't be. She'd know! The tingling in her veins became a screech.

Diya smiled. "You can't bear that thought, can you? Your heart knows the truth even if your head is trying to muddle you."

"Look, my day starts early tomorrow, and I'd rather not get to work with a headache. I have decided to see this through to its dismal end, so that is that. Can we go to sleep now? Good night, Diya."

So saying, Alisha rolled onto her stomach and shut her eyes. She grinned despite the tension pulsing in the pit of her stomach when she heard Diya grumble loudly about workaholics who didn't deserve handsome hunks that graced Page 3 as she left the room.

CHAPTER 6

"Glad to see someone smiling at the world these days."

At sixty-two, Madhuri Tandon looked fifty and exuded health, toughness and the solid wisdom that came through age and experience. She bustled into Alisha's office in a white organdy sari, her black advocate's gown hanging over a bent arm.

"That was quick." Alisha sat up straight in her office chair, embarrassed that her mentor had caught her woolgathering again.

"It was a disaster," MT said. Perspiration dripped down her face, and strands of silver hair that had escaped from her pristine bun stuck to her forehead and neck. She came to a halt directly beneath the frigid blast of the airconditioner. "Would you switch the fan on as well, please? I'm drenched."

Alisha used her iPhone as a paperweight for the stack of loose papers on her desk, then stood up to turn the fan on. "What happened in court?" she asked, turning back to MT.

"To quote Judge Bhatia, 'A stupendous waste of time to even think about adding more amendments to the Dowry

Act when we can't seem to make the last ones work.' Oh and, 'No substance to them.' I knew that. And I still went ahead and wasted my whole day trying to convince him. Bloody idiot!" MT snapped. Whether she meant Judge Bhatia, Shankara Munshi or herself was anybody's guess.

"She is that," Alisha agreed, deciding to go with the obvious. "I'm surprised you agreed to work with Shankara again. I thought you didn't like the way she twisted the law to suit her purposes."

MT threw the gown over the back of a client chair. "I don't like it. But that doesn't mean I can't see that her heart is in the right place—in terms of rescuing women from untenable situations." MT rubbed her temples with all ten fingers. "I have no words to describe what Shankara did today. She even managed to shock Judge Bhatia into silence."

MT pointed a finger at Alisha. "You have my permission to kick my posterior if I ever give in to one of Shankara's mad schemes again."

Alisha suppressed a smile. MT always swore never to work with Shankara, and then she always succumbed to the social worker's pressures and pleas.

Shankara Munshi was a well-known social worker in Mumbai who fought for children's and women's rights, and she felt it was her personal duty to periodically shake things up in the government. Of course, these days it was a red letter day if the government wasn't shook up about something.

"What did she accuse the government of doing, neglecting or corrupting this time?"

Like MT, Alisha didn't approved of Shankara's bullying tactics, but she also couldn't deny that they worked, for the most part. The woman could move mountains with the power of her convictions alone.

"Same old thing. She won't rest until anti-dowry law is

amended to her satisfaction. She's right, blast it! The misuse of certain amendments cause more harm than help." MT drained the whole glass of water before speaking again. "Ah. That should cool my insides. Let's talk about something less aggravating. I want to forget Shankara even exists, much less that I respect her."

"Should I call for tea? Or do you want something cold?"

"Tea. And ask him to bring veggie sandwiches."

Alisha buzzed for the peon on duty and placed the order. While on the office intercom, she noticed her phone light up with a notification from the Scrabbulous app. Which meant Aryan had just played a word, and it was her turn on the board. She nearly reached for her phone before she realized that she was at work, and MT was looking at her with an odd gleam in her eyes.

"Your mother called me last night," she said, the gleam sharpening into diamond points.

Crap. Alisha knew where this was going. Her mother had been dropping hints about meeting Aryan, which Alisha had been copiously ignoring. She wasn't ready to bring her relationship out in the open, or more in the open than it already was. And meeting family was a whole new chapter in the law book of relationships.

"How quaint, but don't you speak every night?"

"She misses you."

Low blow, MT. "I miss her too."

She hadn't had time to visit her mother because she'd been spending every free second with Aryan, including most weekends. She quickly counted the number of weeks they'd been officially dating. Goodness! Five weeks, nearly six, already. Which meant that she'd known him for a little more than six months now. Alisha had never dated someone for so long. Usually she knew within a date or two if the relationship had any potential. No wonder her mother was desperate to find out just what was going on.

MT gave Alisha another once over. "You *do* look happy."

"Why do you sound so surprised?" Alisha shifted in her seat. Was she so hard to please?

"Because I've never seen you like this before, and it makes me happy."

Just then the peon rolled in the tea and sandwiches cart, and set about to serve them. Alisha moved the papers around to make room on her desk. MT came around to sit in one of the client chairs, wincing as she did so.

Alisha shook her head. "Your back seems to be troubling you again. Will you just go to a real doctor, please? That quack you visit for Reiki healing is not helping. You know it."

"Don't change the subject, dear girl. I have orders from your mother to investigate your situation forthwith and conclude the proceedings."

"Oh God!" Alisha groaned around a mouthful of sandwich.

"What do you expect? You've been so secretive about him."

"How is it a secret if I've told everyone that I'm dating? Besides, it's not anyone's business until I decide to make it their business. People should learn to butt out," Alisha grumbled.

MT raised her teacup to her lips, took a sip of chai. "She's your mother. Not people. She cares about your happiness. Plus, she's offended that you met Aryan's grandmother, but won't extend the same courtesy to her."

Alisha gaped. "But, that wasn't a *meeting* meeting. I happened to be in the car with him when his grandmother called and asked for a ride home from the temple. That's all."

"Yes, yes, we all heard the story. Why do you think his grandmother called at such an opportune moment? The old biddy wanted to check out the woman who's sunk her claws into her grandson."

"What utter nonsense! MT, I am surprised at you, gossiping and weaving conspiracy theories from nothing. Isn't this what you abhor about women your age?" Alisha felt not a twinge of remorse for calling MT a gossipy old woman. If the shoe fit. Still, she was shocked by the insinuations. Could Aryan's sweet little grandmother be so devious? And now that it had been pointed out to her, she could understand why her mother felt slighted. Shit.

"I'll go. But I'm not bringing him." They weren't there yet.

"You'd leave your poor mother to suffer like that? When she's dying to meet him? Shame on you." MT was the queen of emotional blackmail.

"Fine. I'll ask him if he's available, and I'll let Amma know when to expect us. Satisfied?" She raised her eyebrows at her mother's advocate in more ways than one.

"Not nearly, but it's a great start. I'll come too. We can all go together."

Alisha's eyes bugged out then. "What? Why?" What the hell was MT up to now? She was a sly old fox, and Alisha was beginning to feel like a cornered rabbit.

MT's smile was serenity itself. "What do you mean by why? I have to meet him too, so why not kill two birds with one stone?"

Why not? Alisha's mind boggled. Because she didn't want to introduce Aryan to her family yet. Because to deal with her mother and MT separately was bad enough, together they were indomitable. And because she really wasn't ready to acknowledge what was happening between her and Aryan. Maybe she'd never be. Oh God!

"I don't think we all need to meet him together. I mean, three women against one poor man?" Alisha said lamely.

"Nonsense. I'm sure he'll be fine." MT pulled out her

phone from her handbag. "I'm sending you my weekend schedule so you can match our free times."

"Fine. Let's just get it over with." Alisha mentally threw up her hands. It might be for the best. Intimidate the hell out of Aryan and watch him run for the hills. Didn't her family want this relationship to work? "Maybe I ought to invite Diya along too. Or better yet, have Krish fly down from Dallas. Big brother ought to check out the man in little sis's life."

The sarcasm was lost on MT. "I don't think he can, dear girl. But ask him, anyway."

Alisha rolled her eyes at the salt and pepper colored hard head in front of her. "I was being snarky."

"Oh? But at least have them talk over the phone," MT instructed, typing into her phone.

"Yes, MT."

"Preferably before the weekend. We should hear what Krish has to say about him too."

"Yes, MT."

MT looked up, finally registering Alisha's militant expression. "Are we pressuring you?"

Alisha didn't bother to nod. "And don't say, *But it's for your own good, Alisha.*"

"Well, it is," MT maintained stubbornly.

"I know what's good for me. Understand this, MT, and help Amma understand it too. I will do things in my own way, and in my own time. And I'd appreciate some support from all of you."

MT's expression softened. She leaned forward and patted Alisha's hand. "We do understand. It's just that we've never seen you so besotted, so we're worried. That's all."

Alisha was too stunned to answer back. Besotted? Goodness, if she seemed besotted it was something to worry about. MT was right. She'd never felt like this before. She didn't just like Aryan, she was *besotted* by him. Maybe it was time to take things to the next level.

Dozens of butterflies took flight inside her stomach at the thought of having sex with Aryan.

Okay. It was time to freak out.

CHAPTER 7

The trip to Pune came together on the following Sunday.

"Turn left and drive down the road to the end," Alisha gave Aryan directions to her mother's house as he maneuvered the car through the last leg of the three-hour journey. "See the iron gates on the right? Go through them and immediately turn right. There it is."

They'd left Mumbai early that morning. Traffic had been manageable, both on Mumbai's busy streets and the Mumbai-Pune Expressway since it was Sunday. They'd reached the outskirts of Pune without any delays, and then hit a minimum of city traffic.

"Are we there yet?" Diya mumbled sleepily from the back of the car.

"Almost."

Alisha had asked Diya to come along on the expedition. She needed her own backup person when dealing with her mother and MT. She also needed Diya to distract Aryan, in case of a family fight. Diya, of course, had gleefully jumped at the chance to be part of the drama. She'd been asleep for most the drive, stretched out in the back, looking cozy and snug as a bug in a rug with her pillow and blanket. Late night parties did that to a person's energy, even one as lively as Diya.

They were all feeling the ill-effects of sleep deprivation. Alisha had stifled a thousand yawns on the drive. She'd stayed up worrying about today's interrogation. Aryan had been uncharacteristically quiet too, though he was being a trooper about the parental visit.

As the passing landscape outside the window began to look more and more familiar, Alisha let out a happy sigh. She missed Pune sometimes. Missed the quieter life. Though she hadn't grown up in this peaceful, residential neighborhood they were driving through with a manmade lake and artificial woodland. Her mother had moved into the gated community after she'd become the principal of the school she'd been tenured in as a teacher.

"Why can't Mumbai be like this?" Alisha commented wistfully.

"Like what?" Aryan asked. He'd dressed up, looking gentleman-like in a yellow and blue striped shirt and dark chinos. His hair had been neatly clipped recently, and he'd shaved. Though Alisha preferred his stubbled roguish look, she appreciated the effort he was making on her mother's behalf.

"Why can't Mumbai be like this?" She pointed out of the window at the tree-lined boulevard and the neat rows of small houses or buildings peeking out from between the trees. "Mumbai is stacked with buildings upon buildings like a concrete assembly line. Every time I go out, another sky-high structure has popped up, seemingly overnight, squeezed into an impossibly small plot of overpriced land. And the noise. Goodness! Isn't civilization supposed to encourage rational development?" She shot a narrow-eyed look at Aryan. "Do something about it."

He turned his head towards her briefly, though she couldn't tell what he was thinking behind his Tom Ford sunglasses. "Exactly what do you expect me to do about it? I'm in construction and home design, Sunshine, in case it had slipped your mind. Those skyscrapers are my livelihood."

"The government should make building buildings in Mumbai illegal. Um, except yours. Yours don't destroy our planet," she added quickly.

Aryan laughed. "Thanks! For a minute there, I thought I'd need to change professions to stay in your good graces." He turned into the driveway she pointed at, driving up behind a white Honda City. He put the car in park, and asked. "This is okay?"

"It's fine. That's MT's car." Alisha twisted toward the back and shook Diya awake, who'd fallen asleep again. "Dee, wake up. We're there."

Diya groaned and sat up. "I'm so tired. Gah! My feet feel like blocks of wood. I shouldn't have worn those new wooden platforms last night."

Alisha got out of the car and stretched. The sun already felt hot and bright on her bare arms, and it was barely eleven in the morning. Summer was nigh and it was only going to get worse—cue the global warming bells.

"All right. Time to face the firing squad," she said, squaring her shoulders.

Aryan was busy extracting the gifts he'd brought for her mother and MT from the trunk. Someone had raised him right. He closed the trunk and grinned at her. He'd been amused at her since she'd tried to explain why she wanted him to meet her mother.

"Don't read too much into it and freak out, okay? She

only wants an introduction. It's all very simple and uncomplicated."

"Yes, *simple* and *uncomplicated* do mean the same thing," he had teased, unruffled by the prospect of meeting her family.

This was a simple Sunday lunch with friends and family, she told herself. Her mother would want to meet any new friend in her life. That's all it was—a friendly meeting.

She wondered if anyone believed it, including herself.

ALISHA COULDN'T BELIEVE what she was seeing. Amma laughing at something Aryan had just said.

As a teacher and the principal of an all-girls school in Pune, Savitri Menon could smell bullshit from a yard away. Not only that, Amma had had a hard life because of the actions of a spoilt, rich man—a man who'd used his money and influence to make Amma's life as miserable as possible. It was the reason Alisha had worried about introducing Aryan to her. In Amma's mind, Aryan was already a spoiled, rich man. She'd already be biased against him.

Alisha had worried over nothing. Why she'd doubted Mr. Suave Charm's ability to handle her mother or MT was a mystery. She'd seen Aryan charm the socks off plenty of women, young and old, numerous times now. The twits at the parties he took her to, the nervous new server who'd spilled water at the restaurant they'd dined in two weeks ago, the old ladies from the temple when they'd picked up his grandmother—he delighted them all.

Except Vallima. Only Vallima seemed immune to Aryan's allure.

Alisha was so relieved that her mother liked Aryan.

"It was fabulous!" Diya exclaimed as she and Aryan regaled MT and Amma about last night's party. "Rasheed and Saima sure know how to throw a party. I had such a great time. And that gorgeous friend of yours, Aryan? Mann? Can he dance or can he dance? We bounced on the dance floor for four hours, nonstop," she said, bouncing on the crowded sofa.

"It was an okay affair. I'd rather have stayed home and watched TV," Alisha grumbled.

"Pooh-pooh it all you want, Leesha, but that party was the bomb. There were a thousand people there. And this dear, dear man knows most of them. And he introduced me to that brilliant artist, Shiva. Oh God! I could shiver. Did I thank you for it? Thank you!" Diya gazed at Aryan with stars in her eyes.

Aryan laughed. "You're very welcome, sweetheart."

"Ooh! If you don't want him, can I have him, Leesh? Pretty please?"

Aryan's ears turned red even as his dimples flashed. MT coughed to cover her grin. Diya slapped her hand over her mouth and mumbled an "Oops. Sorry." Alisha and her mother just shook their heads. They were used to Diya's nonsense by now.

"That party was a bomb—as in an impending explosion. It was crowded, loud and phony. All those intentionally bitchy and brainless people gathered in one place. What a horrendous waste of my time." Alisha's little peeve got her mother's and MT's approval. They weren't party enthusiasts either.

Diya looked down her flawed nose at Alisha. Then she pointedly flared her nose at Aryan, gesturing to Alisha. "See what I have to put up with? How you convinced her to leave her precious depositions and domestic fortress last night is a huge mystery. I bow to you, O Masterful Persuader," said Diya, dramatically bowing before Aryan.

"I'm a proud party pooper," Alisha shot back, defending her choices.

Aryan guffawed, clearly enjoying the ridiculous conversation since he wasn't the one in the hot seat. *Just you wait,* Alisha thought. *Your time will come.*

"You go to a lot of parties?" Amma asked Aryan.

And so it began.

Aryan glanced at Alisha briefly, his laughter abating. "It's part of my job, Mrs. Menon. A lot of my clients come from that social circle. My family is part of that circle too."

Mrs. Menon? Alisha mouthed in amusement.

Aryan shrugged imperceptibly as if to say, *What else am I supposed to call your mother?*

"Only the rich can afford you, is it so?" asked MT.

Alisha didn't know whether to kiss her mentor for sticking to her principals or to hold Aryan's hand. She need not have worried though. Aryan seemed to land on his feet no matter the question.

"It appears so only because environmentally conscious architecture is an expensive undertaking right now, especially in our country. Not many companies manufacture solar panels or green building materials or non-toxic insulation, so the prices are not competitive yet. In the coming years, when more companies get into eco-friendly products, the prices should come down.'

"What about the clients who are interested, but have a small budget? Is there any way to work with them?" asked MT. She was definitely intrigued.

Aryan explained that Prithvi Homes offered a variety of service options to its clients. "The client need not have his whole space done with green products. We could also design it or build it in stages. With the ones who can afford it, we have an all or nothing policy. The good thing about social gatherings is that you meet all the major players in construction in one place. It's a great way to network and to put ideas into people's ears. I also use the parties to hit people for charity. Ask the big players for a donation in front of their peers, and they won't refuse out of sheer pride. That money is then used to finance my rural projects."

Being of a firmly middle class feminist mindset, the explanation totally got MT's and Amma's juices flowing. Alisha was beyond impressed by Aryan's diabolical maneuvering. She'd attended enough parties with him to know that it wasn't a lie, even though his primary objective was to have fun. He thrived at such events, laughing, dancing, drinking, talking business and generally having a blast. He did it all rather spectacularly too. Especially that one particular gyrating dance move that he did with her in his arms. It drove her half mad with lust every time.

At MT's sudden burst of laughter, Alisha realized that she'd missed what Aryan had said next. Whatever it was, it had an even bigger impact on the ladies. They now looked as if they wanted to jump up and embrace him.

Diya was the exception. "Why did you burst my bubble? I thought you were a Page 3 god. But you're nothing but a hustler. I take it back. I don't want him anymore, Leesha. You can keep him."

"Thank you. I intend to," Alisha replied, dryly.

Amma had been more or less silent for most of the conversation, but now she asked if Aryan had always wanted to be an architect, or had his uncle inspired him?

"My uncle had a hand in it. As a boy, I'd trail behind him while he worked. I lived in London until I was thirteen," Aryan paused, took a deep breath, clearly in uncomfortable territory.

Alisha pressed her thigh against his, offering silent support. She knew he found it difficult to talk about his childhood. In fact, he never spoke of it. He mentioned his grandmother, uncle and aunt, and his little cousins daily, but when she asked about his parents—neither one of whom were alive—he changed the subject.

"Circumstances changed, and I moved to Mumbai to live with my grandmother. Her house was always cozy and warm and safe. That was what struck me when I went to live with her. I thought it was such a blessing to feel safe in one's own home. Uncle Sam had designed the place, and I guess my vocation was just a natural extension of that feeling. I wanted to design spaces that were not only functional and socially responsible, but ones that generated feelings of happiness."

His explanation only sparked more questions in Alisha's mind. She wondered when he'd tell her his whole story. What had happened in London for him to feel unsafe in his home?

"What about your parents, *beta*? Are they not with you anymore?" Amma asked gently.

Aryan went rigid at the question. Crap. Alisha had forgotten to warn everyone not to ask about his parents. It was a sore topic with him. Aryan shook his head in answer, his silence eloquent enough.

Amma realized she'd stepped on an open wound and apologized immediately, reaching out to pat his hand in apology. Then she stood up. "All this talk has made me thirsty. Should I make more tea or is everyone ready for lunch?"

Alisha wanted to hug her mother, but it would only highlight what she'd so neatly sidestepped. Krish reacted the same way whenever anyone brought up their father. No wonder Amma knew how to handle Aryan.

"I think lunch, Amma. After that, MT and I need to go over some things. To prepare for tomorrow's meeting," Alisha explained, turning to her mentor while Diya began grumbling. "Stop moaning and groaning, Dee. Look at it like a window of opportunity to go shopping, since you've been talking about it all week." Diya wanted to buy some fancy pair of *chappals* you could only find in Pune. Sheesh.

"Must you work today?" Amma frowned in disapproval, first at her and then at MT.

"It won't take long," Alisha said.

"Is it the Kumar case?" MT asked and Alisha nodded.

"You said you'd come shopping with us, Leesha."

"Guys, you know I wouldn't do this if it wasn't important."

"What's the worst that could happen if you ignored your client? Come on, Leesha."

"I really wish you learned to relax, *kutty*. And don't forget, you have a guest."

"It's all right, Mrs. Menon," Aryan cut in before Alisha's temper exploded. "I don't mind. Diya and I can entertain ourselves."

They all turned to gape at Aryan, whose cheeks went pink at the collective female scrutiny. There really wasn't anything left to discuss after that. And wonder of wonders, a man had had the last word in her mother's house. And in spite of it, lunch was served.

TWO HOURS LATER, Aryan sat in his BMW X3 Hybrid outside a local shopping mall, placating a client over the phone while melting in the sweltering heat of the afternoon. The air outside was stifling, unmoving, searing, even with the windows down. Still, he couldn't justify powering up a stationary car and letting the engine run idly.

He hadn't gone inside the mall with Mrs. Menon and Diya because just as he'd parked the car his iPhone had beeped with a message from his contractor about a crisis he needed to sort out ASAP. He'd stayed in the car and made the call. He should've ignored the bloody message.

The salvaged wood that the clients had chosen after weeks of debating between wood samples for the wardrobes in their master bedroom was apparently not acceptable anymore. Mrs. Bhamra was distressed over the distressed look of the wood, insisting that he'd shown her some other samples, and that she'd never agreed to have dirty old wood in her house. However, even if she was lying about it or seen what she'd wanted to see, and even if she'd changed her bloody mind, the fact was that the wardrobe had been built and installed. The Bhamras would simply have to live with it or pay for a design change. But Aryan couldn't say that to them. He needed to convince them.

He prayed for patience and launched into his soother-slash-pacifier speech. He pandered to Mrs. Bhamra's considerable ego, her sense of style, her hair, her lovely Bermuda tan, and somehow got her to agree that having recycled wood—she could call it antique wood if she so wished—in a never before used finish was just what she could boast about to her friends. She sniffled a little, hemmed and hawed a lot, but eventually was mollified at the thought that she would be the first one in Mumbai to have that particular product in her house.

Crisis solved, Aryan tossed the phone down on the passenger seat and pressed the stereo on. Instrumental jazz spilled out from the speakers; John Coltrane was his all time favourite saxophonist. Aryan tilted the power seat back, relaxed as the music flowed through the car and thought about the four women he'd spent the afternoon with.

Mrs. Menon was almost as tall as her daughter and equally slender. She carried herself smartly, if a bit severely. Her brown and black *kota* sari—he knew about the sari material because Nanu wore the same—had been neatly pinned to her shoulder and wrinkle-free. She wore her hair twisted in a tight bun that accentuated the broad lines of her face. A handsome woman, she exuded confidence, determination and character. And from what Alisha had told him,

Savitri Menon had earned those qualities the hard way. He could easily imagine her keeping the general populace of her all-girls school in line.

Madhuri Tandon, or MT as she wanted him to call her, was another personality to be reckoned with. She'd never married, had devoted herself to the ekeing out of justice and suffered no fools. Alisha's mentor had taken the Menons under her wing in more ways than one. She was close to his grandmother's age, and it surprised him how much she reminded him of Nanu.

All four women had hearts of gold and wills of steel. Even Diya, for all her ditzy behavior and preposterous jabber, was no one's patsy.

Aryan spied Mrs. Menon walking towards the car with a young man trotting behind her, carrying half a dozen bags. Aryan popped the trunk, and got out to help. Once the bounty had been stashed, he shut the trunk and brought out his wallet to tip the boy, earning a sharp glance from Mrs. Menon.

"I've already tipped him," she said. Then she went around and slid into the passenger seat of the car.

As he was getting in behind the wheel again, she began fidgeting. It all made sense when she found his cell phone and handed it to him.

"Sorry. I forgot I put it there," he said, embarrassed that she'd had to grope under her...*err* butt.

"Diya is still shopping. She found the *chappals* she was looking for, and plenty besides." Mrs. Menon's smile was fond and rueful. Diya's shoe fetish was no secret.

Aryan laughed despite the fact that it was weird being alone with Alisha's mother. Not uncomfortable, just weird. He didn't know how he was supposed to treat her. Casually, friendly, or properly respectful? He'd never had issues dealing with a girlfriend's family before. But he did now. It was probably because Alisha wasn't like his other girlfriends. She was his good friend, his Scrabble partner. She was the woman who made the sun shine. His feelings for Alisha were not casual, so he could hardly treat her mother casually.

SAVITRI MENON FOLDED her hands in her lap, and regarded the man sitting next to her. A man who might or might not become her son-in-law. Her daughter was a complicated person, so Savitri could only hope Alisha was considering marriage and not some other convoluted domestic arrangement.

Children these days didn't believe in keeping their lives simple and smooth. Not like the old days where one's parents arranged one's marriage. Where the couple only got to know each other and began living with each other after the wedding. The sequence of events had been exciting, mysterious and yes, romantic in its own way. The couple learned to compromise and sacrifice together, somehow making the marriage work.

These days, couples dated first. They insisted on knowing each other in every possible way before agreeing to marry, and even then they had issues. Commitment issues, lifestyle issues, religious issues. How could they have all those issues if everything had been discussed already?

Just the other day, she'd overheard a student say that she would never give in to anyone. That if one compromised in a relationship, they were dead. It had been heartbreaking to hear such harshness coming from the mouth of such a young girl. How could a relationship survive without compromise?

Maybe relationships themselves had become obsolete—the conventional ones, at least, where people met, interacted and learned from each other. With texting and e-mail and social media, who needed face to face contact? Who wanted the aggravation of a real interaction? In virtual societies one didn't need to compromise. If things didn't go their way, one could simply delete the offender from their contact list. Savitri did not understand the digital age. No wonder the divorce rate in India was rising.

How could she think like that when she herself had chosen to walk away from her marriage? Never mind that she'd been widowed before the divorce became final. That was just a technicality.

And now, her own daughter, Alisha had brought home a man she'd met online.

"You have a very nice house, Mrs. Menon. Not too big. Not small either. Just right, in fact. And surrounded by all that nature," Aryan said, breaking the long silence that permeated the car.

"And I suppose you think you're Goldilocks meeting the three bears or four bears in the woods," she said, making him laugh out loud.

Aryan Chawla made quite an impression. He was good looking, polite, smart and very attentive to Alisha. What more could a mother want for her daughter?

"It was nice of you to come and meet me, and put my fears to rest."

"I wanted to meet you too. And I completely understand your anxiety. My aunt and grandmother are the same. They want to meet Alisha too."

"The ones you live with?" Alisha had told her next to nothing about his family.

"I live on my own now, but yes. My maternal grand-mother and uncle have raised me. My parents." Aryan choked again. It was clear he was still mourning his parents. Poor man. "My mother passed on a long time ago, and I," he slanted a look at her, "don't really talk to my father."

His father was alive? But that's not what he'd implied earlier.

He shifted in his seat, turning to face her. "Mrs Menon, I want you to know that I'm very fond of Alisha. It's not… casual for me. I… She…" He took a deep breath and blew it out, and seemed to wrestle with his thoughts for a few seconds. "There are things I haven't told her. Alisha assumed that my father was dead too, and I've not corrected her assumption. I have my reasons for that," he added quickly when Savitri frowned. "And I will tell her the truth soon. But, until I do, can I ask you not to say anything to her? Can I ask you to trust me?"

Trust him? A stranger? But why had he lied to Alisha in the first place? And why was he telling her when he should be telling Alisha?

This man meant something to her daughter, something important. And he'd admitted to being equally enthralled by her. Savitri measured the man before her who was trying to hide his vulnerabilities behind good manners and humor. In that moment, Aryan reminded her of Krish so much that Savitri's heart melted. And because he did, she believed him.

Alisha had been Savitri's rock in moments of pain and turbulence. Krish had fallen apart, he'd run away. But not her Alisha. Did this young man know her daughter at all?

"Alisha is a strong woman. She can handle anything. Trust her, Aryan."

Neither of them spoke after that. The important things had been said and understood. Not long after, Diya yanked open the back door of the car, and threw in six bags of shoes before jumping in herself, chattering nonstop. Aryan drove them home. His face was a smiling mask of wit once again, though he refused to meet Savitri's eyes. Poor man was embarrassed by his honesty. Like Krish would have been.

One thing was certain though, Savitri Menon liked the man her daughter had met over the Internet.

"I APPROVE OF HIM," declared MT as soon as they sat down to work on the Kumar case. "Your mother liked him too."

"Oh good! I feel so much better now that I have your approval." Alisha rolled her eyes.

"Don't be a smartass. You need our approval, and you have it. Your choice in men has improved, dear girl. This one is good looking, rich, smart and funny. Quite perfect."

Alisha felt obligated to point out, "He's also younger than me."

"Bah! Age is trivial. Irrelevant." MT tapped a pencil against her chin and added, "However, is there such a thing as being too perfect?"

Alisha blinked. "What does that even mean?"

"No one can be that perfect. Therefore, there must be something wrong with him."

Alisha threw her hands up in the air, thoroughly exasperated by her mentor. "I don't believe this. You like him, say he's perfect and now you *want* something to be wrong with him? Stop being such a lawyer, MT."

But the scary thing was that she'd been thinking the same thing for days. That Aryan was too good to be true. Alisha shook herself, forcing herself to focus on her client's problems, and not borrow some for her own. "Can we find a solution for the Kumars, please? I want to get back home and to bed. That stupid party robbed me of sleep, and I can feel a headache coming to roost inside my brain."

"All right. Don't be such a sourpuss. What did Mr. Kumar contest now? Is he kidding?" MT cried after she'd glanced over the papers Alisha handed her, the points of contention highlighted in yellow.

Mr. Kumar was a male chauvinist pig, and a thug to boot. He'd made his wife's life a living hell while they'd been married. To punish her for her audacity to leave him, he was dragging the divorce on endlessly by contesting every little detail. First, he completely denied getting a dowry and called it an investment his father-in-law had made in his business, which he'd promptly lost. Next, he'd demanded compensation for feeding, clothing, and housing his wife for ten years. Then, he wanted sole custody of the kids by insinuating their mother was unstable.

The latest ploy was reverse alimony. Since he'd lost all his money on a bad investment and was now destitute, he claimed that he should be entitled to alimony from his wife who had recently inherited a small fortune from her grandparents.

MT was scratching notes in the margin, mumbling to herself about guns and idiots. "Did you find out whether he was paying off the court clerk or the judge to have the court dates pushed back?"

"It was the clerk. I straightened him out. I don't think we'll have another postponement on this."

"Good. Here, these are the cases I remember. Check their transcripts about what constitutes joint property and wealth. I think that should do it. The bastard cannot get a dime of her money."

Alisha perused the notes. "I was thinking along the same lines except I don't have case numbers filed in my head like you do. I hope this is it, MT. Jyoti Kumar needs to be free. She needs to get on with her life. I don't think she's strong enough to take much more of this."

"She'll be fine once the divorce is final." MT always had amazing faith in the human spirit's ability to deal with misfortune.

Alisha wasn't so sure about Jyoti Kumar's ability. She had

a horrible suspicion that if not monitored every minute of every day, Jyoti would either go back to her husband or kill herself.

Alisha picked up a pencil, adding her own points to MT's suggestions.

"And now that work is out of the way. Tell me, have you slept with him yet?"

The pencil point broke with a loud crack. Alisha took a deep breath and reached for another one as a fierce blush heated her face. "Stop trying to distract me, and it's none of your business."

"You should, you know. Before you commit to him in any way, you need to know if he's any good in that department. Is he any good?"

Alisha absolutely refused to play a game of Go-Fish with MT. "I'm not having this conversation. And don't think I didn't see you this morning hanging at the window like a gossipy old lady spying on her neighbor. Do you know how mortifying it would've been for all of us if Aryan had spotted you?"

MT harrumphed, looking insulted. "It's not spying if you have the best interests of your protégé in mind. I wanted to see what kind of a car he drove. A beemer. Very nice. And who are you calling gossipy and old, you cheeky child?"

"For God's sake, MT. Behave like the successful, dignified lawyer that you are."

MT began to laugh. The stupid conversation was making Alisha grin too.

"So, have you or not?"

"I'm not telling."

"Just blink if you have."

"I think we're done here," said Alisha, putting an end to it. She stood up and packed up everything, fervently praying that Aryan, Diya and Amma were on their way back. MT wasn't going to rest until she'd extracted an answer one way or another.

THE DRIVE back to Mumbai that evening wasn't as sanguine as the one in the morning. They got stuck in horrendous traffic, and by the time they'd dropped Diya off and reached Alisha's house, it was already past dinnertime. Not that Alisha was hungry. Amma's *sappad* was still sitting in her stomach.

Alisha switched the lights on in her bedroom, and kicked off her flip-flops. It had been a long, stressful day. But it was over. Any gatherings with her family could only get easier from now on.

"Just dump those bags anywhere."

"What the hell is in them?" Aryan grunted as he lugged the overfull bags into her room, biceps flexing. He dropped them at the foot of her bed.

"My seasonal quilts, pillows and stuff that I store at my mom's." She grabbed a control from her desk and powered the air conditioning unit; the blast of cool air at once welcoming and shocking.

Aryan fell face first into bed and groaned as if in pain.

"You're pathetically out of shape if that tired you out. The bags were full of fluff. Just like you," she said, walking to the bed. "Mr. Suck Up. That's what I'm going to call you from now on." She nudged him with her knee. He didn't budge. "Get up. I have no sympathy for sycophants."

He opened one eye and looked at her. "You should. Impressing your mother and MT was hard work. You should give me a back rub as a reward."

She jabbed his shoulder a couple of times. "Like that?" When he yelped, she softened her hands and began to massage him. "They liked you," she said quietly.

"I liked them too," he said, his lips barely moving.

Alisha moved to kneel on the bed, so she could put the right kind of pressure on his back. Her fingers decided to run off towards his head and began to thread through the mop of silky hair.

Aryan began to purr. "Your mother's great. You're very lucky," he said after a while.

"I know." Her smile faded as she wondered if he was thinking of his mother. "What was your mother like?"

All of a sudden, Aryan flipped over onto his back and pulled her over him with one hard tug. She found herself sprawled half across his steely abs, her face buried in his shirt.

"Your turn." He started massaging her with ruthless fingers, digging into her back, her waist, moving over her butt, inching her skirt upwards. It tickled more than it felt good and she couldn't help squirming and giggling because she was super ticklish.

"Stop it!" Her plea was muffled, barely audible and completely ignored.

"What did you say, Sunshine? More of it?"

Alisha pressed her hands on a rock hard chest and pushed off, rolling into a crouch on the edge of the bed, wheezing with mirth. He was such a lunatic. She screeched and crawled away as he lunged for her, wriggly fingers threatening to attack again.

"Stop it. You'll give me hiccups."

"I live to give you hiccups. Muah-ha-ha-ha!" He grabbed her ankle and pulled her flat on her back without any effort at all.

His hand on her ankle sent another wave of tickles through her and she began to kick at him, but he held firm and started tickling her insole. Before she could gather the breath needed to scream, he rolled on top of her and started kissing her instead. No more tickles. Thank goodness. He changed the angle of his head, deepening the kiss.

His kisses too had the power to rob her of breath. Alisha closed her eyes and gave in to them.

He was such a good kisser. He was an excellent kisser. She wanted him to go on kissing her, goodly and excellently, forever. Goodly? Oh help! She was losing command of her breath, her mind and her grammar. She bit his lip, punishing him for bringing back the butterflies.

Did she want to go all the way tonight? Wasn't it time they did?

"I've wanted to do that all day," Aryan whispered, lifting his mouth from Alisha's. He looked down at her flushed face, lips wet from his kisses. They reminded him of strawberries —sweet and tart. He loved strawberries. He bent down and took a small bite of the fruit, relishing her taste. He couldn't get enough of her. He'd never get enough.

"Aryan?"

"Hmm?" He nuzzled her cheek, moved to bite her earlobe. Her heart pounded in tandem with his. He felt it through her tank top and his shirt, against his own heart. Her hands clamped in his hair, alternately tugging and stroking. He loved her hands on him.

He scattered wet kisses all over her face, her jaw, her neck. When her legs wrapped around his hips and her back arched, he couldn't help but press himself closer, deeper into the cradle she made. Her head fell back, leaving her neck open for him to nuzzle, to bite, to taste.

"Aryan, please." She bucked under him, skittish. Not yet ready.

He rolled off her immediately. Sitting up, he scrubbed his face with both hands. Too much. Too soon. Their kisses always got out of hand too fast.

"Sorry. I forgot for a minute." He stood up, paced away

from the bed, hoping the distance would settle the riot taking place inside his pants.

Alisha sat up and began to adjust her clothes. He had to look away from her bare midriff, her thighs. She wanted to wait. She'd asked for time, and of course she deserved all the time in the world to make up her mind. He just wished she'd make it up fast. It was already hard to stop at kisses. Already impossible to ignore what their bodies craved.

When he looked back, she was watching him with wary chocolate eyes. "Why do you do that? Why do you distract me every time I ask about your parents?"

Aryan ran a hand through his hair and laughed ruefully. He'd not succeeded, had he? "You want to know what my mother was like? She wasn't anything like yours. My mum attended kitty parties and shopped for shoes all day."

"That's oversimplifying it, Aryan."

"That's the truth, Sunshine."

Sandhya Chawla had been a housewife, pure and simple. She'd kept house for a man who hadn't even wanted her, and she hadn't had the guts to leave her husband and make it alone in the world. His mother had been the exact antithesis of Savitri Menon. She hadn't been the kind of woman who would refuse to live on her dead husband's modest wealth. Alisha had told him that her mother had put away the money she'd inherited from her husband in a trust for her children until they matured. The funds had helped Alisha and her brother buy their Mumbai flat three years ago.

Aryan couldn't imagine his timid mother doing something like that. Besides, he really didn't want to talk about his mother. Or his sleazebag of a father. He didn't want to tell Alisha about the kind of blood that ran through his veins. Not tonight.

"My parents don't matter, okay? Nanu and Uncle Sam matter to me. They are all that matter to me." He sat down on the bed and took her hand in his. "My cousin is getting married on Friday. I have to attend and I refuse to go stag," he said, faking a shudder. "Weddings are wicked things if you attend alone. Invariably, some old lady thinks it's her divine duty to fix me up with some available female. Come to think of it, there was this one time where someone tried to fix me up with their son."

Sunshine snorted like he'd known she would. "You must have had that tulip shirt on that day. It makes you look completely gay."

"*Tsk tsk tsk tsk.*" Aryan shook his head. "That's stereotyping, Sunshine. I expected better from you." He winced when Alisha's nails dug into his skin. "Plus, you know next to nothing about fashion so what you think doesn't count. That shirt happens to be Helen Pal's winter showstopper."

"If I didn't know any different," Alisha eyed the deflating bulge in his pants evilly, and Aryan felt hard-pressed not to squirm, "I'd definitely think you were batting for the other team in that shirt. Ack! Behave, Aryan." She snatched her hand back as he threatened to give her hands-on evidence of his sexual preferences.

But enough monkey business. It was time she met his family. "Will you come to the wedding?"

Quid pro quo, after all.

CHAPTER 8

*A*ryan Chawla, architect extraordinaire, was having a bloody brilliant week.

His jaunty stride in perfect accord with his whistling, Aryan crossed the overflowing parking lot of the Kamala Mills complex and hopped into the BMW when his chauffeur, the ever faithful and fabulous Singh, opened the door.

"Back to the office, Singh."

He'd just finished inspecting his fifth and final site for the day—a residential remodel—a good two hours ahead of schedule, and not even the blips and bumps of an ongoing construction site had dampened his good mood. The work was on schedule. His imagination was bearing fruit, his creations coming to life, all while saving his percentage of the planet. That was enough to make any man happy. But the pièce de résistance, the bloody cherry on top of the chocolate cake with vanilla icing, was the woman who'd come into his life unexpectedly.

Alisha made his heart pitter patter with a smile and his ribs crack with laughter with her snark. She made the sun rise and the moon gleam. She was fast becoming his reason, his purpose in life. His peace, his harmony, his Sunshine, his alpha and his omega and—he'd officially gone off the deep end.

Aryan chuckled at himself, catching Singh's grinning reflection in the rearview mirror.

"I am very happy for you, Sir*ji*," said Singh. "Ma'am is a very nice person."

Apparently, whatever magic effect Sunshine was having on him, she was also having on his staff. She'd bowled them all over. Jaggu, Shyamu, the cook, the watchmen and liftmen in the building, and now Singh. It was bloody disconcerting to see their beaming, overly enthusiastic faces looming about to do her bidding. How did she do it? Did she have a special wand she waved about in secret?

He hadn't done too badly in winning over Mrs. Menon, MT and Diya either. Not to sound conceited, but most women adored him—tall, short, young, old, it didn't matter. The only fly in the ointment who was breaking his stellar record was Vallima. The dragon lady was a tough nut to crack and she wasn't showing any sign of cracking. What was he doing wrong with her? He would have bribed her without any qualms had she seemed bribable at all.

With such weighty thoughts and plots bouncing about in his head, Aryan answered his vibrating phone without checking the caller ID. "Hello!"

"Hello, son. How are you?"

And just like that, Aryan's cheery mood was extinguished.

"What do you want?" he asked, his tone unreasonably harsh. He took a deep, steadying breath and let it out. *Stay calm. Stay cool. He's not worth it.*

The short silence that followed Aryan's question was broken by a hacking cough. Then, "Nothing. Can't I call my son and talk to him without an ulterior motive?" Another cough ended the statement.

The old man sounded tired, meek, but Aryan hardened his heart. "You called, we talked. Goodbye."

"Wait! Don't hang up." Rajaram Chawla broke into another coughing fit. The old man was never sick.

"What's wrong?" Aryan asked, frowning.

"Nothing. Just a cold."

"Have you seen a doctor?" He hated feeling even a twinge of concern for his father. The old man didn't deserve a drop of emotion, not one drop.

"Yes. He prescribed rest and other things. But I called to find out how you were doing? We haven't spoken in two months, son."

Aryan's jaw clenched at the meaningless epithet. A few years ago, he would've shouted at the old man to stop calling him "son." He was older and wiser now, and he wasn't going to show any weakness to this man. "I'm fine."

"Good. That's good. How is work?"

"Fine."

"Any interesting projects coming your way?"

Aryan didn't bother answering. Who was the old man kidding? Did he actually believe that calling every once in a while and inquiring about Aryan's work and life made him a father?

"If that's all, I have to go." Aryan deserved serious brownie points for not losing his temper and for being perfectly polite. He deserved a bloody medal.

There was a small hesitation, a rough breath. "I need you to sign some papers, Aryan. And go over some estate matters. Can you come to London this week?"

Had the old man lost his mind? "You're joking, right? I've told you time and again that I want nothing to do with you or your wealth."

"Aryan, please." His father started coughing violently then.

"Look," Aryan said, a sick feeling snaking into his belly. How sick was he? "You can barely talk, so let's not do this. I don't want anything from you."

"You are my son. My heir." That came out clear and strong.

"You have three daughters. Give it to them," Aryan said coldly.

"You are my first born, my only son."

And where had this deep familial bond been when he'd needed it? Begged for it? After his mother's funeral, after the shock had banked and the hordes of people had left their home, Aryan had gone to his father in search of comfort, for reassurance that everything would be fine. What did he get instead? The old man had fumbled through some ridiculous explanation about needing to be alone. So Aryan had left him alone and gone back to his room and cried himself to sleep.

The next day, his grandmother had informed him that she was taking him to India with her. His father hadn't even had the decency to tell Aryan himself. So, bollocks to the first born son bullshit.

"Don't make me laugh."

"Why do you insist on making things difficult, Aryan?"

"You're wrong. I'm making it easy. I know what roles we play in each other's lives. And I'm fine with it. Better than fine. And if that's all, I have to go and inspect a site."

Rajaram Chawla sighed weakly. "All right, son. Have it your way. I'll send the papers and cheque to Sameer's office like always. Please go over them and sign them at your convenience."

"I told you, I don't want—" Aryan broke off when his father disconnected the line. He drew in a deep, shuddering breath and blew it out.

Bloody buggering hell!

. . .

It was clear something was wrong with Aryan.

She'd known it the second she'd laid eyes on him loitering below her building two hours ago, waiting for her to come home. Apart from a quick greeting and a kiss on her cheek, he'd remained silent as he'd helped her gather her office bag and other things from the backseat of her blood red Tata Nano, gallantly carrying it all up to her flat for her.

"Weren't you supposed to catch up with friends tonight, playing billiards or something?" she'd asked in the elevator, more than a little nonplussed at his disheveled appearance. His short-clipped hair stood up in spikes as if he'd run his hands through it in no set pattern. His light blue office shirt was missing a button. She'd never, not once since they started dating, seen him in a condition that was less than pristine. It was an obsession with him, to dress well, to look good. Both he and Diya seemed to be competing for the World Clotheshorse Trophy—if there was such a thing.

"Change of plans," he'd mumbled, then asked if he could hang around for the evening.

She'd said yes, of course. She could hardly have thrown him out when he clearly looked as if he needed not to be alone? But her surprise at his unannounced appearance had soon given way to annoyance. They'd had no plans for the evening. She'd been looking forward to a night to herself, catching up on work and reading and organizing her closet. And now she had to change her plans because of him? In truth, she'd already been annoyed because of certain things that had happened at work, and Aryan had only tipped her mood lower.

When she'd mentioned her evening plans, he'd assured her he wouldn't get in her way. And he hadn't. After they'd shared a quick meal together—Vallima hadn't been too thrilled at their sudden dinner guest either—he'd left her to her devices, making himself comfortable on her living room sofa with a couple of bottles of beer and the TV for company. He hadn't bothered her once.

Alisha walked over to where Aryan was sprawled lengthwise on the sofa, his eyes glued to the flatscreen TV broadcasting an IPL match.

"What's the matter?" she asked, frowning down at him. Her mood had more or less improved in the last two hours. She wasn't displeased anymore, though she was beginning to get worried about Aryan.

Other than a slight shoulder shrug in lieu of an answer, he didn't so much as twitch. He had a bottle balanced on his flat abs. Maybe that's why he couldn't move.

She removed the bottle and nudged his hip with her knee. She sat on the edge of the sofa when he made a little room for her.

"You're sulking?" It couldn't be because she'd ignored him. He'd come to her like this—face sullen as the Grinch.

His eyes slid to her face, then slid back to the TV which was making soft bleeting sounds because the spectators of the cricket match had gone wild cheering for the batsman who'd just scored a century in runs. She squinted at the score board on the screen, displaying the match stats thus far. The Kolkata Knight Riders were in the lead.

"Do you want to talk about it?" She smoothed the hair that was sticking up in all directions on his head. When he shrugged again, she tried a different tactic. "So, Shah Rukh's team is winning?"

She was blindly loyal to the KKR because of SRK. Aryan usually rooted for the Mumbai Indians. Though, he hadn't done any rooting or hollering or excited fist-shaking at the TV today. The only indication that he'd been watching the match and hadn't fallen asleep had been the periodic movement of his hand as he'd chugged beer.

"For now." Aryan heaved a sigh and sat up, clearly getting

the picture that alone-time was over and it was time to talk. He scrubbed his face with his hands as if to rub his mood away. He'd removed his shoes, socks and belt at some point in the evening, and the discarded items sat in a neat pile under the coffee table. His tidy untidiness was at once endearing and disturbing.

Alisha supposed she was in no position to judge Aryan's messy appearance when her fingers were ink-stained, and her *salwar kameez*, that had started off in a pristine white state this morning, was pathetically wrinkled and food-stained. She didn't even want to imagine what state her top knot was in.

It was yet another indication that something was wrong. Mr. GQ hadn't once commented on her frightful appearance.

"Tell me what's wrong," she asked, softly.

"Headache," he answered, rubbing two fingers across his forehead hard.

He was lying. There was something simmering below the surface. She wondered if he'd explode if she pushed. "Here, rest your head back against the sofa." When he did as she asked, she rose to her knees and began to massage his scalp.

"One of your projects giving you trouble?" she prodded gently as her fingers and thumbs found the pressure points on his temple and pressed. Aryan groaned in appreciation. "Is it your *nanu*?" He'd mentioned that his grandmother hadn't been keeping well.

His Adam's apple convulsed as he swallowed. "No. It's nothing."

"Clearly something is bothering you," she pushed. Her brother, Krish, was the same. Getting him to talk about a problem, especially an emotional one, was like pulling teeth with bare hands.

"It's nothing," Aryan repeated stubbornly. Then he slanted

a lazy look at her from beneath his half shut eyes. "Nothing a kiss won't cure, Sunshine."

So, he wished to change the subject. He was telling her, politely, to butt out of his business. It hurt, but a smart person knew when to push and when to concede.

In a lightning quick move, she straddled his lap. He grunted as her weight settled on him and his stormy black eyes widened in pleasure and relief. His hands slid up her arms and encircled her. "Want to play, huh?"

"Not that you deserve it. But I do after the day I've had." She brushed her lips over his. If he wanted a distraction, she'd give them both one.

He curled a lock of her escapee hair around one finger. "What happened with you?"

She thought about not telling him, but then, she'd be as bad as him. "The usual. Crappy world. Helpless clients. Although, one lady came in today who'd rather have revenge than a peaceful divorce, using her children as leverage. So I gave her references to several other attorneys and showed her the door." Alisha licked Aryan's bottom lip. "Now, unless you want to spill your guts, let's get on with making out."

"Wait! Vallima." Aryan craned his neck towards the kitchen.

Alisha didn't stop her exploration of Aryan's pectorals. She'd already made sure Vallima was out for the night. "She's asleep. It's after eleven."

"Hallelujah!" Aryan's heartfelt prayer made Alisha laugh.

Then he cupped her face in his hands and opened his mouth over hers, diving into the kiss like he'd been granted permission to steal manna from heaven. He nipped, sucked, held her lower lip hostage between his teeth, arousing her, taking her higher and higher with every breach of his tongue. Alisha gave as good as she got and had him groaning within minutes. Tongues dueling and stroking, his hands, broad and sure, whispered over her throat, her shoulders, down her chest to cup her breasts. She hummed her pleasure as her senses fired on all cylinders. His hands were so hot that they burned through her clothes. She arched her back, wanting, needing, begging for more.

He gave her more. He rubbed and kneaded her breasts, pinched her nipples until she whimpered, and all the while their mouths stayed fused in a kiss that demanded and writhed and pushed and conceded.

He drew back first, eyes smoldering, chest heaving. She pulled him back, demanded more, wrapping her arms around his neck. If he wouldn't give her words, if he wouldn't give her his secrets, she wanted his passion. His devotion. His surrender.

"Sunshine," he groaned against her throat, his hands stilling on her breasts.

"Don't stop," she begged. Commanded. Her hands clamped down on top of his, guiding, directing, showing him what she wanted, how she liked it. She couldn't help rubbing herself against him in part frustration, part need.

Oh God! It wasn't enough. They were going too slow. They were moving too fast.

He tore his mouth from hers again. "We have to stop, love."

Why? She didn't want to stop. She wanted—no, she needed him to go on doing what he was doing. Never ever stop. She didn't care that he'd barged into her evening, her life. She didn't care about secrets. She wanted to touch him, skin to skin, heat to heat. She wanted to feel him. Only him. All of him.

"I don't want to stop."

He held her head until she looked at him. "Alisha, are you sure?"

Was she? She'd wanted to wait until they were more sure

of each other before this final step. He'd respected her wishes, hadn't argued about it or tried to convince her otherwise. Not once.

Alisha slid off Aryan's lap. He stared up at her, arousal warring with confusion in his obsidian eyes.

She took his hand, tugged him until he stood up. "I'm sure. Come on."

Aryan didn't need to be told twice. He followed Alisha across her living room and into her bedroom. He'd follow her into hell if she asked him. But, she wasn't asking him to follow her into hell. She was leading him into heaven.

His heart began to race in anticipation when they crossed the threshold of her bedroom and he saw the queen-sized bed with its purple duvet. His body was already taut with desire and wanted release, but his brain wouldn't stop rambling. He wanted to obliterate all his thoughts, destroy all the memories, and rolling around with Alisha all night would definitely accomplish the mission.

He squashed down the twinge of guilt he felt at the thought of using her for such a purpose. But, she wanted this. She'd initiated it. It had to be okay.

As soon as Alisha shut her bedroom door and shut off all the lights save one, Aryan tugged her into his arms and took her mouth again. Naked. He wanted to feel her skin. He dropped one hand to her hips, then lower, and bunching a fistful of her white cotton *kurta*, he began to inch it upwards. Slowly, so she could stop him if she wished. She didn't stop him. Her hands were busy unbuttoning his shirt. With both hands, he began to pull her top over her head. She raised her arms to accommodate him. Of course, the fabric bunched and caught just under her chin.

"Shit. We should have unbuttoned it first," she said a little breathlessly, wriggling to free herself from her clothes. He wanted to rip it off her, but Sunshine had more control.

"Wait. I think the hook is caught in my hair. Can you see it?" she asked, her voice muffled under all that fabric.

Somehow, they managed to get her *kurta* off without tearing it or her hair out. He'd been grinning since their striptease had turned into a comedy, but now his mouth went dry at the vision she made. Proud and utterly unself-conscious, she stood before him in her white *salwar* and plain white bra. He'd never seen anything more beautiful or sexy in his life. She raised her arms and began to undo her topknot slowly, her chocolate brown eyes locked with his. When all the hairpins had been removed and tossed aside, she fluffed out the thick rivers of silky, dark hair.

Aryan tunnelled his fingers into her hair, massaging her scalp as she'd done to him just minutes ago. "It's so thick and soft. And it smells of apples," he said, bringing a handful of her hair to his nose. He'd died and gone to heaven.

"It's my shampoo." She resumed unbuttoning his shirt quickly and efficiently. "Take it all off," she ordered as her hands reached behind her own body to unhook her bra. She dropped it on the floor.

And just like that she was half naked.

Aryan swiped his tongue over his lips for any telltale drool. His hands rose, eager to touch her, but dropped away as he realized she hadn't stopped stripping. He gaped at her as she loosened her *salwar*, pushing it off her hips to let it pool at her feet. She stepped out of it, then turned back to him with her hands on her hips, looking every inch like a lingerie model in basic white cotton panties.

It was the first time that he'd seen her naked. Mostly naked. And she was magnificent—all dusky and willowy, and he couldn't wait to put his hands on her.

"Well?" She raised her eyebrows, when she saw him frozen in place and gawking.

"Well, what?"

She flapped her hand at his pants impatiently. "Your turn. I want to see you."

"You're very bossy, you know?" His Sunshine was a regular firecracker, that she'd be the same in the bedroom, delighted him.

She rolled her eyes, but she couldn't quite conceal the tremor that rippled through her.

Not so nonchalant then, was she? He shrugged out of his shirt, angling his body to bring his chest and biceps into sharp focus. He heard her swallow a gasp. Nope, not nonchalant at all. He brought his hands to his waist, unhooked his pants with a flick of his thumb while her eyes tracked his every move. He stifled a smile. He had her in his clutches now. By her own previous admission, she was a novice when it came to bedroom games compared to him.

He rubbed the zipper with his forefinger, up and down, up and down, before grasping it and pealing it down, the sound loud and daring in the absolute silence that surrounded them.

Sunshine licked her full bottom lip. Her nipples had turned into dark little pebbles. Aryan's mouth watered. He needed another taste of them. Soon, he'd have his fill. Right now, he was enjoying putting on a show for her. He loved the dazed look in her eyes too bloody much to hurry things along.

He hooked his thumbs over his pants and briefs, and in one fell swoop he pushed both down. Sunshine wasn't the only one with a dramatic flair. He placed his hands on his hips when he straightened, mirroring her pose, and waited for the verdict.

Hot. Cold. Everything. Alisha felt everything at once. She wanted to whistle like a roadside Romeo. No, she wanted to say something witty and blasé, but her brain had shut off.

Good lord, the man was built. Hard, lean muscle rolled

over broad shoulders, a wide, well-defined chest, narrow waist and strong, thick legs. He looked like a mythical god. A gorgeous, aroused god bent on mayhem.

She had to touch him. She tried to control her quivers, but her hands shook when she placed them on his rock hard chest. She shuddered out a breath, spreading her fingers wide, feeling the soft, springy hair sprouting from his skin. He caught the hand pressed over his heart and brought it to his lips.

"How far?" he asked gruffly, letting her know she was still completely in charge.

Her heart melted. "All the way." She wanted them to go all the way.

Aryan nodded jerkily, then froze as a little technical detail popped into his head. He wanted to kick himself. He was such an idiot.

"I don't have any condoms on me," he admitted. "Let me go and get some." Bollocks. He hoped the minor glitch wouldn't ruin the mood.

"Don't worry. I do." Sunshine pointed to the nightstand by the window.

Of course, she had condoms. Alisha was the epitome of practical efficiency and ruthless organization. When she'd decided to move their relationship to this level, she would have prepared accordingly. Which meant, she'd been thinking of bedding him for a while. Aryan grinned. He was coming to love her thoroughness. Her thoughtfulness.

"All right then. Strip it all, love. Panties off!" It was time to show her who was boss.

At his order, Alisha turned a pretty shade of red. Sort of like the inside of a beetroot.

Aryan couldn't believe his audacious Sunshine was bashful of being naked in front of him.

"Give me a minute," she said. Sliding her arms around him, she hid her face in his shoulder.

A variety of emotions spilled over from his heart. They absolutely delighted him, these paradoxical traits of hers. They certainly kept him on his toes.

He wrapped his arms around her, kissing her cheek, her eyelids, her forehead. "Why are you embarrassed?"

"Don't know." She began to stroke his back.

"Don't be shy. Not with me." He bit her earlobe, sucked it into his mouth.

Giggling, she squirmed away, but he followed her, moth to her flame. She got into bed, scooted to make room for him to crawl in behind her. He took her in his arms again or she took him. He didn't care which. They pleasured each other with long, drugging kisses and addictive, leisurely strokes. Sometimes, he was the aggressor and sometimes she. Sometimes, he'd wind up on top and sometimes she.

He discovered a tattoo on her right hip, a small red and black scroll with LEX written on it in black. Every day, he found out something new about her. Every day, she managed to surprise him.

"When did you get this?" he asked, tracing the tattoo with his tongue.

"A symbol to mark my twenty-fifth birthday," she answered breathlessly, her fingers digging into his shoulders.

He kissed it. Tongued it. Kissed it again. "Never took you for a tattoo person."

"You're under the mistaken assumption that it was my idea. It was Diya's. When we both turned twenty-five and," she paused, shuddered as he pressed more kisses, travelling closer and closer to her center, "the year my mother turned fifty."

Aryan stilled, did a double take. "No, your mother couldn't possibly have a tattoo."

"She does," Sunshine confirmed, grumpily. "A tiny flower on her wrist that she covers with her watch. Not because she's embarrassed, but because of being a principal. She's actually quite proud of it. It was a major miscalculation on my part. I only accepted Dee's challenge because I never thought Amma would do it. But, who knew my mother is a little rebel?"

"Well, to my extreme delight, I'm glad you lost the gamble. I love it." Then, his tongue ran away from him and confessed, "As I'm beginning to love you."

If he hadn't been staring right into her chocolate brown eyes, he'd have missed the brief flare of panic in them. She covered it up by deliberately misinterpreting his words.

"Why don't you finish loving me then?" she said with a vixen smile.

Her response—or a lack of one—confused him, but he left it alone because she tunneled her fingers into his hair and pulled him down for a blistering kiss. His thoughts scattered.

Matters heated up swiftly after that. He rolled on the prophylactic and positioned himself above her. When he began pressing in, she instinctively tightened up.

"Relax, love," he crooned hoarsely, pushing in further.

"I am relaxed," she argued, even while her body stiffened at the invasion.

Aryan tilted his hips and felt something—something he shouldn't have. What in the world? He changed the angle and tried again and…he felt it again. This time, he froze.

What the hell?

One moment, Alisha's arms were full of Aryan who was making her feel all sorts of fearless and diabolical things, and the next, she was clutching at air because he'd rolled off her and jumped out of bed.

She looked about in confusion, her body suddenly bereft and cold. "What happened?"

Aryan was glaring at her. No, not her. He was glaring at the bed.

"Something is vibrating in there. Your phone. It's your phone," he said, breaking into a relieved chuckle. "For a minute there, I thought it was…" He broke off, shaking his head.

Alisha sat up, looking about. Had she left her phone here? She rooted through the bunched up quilt. "I can't find it. Was it ringing?"

Who could be calling her at this time? It had better not be Diya. Not if she still expected them to remain best friends.

"It's there. It zapped me."

"Oh." Her hand stopped searching. Her eyes slid to Aryan who remained standing by the bed, only now one of his hands covered his private part protectively. "It zapped you… there?" A snigger burst out of her. No wonder he'd shot out of bed as if it was on fire.

"Not funny, Sunshine," he said ruefully. "We're delicate creatures."

Her snigger turned into a chortle. Then her phone buzzed again, and she pounced, raising it over her head in triumph when she found it. "Ah ha!"

But her elation died swiftly when she saw it was Jyoti Kumar calling. At nearly midnight? Alisha's belly fluttered in dread. She shot Aryan an apologetic look. "I have to take this. Sorry. It's that client I told you about." She pressed accept, her thoughts whirling a mile a minute. "Hello? Mrs. Kumar? Jyoti, has something happened?"

"I'm… I… I'm sorry for disturbing you so late." The voice was indeed Jyoti Kumar's.

"That's all right. Tell me what's wrong."

When Jyoti didn't say anything, Alisha tried to bank her impatience. Of all the nights to call. But, Jyoti Kumar needed patience and support, and Alisha was there to provide both.

But seriously, the woman had chosen the worst possible moment to make this call.

"I…can't sleep."

Alisha felt her gorge rise at the mewling tone. A wounded animal sound. "That's understandable, isn't it? You've taken a big step. It's normal to feel scared and unsure."

Aryan picked up his pants and drew them on. Alisha pouted. He pointed to the locked bedroom door. Should he stay or go?

Stay, Alisha mouthed, and patted the spot next to her on the bed. Hopefully, she'd be done in a few minutes and they could resume tuning each other up.

She pouted even more when he shrugged on his shirt, buttoning it up. She wanted him naked. He looked amazing naked. He should burn all his clothes.

"He called me today," Jyoti Kumar mewled again. "He was so angry. He is going to kill me."

Alisha sobered up instantly. "He's trying to scare you. We spoke about this. The judge said he can't come anywhere ear you." Not if he wishes to get his hands on her money.

They were in the process of negotiating a reverse alimony payment on Jyoti's insistence. She simply wanted a divorce and wanted her husband out of her and her children's lives. Of course the bastard was taking advantage of the fact.

Alisha felt like a failure because she hadn't been able to protect her client from being leached and abused again. This time for money.

Aryan sat on the edge of the bed, pulled out his phone and began playing a game on it. Not Scrabble. They'd both decided on complete Scrabble monogamy with each other.

It occurred to Alisha that while one relationship was disintegrating at one end of Mumbai, another one was being forged. The neverending cycle of life.

He waited the whole time. For more than an hour, Alisha

listened to, counseled and encouraged a broken woman while Aryan waited. Then he wished her a good night, sternly instructing her to go to sleep and left without demanding a reward for his patience or harping about the inconvenience the phone call had caused him.

Life had never claimed to be ordinary, but with Aryan, it became almost simple.

Now, if he'd only find the courage to tell her his secrets, life would be perfect.

CHAPTER 9

"Wow!" Diya said for the fifth time in two minutes.

Alisha shot her friend an irritated look. "Stop saying that."

Tonight was the night. It was Friday and Alisha was going to meet Aryan's family in approximately three hours. She was nervous, of course, but more than that she was annoyed. At Diya.

Her insane best friend had harangued her until she'd agreed to ditch work early and come home to be primed, scrubbed, plucked, waxed and polished to her best shine. Guilt made Alisha moan as she thought about the piles and piles—mountains really—of paperwork she'd left to marinate in her office. She'd simply have to go in over the weekend and get to it.

And why was she in this predicament? Because, apparently, she couldn't be trusted to make the right decisions regarding fashionable wedding wear and which bling would best enhance the outfit.

Alisha's annoyance reached a new level.

Whatever happened to brains winning over beauty?

Appreciating the more profound faculties against pandering to the purely superficial? And where in the world had all her South Indian silk saris gone? They'd been kidnapped, that's what, and replaced by the yellow net, overly embroidered, stitched sari that had a *choli* that could only be described as a bra. The only redeemable quality that the outfit had was its color.

'Waa-a-ow!' Diya repeated, drawing out the word in three long syllables. She sat cross-legged on the bed, wearing black bike shorts and a pink tank, a decorative purple pillow clutched to her middle. Diya had come straight from the gym, all flushed and energetic, and had started bossing Alisha around immediately. All around the room lay a plethora of accessories that just *had* to be worn with the outfit that Alisha just *had* to wear that evening.

Who'd died and made Diya the fashion police, Alisha wanted to know.

"If you say 'wow' once more, I swear I'll stuff that bra in your mouth." She was beginning to regret her girl talk session with Diya.

Alisha unwrapped the damp towel from her head and tossed it into the bathroom. It was too hot, even with the air conditioner blasting, so she'd shrugged on a thin cotton robe over her panties until it was time to get ready. No bra as she apparently didn't need to wear one under the *choli*. Naturally not, since it was a bra itself. Goodness, she was going to feel naked without a bra.

"Why can't I wear something else?" she shot her BFF a pleading look.

"You just can't," Diya retorted without sympathy. "Your life sure has become bizarre since you met Aryan."

"Like it's any less weird with you around, Ms. No Bra." Alisha began to brush out her semi-wet hair. She was pretty sure Diya would blow-dry it at some point.

"True. But still. What I can't get over is that your mobile phone zapped his…*ahem.*"

The image of a gloriously naked Aryan popped into her head and she nearly swooned. He'd been great. He was wonderful.

The doorbell rang, and Diya jumped up from the bed and ran out of the room. Before Alisha could even wonder what was going on, Diya hurried back with one of her supermodel girlfriends in tow. The woman was very tall, very skinny and very beautiful. Her hair had been snipped off in a short blunt and had fat streaks of red running through it. She carried several miniature suitcases which she set up on the dressing table.

Alisha frowned as the woman opened case after case. "What's all this?"

Diya waved her hands in the air. "Alisha, meet Millie. Millie, this is Alisha."

"Hi, Millie." Alisha crossed her arms over her chest. "I repeat. What's all this?"

Millie pulled out tubes of gloss, kohl pencils, compact powders, brushes, bottles—goodness, was that an eyelash curler? Her bedroom suddenly felt and smelled like the backstage of Lakme Fashion Week. She'd been to some of Diya's events and the organized chaos of a fashion show's "labor room" as Diya fondly called it, always left her quaking. It finally dawned on her what they were about.

"Absolutely not. I draw the line here."

Diya ignored her, and began chatting with Millie, pointing at the clothes, the bronze-heeled shoes, the accessories lying on the bed and at her.

"No!" Alisha snarled. "Thank you, Millie. So sorry we wasted your time, but you can go."

Vallima came into the room holding a tray laden with three glasses of orange juice and a bowl of ice. She set it down on the desk, whispered in Diya's ear and left. Alisha glared at her retreating back. The woman was driving her crazy with her silent treatment. Alisha strongly suspected Vallima had guessed what had transpired—or would've transpired two nights ago if Jyoti Kumar hadn't called.

Of course, Vallima was upset. She was an old fashioned woman and had old fashioned ideas. She put store in traditional values and just because the world was changing around her didn't mean that she had to change or approve of the change. Alisha understood and respected Vallima's feelings and tried to shield the older woman from various upsetting realities.

Except Aryan had crashed into their lives like an asteroid and they were all scrambling to deal with the aftermath.

Vallima should be slightly mollified by the fact that Alisha was meeting Aryan's family tonight. It seemed a very proper and traditional thing to do. But, she'd worry about Vallima on another day. She had bigger problems looming in front of her.

"I mean it, Dee. Don't test me."

Diya let out a long suffering sigh, gave Millie an I-told-you-so look. She put her hands on Alisha's shoulders and shook her. As they were more or less the same height, they stood eye to eye. "One, Aryan and his family are super rich. Two, you are meeting them for the first time. Uh-uh, no arguments." She held up a hand and went on when Alisha narrowed her eyes, but shut up. "Three, you're meeting them at a family wedding. Four, do you really want to embarrass him? Five, do you really want to feel like an odd duckling?"

Alisha thought about it for a second. "I will stun them with my brain."

"Good, you do that." Diya patted Alisha's shoulder. "But first, dazzle them with your looks."

"I really don't care to," she said just to be contrary. Though, the points Diya mentioned had hit their target.

"You will. Trust me, Leesha. If you show up at a society wedding in one of your South Indian silks, you'll want the ground to open up and swallow you whole the second you cross the threshold."

Millie giggled. "Listen to Dee Dee. She knows everything."

Diya gave a modest shrug. "Come now, Leesha. I promise it'll be painless."

It turned out that Diya had lied about it being painless, but had spoken the truth in every other respect.

SUNSHINE WALKED out of her bedroom, looking irked as hell, incredibly tall in her killer heels, and so freaking beautiful in a gorgeous yellow sari.

She staggered him.

Twenty minutes later, enroute to the wedding, he still couldn't keep his eyes off of her. Singh was doing his best to battle Mumbai's evening traffic, but progress was slow. Not that Aryan was complaining. He'd happily spend an eternity in traffic if he had Alisha by his side.

She'd barely said a word since he'd picked her up, and now sat stiff as a board next to him, pointedly staring out of the window. Aryan pressed his lips together lest he burst out laughing. He knew what was going on in that wickedly clever mind of hers. She was angry at the general superficiality of the world. Possibly irritated at Diya for convincing her to be part of that circus. Though, he wouldn't hold much hope for himself. After all, she was bedecked and on display because of him and his family.

Aryan wanted to tease her about it, but he was pretty sure she'd bonk him on the head with the jewel-studded metal clutch she was mauling between her hands if he did. So, he contented himself by silently basking in the sublime appreciation of her person. Hair that shimmered in a straight line down one bare shoulder. They'd used a flat iron to achieve the effect as her hair was naturally wavy. Her bodice peeked from behind the drape of her sari, giving him tantalizing glimpses of her cleavage whenever she moved or shifted in her seat. Then there were her delicate collarbones and long slim arms. He hadn't imagined collarbones could be so sexy.

But the feature that made his heart stop, then speed up, were the big brown eyes on her beautiful gamine face. Two chocolate-colored windows into her soul. His Warrior Queen was nervous, they told him. It brought out his macho instincts. Not that he was fool enough to act on them.

"Nervous?" he asked, taking her clammy hand in his so she wouldn't bruise herself on the clutch.

She flicked him a glance. "Were you when you met my mother?"

"Not exactly, no."

"Hmm." She turned to look at him, her brows creasing when her distracted gaze finally noticed what he was wearing.

Aryan stifled another laugh. "Yes, it does." Her eyes narrowed, and he elaborated, "Diya sent a text with instructions to wear a golden yellow tie and a dark suit. To match your sari."

Alisha's eyes bugged out. Aryan couldn't hold back his amusement any longer, but he covered it up with a fake cough when she growled at him.

"You both are unbelievable." She shook her hand free of his and flung it up in the air, bangles jingling, nearly clipping him on the chin. "What is it with the two of you and clothes? Why must everything match?"

"Because we're fashionistas, Sunshine." His shoulders

shook as another growl rumbled out. He laced their hands again. "Don't worry, love. We've got you covered. You go be a lawyer, and Diya and I will take care of your wardrobe."

"Ha ha! So not funny." She turned her head to the window again, but she kept their hands laced together.

"Seriously, don't worry," he said as Singh pulled up the car in front of the Taj Mahal Hotel. "I'll be right next to you the whole time. And if for any reason you feel uncomfortable about anything, we'll leave. Okay?"

Alisha nodded and Aryan squeezed her hand, then helped her out of the car.

ALISHA TRAVERSED the Taj's bustling lobby, sticking as close to Aryan as she could. She needed his support tonight, in more ways than one, because every time she glanced at him, she stumbled over her own feet—or the stupid pleats of the stupid sari—while her vital organs started dancing like marionettes.

Handsome was too tame a word for how he looked tonight. His suit fit him flawlessly, enhancing the strength of his shoulders and the tapered width of his waist. He pressed his hand to her back, supporting her ascent as they began to climb up the carpeted grand staircase leading up to the Ball Room where the wedding was taking place. He'd sprayed a sinfully decadent cologne tonight, and it was all she could do not to curl into him and sniff his neck like a dog in heat.

She was beginning to resent the power Aryan had over her organs.

"There they are," he murmured into her ear, making her shiver. Goodness, she wanted him to move far away from her, and yet she needed him to stick close and not leave her to the wolves.

"Relax. They don't bite," he said, raising his hand to wave at them.

Easy for him to say, Alisha thought, her heart beginning to pound with every step she took. He wasn't the one who'd stepped onto an alien planet.

Aryan's family waited at the top of the staircase. As the only man in the group, Uncle Sam had to be the elegant man in the dark blue *jodhpuri*. He bent to help Aryan's grandmother up from the ostentatious diwan she'd been sitting on. And the short, pretty woman in the lime green *sharara* had to be Aryan's aunt, Neeta Vaidya. She wasn't much older than Alisha. As they neared, the diminutive woman held out both hands to Alisha and basically took over.

"We finally meet! You both look lovely." Neeta Vaidya gathered Alisha in for a gregarious hug and kisses on both cheeks. Alisha had to bend nearly in half to hug her back.

"Lovely to meet you too. And congratulations," Alisha said. "Aryan mentioned another little one on the way?"

"Yes. We're very excited," Neeta Vaidya went a pretty shade of pink as she looked at her husband. She wasn't showing yet. It was early days.

One down, two to go.

Smiling, Alisha folded her hands respectfully in front of Aryan's jovial-faced grandmother as she would with any older member of her family. "Namaste, Aunty*ji*. Good to see you again."

"Namaste, *beta*," she replied, pulling Alisha in for a warm hug and a pat on her cheek. Exactly like she'd done with Aryan.

Finally, she turned to the older man standing shoulder to shoulder with Aryan. They looked nearly identical, standing so close. They had the same tall frame, the same broad boned face complete with dimples. Aryan was a younger, taller version of his uncle.

"Alisha, this is my uncle, Sameer Vaidya," Aryan introduced formally.

For one awkward second, Alisha didn't know what to do or say. Hug his uncle? Too familiar. Bow to him? Too respectful. He wasn't an uncle*ji*. She settled for shaking Sameer Vaidya's hand. "I've heard so much about all of you that I feel I know you already."

It was the right thing to say because Uncle Sam grinned. His smile was so much like Aryan's, so completely genuine, that all the butterflies in Alisha's belly flew away. Hopefully forever.

"Same here, Alisha, same here." He surprised her by kissing her on the forehead. Then, out of the blue, he said, "Let's skip the damn wedding and go out for dinner. It's too noisy in there to talk."

"Just what I was thinking," Aryan seconded.

"Absolutely not!" the two Vaidya women vetoed.

"Don't even think of skipping out on the wedding. That's my cousin's daughter getting married in there. A cousin you are very fond of, I might add." Neeta Vaidya poked her husband in his chest.

Uncle Sam grumbled and argued for a few minutes, but eventually his wife won the case. With the sigh of a martyr, he escorted his mother into the Ball Room.

"I think I've fallen in love with Uncle Sam," she whispered to Aryan whose eyes twinkled in mock outrage. But before she could take his hand again, his aunt hooked her arm through Alisha's and started walking. Alisha had no choice but to tag along.

"Stick to me. I'll introduce you to everyone."

As what, Alisha wondered inanely. *Oh God, here goes nothing.* She looked back at Aryan helplessly just before she was gobbled up by the humming, throbbing wedding crowd.

· · ·

THE BALL ROOM was bursting at the seams with people who seemed to be sparkling in one way or another. Dazzling chandeliers hung from high ceilings that compensated nicely for the jammed square footage. The ambience was modern and romantic with pots full of sweet smelling freesias and roses. White silk bows held violet drapes together with tea lights and rose petals floating in enormous water-filled containers along the walls. A *shehnai* played softly in the background, overriding all the chatter.

"Family and divorce law," stated Uncle Sam as they milled around the wedding stage to watch the ceremony. It was quite a crush, but the combination of a Hindu priest and a Catholic priest working in tandem to get the Hindu bride and Catholic groom married was a novelty no one wanted to miss.

Alisha nodded, feeling shy again.

"Your practice must keep you busy what with the state of marriages these days." Uncle Sam winked at his wife, and a silent, married joke passed between them.

"Quite busy," Alisha answered, then turned to Neeta—who'd insisted they not stand on formality and call each other by their names. "If you ever need one, I'll represent you. Pro bono."

Uncle Sam burst out laughing. Aryan gave her their version of a private wink. Alisha began to smile too until she realized that Aunty*ji* had also heard the exchange.

"I was joking," she clarified lamely, embarrassment burning her ears. What must his grandmother think of her?

Neeta Vaidya shook her head, her long diamond earrings swishing to and fro. "I see your sense of humor matches my husband's and nephew's." She didn't add the addendum, but her expression clearly said, "God help us."

True to their word, Aryan and Neeta made sure Alisha was never alone. Alisha met so many people—as a friend of the family—that the names and faces started glazing over. Everybody in the whole gigantic space was dressed to kill. *Note to self: thank Diya for her foresight.*

Aryan was completely in his element.

In her experience, most people projected different personas under different circumstances. Maybe not different personas so much as different traits in their personalities dominated in different surroundings. As the faceless Wordfreak, Aryan had been glib and flirtatious. As a man on a date, he was courteous and charming. Amongst friends, he was fun, often frivolous. On rare occasions, he was aloof and moody, and she'd found that those moods could easily be reversed. He called her Sunshine, but it was his nature that was sunny.

Here, Alisha was introduced to Mr. Confident-and-Cocky and Mr. Over-the-top-and-Pseudo.

"Jazzy Aunty! I swear you are Meryl Streep's twin sister. I love your sari, the color looks stunning on you, really. This is Soni? Our little Soni?" When Jazzy Aunty insisted the shy little girl was indeed her daughter, Aryan went on with his ridiculous superlatives. "You don't look old enough to have a daughter old enough to be in college, Jazzy Aunty."

Alisha wanted to pinch his arm, hard, even though the theatrics were entertaining.

Aryan also had a subtle mean streak that he wielded like a weapon, and most people didn't even realize they'd been insulted. Alisha herself had a more direct approach for nasty people and situations, but she was quite impressed by Aryan's barely noticeable snark-darts. Uncle Sam had the same proficiency with sarcasm and Alisha had noticed his wife freezing every so often, when he delivered some such comment, waiting for the recipient to punch her husband.

"Who was that again?" Alisha asked, watching the glamorous woman in a purple and pink *lehenga* walk away to air kiss another woman. She'd come and fawned over Neeta's outfit. The two petite women had spent a considerable amount of time oohing and aahing over each others' outfits, jewelry and hairdos. The woman had departed, completely ignoring Alisha even though Neeta had introduced them.

"The bride's sister, Brinda."

"The barracuda," Uncle Sam added as the men joined them again, each holding a glass of amber colored liquid in one hand. Aryan also carried a champagne flute that he passed to Alisha.

"Cheers." He clinked his glass to hers, giving her a very strange look.

Aunty*ji* tut-tutted at her son for his comment about Brinda. "Don't call her that. She's a sweet girl. A little spoiled, but she's still young."

"Behave yourself, Sam. People can hear you," his wife admonished.

Uncle Sam shrugged. "Well, she is. Just because she's nice...way too nice to you two," he waved his glass between his spouse and his mother, "doesn't mean anything. We've worked with her on her bedroom renovation. Ask Aryan. She's a nightmare to please."

Everyone looked at Aryan for a confirmation, but he'd taken a sudden riveting interest in his scotch. When his uncle prodded him, he pretended not to understand the question. "What?"

Alisha's gut flipped over. It was like that, was it? No wonder the woman had ignored her. As she mulled over Aryan's past and the secrets he kept from her, she came face to face with her current nemesis—Mr. Kumar. Alisha was so taken aback to see him, that she actually stepped back.

He stood with a group of powerful looking men about twenty feet away. The malevolent glare he shot her sent a shiver down her spine. She absolutely loathed the uncouth, nasty man. Ghastly, odious man, she thought, turning her back to him.

"What is it?" asked Aryan, making her jolt. He was looking at her curiously, apologetically. Probably because of the barracuda.

"Nothing. Please excuse me, but I need to powder my nose," she said to the whole group. When Aryan made to go along with her, she whispered. "You don't need to carry out your chaperone duties quite so avidly. I can get to the bathroom and back on my own."

His face tightened at her brush off, but he let her go. She made her escape to the washroom, suddenly desperate to be free of all men—nasty ones and secretive ones. She immediately regretted snapping at Aryan though—it was hardly his fault for having a past. Still. He should have warned her that they'd be running into his ex.

She pushed the washroom door open and, just her luck, she had the unmitigated pleasure of confronting his past. The bride and her sister were inside. Alisha's foot caught on the hem of her sari as she walked in, nearly pitching her flat on her face.

"Careful," the bride yelled in a high-pitched voice, grabbing Alisha's arm to break her fall.

Alisha's heart hammered inside her chest as she found her balance. "How clumsy of me! Thanks for catching me."

"My pleasure, darling. Don't want any of my guests falling and ending up in a hospital. I'm Myna, the bride." Myna divulged her marital status with such relish that Alisha laughed.

"I know. Congratulations on your wedding. It was a lovely ceremony."

"Thank you. It was difficult to convince the priests to work together, but the end result was amazing, wasn't it?" Alisha nodded, smiling at the sassy young girl in a fussy,

Cinderella-like gown. Myna looked too young to be a bride. "And you are?" she inquired happily.

"She's Aryan's latest," Brinda, the barracuda, answered before Alisha could open her mouth. Insolently, she looked at Alisha up and down through the vanity mirror while applying fresh lipstick on her lips. Then she turned around and swept out of the room in a huff.

Alisha counted to ten. His past was his past. Nothing to do with their present.

Myna watched her with some sympathy. "Don't mind my sister. She's had a thing for Aryan since Neeta Aunty married Sameer Uncle."

Alisha dismissed the apology with a wave. "Don't apologize. It has nothing to do with you."

"She'll get over it. Maybe," Myna said, sighing. "I'm afraid my sister likes to hold a grudge."

"Seriously, don't worry about it. I usually have my gun on me. It didn't fit in this tiny purse today." Alisha brandished her clutch in the air like a weapon.

Myna gave a sharp, shocked giggle. "I can see why he likes you."

"I'm Alisha." She offered her hand, ignoring the praise as she'd ignored the other sister's insult.

"So nice to meet you. Please, don't leave before the show, okay? It'll start right after dinner."

Alisha smiled at Myna, gave the appropriate response, and went into one of the free bathroom cubicles. When she came out, the bride had gone. Alisha adjusted her drape and her pleats, dabbed the oil off her nose and chin with a tissue, and gave herself a once-over. Everything was still in place, nice and presentable, but just as uncomfortable. Then she swept out of the washroom, much like the barracuda, and stopped dead right outside it.

Aryan stood diagonally across the hall, a grim, unapproachable cloud hanging over his head. Brinda, the barracuda, stood in front of him, jabbering away. From Alisha's vantage point, Aryan looked like he was getting ready to smash his scotch glass on the wall, or smack the barracuda across her face.

Alisha sincerely hoped the glass shattering would win as she absolutely could not be with a man who hit women, even women as provoking as the barracuda. She made her way across the hall towards them. Aryan hadn't seen her exit the washroom, so her sudden appearance by his side startled him. Then a dark flush crept into his cheeks as he wrestled with a riot of emotions all at once.

Alisha was totally intrigued.

Brinda finally noticed her as well. Goodness, the woman was short and delicate like a porcelain doll. Was she the kind of girl he usually went for?

Aryan took Alisha's elbow. "Shall we go?"

And then it got interesting.

Brinda grabbed his other arm, the one holding the glass. Liquid sloshed violently as she shook his arm. "Don't you dare ignore me, Aryan Rajaram Chawla."

His whole body stiffened. "We just spoke for five whole minutes, how is that ignoring you?"

Brinda, the barracuda, deigned to talk to Alisha then. "Do you shut the lights when you leave the room? Do you leave the water running when you brush your teeth? Do you recycle?"

Alisha could only shake her head in confusion.

"Bloody hell, Brin," Aryan said, sounding thoroughly aggrieved.

Brin?

But Brin was beyond reason now. "What's your carbon footprint? Tell me. Tell me!"

Alisha looked between her and Aryan and took a cautious step back. Was the woman mad? "I have no idea."

Brin lost it then, rounding on Aryan in outrage. "You didn't lecture her on saving the planet? How one must only take what one needs and nothing more? On using solar panels and reprocessed wood and saving the frigging planet one footprint at a time?" Brinda folded her arms across her chest and sneered at him. She was very good at sneering. "Typical Aryan. A charming bastard when he's pursuing a woman but once he gets what he wants, it's over. Where is your conserve and use as little as possible policy when it comes to bedding women, huh?"

Aryan's blush turned a fiery red and spread all across his face and neck. Alisha wondered if she could be a witness as well as his defense lawyer when he murdered Brin, the stupid, grudge-mongering, barracuda.

A bright light suddenly flashed across the room, startling all three of them.

Aryan's "Bloody buggering hell!" was heartfelt and resounding.

THE MINUTE SINGH put the car in gear and they rolled forward, Alisha doubled over and howled with laughter. The hiccups came, and there were tears, but she couldn't stop. She didn't want to stop. How she'd controlled herself until they'd dealt with the press photographer, convincing him not to use the photo in any nefarious way, then delivered a somewhat calmer Brinda to her sister, and said goodbye to the Vaidyas, she'd never know. But she was thankful for that steely control.

Aryan slouched in his seat, staring broodily out of the window. His sense of humor seemed to have deserted him. Poor baby, thought Alisha, hiccupping, although her howls were now spurts of laughter. Women were the bane of his existence.

"Are you quite finished?" he inquired politely.

Alisha hiccupped. "Al-*hic*-most." She patted his hand. "I'm sorry."

He gave her a baffled frown.

She waved her hand between them. "For laughing…*hic*… at your expense."

He gave her a lopsided smile, and began to loosen his tie and undo his collar button.

Finally, Alisha gave a hearty sigh as the last of the hiccups disappeared into the good night. "Diya and I were just discussing how my dull and ordinary life has changed since I met you." She'd nearly made her Page 3 debut tonight. Diya was going to go green with envy.

"My life is equally dull, believe me. She…" he cleared his throat. "This was an aberration."

Alisha didn't believe him for a minute. A man who air-kissed and backslapped half of Bollywood, who stood shoulder to shoulder with the top one percent of the one-percenters in India could not have an ordinary life if he tried.

"A woman scorned?" she asked, just to clear it up.

He snorted. "Hardly." His eyes whipped back to her face, black and glittering. "Tell me you believe me."

"As opposed to her?"

"Alisha."

"Believe what? That you're an anal-retentive, planet-saving jerk?" She paused for effect. Teasing him was too much fun. "I have known you these past several months, you know."

His lips twitched. "And the last part?"

Alisha wanted to laugh again, but she couldn't take another round of hiccups. "Is it true?"

"Don't tease me, Sunshine."

"But it's so easy." She grinned, letting him know she wasn't upset. His past wasn't her burden to bear. Neither was his conscience.

Aryan frowned. "You're not jealous at all?"

"Of that twit? Give me some credit." It was like she'd trained for an Olympic gold in swimming and he was asking her to be insecure about the local swim team.

He rubbed his nose. "She is beautiful. And a lot of fun to be with…when she's not having one of her episodes." He said the last bit curtly, clearly remembering Brin's latest episode.

"You want me to be jealous of a beautiful twit who's also a little bonkers? Thank you, but no."

Aryan laughed huskily, then scooted closer to take her hand. "Will you come away with me."

Alisha's heart tittered. She was falling, sliding, deeply into love. "On one condition."

"Anything." He brought her hand to his lips and kissed it. To seal the deal.

"You have to measure my carbon footprint."

CHAPTER 10

"Shit. Shit, shit, shit, shit!" She was terribly, terribly late.

Alisha dashed into her bedroom, stripped off her work clothes and pulled on a T-shirt that said *Lawyers have feelings too (Allegedly)* on it's front. She hopped into the bathroom with one leg in her jeans, did her business, splashed and dried her sweaty face, and hopped back out to finish dressing.

This is it, kutty. *No turning back now.* And hopefully zero inopportune phone calls will follow them to Aryan's farmhouse.

Alisha gulped down the glass of orange juice Vallima brought her. "Thanks. My cell should work there, but just in case, you can reach me at the farmhouse. I've left the number on the fridge."

Vallima harrumphed and retreated into the kitchen. She'd been expressing her abject displeasure and disapproval about the weekend thusly, even though Alisha hadn't specified with whom or why she was going away.

Alisha brushed her hair out, and began to pack her

remaining toiletries into her kit, and the kit into her overnight bag which lay open on the bed. She dumped in extra batteries for her laptop and her phone. Aryan's farmhouse was in rural Maharashtra, electricity would be unpredictable at best.

She checked her watch. He'd be coming to get her anytime now and she wasn't ready. She'd planned to come home two hours ago, hoping to catch a nap and then soak in a relaxing bath. But at noon, Jyoti Kumar had come into the office and fudged her plans.

Alisha rubbed a hand across her stomach, remembering the afternoon's chaos which was still causing a nasty reaction in her belly. A preternaturally calm Jyoti had walked into the office, informing Alisha to stop the divorce proceedings. "I'm not ready to give up on my marriage. I don't want a divorce anymore," she said stonily. Alisha had asked Jyoti to sit in her office, then she'd asked MT to join them, as well as Jyoti's counselor, so that they could get to the bottom of Jyoti's change of heart.

It hadn't taken long for Jyoti to confess everything while sobbing hysterically. She'd only said it under duress, she confessed. Her bastard of a husband—soon to be ex—had barged into her sister's home, punched Jyoti in the stomach several times and warned her to reconsider her actions. Unluckily, he'd caught her alone. Sheela had taken the kids out for lunch and a movie. Luckily, the children hadn't been home to watch their father beat their mother this time.

By late afternoon, reports and complaints had been lodged, logged and filed against Mr. Kumar. The police and the judge had been informed of his behavior. Mr. Kumar's advocate was reprimanded on his behalf. Sheela had come to take her sister home and Jyoti Kumar had left their office looking like the walking dead.

Alisha balled a T-shirt in her hands as pity and fury

welled up within her for Jyoti Kumar. Alisha had hated seeing her in that state—beaten, broken, blank. The last two just like Amma. Alisha had very nearly cancelled the farmhouse trip, but MT had literally pushed her out of the office, ordering her to go and enjoy the weekend, promising Alisha that she'd call if anything needed urgent attention.

Guilt wormed its way between the pity and fury. How could she go off and have fun when her client's world was falling apart?

How could she not for those very same reasons?

There would always be a crisis at the office or in the world. Didn't she deserve to enjoy the sweet, wonderful things Aryan made her feel when there was precious little that made her feel that way?

Her iPhone buzzed. It was a text from Diya, self-appointed connoisseur of all things quixotic.

Two words: SLUT WEAR.

Alisha rolled her eyes and texted back. She absolutely, categorically refused to pack the lingerie Diya had purchased for her.

Please return the silly scraps of nothing and get your money back.

Besides, what was the need of a garment she wouldn't wear for more than two minutes?

Alisha zipped up her roll-on bag, then placed her supple leather briefcase next to it. Of course she was taking work along. Forty-eight hours was a long time just to be—

The thought of what was going to happen over the weekend made her feel warm and wobbly all over. Oh yes, she was definitely ready and willing to feel all kinds of things for Aryan Rajaram Chawla.

. . .

ARYAN'S FARM was on a plot of land somewhere between Mahabaleshwar and Panchgani, approximately six hours away from Mumbai. Alisha slept through most of the drive. Dealing with the Kumars had exhausted her. Aryan had woken her up for a quick dinner at a *dhaba* along the Mumbai-Pune expressway, after which she'd promptly fallen back to sleep.

They arrived at the farmhouse well after midnight.

"Wake up, love. We're here," Aryan said, shaking her gently.

"I'm awake." Alisha yawned, rubbing sleep from her eyes. Not that she could see much. Everything was pitch-black outside the windshield. A dozen steps away was a dimly lit, single story structure with stucco walls and a gently sloping roof. She yawned again, and stretched until every bone in her body realigned.

Well, certainly looks like a farmhouse, she thought. And sounded like it too. The cricking of crickets drifted into the BMW when Aryan got out, along with the sweet fragrance of the night jasmine.

Aryan's yawn threatened to crack his jaw as he too stretched in his sexy, languid manner. Then he gave a loud whistle and a commotion of barks drowned out the cricking crickets as a trio of dogs raced towards him in joyous welcome. Alisha pushed the passenger door open and was about to climb out when Aryan blocked her exit.

"I forgot to ask. You okay around dogs?"

Whimpering and barking, the dogs butted their heads against his legs trying to get to her—her new scent a stimulating lure. She pushed Aryan out of the way and held out her fists, knuckles up. "I grew up with dogs. My brother had aspirations to become a veterinarian so we had all kinds of animals parading in and out of our house at any given time."

Aryan crouched down to vigorously rub the smallest of the dogs, an adorable bug-eyed pug, on his head. "Isn't your brother an accountant?"

"Sadly. He lost his way somewhere." Alisha crouched too, letting the labradors lick her face.

Aryan laughed huskily when the little pug tried to jump into her lap, yapping for all he was worth. "Meet Kirk. The black labs are Spock and—"

"Don't tell me, Scotty," Alisha finished, grinning at the Star Trek junky.

Aryan spread his arms in front of him. "What can I say? I wanted to be an astronaut when I grew up. Blasting off into Space, the Final Frontier." He began to whistle the Trek tune, making the dogs yip with excitement and her laugh.

Yes, she'd needed this reminder that life could be fun too.

Alisha went to help Aryan when he began unloading the car. "No staff at your farmhouse? Who takes care of the dogs?"

"The caretaker's cottage is down the road. The dogs live with him and his family. No overnight staff. The village is not far, and someone will be here in the morning to help."

Aryan picked up the bags, two in each hand. Alisha tried to extract her roll-on from him, but he wouldn't let go. So, she took her laptop bag, and allowed him to be chivalrous. The labs bounded around their master in circles as they walked, but Captain Kirk had attached himself to her. When their entourage reached the front porch, Aryan turned the carved door handle and pushed the main door open.

He gestured for her to go in first. Alisha walked into a wide, airy foyer with bamboo floors and white stucco walls that were adorned with Japanese lanterns and wrought iron wall art. The décor was minimalistic and rustic with stone and wood everywhere.

"It's beautiful. Very Zen."

"No muss, no fuss." He nodded to the right. "It has an open floor plan. The great room and kitchen are that way. The bedrooms are this way." He turned to the left and started walking. "I'll show you the rest in daylight. Right now the lights are on energy-save."

That explained the dimness. Despite it, whatever Alisha could see looked amazing. The dogs dashed from one room to the next and finally disappeared down a corridor. Except Kirk, who remained glued to her heel.

Aryan halted in front of a dark wooden door. "Sharing a room, right?" he asked, solemnly.

Alisha raised her eyebrows in answer.

He caught her chin in his hand and planted a quick, hard kiss on her lips. "Just checking. In case you'd changed your mind." He opened the door and switched on the lights.

If the foyer had impressed her as Zen, Aryan's bedroom was a veritable paradise.

"Goodness gracious, Aryan," she gasped in awe at the size of the room which was nearly the size of her Mumbai flat. Half of it anyway.

The minimalistic Oriental theme carried into it. A massive bed, the star attraction, had been positioned against the far wall and was flanked by floor to ceiling windows. Concentric layers of a Balinese lotus had been carved into the superimposing headboard that rose like a colossus from the bed frame right up to the vaulted open-beam ceiling.

An entertainment area made up the bottom right of the room, complete with theatre-style chairs, a humungous TV and a game center. Four massive wardrobes in the same thick, dark wood as the door ran along the left, ending in a recessed door. A floor mirror in a bamboo frame leaned against one wall near the wardrobes. Light bamboo flooring, smooth walls painted in a shade between gold and peanut and more Japanese-style light fixtures completed the room.

She took in everything, but her eyes kept bouncing back to the enormous bed with a red and black spread, currently loaded with dogs. Alisha gulped, suddenly nervous at what was about to happen in it. Aryan walked past her and dumped their bags on a padded bench by the wardrobes.

Blushing, she busied herself by unzipping her bag and pulling out what she needed. What did she need exactly? "I should take a shower." Right. She was dusty and grimy from travel.

Aryan pointed at the recessed door. "Bathroom's through there."

Alisha locked herself in the bathroom and blew out the breath she'd been holding.

"It'll be all right. You'll be fine. It's like cooking. You don't need to make the dish every day or know it's recipe by heart to cook it well." She hugged her pajamas to her chest and groaned. Why was she giving herself a pep talk with cooking metaphors?

She groped for the light switches, flicked one on and was stunned again.

If the farmhouse was a retreat and Aryan's bedroom a wild dream, the bathroom suite was the ultimate luxury spa. It was a space one could happily wallow in. Live in it too. It was big enough.

Dirty-green concrete covered the floor and was warm beneath her feet. Two beautiful porcelain vessel sinks had been sunken into the concrete countertop that served as a vanity. An alcove in a corner housed the toilet. Next to it was a spacious mosaic-tiled shower done in green and black. And in the middle of the bathroom was an enormous sunken Jacuzzi.

Alisha promptly ditched the idea of a quick shower, the

tub completely seduced her. She filled it to the brim, sprinkled a spoon of eucalyptus bath salts she found on a tray on one side. She slid in, switched on the jets and moaned in ecstasy as pistons of hot water massaged her from shoulders to thighs. An eternity later, she shampooed and soaped herself.

Next, she jumped in the shower and washed off any lingering soap scum from her body, and while she was at it, she ran her hands over her legs and arms. No need to bring out the razor, her body was still hairless from the waxing a week ago. She applied cucumber scented body lotion, semi-dried her hair, brushed her teeth, flossed and gargled with mouthwash.

It was easier to tick off actions on a list. Pee—check. Bath—check. Brush—check. Focusing on her nightly ritual soothed her otherwise ready-to-revolt stomach. If she thought about *it*, she'd turn into a puddle of goo.

She unfolded her black and yellow emoji pajamas. They looked ridiculous dangling from her fingers. Was she really going to seduce Mr. Page 3 wearing that? Alisha made a face. She should've gotten off her high horse and packed the slut wear.

Oh well. She'd simply have to improvise. She pulled out a fresh towel from the ventilated linen closet and wrapped it around herself.

"It's just sex, *kutty*. No big deal."

Alisha stepped out of the bathroom and made her move.

ARYAN WAS MORE than aware of Sunshine's gaze on his towel-clad butt. Even so, he didn't turn around and continued to light the candles on the nightstand and along the window sills. He wanted to create the right atmosphere—soft music, scented candles, a single red rose on the bed. Just a little bit of enchantment for a night of passion. He'd taken a record two-minute shower in one of the guest bathrooms, and rushed back to set the stage.

He jerked upright when he felt more than Sunshine's gaze this time. Shivered when a fingernail traced the column of his spine from his nape to where it disappeared beneath the towel. Still, he finished lighting every single pillar of light before he turned around and met a pair of delicious chocolate eyes.

His mouth split into a wide grin, taking in her attire. Her eyebrow arched when he began to chuckle.

"I was wrong," he admitted, shaking his head. The eyebrow went impossibly higher. "I imagined what you'd wear tonight. Speculated between red lace and black lace, decided that a sheer mauve and black babydoll would look amazing on you. It would," he rubbed his thumb across her fleshy bottom lip as he spoke. "Then it hit me who I was fantasizing about and I was sure you'd wrap yourself in flannel pajamas just to make a point." He pulled her flush against his chest, towel and all. "Guess I don't know you as well as I think, Sunshine."

He kissed her. Gently, at first, then took it deeper, stronger. She tasted minty.

She was warm from her shower. Soft. Fragile somehow. He sucked on the dewy-fresh skin of her shoulder. She put her hands on his chest, igniting his already sensitized flesh, and beamed at him.

"I love him, you know. He's my ultimate fantasy lover."

He? "Who?" Aryan would murder the bastard, fantasy or not.

Alisha cocked her head at the entertainment system. An instrumental version of a song from one of SRK's movies played in the background. "Shah Rukh Khan. Well, it's a toss-up between him and Ranbir Kapoor. I can't decide who gives me the bigger feels."

Apparently, Sunshine had a Celebs-I'd-Like-To-Shag list. He wanted to laugh.

"Can I vote?" If anyone was going to reap the benefit of her superstar fantasies, it was him. He resumed kissing her shoulder, her neck, her beautiful collarbone.

"When I look at him, my ovaries stand up and cheer," she stopped teasing and gripped his biceps. "Aryan?"

"Hmm? Are your ovaries cheering?"

"How come you don't know him? You know most of the movie stars—Wait. Just wait! What's that look on your face?" Whatever she saw on his face made her own light up like a house on Diwali. "*You know him!* Oh my God! You know Shah Rukh Khan." She screeched, her nails digging into his skin deep enough to indent. She started bouncing in place. "Please, you have to introduce me. Please, please, please."

He bent his head and fused their mouths together. The only man she should be thinking of was him. Two quick tugs and he had them both naked, towels discarded to the floor.

She broke the kiss and gulped in air. "Dogs?"

"Outside, with the caretaker," he said, touched that she'd worry.

He pulled her close again and turned up the heat. He touched her all over, producing a friction that had her squirming, gasping against him and his heart jack-hammering. They were both beyond ready. He grabbed a foil packet from the nightstand, rolled on the condom. Planting a large hand between her breasts, he nudged her backwards, tipping her over the bed and joining her there. *At last.* He shuddered as he settled between her legs.

Still, he asked, "Yes?" He had to be sure. He needed her to be sure.

She nodded jerkily, hugging his hips with her legs. "Yes. Aryan, please."

That's all he needed. With one impatient thrust, he joined their bodies together, putting an end to their weeklong—hell, months-long foreplay.

And then there was no more talk, no more thought, there was only Sunshine.

"YOUR HAIR CURLS when it's wet."

He felt a hand pet his head. He should move. He was crushing her, but he couldn't find the strength. He nuzzled her throat because it was right there. She purred in approval and tilted her head, granting him an all-access pass to the party.

He breathed her in. Her skin was hot from their exertion, wet and female and smelled like...

"Why do you smell like a salad?" He drew back, just enough that he could see her sweet face.

She smiled her siren's smile. "Probably my lotion. It's cucumber and avocado."

He bent back to his work, diligently licking his way from her head to her toes. His blood no longer frenzied, he came to know her body thoroughly. Intimately. She followed his lead without arguments or opinions. It amused him, this timid version of Sunshine. It made him feel protective towards her, possessive of her.

He aroused them both slowly this time, relentlessly, until they were poised on the edge of annihilation once again. His Sunshine, he thought as he spread her legs apart with his knees and touched her until she was writhing and senseless beneath him. Until her voice turned hoarse from screaming.

"I want to hold you down. Will you let me?" he asked, his voice equally harsh.

Lust filled every molecule of air between them. She heard him. Locked eyes with him. Said yes.

Only then, he held her hands tightly on either side of her head and like a conquering hero, he began his possession of her.

Alisha's eyes went dark, then blank as she yielded to him. Utterly.

CHAPTER 11

A rambunctious *cock-a-doodle-doo* woke Alisha up the next morning.

She rolled onto her side while her consciousness jump-started her brain. She was usually up on the first ting of the alarm, albeit grouchily, so no wonder she'd woken up with the first crow of the rooster.

Not a rooster. There were several of them, and all of them in discord with each other as the crowing gained volume. Manic barking joined the early morning chorus. The dogs were chasing the silly fowls who were bent on waking the dead.

Alisha sure did feel dead. Boneless. Delirious. She was drunk on sex. Maybe love, but definitely sex. At least she didn't need to get out of bed and start prepping for the day. It was Saturday. She could wallow in bed all day long, if she wished. She stretched out her legs, making them stick out of the quilt wrapped around her body.

Thinking of bodies, hers throbbed and twanged in weird places. Her muscles ached and her skin felt bruised, used, and yet she'd never felt better. She wanted to jump up and crow with the roosters. Now, if only her limbs and vocal cords did as she directed.

Prying her eyes open, she blinked groggily at the still burning candles on the nightstands. The room reeked of vanilla, they'd have to air it out soon. Restless now that her brain was semi-awake, she rolled-stretched again and hit her nose against Aryan's granite shoulder, hard enough that her eyes watered. But, when they cleared, she was greeted by the most dazzling early morning vision of her life.

Mr. I'm-too-sexy-for-my-clothes was sound asleep on his stomach. He slept on his stomach, just like her. Candle light had turned his skin to gold last night. This morning, dappled daylight made him a silvery shadow of light and dark. One sinewy arm was flung upward and the other—the one attached to the shoulder she was inhaling—was buried under a fluffy black pillow. A sigh escaped her lips and she raised herself on an elbow to inspect him better.

A straight, thick brow slashed wickedly over one closed eye accentuated with dense, inky lashes; the counterparts hidden from her view by the pillow. His razor-edged nose flared and deflated with every breath. He had an inch-long scar on the curve of his shoulder; an old injury that had probably needed stitches. She leaned in, kissed it. Then she licked him. He tasted salty, smelled musky. They'd both perspired profusely last night.

Alisha's body hummed in rememberance of all they'd done, all night long.

She should get up, take care of her body's demands, before they started doing it all over again—and she had no doubt they would. She sat up with a sigh. Lethargy filled the pockets of her body that weren't throbbing. Was it imperative to pee? She flopped back down and stretched luxuriously.

Right. She definitely needed to pee. She sat up again.

"Stop fidgeting," Aryan growled sleepily.

"Oh! You're awake." Giddy to engage with him again, she smiled down at him.

"No, I'm not." His eyes were shut. Only his lips moved —barely.

Alisha pouted. Now that she was awake and semi-functional, she wanted to get up, dance, have breakfast and explore the land. Make love again and again. She poked his shoulder.

In a lightning quick move, he clamped a large, warm palm around her arm and wrestled her flat on her back, flinging one hairy thigh across her legs when she started to shriek.

"I want to get up." She pushed at his leg, at his shoulder, and couldn't so much as budge a hair on his body, much less shove eighty-seven kilos of muscle off her.

"I hate cheerful morning people," he mumbled into the crook of her shoulder.

A delicious shiver rippled through her. "I'm definitely not one of those creatures. I can't function before two mugs of tea, minimum."

He opened one bleary eye. "Then why the hell are you so perky today?"

Her stomach growled in answer.

"God woman, it's not even six."

"Tell that to my stomach. I think we each burned several thousand calories last night and my body needs replenishing." In more ways than one.

She noticed the roosters had gone silent. Serves them right if the dogs had had them for breakfast. She wanted breakfast too. And she wanted Aryan. She couldn't decide which one of her hungers she wished to sate first.

Aryan patted her tummy. "I'm sure it'll survive a fast or two."

"Don't be mean. I want to use the bathroom. Let me up, you oaf."

"Oaf, am I? What happened to, 'You're a god, Aryan. You're the best. You're so good, Aryan?'"

"I never said any of those things." She struggled to get free, but his arms were unrelenting.

"Close enough."

"You're such a liar." She would not shriek again. She wouldn't give him the satisfaction.

Not that it stopped him from snaking his arm around her stomach and flipping her on her side, so she faced away from him. Alisha struggled anew, but only succeeded in fitting their bodies closer together, her back to his front. She realized his intent then, could feel it against her back. And because he asked oh so politely and explicitly, she let him drape her like he wanted; one leg straight, the other bent for easy access.

Who knew his asking and her granting permission could be an aphrodiasiac?

After he'd arranged her to his satisfaction, he curved a hand over her hip, just below her tattoo. He brushed her hair off her shoulder with his chin and his teeth scraped her neck, then sucked hard. Her back arched like he meant it to, and she gasped.

"Now," he said, his voice dark with promise. "Let's see if I can make you say those things again."

Alisha clamped a hand over her mouth refusing to boost his ego any further, and fell asleep as soon as Aryan finished turning her brains and bones to mush once more.

THE STAR TREK crew woke them up just after eleven o'clock. They barked and scratched at the door until Aryan had to get up and let them in. The canine trio proceeded to leap up on the bed, creating a rumpus that put an end to their laziness.

Alisha showered alone much to Aryan's irritation. Some things should be private, she'd told him firmly. She put on denim shorts, a yellow T-shirt and went so far as to paint her toenails a bright yellow-orange to match her outfit. The fashionistas would be proud.

Then, she went in search of breakfast—lunch now—while Aryan took his turn in the bathroom. She found the kitchen, the cook and a pot full of caffeine. She was on her second cup of tea when Aryan sauntered into the dining room wearing cargo shorts and a blue and white checked shirt with the sleeves rolled up. He looked good enough to eat.

"Thank you, Mira *bai*," he said in accented Marathi to the caretaker's wife when she set his breakfast and black coffee in front of him.

Mira *bai* replied in equally accented English, "You are velcum, AB."

"AB?" asked Alisha, thoroughly amused by the exchange.

"Aryan *bhauji*. They won't call me by my name and I refuse to answer to *bhauji*," explained the liberalist consuming his breakfast with remarkable speed.

They were both starving. She demolished several toasts with jam, a cup of semolina *upma* and a couple of *samosas* with equal gusto. Aryan had two cheese omelettes in addition to all of that.

"What do you want to do today?" he asked, once their hunger wasn't as acute.

"Whatever you want as long as I have a couple of hours in between to work." Captain Kirk rolled belly-up at her feet. She obliged him by rubbing it. "He's adorable. Does he ever come to Mumbai?"

"He started off there. I got him when I moved into my flat. But when I got the labs for the farm two years ago, he just took to them. He refuses to come back, starts whining whenever I put him in a car without his posse."

Alisha sat on the floor—which was unnaturally warm just like the bathroom—so Kirk could climb into her lap. She asked Aryan what the deal was with the warm floors.

Between bites of omelette, Aryan explained how the farm was rigged on a geothermal energy system. Meaning, ground heat was sucked from the earth and pumped out to the hot water boiler, the generator and the piped floors at night to store energy or keep them at a certain temperature. The reverse happened during the day. Uncle Sam and Aryan owned an impressive chunk of the surrounding land, most of it running on clean, renewable energy.

Aryan stood up once he was done eating. "Come on, I'll show you around."

It was a no muss, no fuss house indeed. It didn't need fuss, not with the rows and rows of windows on the walls that allowed light to pour in from every direction, and show-cased spectacular views. The Sahyadri Mountain range, so dark and foreboding last night, was picture-perfect in daylight.

"If going green looks this good, it's a wonder why more people don't opt for it," she said, looking around in awe. He gave her a sweet peck on the cheek, clearly happy with her remark.

They went outside on the verandah where the April sun blazed down on the crisp earth. It was so hot that she found it difficult to breathe even in the shade. Still, she followed him around the farmhouse because she wanted to know him better. He'd built quite a place, blending style with principles, and she told him so.

"Not bored by my sermon on ecologically sound construction?"

She made him stop walking and face her. "If you're

comparing me to the brainless barracuda, I'll have to kick your ass."

His mouth slanted up in a wicked smile. "Wouldn't dream of it." After a moment, he asked, "You aren't jealous at all?"

He was such a *guy* sometimes, needing his ego petted. She rolled her eyes. "Nope."

"Why not?" Teasing Sunshine was soon becoming one of Aryan's favorite pastimes, along with kissing her and making love to her.

"Because I trust you," she said.

He'd expected a droll rejoinder, not…honesty, he thought, surprised. So, she'd speak of trust but she wouldn't speak of love. Not even after last night. Didn't she realize love was easier than trust?

"Goodness, it's hot." She bent at the waist and caught her mane of hair in a fist, deftly twisting it into a topknot and securing it with an orange-colored *Juicy* ball cap on her head. Kirk staggered around her in a circle, then collapsed at her feet.

Aryan was pretty close to doing the same.

"He's fallen hard. Maybe he'll come back to Mumbai now." He wanted to tell her the truth, earn her trust as well as her love. He slipped on his aviators instead.

"I love him too. Yes, my poochie. I love you. Yes, I do," she crooned, rubbing Kirk's belly who was shamelessly writhing on the ground.

Once Sunshine was done loving his dog, Aryan showed her around the rest of the property, starting with the greenhouse where they grew their own produce. The gardener and his two teenage sons waylaid him about a problem. There was always something that needed fixing or his input. This time it was the new roofs he was meant to install in the village before the monsoons struck. He hadn't forgotten, he assured them.

They passed the cow shed and the chicken coop—it was a working farm—and headed toward the northeast end of the property where Uncle Sam's bungalow sat high up on a hill.

"The view must be amazing up there," she said, sighing.

"If you like heights."

She had caught something in his words because she turned to him. "You don't like heights?"

He shrugged. His aversion to heights wasn't a phobia exactly, but the story was another one in a long list that came under the heading: Mother, Father and Stuff Better Left Buried. Aryan didn't know how to even begin telling her, though he knew it would have to be soon.

He kissed her, delaying the inevitable. Strands of her hair had escaped from her ragtag bun under her cap. She was flushed from the heat, her upper lip dotted with sweat. A couple of flies hovered over them, so he pulled her away.

The stillness of the land was beautiful. Peaceful. The quiet only broken by the occasional moos and clucks or a distant road bike or the sound of their feet shuffling through the dry vegetation.

Alisha seemed to enjoy the silence too. He liked that she didn't fill it with forced chatter.

Did she realize he was different here? In Mumbai, he was the quintessential young urban professional, or damn close to it, with his jet-set lifestyle and phenomenally successful career. He loved all that too—the parties, the schmoozing, the race to the top and the constant movement. But here on the farm, life was uncomplicated. Here, he could walk the earth in bare feet.

Alisha didn't have his duality of nature. She was a pragmatic, self-assured lawyer just about anywhere. She had no doubts about who she was or where she wanted to go, and that steadfastness drew him like nothing else.

He knew too many people who were confused and lost

and ungrounded. He saw his mother in all of them. Weak-willed people disgusted him. They always spelled trouble.

But not his stable, no-nonsense Alisha—she was trouble on an entirely different level.

"Aryan, are those kids waving at you?"

He followed her line of vision back to the house where a gaggle of kids played on the verandah. Oh, yes. He knew those hooligans well and what they wanted from him. And since Alisha wished to work that afternoon, he had a few hours to kill, didn't he? Aryan rubbed his hands in glee and hollered a greeting at the kids.

Where on earth had he trotted off to with all those kids? Alisha wondered for the umpteenth time.

He'd deposited her at the house after the tour, given her a vague explanation about the kids and a clubhouse, then he'd sailed off like a galleon at sea with thirteen tugboats of various shapes and sizes, and Scotty and Spock in tow. Kirk had refused to leave her side, her loyal sweetheart.

Three hours later, Captain Kirk was still prostrate at her feet, snoring gently, while AB was still missing in action.

Alisha began sorting her work papers into piles—finished, unfinished and junk. The junk pile she left for Aryan to deal with as he recycled paper products. She stuffed the finished pile back into her briefcase and left the last pile on the desk to work on later—she'd taken over a guest room that doubled as an office to work. Mira *bai* had supplied her with enough lemonade to fill the Jacuzzi, which she'd consumed in its entirety. The cold drink had helped cool down her overheated body, and deterred the migraine she usually suffered after walking about under the scorching sun.

She was not ashamed to admit that she had a delicate constitution and was mostly a sedentary person. The only forms of exercise she could handle was an occasional Yoga class or shopping. Yes, she considered shopping exercise; you walked for hours carrying weight, what else would you call it? Gyms and sports had never held any appeal for her, and she'd been blessed by Amma's skinny genes. Diya hated her for it, but such was life.

Aryan ran every day. He also swam, played tennis and football. The guy was a fitness freak, and loved to work up a sweat.

Diya and Aryan were like two peas in a pod, in that respect. In fact, they were similar in a number of ways. They loved to party, they actually loved to exercise, and they were both obsessed with clothes. How strange she'd connected with two people who were her opposite in every way.

While Alisha used the bathroom, Kirk kept a vigil on the other side. She wondered if Aryan had meant it about bringing him back to Mumbai. If Kirk wanted to come home with her, she'd take him gladly. His master, too.

She bit her lip, and quickly turned away from the vanity mirror. She wasn't ready to face what was so obviously on display there. She brushed and braided her hair and changed into a sweat-free top.

Then she went in search of AB, Kirk tottering behind her.

CHAPTER 12

The gardener pointed her in the direction of a woodland on the far edge of the property where Aryan and his gang were hard at work. On what, she still had no idea.

The woodland was dense with foliage, blocking out most of the late afternoon sun as she tramped through the undergrowth. Jackfruit trees swelled around her, the scent of the fruit, strong and tangy. The humidity was bearable, still, she'd been smart to pack six T-shirts for a two-day trip. She'd have to shower again before dinner.

She heard them before she saw them. Laughter mingled with barks, interspersed with sawing and hammering. The sounds filled the woods, giving her an audible direction. When she saw them and their enterprise, she stopped to admire the delightful view.

They were making a treehouse. A gigantic treehouse.

There were six platforms resting on the thickest branches of a massive tree, each about fifteen feet or higher from the ground, and in various stages of completion. The larger, older boys were up on the tree, one on each platform, hammering away. The smaller boys were sawing wood and cutting planks into different sizes safely down on the ground.

Aryan was up there as well, on the largest and highest of the platforms, yelling out instructions. He hadn't noticed her yet, because his attention was on the boys and their safety.

"AB, the girl is here," a little boy, around twelve, shouted in Marathi as he spotted her.

Alisha smiled at the boy, who grinned back, displaying crooked white teeth.

"Hey you," AB gave her a mock salute from his perch. Then swept his arm across, gesturing broadly. "You like?"

He was shirtless and sweaty, his chest streaked with sawdust. Oh yes. She liked it very much.

Her heart went thumpity-thump as an ocean full of emotions surged inside her, wiping the smile off her face. How had she let this happen? How had she given him such control over her heart?

"You want to come up?" He stood on a floor with a partially finished wall on one side. It had a huge hole in it, presumably for a window.

"Not particularly," she said and forced her gaze away from him.

"Thought so. A girl can't climb so high, can she?" said another scruffy-looking boy missing a few front teeth. He barely came up to her hip, but clearly, was a male chauvinist in the making. Some of the kids snickered at his wit.

"That's not true. Girls can pretty much do anything a boy can." Teach them young and maybe the world would be a better place.

The boy, whose name she learned was Amit, looked at her suspiciously. "That's not what AB told us. He said boys were stronger, smarter and more talented." Amit looked at his mentor for validation. Alisha looked up too, brows raised at the child's dubious guru.

Aryan winced and shook his head at the boy. "I should've also mentioned that some things were meant to be kept within the boys club." But his shoulders shook, betraying his amusement.

Alisha sneered. "No wonder God has to repeatedly send down messiahs and avatars to save the world. Even She knows you men botch things up spectacularly."

Aryan's laugh boomed out, the implied insult bouncing off his tree trunk-sized ego. The boys wanted a translation to the English joke that had made AB laugh so loudly. So she told them. Unfortunately, they were too young to understand the finer points of feminism and no one laughed. Though one or two faked a chuckle.

"So, are you chicken or are you game?" He taunted from on high with his hands on his hips where a tool belt was slung rakishly. He looked like Tarzan. He wasn't even holding the trunk, the idiot! What if he fell?

"Fine, fine," Alisha said crossly. "I'll come up. But if I fall, I'm suing you for damages."

She walked around the tree, looking for the ladder. A thick rope came swinging down nearly rapping her on the head.

"You're joking." She stared at the rope in horror. Goodness. What had she just agreed to do? She reached out to touch it gingerly, hoping it would disappear on contact.

"We haven't gotten around to making a proper ladder, yet," explained Aryan, tongue in cheek. He was clearly enjoying himself. The ass.

Alisha cursed under her breath. Of all the foolish things Diya had forced her to do in her life this one, that this mad man was making her do, took the cake.

"You know what? I'll just help these little kids cut up wood. Yes, that's what I'll do." Aryan should appreciate her thoughtfulness and practicality. She was saving him from paying her a zillion rupees when she fell, broke her body and sued him.

"Just hold that knot tightly and I'll pull you up."

What? This was getting worse and worse. Alisha looked around for an escape, an excuse, anything. Why the hell had she stopped working on those briefs? She was a workaholic with no muscle mass, not a chimpanzee with opposable toes.

The boys stared at her in varying degrees of doubt. And Hulk Hogan up there was the worst. How dare they think her a scaredy cat even if she was one? She could do this. She would show them. For all women all over the world, she squared her shoulders and grabbed the rope. "Ready," she squeaked.

"Alright...one...two...and...three!"

He pulled her up without dropping her on her head. When she almost reached his platform, he instructed her to gain a foothold on the nearest branch and push upwards as he grabbed her under her armpits and dragged her the rest of the way, until she was sitting on top of the wooden floor.

"Okay?" he asked, chest heaving.

Alisha slowly moved to sit cross-legged, letting her pounding pulse settle down. She couldn't look down. Not yet.

Aryan hunkered down and kissed her forehead. "Good girl."

She shouldn't feel pleased by his praise. It was pathetic. She shouldn't notice how masculine he smelled, of sweat and dust and a trace of cologne thrown into the mix. It was pathetic how she wanted to lean into him and inhale the aroma.

The youngsters watched, giggling and poking each other, until Aryan told them to get back to work.

Aryan sat down next to Sunshine and dangled his legs over the edge of the platform, giving her time to right her bearings. Heights did strange things to people. At the least, it skewed perception.

"Have you seen the movie *Robin Hood*? The one with Kevin Costner?" he asked, and she nodded. "Remember the tree house in Sherwood Forest? That's what we are attempting to build here."

A slight breeze billowed around them, cooling and drying his sweat-soaked skin.

Twisting to and fro, she took it all in. "Impressive undertaking. Your idea?"

"Mine had been to install one tree house. But there are too many boys…and girls in the village," he said. Contrary to what it looked like, he was not a Neanderthal. "One such set up isn't enough. So, once this one is built, we'll scout for another tree like this one and build more."

"It's a gigantic and sturdy-looking tree, but it's shaped funny. What is it?"

"*Parijaat* or baobab. The thinnest branches are two feet wide that's why I chose it to build on. It's an old tree, more than a couple hundred years at least."

"Really? Is that why it's leafless? Is it sick?"

"No, baobab live for thousands of years. It blooms only in the monsoons. It's a super hardy desert tree, originally from Africa, and it stays leafless for most of the year." He would bring her back in the monsoons so she could witness its glory with her own eyes. The baobab was magnificent in bloom. "It's supposed to bear strange, hairy flowers and jack fruit-like fruit, but I haven't seen it happen yet."

Alisha crept closer to the edge and dangled her feet over,

mirroring him. He noticed her bare feet and cautioned her about splinters since they were sitting on raw wood.

"Why tree houses?" she asked while playing footsie.

His Sunshine was damned intuitive. She'd plunged the arrow straight into the bull's eye.

"My father and I built one when I was five. We'd come back from a trip to Nottinghamshire where we visited the absolute best tree house in the world. I wanted one just like it and I threw hellish tantrums until I got what I wanted. We lived in an apartment and couldn't actually build a tree house since…no trees. So we improvised and built a clubhouse on our private terrace. I remember the three of us laughing through structural mistakes and mishaps all summer long."

He rarely brought up his parents so he knew he'd surprised her by doing so. She didn't even tease him about being a spoiled little tantrum thrower.

She took his hand in hers and laced them together. "And now you want to give these boys the same thing. A summer of fun and laughter."

He shrugged. He didn't know why he'd started this project a few months ago. It had just happened. If his father had called at the farmhouse that day, it was only a coincidence.

"You're good with children," she said after a while.

"How many should we have?" He couldn't resist teasing.

"Shut up, Aryan."

"Ah, I forget. You're not sure you want any." She'd intimated it in one of their chats.

His little cousin Lara's favorite nursery rhyme came to mind. *Aryan and Alisha sitting in a tree; K-I-S-S-I-N-G!*

He'd make the ditty a reality if not for the boys. They didn't need those kinds of lessons just yet.

"What kind of wood are you using?" A pointed change of subject.

"Teak. And for every tree we cut down, we've planted five more in another area." Always environmentally conscious.

"These are the windows?" she asked about the rectangular holes in the walls.

There weren't going to be any, he explained. The openings were for ventilation. And no, it wouldn't be dangerous to have random gaping holes in the walls. The boys needed to learn responsibility and caution at some point, didn't they?

"The tree houses will connect to each other with rope bridges, exactly like in *Robin Hood*."

"You've built an amazing play area for these kids. I can't wait to see it finished." She froze after she said it, but recovered quickly. "You're a sweet man, AB."

He turned up the sweetness to show her that he too was thinking in terms of forever. "I'm imagining our sons playing here, love."

She didn't take his teasing well and tried to pitch him over the edge. The boys noticed the scuffle and the woods suddenly resounded with threats and shouts and boisterous giggles.

They spent a long time in the tree house, talking, arguing and working. He showed her and the boys how to build walls and she took to hammering nails like a champ.

"This was nice," Sunshine said when they wrapped up for the day, stowing the tools, covering the danger zones in tarp.

It had been more than nice. He loved being with her, challenging her, and he was sure the feeling was reciprocated. That wasn't the issue.

His skin cooled fast as he accepted there was an issue. He needed to tell her about his parents. Frankly, he wanted to. He'd tried to several times over the past months but he just couldn't settle on the right words. Some Wordfreak he was turning out to be.

Ever the coward, Aryan taught Sunshine how to rappel down a tree instead.

Turnabout was fair play.

Aryan had tormented her all day long. He'd won all three Scrabble games they'd played before and after dinner. Unfairly, she might add, by making her lose her mind with his smoldering teases and toe-curling kisses. And that last verbal volley he'd shot at her during dinner?

It's your move, Worddiva!

She couldn't let him get away with such smugness now, could she? So, she'd seized the upper hand and laid down the law—her law—in his bedroom.

So far, he'd done everything she'd commanded, demanded of him, without a peep or a groan. Not very sporting of him, she thought with a pout. A hostage should make some sounds of distress. She wanted him begging, maybe even roaring, by the time she was done. She wouldn't be the only one screaming tonight.

She stripped him slowly, then asked him to lie down on the bed. She ordered him to close his eyes because even that dark, devouring gaze was like a caress on her skin. She didn't want to be the one trembling. Not yet.

But he was shaking, she saw with some satisfaction. Moisture had popped up across his skin, making it glisten.

She looked down at the picture he made from her straddled perch. He was a veritable feast of muscle and bone and gorgeous man—all hers to do with as she pleased. Still, she asked his permission before touching. Described what she was about to do before raising his hands to her lips, kissing his palms, sucking each of his fingers in turn as he'd done to hers last night. His breath stuttered and he throbbed beneath her, but he didn't move, didn't take over. Didn't make a sound.

Last night, she'd been set adrift in a sea of sensations. He'd allowed her no surcease.

She began to move up and down his body, nibbling, licking, taking tiny, tasty bites of his flesh. His arms jerked like a marionettes and she pressed them down flat on the bed.

"You promised. My turn," she whispered, giddily steering his surrender as thoroughly as he'd induced hers. "Open your eyes now."

He obeyed instantly, almond-shaped eyes locking on hers. Compelling. Beguiling. She loved his eyes. Black as sin, burning with a desire that threatened to send them both up in flames.

She bent and kissed him. His mouth opened and she pushed her tongue in. They both groaned; she mewled, but the sound that ripped from his throat was a sensual, guttural assault on her senses.

Sounds he was making because of her. For her. She was going to lose her mind if she hadn't already. She couldn't handle him for much longer. She wasn't skilled enough or experienced enough.

How did he do it? Why did he have such control over her body?

She'd build up to it, she swore. She'd get better at this game and then she'd play to win. He couldn't always get his way.

She fumbled then, grew clumsy and shy when her own desires started working against her.

"Aryan," she whispered.

Somehow, he understood her unvoiced demand. He clamped his hands on her hips and drove into her deep and strong, giving her the release she wanted so desperately even as she craved his surrender.

It wasn't about winning, she realized as she fractured into a million pieces, taking him with her. It wasn't about him roaring his love for her or her coming undone by him. The true beauty lay in compromise.

And once she grasped that, the inevitability of their next move was clear as crystal.

CHAPTER 13

When Aryan woke the next morning, Sunshine wasn't in bed. But he could hear a jubilant commotion going on outside between woman and canine. Groggily, he rolled out of bed and yanked open the satin curtains, flooding the room with sunlight. And just like that, sleep vanished from his mind.

There they were—his love and his dogs.

Barefoot, wet and absolutely perfect, Sunshine danced about in middle of the lawn with a hose in her hands and a towel over her shoulder as she gave Scotty and Spock a thorough scrubbing. Being water hounds, they were having the time of their lives, while Kirk, the dignified leader of the crew, was keeping an eye on the spectacle from the dry verandah.

Gilded laughter lit up her face, making her look even more beautiful this morning. Every day he fell deeper in love with her—his Sunshine, Alisha Menon, Worddiva and dog lover.

A fist full of need slammed into his gut and he barely managed not to gasp out loud. He wanted her again and in a way that had nothing to do with sex and yet had everything to do with it. Last night, she'd destroyed him with her lovemaking, and when she'd handed the reigns back to him —fuck.

He turned from the window, rubbing his chest, trying to sooth the panic beginning to set in. Lust or love was one thing. He could handle that. What he hadn't expected was the manic possessiveness he felt for her. He wanted to consume her, own her mind, body and soul. He couldn't imagine his life without her anymore and that scared the bejesus out of him. What would he do if he lost her?

He let loose a blasphemy Nanu would box his ears for and stalked into the bathroom. He wanted to bloody punch something. He needed to let off steam. A swim. He'd go for a swim.

He changed into a pair of black and orange Oakley trunks, and shoving his feet into his slippers, her made his way down to the pool house and gym annex behind the house.

He'd installed an indoor pool at the farmhouse because it was easier to maintain, a whole lot cleaner than an outdoor one, and not subject to the vagaries of the weather. Aryan kicked off his slippers, and dove into the warmish water. He started doing laps in a strong, steady crawl.

If he was being honest—and why shouldn't he be as he was conversing with himself—he was in over his head with her. What had started as a simple online flirtation had become a complicated emotional affair—a bond Alisha categorically refused to even acknowledge. Verbally, at least.

She was afraid of commitment. Afraid that a relationship would hinder her life and goals. Love was a commitment. Marriage an even bigger one, and babies were the ultimate, irreversible commitment a person could make. By her own admission, she wanted nothing to do with any of the three if they became hurdles in her path.

But, she trusted him.

He stopped to catch his breath at the shallow end of the pool, water sluicing down his face.

So, where the bloody hell did that leave them? Their families clearly expected something to happen. Quite frankly, taking their relationship forward wasn't unappealing to him. But…

He pushed off the wall and started the next round of laps in a butterfly stroke.

Nothing was simple with her. And, damn it, he wanted life to be simple. He'd made his life simple. If a complication arose, he shoved it into a corner and ignored it until it went away. Not that his father got the hint. The old man had been persistently calling for the last ten days.

What was she afraid of? What wasn't she telling him? Well, he hadn't told her the whole truth either, had he? *Fuck.*

What did it mean that they were both hiding something from each other?

Nothing. Absolutely nothing. He should stop the amateur psychology. And it wouldn't hurt to take a step back for now, shut a few doors, rebuild some walls. And no, it wasn't retreating. He was just being cautious. Alisha liked level-headed people. She didn't approve of craziness. And she'd roast his balls for breakfast if he so much as looked at her possessively.

So, new plan. He'd harness the mania, the passion and the love for her sake.

EXHAUSTED BY THE DOGGIE ABLUTIONS, Alisha sprawled out on a towel on the verandah to sun dry. The dogs, clean and odor free but equally exhausted, slept in a heap by her feet. If she didn't care that she'd burn to a crisp within half an hour, she'd happily start snoring too. But her skin was already several shades darker due to the amount of time she'd spent outdoors this weekend, and she didn't want to burn herself. Ten minutes of lethargy, that's all she could allow herself.

Just as she closed her eyes and let herself go boneless, droplets of chlorinated water began to rain down on her face. She opened her eyes to see Aryan shaking himself like a dog over her. He was in a pair of dripping wet swimming shorts.

"Don't be a buffoon." She screened her sun-warm face from the cold drops. "You went swimming?"

"You robbed me of my beauty sleep again, Sunshine," he said as he stretched out beside her, using a rolled up towel as a pillow. He pushed his aviators back in position on his nose and folded his hands neatly on top of each other on his stomach.

"What's so funny?" he asked lazily when she laughed at him.

"You are, Mr. Fashionista." She rolled onto her stomach and propped her chin on her fists. Even tanned, he was several shades lighter than her. The quintessential difference between them; he was a North Indian, an Aryan, and she was a South Indian Dravidian.

If he were a photograph, she'd meme it, *The Sun God in repose.* He was all sun-kissed skin, sculpted muscles and sleeping arrogance. All hers.

He grabbed her hand, kissed it and placed it firmly on his chest when she began to tease the scar on his shoulder. Wet chest hair tickled her palms and she couldn't help snaking her fingers through the thatch.

"You should use it as your handle on social media." Feeling impish, she fisted his chest hair and pulled, making him grunt while his brows drew flat above the aviators.

"What?"

"Mr. Fashionista. Your forty thousand Instagram followers will double overnight." She sat up and began dabbing the wetness on his chest and arms.

"Are you implying I have more beauty than brains?"

"If the shoe fits." Alisha yelped as he pinched her thigh. She tossed the towel aside. She was dry, except for the folds of her skirt. "Hungry?" she asked, excited about the surprise she'd planned.

No response. Alisha poked his rock-like abs. "I made you breakfast."

Last night, he'd told her that they'd have to fend for themselves for breakfast because Mira *bai* didn't come to work until later on Sundays. Alisha had woken up early to prepare the meal but the dogs had sidetracked her.

"Did you?" He still didn't move. In fact, he resembled an Egyptian mummy.

She poked him again. "Did you hear what I said?"

"Will it poison me?"

"Shut up!"

She rose to her feet and headed for the kitchen, her happy mood getting happier by the minute. With a spring in her step, she flitted about the kitchen, whisking egg batter, pouring it on the heated skillet, grilling sandwiches and arranging everything on the tray she'd readied earlier. Aryan sauntered in as she poured freshly-squeezed orange juice into two glasses.

"Coffee?" He pulled two mugs out of a cupboard above the sink when she nodded.

"A macchiato, please." She'd already had her tea. Coffee would do nicely with breakfast.

Since their clothes were still damp, and it was pretty outside, they shared the first meal of the day out on the verandah's seating area.

She could be with this man, Alisha thought suddenly. Without a thought in her head or a care for the future, she could simply be with him like this for a long, long time. He demanded nothing from her. He didn't need constant attention. He didn't expect to be waited on hand and foot.

He wasn't like any man she'd known. He wasn't like her father.

Everything was falling into place. They fit together so well. So why was she hesitating to tell him how she felt?

Aryan took a giant bite of his sandwich and decided he'd live after all. "This is good," he said around a mouthful of bread.

"Don't sound so shocked. Besides, how hard is it to get a grilled cheese right?" Sunshine replied.

"I'm serious. You've sprinkled herbs and everything like a true gourmet." His personal chef preened a little, so he teased her. "You should be proud of yourself for performing your womanly duty with true diligence. Waking up early, cooking for your man, even bathing his dogs. I bet that's worth some serious brownie points in *pativratta* heaven."

He laughed when her nose went up in the air and she sniffed. "And here I thought you were an enlightened man."

"Enlightenment comes easier on a full stomach, love. There," he paused, popping the last morsel into his mouth. "Enlightened once again. And now that you've fed me, how about washing my back?"

"I've got the hose and towel at the ready. Bring it on."

Aryan grinned. "Are you calling me a dog, Sunshine?"

She fluttered enormous chocolate eyes at him. "I'd never insult the Star Trek crew like that. You, Mr. Fashionista, are a pig."

Aryan snorted piggishly, piling empty plates on the tray and carrying it all into the kitchen. "Are you claiming pigs don't take baths?"

"We are not bathing together," she said unequivocally.

"I'm not picky. We can share a shower." He wasn't taking no for an answer today.

"What are we, two, that we need to share bubble bath time?"

He tossed his sunglasses on the kitchen counter, tension streaming through him again. It was as if the swim hadn't helped at all. "Alisha."

She put the coffee mugs in the stainless steel sink. "What?"

"Your carbon footprint is burning a hole in the ozone and I cannot in all consciousness allow you to waste any more water."

"And sharing a bath is your great solution?" Her mouth trembled with mirth, belying her reprimand.

He bent, grabbed her around the knees and boosted her onto his shoulder. He was done arguing.

She shrieked right into his ear. "Let me down, you big fat oaf!"

"I will in a minute." He patted her round, high bottom while she kicked and screamed and pounded his back all the way to the bathroom. She was a lightweight for all her height and larger-than-life convictions. He locked the bathroom door, then dropped her on the Indonesian teak wood bench.

She jumped to her feet immediately. "What kind of infantile behavior is that?"

"Shower or Jacuzzi?" Their eyes locked in a showdown. He wasn't backing down this time.

She opened her mouth to huff and puff, but she closed it again without saying anything. And she didn't leave. "Shower," she said after several minutes.

He took off his clothes first and then hers. "Warm or hot?" He turned on the rain shower.

"Hot."

Alisha stepped under the steaming spray and tipped her head back, letting the water cascade down her body. She wet herself thoroughly while taking wary peeks at Aryan who was doing the same.

What had gotten into him? Why had he suddenly gone all caveman on her? He'd been mocking her on the verandah and then—bam—he'd literally carried her off into his lair.

She reached for the bar of soap in the wall niche but Aryan got to it first. He lathered up his hands and began soaping her front.

"It tickles. Let me do it." But watching his hands move over her body was…not bad. Not at all.

He smiled like he'd read her mind. "I'll be careful not to tickle."

It was ridiculous. He wasn't pushing exactly. Or was he? What would happen if she pushed back? Would he back off? She didn't think so, not in his current mood. And yet, she knew without a shadow of doubt that he'd stop if she asked him to.

She didn't ask. She closed her eyes and gave in to the sensations instead. All in all, it was a pleasant experience— once she got over being embarrassed—to feel a large pair of hands massaging her body. Aryan definitely had a knack for it. He turned her this way and that as he washed her from hair to toes, and if he paid attention to certain areas more than others, Alisha found she didn't mind so much.

He handed the sandalwood soap to her, clearly expecting the same treatment. She obliged, running soapy hands all over him, tracing the textures and temperatures of his skin so different from hers. He was rough and warm, smooth and cool, and as she touched him, her own pulse quickened.

He was aroused. They both were right from the start. How could they not be?

"Satisfied?" she asked, checking his body for any leftover suds.

"Not nearly." His voice was rough and low pitched. It abraded her skin like a loofah and lathered goosebumps all over her.

Aryan switched off the showerhead and turned on the concealed jet sprays along the mosaic-tiled shower walls. The cubicle was a masculine space, done in rich earthy green, black and brown, and was large enough to accommodate an orgy of six. It had seemed like overkill when he'd designed it, but right now he was damn glad to have indulged in such decadence.

"I thought the object of the shared shower was water conservation." Sunshine eyed the ten jettisoning spigots.

"The water will help with the friction," he said and nearly laughed at her suspicious expression.

"Friction? We are both clean now. In fact, I'm squeaking."

"And now I want you squealing."

She opened her mouth, shut it, and opened it again. "All right, I can squeal. But why can't I do that when I'm dry and in bed, preferably under those lovely silk blankets?"

"Because it's my fantasy, Sunshine." She'd argue even now when they were both ready to burst into flames.

She seemed abjectly let down by his answer. "Why can't you have a comfortable fantasy?"

He gathered her in his arms, pressing kisses over her shoulder even as he shook with laughter. He ran his hands over the globes of her buttocks, pulling her closer to rub their bodies together.

His Sunshine had become bolder over the weekend, no longer content to be a passive spectator in their games. Heat exploded through him when she stroked him exactly as he liked it, long and strong. He groaned. One touch, sometimes just a look and he was gone. How was he supposed to moderate this? He sucked her lower lip, then licked the sting away.

"Ready?" He dropped his hands to her hips.

"Or not, here we come." She giggled at the double entendre, but curled her arms around his neck.

He boosted her up. "Wrap your legs around me."

"Any fool knows how this works. Stop giving instructions."

He took a bite of her cheek. "It was a suggestion, not an instruction."

"Whatever." She pistoned her hips suddenly and he saw stars.

"Jesus. Don't do that or it'll be over before it even begins." He pressed her back against the wall for traction and also to restrict her movements. Now, he'd go as slow as he wished. Drive them both mad for a long eternity. In and out. In and out. Slow, beautiful and easy.

"Aryan," she moaned into his ear after three strokes, her legs trembling around him. "Faster. Please. Harder."

He discovered he had no control over any of it. Not his heart. Not his conscience. And definitely not his Sunshine.

THEY WENT HARD and fast in the shower, then slow and easy on the bed, later. Alisha was nearly comatose by then and completely malleable. Aryan couldn't decide whether he liked her sassy and sharp-tongued better or passive and pliant.

Her head rested on his shoulder and her arm was wrapped around his waist. He slowly caressed her back. "Have I ever told you that this is where we met first?"

She stirred and he felt her breath against his neck. "You came all this way to play Scrabble?"

It had been early October. Uncle Sam and the gang had

gone to Singapore for a holiday. He'd been fidgety and ill tempered for weeks, and instead of foisting his mood on the family, he'd bowed out and left for the farmhouse. Actually, Nanu had forced him to go with instructions to straighten his head out whilst there.

He'd spent a week there, swimming, hiking, mingling with the men from the village, eating Mira *bai*'s excellent food. The amount of food she'd fed him. He'd had a nasty stomach for days.

That first night at the farmhouse, after four mind numbing hours of Call of Duty, he'd browsed the Web in utter boredom, looking for something, anything, to keep the monsters at bay. He'd stumbled on the Scrabbulous app and because he'd been thinking about his mother and how much she would have loved the app, he had accepted a quick game with Worddiva.

She'd been just what he'd needed, then. Now, she'd become as necessary as air.

Sunshine had unlocked something in him that night. The part of him he'd left behind in London.

"It was my birthday," Alisha said softly.

"On that day?" He shifted, tilting his head down to look at her.

A slow smile curved her lips. "Serendipity or what?"

Knots of fear cleanched his gut. "I came here to find peace and I found you."

Her brow tweaked up. "Are you being sarcastic?"

"It was either Scrabble or a porn," he said desperately. *Keep it foolish. Keep it simple.*

She pinched him, giggling. "Such a guy thing to say."

"I thought I was playing against a porn star."

She struggled to sit up. He held her fast.

"What nonsense. Why would you think that?"

"Diva? And you wrote some pretty salacious stuff in our little chat box." She'd been naughty, but sweetly so.

The giggles turned into spurts of laughter. She was clearly remembering the chat. "Stop! You'll give me hiccups."

"My poor brain couldn't handle all the wicked things you were saying… So I lost the game."

She was digging her nails into his forearms and wheezing. Any minute, the hiccups would make an appearance.

"Do you know, I had to…*ahem*…in the middle of the game because of that position you mentioned from the Kama Sutra? What was it, something about the woman being upside down and on a swing? Want to try it? I have a swing outside."

"I never ever…*hic*…wrote…*hic, hic*…any such thing. *Hic.*" And there they were.

Aryan grinned. Love could certainly be fun and foolish. He just had to make sure to keep it that way, for both their sakes.

THEIR IDYLL CAME to an end that evening when they pulled up outside Mumbai's domestic airport. Alisha got out of the passenger side of the BMW, and met Aryan by the trunk. He took out a different overnight bag from it. He was flying to Bengaluru on business, and she was going home alone. She wouldn't see him for four days.

"Drive carefully," he said, his voice gruff and soft.

She bent her head, pretending fascination for her white Kolhapuri *chappals*. If she looked at him, she'd start weeping again like she'd done that afternoon when she'd said goodbye to Kirk. He hadn't wanted to come back with them.

"I'll miss you, Sunshine."

Alisha's eyes blurred. Oh God! *Please don't go. I'll miss you too. I love you.*

But the words stuck in her throat and she took the coward's way out. "Have a good flight. Call me when you reach Bengaluru."

He gave her a lopsided smile, tucking a stray strand of hair that had escaped her braid behind her ear. Then he was off, walking toward the terminal, but just as the automatic glass doors slid open, he whirled around and jogged back.

He cupped her face in his large, warm hands. "Move in with me."

It shocked her that she wasn't shocked at all by the proposal.

"Can I think about it?" Damn it. This was no time to be a coward. "I am thinking about it," she clarified, her heart flip-flopping wildly.

His eyes bugged out and he dropped his hands to her shoulders. "What? No arguments? I didn't even need to present my case?"

He made her giggle so effortlessly. "Why don't you present it anyway?"

"Ledies and gentullmen of the jury," he began in an absurd nasal vernacular you often heard in Mumbai's courts.

"India abolished jury trials in 1960," she felt duty bound to point out.

"Do you mind?" He glared at her for interrupting his flow.

"Sorry. We'll pretend we're not in India." Alisha waved at him to continue.

"Thank you. Leddies and gentullmen, we are gathered here today—"

She burst out laughing. "You've morphed into a priest now."

"Stop interrupting me, Sunshine. Lawyer or priest, I'll say the same thing. Move in with me. Make a home with me. A life." Fake accent gone, his eyes held hers in their thrall.

She couldn't look away. Didn't want to. "I agreed to think about it. You think too."

"We'll reconvene when I come back." Then he kissed her nose and strode away and she watched him go until he disappeared behind the sliding doors of the terminal.

Sighing, Alisha climbed into the driver's seat. She had until Thursday to talk herself out of it. Or into it. The omnipresent butterflies decided to throw a party in her belly.

"Don't be a coward. Don't be a coward," she berated herself all the way home.

CHAPTER 14

She felt his absence acutely, like she was missing a vital organ in her body—mainly her heart. It was ridiculous how much she missed him even though they kept in touch constantly through the million and one forms of communication of the era.

Thank goodness the sappiness was restricted to evenings only. During the day, she was much too busy to think of him or chat for any length of time. But the nights—her nights were plagued with cravings and dreams that only a three-dimensional, hands-on Aryan could satisfy.

Diya had been on a modeling assignment in Delhi for three of those four days, magnifying Alisha's aloneness. But, Diya was back and was expected for dinner at any moment.

The phone in her hand buzzed, and Alisha contemplated Aryan's latest text.

Electric blue or mauve?

Neither?

That's not an answer. Which color do you prefer?

Both.

You're trying my patience, Sunshine.

Her phone buzzed another incoming text before she could type a reply.

Are you still thinking?

She answered the first question, ignored the last and slipped her phone into her pant pocket when the doorbell rang.

"I had the most stupendous trip!" Diya ramp-walked into the house in a chic, pink and mauve—what was it about that colour?—day dress. Her metallic purple platform heels gave new meaning to the word platform.

Alisha glanced down at her at-home attire of loose beige pants and a dark brown tank top. "Were we supposed to go out?"

"No, no. I've come from a meeting with," Diya paused, then trilled, "L'Oreal!" She threw her hands in the air and jiggled her booty.

"Oh, my God! They signed you for their new product line?" Alisha joined the jiggling party. It was a huge deal for a new model.

"Yes, and yes. I could dance. I could sing. I...come here. Hug time."

They hugged and jiggled and squealed. Vallima added her congratulations too—no jiggles.

"I have news too," Alisha said when they'd jiggled enough for Diya.

"Aryan proposed to you!" Diya's massive shriek made Alisha's ears ring.

Alisha nodded and Diya shrieked again. "But, not in the way you mean," Alisha yelled. If she didn't take control of the conversation, Diya would continue bouncing and screaming. "Sit!" She pointed at the dining table where Vallima was setting their dinner of tomato soup, *paneer* sandwiches and *bhel*.

"I have so much news, both home and office front. Jyoti

Kumar's divorce went through today." Oh! These were glorious times. Alisha grinned madly.

"Good for her!" Diya cheered.

"Yes. She can begin again. Be the woman she could've been."

And so could Alisha. She'd been too involved with Jyoti's case. It had hit too close to home. Her father hadn't physically abused her mother, but Alisha remembered how his drunken words had ravaged, leaving bruises and scars just as painful, if not so immediate.

If Aryan ever spoke to her like that—her back went up. She'd *never* allow anyone to treat her badly. That was one thing she'd never compromise on.

"How was it?" Diya asked once Vallima was in the kitchen and out of earshot.

"How was what?" Alisha bit into her sandwich so she wouldn't laugh.

"You know what." Diya waggled her eyebrows suggestively.

"Well, not to brag, but..." Feeling thoroughly smug, Alisha spilled all the juicy details. She flaunted and flashed and was generally shameless, and she had the great fortune to confirm that slut wear was indeed a redundant commodity. "I hope you returned it and got your money back."

Diya's jaw had dropped a while ago. "Seven times? That's...not normal. Is it?"

Alisha decided that normal was officially kaput. She missed a man. How normal was that? She couldn't wait for tomorrow night. Aryan was coming to see her straight from the airport. She'd asked him to stay the night. She'd deal with Vallima's wrath somehow.

"I feel completely changed, Dee. I mean, I am myself, but I am different too. Does that make sense?"

Diya smiled, nodding. "Absolutely. I'm so happy for you,

Leesh. I was so cynical about your blind date. But I'm glad—ecstatic that I was wrong. So, when are you moving in with him?"

Oh God. Butterflies. "Well, there's stuff to…"

"Uh-uh. No sorting stuff. No thinking. No analyzing. There's no way we'll allow you to screw this up," Diya said imperiously.

"What do you mean, 'we'? Whose 'we'?" And why the hell wasn't she annoyed by the conversation? Why was she smiling?

"Me, MT, Aryan, Uncle Sam… You get the drift."

She did. Still. "There are so many things to sort out. Like, do we live at his place in Bandra or here? If I move to Bandra, my office commute will increase by an hour each way. Two hours in heavy traffic. My place makes more sense for me, but it's smaller than his. Plus, his apartment is absolutely beautiful. And…"

Diya grabbed her hand. "Stop hyperventilating. You'll work it out."

Alisha gulped. "I was thinking to look for a place halfway between our places if he's okay with it. See? It's not straightforward."

"As long as your trying to work it out, it doesn't matter." Diya stared at her in amazement. "You're really going to do this, aren't you? You're not even trying to talk yourself out of it."

"I know. I want him, Dee. So much. I want to be with him." They both got silly again. "I should tell Amma and MT and…" Alisha slapped her hands on her cheeks as a horrific thought struck her. "Vallima. What if she refuses to move in with us?" Vallima would never approve of wishy-washy domestic arrangements.

Diya gasped, grasping the true horror of the situation.

Then they both started giggling until they heard the doorbell ring a few times in rapid succession.

Alisha hiccupped. "Vallima, are you...*hic*...getting the door. *Hic?*"

"What if it's Aryan, Leesha? What if he's come home early to surprise you?" Diya bounced in her chair. "He couldn't wait one more day to be with you."

Alisha's heart soared for a second before practicality won out. "Nice...*hic*...imagination. But can't possibly be...*hic*... him." She went to answer the door because Vallima seemed to have disappeared.

Oh, how she wished it was Aryan at the door.

With her head full of happy fluff, Alisha forgot to peek from the peephole and simply yanked the door open on a hiccup. The next second, a pudgy hand, smelling strongly of tobacco, swung out and slapped her hard across her face. Her left cheek, to be precise.

Her head snapped to the right and she stumbled back, her heart thundering. A roaring started in her left ear. She lifted a hand to her hot cheek while cold fear settled in her belly. A zillion thoughts lifted off and flapped about in her head and then fused into a single scream that didn't even come from her. Diya was shouting in the background.

All at once, Alisha came out of her shock as if someone had switched on a lightbulb in her dark, blank mind. She straightened up from her frozen, awkward crouch with rage in her heart. The fucking offender was dead, blasted to smithereens. Her eyes locked on a pair of slimy ones and a horrible tightness lodged in her throat, robbing her of air once again.

Mr. Kumar was at her door, arms akimbo, an ugly sneer twisting his rotund face. His grotesquely round belly rose and fell under a blue-black shirt. He looked like a fat, angry hog. Two thugs flanked him. One tall, one short. One smiled nastily, the other looked terrified. They were both blocking her main door.

If they were standing right under the frame of the door, they couldn't shut it. Her mind registered the fact and somehow it made her feel better. If the door was wide open, more chances the neighbours would hear the screams.

Help. That's what they needed.

Mindful of the danger, Alisha tightened the reigns on her temper and her panic and stared Mr. Kumar down. Play it cool, play it safe. *Do not antagonize him.* She wasn't stupid, not at all. Her cheek still burned, she noticed vaguely.

Alisha didn't dare turn around to check on the others, but she heard Diya and Vallima's outraged voices behind her. Diya had called the police and was giving them their address. *Well done, Dee.*

Mr. Kumar must have heard Diya too because he took a step closer to Alisha. He smirked, clearly thinking the same thing she was. It didn't matter who they called. They wouldn't get there in time.

"*Saali! Tum apne aap ko badi issmart samajti ho?* How dare you interfere in my family affairs? How dare you instigate my wife against me? Now we shall see just how smart and slick you are," he spewed his vitriol in Hindi, his voice getting louder and harsher with every sentence.

Her focus on Mr. Kumar, Alisha still heard Diya order Vallima to get a butcher knife from the kitchen. Alisha stopped breathing. He'd take it as a threat. What the hell was Diya thinking?

The taller goon cracked his knuckles in a caricature of menace, and the boy darted his eyes about in fear as if he couldn't quite believe what was going on. Mr. Kumar's hand shot out to push her. But Alisha was prepared this time, and stepped back just as he did. His hand grazed empty air.

"Mr. Kumar, this is highly inappropriate. There will be

severe consequences to your behavior. I suggest you leave now." She kept her tone low and non-antagonistic.

But Mr. Kumar hadn't come there to be soothed. He started yelling, calling her foul names and threatening various nasty scenarios. Some of them were highly improbable to carry out in reality, but Alisha kept her face blank. Showing anger, amusement or skepticism would not help the situation. She allowed him to release his anger verbally, right up to the point where he brought up Aryan.

"Gold-digger. You think spreading your legs for that rich boy entitles you to be haughty and butt into other people's lives? Let me show you what people think of you, you two-bit whore."

Enough was enough. "Look here, Mr. Kumar, I understand you're upset." She broke off on a gasp when Kumar bulled forward, pushing her with both hands. Hard enough that she fell on her bottom with a thud. He straddled her ankles, his sagging belly jiggling with every breath. He reminded her of Moto Moto from *Madagascar*.

Alisha bit her lip hard. Laughing would be like waving a red flag in front of a primed bull.

He hunched over and caged her in when she tried to stand up, screaming abuse until orange-tinted spittle flew out of his mouth. The rage emanating from his body made her huddle back in fear, and that only made her more mad.

A thought dashed into her head out of nowhere. How strange that the same action performed by two different men set off such opposing reactions in her body. When Aryan caged her in, she felt cherished, protected, loved.

Diya and Vallima ran at Mr. Kumar, brandishing their knives. The steel flashing yellow beneath the lights while they forced Mr. Kumar back. The larger goon raised his fists.

Good grief. Was she having a Bollywood-style nightmare? What was wrong with everyone?

"Mr. Kumar, just go home." Alisha rose to her feet, hating the fact she had to be reasonable and polite to the creep in front of her. But the alternative would be worse.

"*Chudail*, what home? You stole my home and my family."

He'd start frothing at the mouth soon, or keel over from a heart attack, she thought dispassionately. She gave him one last undeserving chance. "Go home. And we'll forget this ever happened."

Mr. Kumar, it turned out, was not only boorish but also infinitely stupid. He charged at her, arms raised murderously in front of him, and bellowed profanities. Alisha did what she had to in the name of justice. She manfully took the punch aimed at her jaw—he grazed it, nothing more—without retaliation. She dodged and ducked, ignoring the hysterical shrieks rising around her as he tried to grab her throat. But the straw that broke the camel's back was the sucker punch he landed on her stomach. Alisha gasped and doubled over in pain. Then blind rage and survival instincts kicked in.

That was it. Three strikes were enough. He'd used up all his get-out-of-jail-free cards.

She came up grunting in pain and fury, the heel of her right hand connected with his nose even as she lifted her knee and smashed it into his groin.

Someone screamed. Alisha wasn't sure who. She felt vaguely euphoric, yet hideously nauseated. Everything slowed down like a slow motion video. Her lungs trembled, her limbs throbbed, her vision blurred and her head felt like a supernova had imploded inside it.

Mr. Kumar lay at her feet, bleeding and whimpering, rolled into a tight, oversized ball. Pathetic. The man was beyond pathetic.

Alisha felt Diya's hand at her back, patting and rubbing, murmuring gibberish. She shuddered one last time before letting all the strain seep out and numbness take over. She finally looked up and blinked. The goons were nowhere in sight but her neighbours were there—all five of them minus Little Chucky. Rakesh *bhai*, Ami *didi*, Rohit, Manan and Sweetu crowded her doorway wearing varying expressions of shock, surprise and horror. From what she could tell, they had grabbed and pitched the goons aside to get into her apartment.

There! That was what real relationships looked like. Unconditional love and support from one neighbour to another, from one human to another. But because of scum like Mr. Kumar, humanity was still an underachiever. Alisha tried to smile at them but it hurt too much.

"Come on. You need to sit down." Diya wrapped an arm around her waist.

On the floor, Mr. Kumar groaned and whimpered, each hand protecting an injured area.

The room began to spin clockwise, so Alisha leaned into her BFF. "The police are on their way?"

"I certainly hope so," Diya replied, her lips twitching as if she was about to laugh.

Alisha glared at her friend. They couldn't laugh yet, it would only worsen the situation. But Diya didn't laugh, and Alisha gladly put herself into her friend's capable hands. Her engine's steam had run out and wanted to rest. She shuffled to the sofa and collapsed on it. Vallima brought out her comforter and covered her from neck to feet, and began applying ice to her face and knee.

Alisha touched her cheek and jaw gingerly and winced. She was going to bruise. She'd look hideous for the next few days. Aryan was going to be horrified. She groaned. He was going to revert to being a caveman. She closed her eyes. Her energy reserves were low. She couldn't think about Aryan's moods anymore.

She woke some time later, how much later she couldn't

tell. She shifted, expecting her body to throb with pain, but it didn't. The painkillers had kicked in. "Are the police here, yet?" she mumbled, looking around for Diya and Vallima.

Diya came around to sit next to her. "They should be here any minute. Rohit, Manan and Rakesh *bhai* are keeping a vigil." She broke into a smile. "They're fabulous. They hog-tied the thugs."

"They are fabulous." God! It hurt to smile.

Diya winced. "You have a bruise blooming, Leesha. What about your stomach? Feel any broken bones, bruised ribs, sore muscles?"

Nothing felt broken, everything just felt sorely abused, and she said so.

"Dr. Mehra should be arriving soon too."

At that, Alisha struggled to sit up. "Why did you call him? I don't need a doctor, Dee. I'll be fine in a day or two."

"And Dr. Mehra will confirm that. I've also called your mother and MT. Your mother's on her way to Mumbai and MT should be arriving any minute."

Her mouth dropped open. "What have you done? Why did you call them? They'll be so worried. You should have asked me first." What an unmitigated disaster.

"Alisha, do you have any idea how badly this could've gone? How bad you look?"

"I know, damn it. I can feel how bad I look." Her mother and MT were going to lecture her. She couldn't deal with them in this state. "You should have asked me, Diya." Then a thought struck her. "You didn't call Aryan, did you?" She'd kill her BFF if she had.

"I didn't. Believe me, I want to but I'll leave him to you. Call him, Leesha. Right now. He should know about this."

Alisha shook her head and winced. Dear God, her head was pounding. "No need to worry him when he has an important meeting in the morning. He'll find out soon enough. It's over and done. What's the point of harping on it?" She felt a twinge of *something*, but she ignored it. Tomorrow *was* soon enough.

Diya frowned in disappointment. Alisha closed her eyes and snipped the argument before it even began. She was too tired to bother about anyone or anything tonight.

MT, Dr. Mehra and the police barged into her house within moments of each other. Good, Alisha thought dimly, lolling her head in their direction. She only needed to talk about the whole disaster once.

CHAPTER 15

The sky was a glorious shade of mauve when Aryan landed in Mumbai. It was the same shade as Sunshine's gift. He exited the plane imagining her in it. He couldn't wait to see her again.

Heat punched him in welcome when he walked out of the arrival's terminal, his body temperature going from air-conditioned cool to humid hot in seconds. Despite it, he was glad to be home. A few days away out of Mumbai and one missed the messy metro.

Bengaluru had been hectic—he hoped productive—and welcoming. But home was where the heart was. And his heart was with Sunshine.

He sent a text to Singh, letting the driver know he was out of the terminal. Almost instantly, his silver BMW materialized in front of him. He grinned at the familiar faces inside.

"This is a nice surprise. Hey! Uncle Sam, Nanu. Thanks for picking me up." Aryan handed his bag to Singh and climbed in the back next to his grandmother, giving her soft, old cheek a smacking kiss. "This reminds me of the times I'd come home from college. Did you bring *samosas*, Nanu? I'm starving."

Of course she'd brought *samosas*, along with ambrosia or coffee. Aryan gave her cheek another grateful kiss and poured himself a cup.

"Eat, *beta*," she said, smiling at him. Though her smile felt a little subdued.

Aryan shot Uncle Sam a speaking glance whose only reaction was to flare his nostrils. Singh pulled the car away from the curb into the exit lane.

A short detour, Aryan thought. He'd drop his family off and then head back to South Mumbai where Sunshine was waiting for him. He'd spend the drive fueling up for the night to come with the *samosas* and coffee.

"There's another thing that hasn't changed, your cavernous appetite," Uncle Sam remarked from the front seat. He twisted around and stole one of Aryan's *samosas*.

"Jealous?" Aryan taunted, wolfing down three *samosas* before his uncle stole them all. As he ate, he caught a strange look exchanged between his uncle and grandmother. "What is it?" He looked at his grandmother. Was she sick? The *samosas* stuck in his throat.

"What's the status of the project in Bengaluru?" Uncle Sam asked.

"Suffering from memory loss, Mamu? We spoke about it not even three hours ago."

Prithvi Homes had bid for a contract to build a cooperative green housing colony on the outskirts of Bengaluru. The project was right up Aryan's alley—five hundred apartments spread around twenty odd acres of land, the whole complex rigged on renewable energy. His designs and proposal had been met with enthusiasm but there were three other contenders for the project. He'd have his answer soon.

"No need to get testy. You could have got an answer in that time."

Aryan narrowed his eyes. "No, there's been no change. You want me to call them again?"

"Sameer, stop irritating him." Nanu's request was met with instant obedience.

Okay. Something was definitely off.

"What is it?" he asked again.

"It's your father. He's had a stroke. It looks bad," Uncle Sam said bluntly.

Aryan's stomach curdled. "How bad is it?"

"They don't know, *beta*," Nanu said with an unhappy sigh which told him exactly how bad it was.

He whipped his head about to stare out of the window, trying to battle and subdue the ugly feelings rising within him. The car stopped at a red light and suddenly hundreds of pedestrians were crossing the road, going about their daily business. He thought about jumping out and joining the throng. Getting lost in the multitudes. Escaping from his life. He wondered how it would feel to be Wordfreak for real and not his father's son.

Was this why the old man had been calling? But he hadn't mentioned being sick. He'd been coughing, that was all. *Come on, dude, be honest. When have you ever been interested in anything the old man had to say?* Aryan closed his eyes as a fresh wave of guilt swept through his gut.

"I'll call him. Tomorrow," he said brusquely. It was too late to call London now.

"Aryan, he's suffered a stroke. His left side is paralyzed and he isn't showing any sign of improvement. He's asking for you. You need to go to London tonight," Uncle Sam said slowly as if he were talking to Riana.

Aryan shook his head. No. He was not jumping on a plane for *him*.

"You must go, *beta*." His grandmother squeezed his hand.

He couldn't breathe. "It's your birthday on Saturday. I won't miss it for anyone. After that," he clenched his fists, "if I need to, I'll go." That would have to be enough.

His grandmother was disappointed by his answer. "A birthday is not important, but okay, I will not argue. Then we both fly to London on Sunday. Sameer, please make the arrangements."

"That's not necessary, Nanu. I can go by myself."

"I will come with you," Bharati Vaidya said in a tone that brooked no argument.

His grandmother had made up her stubborn mind and Aryan felt irritation on top of all the other emotions roiling around inside him. For the rest of the drive, he ignored everyone in the car. Uncle Sam called their travel agent and managed to book their tickets in the span of ten minutes. Boo-fucking-yah.

It seemed he could not escape his life or his relatives.

ARYAN DROPPED his uncle and grandmother off, then headed to his own apartment where he downed two stiff whiskeys, showered his travel grime off his body, and debated whether he should go to Alisha's so late and in his current mood, or go to sleep.

Sleep was a joke. He wasn't going to sleep tonight. So he went to Alisha's. He'd let Singh go and drove to Breach Candy himself. He liked driving. It relaxed him.

By the time he buzzed her doorbell, it was after 11:00 p.m. He'd texted her, letting her know that he was on his way. She'd replied with a thumbs-up icon, so she knew he was coming.

He cracked his neck by cocking his head to the left and right, easing the tension. He'd have to tell her everything. She needed to know about his parents. Tonight. He'd let it lie for far too long already.

He straightened up when he heard the locks turning, several of them. The door opened a fraction, and a single eye blinked up at him. Then the door slammed in his face and Aryan was taken aback. Finally, a chain lock slid open and so did the door and his nemesis stood there, glowering at him.

"She's sleeping," said the mean-spirited apparition shrouded in white.

"Vallima, she's expecting me."

She stared daggers at him, mumbling in Malayalam like she was cursing him, but she let him in. He left her muttering at his back and let himself into Sunshine's bedroom with a quiet knock. The room was dark and the TV was on. She was sitting up in bed, wrapped in a quilt, her back to the headboard.

"Hey, sorry I'm late," he said, walking in. "And sorry again, but brace your eyes, love. I'm turning the light on. We need to talk."

"Aryan, wait!" Alisha croaked, hiding her face in her hands.

"It's important, Sunshine." He had to see her face when he told her. She nodded, still protecting her eyes, and he flicked on the desk lamp which wasn't too bright, but would serve the purpose. When he turned back, her hands were no longer covering her face. He saw her face—really saw it, and his already frayed nerves shredded into sawdust.

"What the hell happened to your face?" He stalked to her, tossing the bow-tied package he held on the bed. He sat down on the bed right next to her and carefully took stock.

One eye was swollen shut. Split lip in the left corner of her mouth. Long, thin gouges on her neck. Whatever skin wasn't black, blue or green was fiery red—due to medicated ointment. Not tincture of iodine, it didn't smell like it.

Someone had hit her. Not by accident. It had been delibrate.

Someone had tried to strangle her.

She'd nearly died.

Fear burned away everything else he was feeling. He'd almost lost her.

His mother had died on him. His father was dying while he dithered. And now Alisha was in mortal danger. Was it him, he wondered as bile rose in his throat. Did he bring death to people?

"What the hell happened, Alisha?" When had this happened?

Alisha flinched at Aryan's tone. He was so angry. But he was here. And, God, was she glad that he was here within touching distance.

"I missed you." She wanted to hug him, kiss him, but the slightest movement hurt. So she opened her palm on her lap, and he slipped his hand in hers.

She told him everything before he asked again, and as she did, his expression grew more and more stony. Coldly furious, actually. He stood up and moved away to stand by the windows as if he couldn't bear to be near her just then. Dread spread through her heart.

"Why didn't you call me?" he asked, his arms crossed over his chest.

"You were busy. I didn't want you to worry needlessly." *Please understand,* she pleaded silently.

He expression turned incredulous. "You didn't want to *worry* me?"

It sounded pathetic even in her own ears, but it was the truth. "Yes."

He shoved his hands in his jeans' pockets, his eyes flashing fire. "Let me get this straight. You're of the opinion that if—no, *when* one of us is in trouble and the other one isn't available immediately, then we should just blithely carry on with our lives. Is that it?"

"Not exactly. But..." Before Alisha could explain, he cut her off by slashing a hand in the air.

"What were you afraid of, Alisha? That I'd jump on a plane and come running back to hold your hand? That I'd have the sheer gall to offer some kind of support and, God forbid, some comfort?"

She wanted to get up and go to him, but couldn't. Her damn knee was swollen, and Dr. Mehra had forbidden her to put weight on it for two days minimum.

"Don't worry, Alisha. I know the rules of the game. I know you don't need me—you don't need anybody. You're strong, resilient, capable. But for once, Alisha, you could have swallowed your goddamned pride and called. It wouldn't have killed you. But no, that's a line you won't cross. Ever."

"Aryan," her shocked whisper went unheard.

"I'm sick to death of your goddamned boundaries. I'm sick to death of trying to dance around them. Always worrying when I'll overstep my bounds and you'll shut me out of your life completely."

There was a volcano bubbling inside his heart and he couldn't stop it from erupting. Every time Aryan looked at Sunshine's face his rage grew, and it only magnified his help-lessness, his redundancy.

"What are you talking about?" she asked, staring at him as if he'd gone mad.

"The rules, Alisha, the bloody lines that you've drawn around your life. You don't compromise. You don't allow for mistakes. You don't want to hear any opinions that don't merge with your own. You hate it when I say I love you, and you've never said it back to me. Not once. You bloody won't even let me change my relationship status on Facebook. Everything has to be done your way or not at all." He realized he was shouting, but he was beyond caring anymore. *She'd almost died.* "When will you let me in? When will you really trust me?"

Straight and stiff, she glared at him coldly. "Stop talking nonsense."

She was angry? Well, she could just stuff her anger back where it came from. He was through trying to please her. "I'm not talking nonsense. You were wrong by not calling me. In fact, you are totally wrong in assuming that you're in any way as strong as a man. Not to mention, smart. Is this how you prove your intelligence? By letting a maniac into your home, by allowing him to beat you up? Wow, Alisha. Should I applaud your superior reasoning ability?" *Didn't she understand she could have died?*

"I didn't allow him to beat me up, you jackass!" Alisha wanted to jump up and kick Aryan's ass to Mars. How dare he talk to her in that fashion?

"Don't you have any sense, you stupid woman? That asshole could have snapped you in two, like that." He stalked back to her and snapped his fingers in her face.

She shoved his hand away—to hell with her ribs hurting. "In case you didn't hear me clearly, I won. I stood over your strong man-pal while he lay bleeding and squealing like a pig at my feet and is currently crying his eyes out in jail."

"That was just dumb luck. You cannot go haring off into a fistfight with a man. All your silly notions about equality... What can you do if I grab you like this? Answer me." He grabbed her upper arms, pinning her to the headboard, quilt and all. In his daze to prove his point, Aryan missed her cry of pain. He jostled her, repeatedly, trying to scare sense into her.

She couldn't make him stop. She was in too much pain.

"Can you fight this? Can you fight me?" he shouted like a crazy person.

Alisha was crying. The fact somehow registered in Aryan's fear-logged brain. What the hell was he doing? He released her at once, a sick, nasty feeling snaking into his gut.

"Alisha...Fuck...I'm sorry. I'm so fucking sorry." Remorse and shame burned his skin.

"Get out." She didn't scream or shout but her words cut into him like a serrated saw.

"Alisha..." She recoiled when he reached for her. That stopped him in his tracks.

What had he done? What the fuck had he done?

"I said, get out. And don't ever come back," she screamed then, and buried her face in her hands.

He watched her weep as if he were watching a movie—a melodramatic enactment apropos of Bollywood. When he couldn't take it any more, he turned on his heel and walked out of the room. There was no need to talk about the old man anymore, he thought, closing the door behind him.

SAVITRI MENON ROSE from the sofa when Aryan came out of Alisha's bedroom. His stride faltered when he saw her, and when he realized why she must be there, his stunned expression turned bleak. He nodded politely, and let himself out of the flat without saying a word.

Savitri heaved a sigh. It hadn't gone quite as Alisha had expected, had it? Her daughter had some strange notions about people, especially men.

Vallima locked the main door again. Two new locks had been installed that morning.

"Go to bed, Vallima. I'll see to Alisha for the rest of the night."

"He won't come back, will he?" Vallima asked with a half hassled, half fearful scowl.

"I don't think so. Not tonight," Savitri answered. But he'd come back, of that she was sure.

Savitri's heart ached as she pushed open the door of Alisha's room and saw her tougher-than-nails daughter curled up on her bed, wailing like her heart was breaking. She hadn't heard Alisha cry like that since the day Krish had taken away the kitten he'd given her. Not even when her father died, had Alisha cried.

Savitri sat on the bed and ran her hand over her daughter's back. She wiped the tear-stains from Alisha's cheeks with the edge of her sari foregoing the box of tissues that was within reach. Her sari *pallu* was stained red in several places from the poultice she'd been applying on Alisha's face and body. Madhu had procured the ointment from her Ayurvedic doctor and it seemed to be helping with the swelling.

"Shall I heat up the poultice, *kutty*?" Savitri brushed Alisha's hair off her face.

"No. That's not what's hurting."

"It's okay, *kutty*. It was just a fight. Once you've both calmed down, you will forget all about it."

In slow circular motions, Savitri stroked Alisha's back, letting her cry, get it all out. After a while, Alisha shifted and put her head on Savitri's lap. Savitri ran her fingers through her daughter's lovely, long hair, the texture and thickness so like her father's. "Better?"

"I don't know," was Alisha's muffled reply.

"Do you want to talk about it?"

"Not really, Amma."

"Okay. Then just listen." Savitri bent her head and kissed her daughter on her forehead to take out the sting of her words. "You should have called him and told him yesterday. You were wrong, *kutty*."

As expected, Alisha stiffened and struggled to sit up, then gasped when she hurt, "Oh God, Amma. It still hurts so much." She pressed her hand against her bruised ribs and stayed curled up.

"Do you want a painkiller, *kutty*?" Savitri rocked her daughter.

Alisha shook her head, and fresh tears rolled down her cheeks. Alisha took the corner of Savitri's *pallu* and wiped her face. "It will pass. Help me up, Amma. I want to sit up. It's less painful."

Savitri wondered if she should postpone the lecture. But no, delivering it now, when everything was fresh, would be best.

"Did you hear what I said?" she asked, helping her daughter sit back against the headboard.

"Yes, Amma."

"Why didn't you call him, *kutty*?"

"I don't know," Alisha said in frustration. "Honest. I just don't know."

"Do you want to know what I think?"

"No. But I know you're going to tell me regardless."

"Cheeky girl." Savitri smiled. If Alisha was grumbling, things were returning to normal already. "I think everything Aryan said was relatively true. Yes, I could hear you both clearly. You were rather loud. I think even the neighbors heard you fight."

Alisha covered her eyes with a hand. Savitri removed it gently. "Call him back, *kutty*. He can't have gone far. Call him back and sort it out."

"No, Amma. I may have been wrong in not calling him yesterday. And he certainly is entitled to feel slighted or have opinions, but he had no right to talk to me the way he did. And the way he behaved? Like a…a hooligan. He acted no different from Mr. Kumar." Alisha shook her head. "I cannot forgive him for that. I was so wrong about him. So wrong."

"Alisha *kutty*, don't you pride yourself as a good judge of character?" Savitri handed her daughter some tissue so she could blow her nose. "What made you defy your common sense, defy all of us and meet him all those months ago? What made you keep dating him after that? You trust him or you would not have let him get close to you. You love him, everyone can see it," Savitri paused, allowing her words to sink in. "*Kutty*, he was upset and scared for you because he cares. Have you seen your face in the mirror? Ravaged is a euphemism for it." Savitri touched Alisha's swollen cheek with care and love. "When I saw you last night, I was horrified and upset and scared. I yelled at you for being reckless, remember? Madhu was angry too. It was just luck that Kumar didn't find you alone. What do you think would have happened if Diya wasn't there?"

"But she was. And Vallima is always there. And I took care of Kumar. Contrary to what you think, I did not take a foolish risk. It didn't happen like that. So why get paranoid unnecessarily?"

"Love and fear go hand in hand, Alisha. When you care about someone, you fear for that person. And not everyone reacts with logic and reason in stressful situations. Not everyone faces monsters in the night. Most people run away from monsters."

The words seemed to strike home because Alisha closed her eyes and rested her head on the headboard. Good! Her daughter needed to think about such things.

In the meantime, Savitri flipped the quilt exposing Alisha's injured knee. She checked the poultice tied around it and was happy when she saw that the swelling had gone down even more. Dr. Mehra had assured them there was nothing to worry about. Alisha's wounds were largely superficial, he'd said, and she would be good as new within a week.

"I know what you think about men," Savitri said when enough time had passed. "I know what you think about relationships. Alisha, you cannot hold my marriage, your *achan's* and mine, as a what-not-to-do guide. That was our marriage and our failure. And, *kutty*, you do understand that a lot more went wrong in it than just a few badly spoken words?"

"I know, Amma. But that was the beginning, wasn't it? The fights, the arguments, the meanness?" Alisha said, sounding sad. "I made a promise to myself years ago that I'd never allow anyone to treat me badly. Or to speak to me like I was an idiot. I will not allow anyone to dictate my life."

"Does he do any of that? Can't you understand why he said what he said tonight? Don't ruin what you have, what you love, because of the past. Don't be afraid, *kutty*."

Savitri hated that her child—both her children—were paying for her mistakes. She smoothed Alisha's hair off her face and forced her daughter to look into her eyes. "It's not easy living alone. It's not a bad life or a lonely one when you have work and friends and children. But to have someone share your life, someone good and decent, someone who cares, is a better way to live. Will you think about it? Your life with or without Aryan?"

Alisha shuddered out a tired sigh. "Fine, Amma. I'll think about it."

"Good." That's all she wanted.

Alisha narrowed her good eye. "Why am I the only one thinking about it? Why am I developing a headache with all these life-altering decisions? Why didn't he get a lecture? He was the one who messed up, after all. He was the one who went stark raving mad. The one not making a whit of sense. Did you hear some of the things he said? Utter garbbage!" Alisha railed in outrage.

Savitri supposed anger was better than desolation. "*Kutty*, he is thinking about it. And, believe me, he is kicking himself as we speak."

"He better be. And he better grovel for all eternity. And I

refuse to apologize for not calling him last night. I absolutely draw the line there."

"I'm sure he'll be thrilled that you've drawn one more line for him to toe."

"That's not remotely funny, Matashri. And he's a big one to talk about lines."

Savitri's heart warmed hearing the silly nickname her children had given her long ago. "Of course not. Matashri couldn't possibly have a sense of humor, right?"

Alisha grinned and wrapped her arms around Savitri, wincing as she did. But she didn't let go.

Children never stop needing their mothers. And there wasn't a bigger comfort to a mother than providing solace to her children. No matter how old they were.

"Thank you, Amma. I needed that. I love you."

"My pleasure, *kutty*. I love you so, so much."

CHAPTER 16

*A*ryan had no options left but to drink himself into a stupor, and who better to get hammered with than his rock-solid best friend, Mann Singh, whose capacity to consume alcohol was legendary and secondary only to his inexhaustible patience in dealing with Aryan's moods.

Mann picked up the phone on the first ring. "*Bhiddu,* you back from Bengaluru, *kya?*" came his cheery rumble through the speaker.

"Meet me at the St. Regis lobby in twenty minutes," Aryan barked out and disconnected the line.

Going to Luna to get smashed made the most sense as it was one of the few bars that remained open past midnight in Mumbai. Located on the thirty-seventh floor of the hotel, it boasted magnificient views, decent food, mind-numbing music and masses of giggly people one could lose himself in.

It was close to midnight and the streets had thinned of traffic, so he drove fast, zigzagging between the cars, gripping the steering wheel with hands gone cold.

His mind kept flashing back to Alisha's black and blue face. *Fuck, fuck, fuck!* He'd made her cry. He'd terrorized her.

Aryan turned up car stereo, hoping the fast-paced EDM would drown out the hideous sounds in his head. His voice raised in ugly accusation. Alisha's weeping. How could he have lost control like that? He smacked the heel of his hand on the steering wheel.

What the fuck had happened to him? Why had he behaved so abominably? He'd been enraged, yes. Afraid? Most definitely. But the anguish twisting his soul, slicing him apart—what was that? He felt choked. Smothered. He wanted to crawl out of his own skin.

He took a sharp left, overtaking a slow-moving Santro. Then he floored the pedal again.

His heart pounded in time with the music. He was going to have a heart attack if he didn't calm down. Which was a cheerful thought. If he was dead, he'd be sensation free finally.

He'd lost her.

His vision blurred, his eyes stung. Yes, he'd welcome death with open arms.

"What the bloody fuck are you thinking?" He pressed the brake hard, tires squealing in protest as he wrestled the car to an abrupt halt. Horns blasted behind him, drivers spewed invectives. He raised a hand in apology and pulled to a stop alongside the Haji-Ali Seaface.

He got out, gulped in huge mouthfuls of damp, salty air. He needed to get himself under control before taking the wheel again. He needed to stop thinking.

Walking over to the ledge that divided the pavement and sea, he pressed his fists down on the rough wall. Ragged shards of stone and debris pushed against his skin, and he embraced the pain, staring at the black waves crashing against the jagged rocks below. The moon, full and bright, shone down on the endless ripples of water, broken only by the ghostly silhouette of the *dargah*, rising from it in the middle of the bay. The mosque looked cold and all alone.

Just like him.

He'd suffered a double whammy today. First, the news about the old man had upset him whether he wanted it to or not. And second, the absolute shock of seeing Alisha broken and frail had shaken him to the core. In his mind, Sunshine was strong, resilient, unbreakable—she was Wonder Woman —and to see her otherwise had shattered him. He'd lost his mind, and he had lost her.

No one was safe, were they? Life held no guarantees. He'd known that since he was thirteen.

He looked up at the dark, starless sky and forced his mind to go blank. He filled his ears with the the soothing music of the waves; it's ebb and flow, forward and retreat. He noticed the stench of human filth and fish next. Garbage, even here, near a place of worship. Why couldn't people clean up after themselves?

Aryan froze. That's it, he thought, as an idea took root in his head. He had to clean up after himself.

He dialed Mann again as he got back in the car and roared it back on the road.

"On my way, *bhiddu*. What the..."

He cut off his friend rudely. "Change of plans. Meet me at the Malabar Hill Police Station."

"Police station? Are you in trouble?" Mann was his 2 a.m. tag, his irrefutable backup.

"I'll explain later. Just get there." He disconnected the phone, smiling grimly.

He'd found a better—no, a more deserving target for his ire. He was going to make sure Alisha was safe from that beast. He'd do that much before getting out of her life. He turned up the EDM to ear-popping levels and floored the pedal toward his new destination.

He had a new plan. He had no use for emotions now.

THE STUPID MAN WAS SULKING.

Alisha couldn't believe Aryan wasn't answering her call —the fifth one, she might add. She glared at her iPhone while it rang and rang on speaker. He hadn't returned any of her calls or voice messages or texts for the past two days. They'd clashed on Thursday night, it was Saturday afternoon.

She threw the phone on the bed and hobbled into the bathroom. At least she was back on her feet and the various aches and pains all over her body had subsided into a dull soreness. What remained of her idiotic encounter with Kumar was her colorful face—it was now mostly black and even that was fading.

She checked her reflection again. Except for the slight puffiness and discoloration under her left eye, she looked fine. Maybe her lips looked a bit funny as if she'd plumped them up with fillers—which she'd rather die than ever do. Anyway, the point was that she was a thousand percent better.

Except, Aryan Rajaram Chawla was AWOL.

Alisha pouted into the mirror, the fuller lips making her look like a cartoon character. She'd expected him to barge into her home yesterday—shame-faced, sorry-eyed, on his knees or maybe prostrate at her feet, groveling in abject agony over his tantrum. None of that had happened.

She shuffled back into the room and collapsed into her desk chair. She should check if he'd started another Scrabble match but her stomach soured at the thought of being needy.

A week ago, they'd been rolling around making love under the baobab tree, figuratively speaking, and today they weren't even talking. She felt bewildered, betrayed and hurt by his behavior, his cold shoulder. Honestly, it felt so much worse than what Kumar had done to her.

So she'd made a mistake in not calling him after the incident. She'd erred in judgment about the importance of full disclosure. In her defense, she hadn't thought the skirmish was that big of a deal, nothing to warrant frantic phone calls in the middle of the night to a boyfriend in Bengaluru. She'd handled the situation like she'd been trained to do, so why was everyone so upset and touchy about it?

Wasn't this exactly why she avoided romantic relationships? This whole ridiculous situation where one had to predict and/or anticipate the significant other's frame of mind.

A sigh escaped her puffy lips. Relationships were tough business. Mistakes were bound to occur, on both sides. Such was life. And who knew better all that could go wrong in such dealings than a divorce lawyer?

Mistakes happened and you dealt with them. Some people resolved them, others ran away. Alisha had never run away from anything in her life. It had taken her one good cry and a firm talking-to from her mother to clear her head.

She loved Aryan. She knew that beyond the shadow of a doubt. To imagine a life without him was untenable, unacceptable. Somehow, he'd broken her defenses and lodged himself in her heart. She needed to tell him that. If the stupid man would stop running, that is. *Why wouldn't he call back?*

She bent at the waist, gathered her hair up into a loose chignon. Her ribs didn't yelp at her movements. She sat up, poked her stomach. Nothing hurt anymore. There had been no earthly reason for everyone to panic and overreact, and hadn't she been telling them just that?

And didn't the stupid man get that the whole stupid fight was his fault? Well, if he ever called her back, she was going to give him a piece of her mind.

Diya sauntered into the room with two glasses of lemonade, handing one to Alisha. "You look like a mottled space creature in that orange T-shirt."

Coming from a woman wrapped in a peachy, frilly blouse that did lovely things to her alabaster complexion, it was just mean. "And your point is?"

Diya shrugged and sipped her lemonade. "Savitri Aunty reached Pune?"

Alisha drained her lemonade in one shot and set the glass down on her desk. "Yup. She's coming back in two weeks, when summer holidays begin. Year endings are the worst times at her school. The two days she spent here were two days she couldn't afford to waste." She looked at Diya pointedly.

Diya yawned. "Let's move on, shall we? Got hold of Aryan yet?"

Alisha's pout firmed. "No."

"Give him time, Leesha. He's upset."

"*He's* upset? I was the one beaten up!"

Diya tut-tutted. "You're so pig headed. If the tables were reversed, what would you have done?"

"Answered the stupid phone, that's for sure."

"Really?" Diya raised an eyebrow. "You want me to call him?"

"Do not call him, Dee. If he wants to talk to me, he'll call."

"And if he doesn't?"

Alisha gulped down acid. "I'll deal with it."

Gracefully, Diya scratched her right eyebrow. "Isn't his grandmother's birthday party tonight?"

Alisha nodded. She'd even bought a new outfit for it on Monday.

"So go there and confront him. You're invited."

"Are you mad? I'm not going to land up there when he

won't even answer my missed calls." Talk about embarrassing. What if he asked her to get out like she had?

"Look, babe, for this to work, one of you has to give in."

"What do you think I'm doing? I *am* giving in. I'm giving him another chance." That itself was a wonder. She never gave stupid men second chances.

"Leesh…"

Whatever advice Diya was about to impart was interrupted by Alisha's marimba ringtone. She pounced on it and tried to stem her disappointment when the caller ID indicated that it was her brother, Krish, on the line.

"Hello, big, ugly *sahodaran*," she said with false chirpiness. Krish and she had this weird and wonderful language of their own. A mix of English, Hindi and Malayalam. "You don't need to call twelve time a day. I'm absolutely fine now."

"Just want to make sure my ugly baby *sahodari* hasn't gotten uglier. How do you feel, truly?" Krish's voice was husky with sleep. It was well after midnight in Dallas.

"Fine. Better. Great," she answered, both touched and irritated that even he was treating her with kid gloves. "Are you up late or up early?" Like all Menons, her brother was a workaholic.

"I was out with some friends, actually."

"You were at a party?" When he confirmed the aberration, Alisha sent a shocked look toward Diya, who was pretending very hard not to be interested in the conversation. Dee had had a crush on Krish forever, but the stars refused to align for them.

Alisha spoke to Krish for several minutes, then tried to play matchmaker for the millionth time. "Here, talk to Dee. She'll tell you that I'm much better."

Diya spun around from the window, frantically shaking her head and mouthing, "No!"

Alisha frowned at her friend. Since when did Diya not want an opportunity to torment Krish?

"Diya's with you? That's good since you refused to go to Pune with Amma."

"Um, she's not here right now. But I'll say hi for you." Alisha couldn't stop staring at Diya, who was once again staring out of the window and oh-so-casually sipping her lemonade. Her shock multiplied when her *sahodaran* made the strangest comment.

"So who's with you? Aryan? I've been trying to get hold of him. Hand him the phone, will you?"

Since when did Krish and Aryan chat? "Why do you want to talk to him?" she asked carefully.

"Man talk," came the cryptic reply.

Alisha narrowed her eyes. "Krish, keep your Menon nose out of my affairs. I can sort out my own problems, thank you very much."

"Kumar will be out on bail soon if he isn't already. I want to make sure someone's looking out for you because I know you haven't grasped the gravity of the situation yet. You think that laws and rules are on your side, are enough, but not everyone in India abides by them...as has been proven."

Had everyone gone mad? "I'm quite safe, Krish. This isn't a Bollywood flick where the villains can do as they please without repercussions. I've always been careful and I'll be extra vigilant now."

"And that's a relief, *sahodari*. But I still want to talk to him. Hand him the phone."

Alisha rubbed her right temple. "He's not here. We've quarreled."

A small silence followed her mumbled pronouncement which was followed by a sigh. "Only you, *sahodari*, can piss off someone at such a time."

Great! Why did everyone automatically assume it was her fault? "Whatever. Goodbye."

"Take care. I'll talk to you tomorrow." Krish hung up on that note of obnoxious amusement.

Alisha glared at Diya, daring her friend to comment. Diya wisely refrained, resting her miniscule denim-clad butt against the windowsill.

Her phone rang within seconds of Krish's call. This time it was MT. After a short, succinct conversation on various work-related issues, and some personal assurances and impractical promises, mostly on her part, Alisha disconnected. She'd been ordered to make use of her sick leave for an entire week. What was this? Why was everyone ganging up on her?

"What is the matter with everyone?" she asked, perplexed.

Diya grinned. "Well, it is a rare event for you to be needy, so we all want to squeeze lots of pleasure out of it."

"Oh yah, I am such a victim." Alisha rolled her eyes.

"Isn't that what you are, Leesha? It doesn't matter that you rescued yourself and came out on top. What happened… was awful. And it could have been so much worse."

"How long must I endure this tragic treatment? And if that's the case, why isn't everyone fighting to press my feet and head and massage my back?"

"Do you want us to?"

"Goodness, no," Alisha said quickly. "All right. One week. That's my limit. Then I start blasting you twits. By the way, at least one mystery is solved. The two men with Asshole Kumar have been identified. The taller one is a distant cousin of his, and the scared-looking young man turned out to be Jyoti Kumar's younger brother. Apparently, Mr. Kumar coerced him into gleaning out my address from Jyoti. MT called Jyoti to tell her what had happened and to warn her to be careful. That's when they put two and two together."

"What an unbelievable mess. What is it with this country and its all-boys clubs? Is there no room for family loyalty with those idiots?" Diya asked, as incredulous by Jyoti's brother behavior as Alisha.

"MT said she blames herself for bringing bad karma to my doorstep. After all she's gone through, she doesn't need to feel guilty because of her ex and her stupid brother." Alisha sighed. "The other day, she said she had nothing left in her. That she was nothing but an empty shell."

Alisha couldn't think of Jyoti Kumar and not feel pity. But there was hope mixed in it too. Amma had pulled herself up from ground zero, hadn't she? There was always hope. And help if you needed it.

"She has her sister, her children. She has you. She'll be fine," Diya said, echoing her thoughts.

Alisha nodded at her friend who'd always been there for her. Her eyes blurred. Crap, why wouldn't the waterworks stop?

Where was the bloody man?

"What will I do if he doesn't call back? What if he never wants to see me again?"

"Are we going to let that happen?" Diya arched her brow.

Determination sprouted inside Alisha, uprooting the pessimism. "Definitely not."

CHAPTER 17

"You know, when I said 'we' I meant it figuratively," Diya grumbled while parking Alisha's Tata Nano in the vivitor's spot under Uncle Sam's building.

"I can't waltz into the party alone, looking like a disaster victim. Besides, Dr. Mehra forbade me to drive until my knee stops twinging." Who knew kneeing a man would hurt so much?

Alisha shoved open the car door and limped out. She hadn't been able to wear the new sleeveless gown she'd bought for the party because her upper arms were dreadfully bruised. She was in a simple long-sleeved tunic and black leggings. Nothing fancy, since she wasn't staying long.

She was only there because Aryan's grandmother had called an hour ago, asking what time they'd be arriving at the party.

"Who's they?" Alisha had asked stupidly.

"Why, Aryan and you." Bharati Aunty's answer had only added more confusion to the cauldron.

Apparently, Aryan was incommunicado with his family too. He hadn't been seen since Thursday night.

"What's going on with him? Where could he be?" Alisha wondered aloud while riding the elevator up. She caught Diya scanning her face. "I look awful, right?" She'd tried to conceal the bruises with foundation as best as she could.

"A little. What will you tell them?" Diya pointed upwards.

"The truth. Aunty*ji* is genuinely worried about him. He's not at the farmhouse. She checked. I hope everything's fine, Dee. It's not like him to disappear, I don't think. He'd never, ever worry his grandmother, that's for sure." A horrible tension gripped her body, making it flash hot one minute and cold the next.

"You're not going to faint, are you? Breathe, Leesha. Hold my arm." They got off on the twelveth floor.

The entire floor belonged to the Vaidyas. Pandemonium reigned inside the open mahogany double doors. Men in brown uniforms rushed about the residence, arranging bouquets, rearraging furniture for the party. No one paid any attention to Alisha and Diya who'd burst in a full hour before the start time.

Alisha tried not to hobble as Babu—a servant she recognised from a previous visit—led them into the living room, then hopped off to fetch Aunty*ji*. The sprawling Pali Hill apartment had windows aplenty and the living room opened to a large terrace overlooking Bandstand. The décor was opulent and ornate, not really her style, and not Aryan's either. Lots of glass and silver, lots of silk and brocade—a veritable rajah's *haveli*. Even the wall paint had a silvery tint to it.

"OMJeez. That's one by Shiva!" Diya was gawking at the paintings on the walls. Art was her latest obsession.

"Alisha *beta*, thank you for coming so fast. And thank you for the lovely flowers you sent. I have them in my room," said Aunty*ji* as she hurried into the living room. Her cream silk sari was simple, the solitaire diamonds flashing from her ears and neck were anything but. She totally went with the décor, Alisha thought, idiotically.

"This is so troubling. Where has he gone?" Then Bharati Vaidya got a good look at Alisha and that was that. "What happened to you?" She took Alisha by the shoulders, studying her face with wide, shocked eyes.

"Yes…well…it…" Alisha stammered. And before she could begin explaining coherently, Neeta Vaidya walked in and screeched. Alisha sighed when Aryan's aunt ran towards her. How she managed it without tripping over her heavy Lucknowi sari Alisha was a mystery. Was she allowed to run with a baby inside her?

"Oh, my God! Alisha what happened to you?"

So much for thinking she'd camouflaged the bruises.

"I'm fine, really. Let's focus on Aryan because Diya and I need to head back soon." Preferably before the guests arrived. She had no intention of becoming the circus act of the evening. Unless, Aryan begged her to stay.

The Vaidya women wore matching frowns on their faces. "Aren't you staying for the party?"

"What's this? A pre-party party? Ladies, every one of you looks stunning," Uncle Sam boomed out as he walked into the living room by way of the terrace, looking dapper in a cream silk *kurta-pajama*.

The terrace was festooned with baskets of flowers and candles glowing inside petite hurricane lamps. High-backed chairs with big red bows had been arranged around a small curved stage that had been set up in a corner. Someone was testing the mic and sound system to get it ready for an evening of *ghazals* and old Bollywood songs—Auntiji's favorite.

Though hot, it was the perfect way to celebrate sixty-five years of a life well lived.

Alisha pulled her eyes away from the happy prospect

Aryan had planned it all with such excitement. He wouldn't ditch his *nanu*'s party. He wouldn't.

"As I was saying," she began only to be interrupted again.

Uncle Sam came up to her and winced in sympathy. "He did a number on you, didn't he?"

Alisha stared. Uncle Sam had known about it?

"What?" he said as all the women glared at him. Except Diya. She was trying hard not to giggle.

"You knew? I mean, you know what happened?" Alisha gestured to her face.

"Aryan told me. Nasty business, Alisha, but it's over and that piece of garbage will never be able to show his face in Mumbai again. I guarantee that. He won't get away with what he did."

The suddenness of the disclosure created a monstrous hullabaloo.

"What do you mean? Someone beat you?" Neeta asked incredulously.

"Is that true, *beta*?" Bharati Aunty looked even more worried.

"Yes. But, I'm fine now. If we could all focus on…"

Neeta Vaidya rounded on her husband. "You knew about this and you didn't tell us? If you say *oops*, Sam, I swear to God I'll punch you. Do not mess with a pregnant woman."

Diya burst out laughing. Alisha heaved a sigh and sat down on the sofa. She needed to be off her feet, and there was nothing to be done until everyone had calmed down.

"Sameer, you are too much," Aunty*ji* admonished her son as if he were six and not thirty-six. She took the seat next to Alisha and patted her hand. "What happened, *beta*? Tell us everything."

Alisha stuck to the basics, but recounting the incident brought it all to life again. Unbelievably, it still had the power to knock the breath out of her.

"My God! Alisha, that's so scary. You were so brave," Neeta said, still in shock.

Their concern warmed her heart. "I am fine now, really." Now came the sticky part but she squashed down her embarrassment. "We fought. Aryan was very upset with me."

"Where is he, Sam?" Neeta asked her husband. "None of us have heard from him or seen him in two days. He hasn't even wished Ma today."

"He's in London." Uncle Sam nodded at his mother and she sighed in relief.

"Oh. That's good. That's very good," she said.

London? "He's there for work?" Alisha was confused.

Aunty*ji* patted her hand. "No, no. He's gone to see his father, *beta.*"

"Raj had a stroke last week and is in the hospital. Didn't Aryan tell you? He should have flown out on Thursday night itself but you know how he is about his father." The look Neeta gave her indicated that Alisha should know exactly what she was talking about. She so didn't.

She crossed her arms over her stomach as her gut spasmed. What were they saying? His father was alive?

"I thought…" She cleared her throat, suddenly close to tears again. "He's never spoken about his father to me. I thought both his parents were dead," she said numbly.

A horrible silence followed her disclosure. She wanted to go home. She wanted her mother. She wanted to curl up on her bed and sleep forever.

Neeta started whispering in Uncle Sam's ear. He shook his head, frowning at his wife.

Diya leaned in to whisper in her ear. "Good thing you practiced that knee maneuver on Asshole Kumar. You'll need to perform it again on Aryan. Gently though, you don't want to permanently maim the family jewels, just bruise them a little bit."

Alisha choked mid-breath, her sob turning into a gurgle or mirth as she glared at Diya. Trust Dee to make a comedy out of an almost tragedy. Aunty*ji* started rubbing her back and murmuring reassurances. It dawned on Alisha that she thought Alisha was weeping. It would not do to laugh out loud now. They'd think her mad. She doubled over, hiding her face, as she broke into silent giggles.

"Are you all right, Leesh? Do you want some water?" Diya inquired politely, the devil trying to sound innocent.

She wanted to kick her friend, yet hug her tight at the same time. She felt a whole lot better, her brain a whole chuck clearer, thanks to Dee.

Aryan had lied to her, albeit by omission. Yes, it hurt that he'd ghosted her instead of talking to her, and she'd make him pay for it in a diabolical way. She might not understand why he'd run, but she finally understood why he wasn't calling back. It had nothing to do with her. Or very little to do with her.

"Why didn't he tell me?" she wondered aloud.

"It's just his way, *beta*. He tends to bottle feelings up until he can't ignore it anymore. Do you want to know about his father?"

"Don't interfere, Ma," Uncle Sam cut in but shut up when his mother held up a hand.

"It's only fair that she knows everything, Sameer."

Alisha shook her head. "No, Aunty*ji*. I don't want to put any of you in the middle. Aryan should be the one to tell me...if he wants to."

"I'm glad you see it that way." Uncle Sam smiled in approval.

"This is silly. Alisha, he's not going to tell you unless you force him to," Neeta said.

"Well, I'm certainly not going to force him." He had to trust her with his secrets or they had nothing worth salvaging between them. The crunch of it was that she'd expected her own inability to trust men to be a problem in their relationship. How naïve of her to never question whether he trusted her or not. And how selfish of her to think of their relationship only in her terms—her issues, her needs, her vulnerabilities. She'd never once considered Aryan might be vulnerable too.

"Sam, you know he doesn't talk about his father. You know him. Tell her," Neeta begged, clearly frustrated by everyone.

"I am flying to London tomorrow, just like we planned on Thursday," Bharati Aunty said while staring at her dead daughter's portrait hanging on a far wall. Alisha's heart went out to her. What kind of birthday this was turning out to be for her? Aryan's *nanu* turned to her then. "I want you to come with me, *beta*."

Alisha gaped at her, speechless. "Huh?"

Uncle Sam burst out laughing. "And, that's my Ma. See, Neetu, you don't need to do Aryan's dirty work for him. You just back him into a corner, so he can't slither out. God, Ma, you're devious. I'm so proud."

"I...um...I can't just hail off to London." Could she? She did have a week off. Alisha's mind scrambled for purchase, landing on her BFF. Diya looked as amused as Uncle Sam and her expression seemed to say, *Go Leesha, go! Practice your boxing moves!*

They were waiting for her answer, only Neeta looked worried. They wanted her to say yes, take the leap. This was madness. From what she could tell, Aryan had a nonexistent relationship with his father, a man who was gravely ill, possibly on his deathbed. She couldn't just land up there and add to the familial tension. How could she do that to him? If he ever did something like that to her, she'd kill him with her bare hands. There was no way she was going to London.

Thankfully, she was saved from making a decision when Mann waltzed in to join them.

"Hello, hello." He waved cheerfully. "Happy birthday, Aunty*ji*." He bent to touch Bharati Vaidya's feet, then kissed her cheek.

Alisha's head spun as a feeling of déjà vu swept through her.

Mann's face was as colorful and raw as hers. A lovely apple-sized purple bruise bloomed on one cheek, his right eye was swollen shut and his lips resembled fat burgundy grapes.

"What happened to you?" Did she look like that? No wonder everyone had freaked out.

"Oh! This?" Mann pointed at his face and grinned. "You should see the other guy."

Manjeet Singh—Mann, to his friends—was a "cut Surd"— a Sikh who didn't observe all the tenets of Sikhism like never cutting his hair. He was tall and brawny. He was also a sweet little puppy dog. He'd never instigate a fistfight, though apparently, he didn't mind participating in one.

"Shit! Alisha, we could be twins," he said while hugging her. "Aryan didn't tell me how badly you were hurt. No wonder he went berserk."

A bad suspicion crept into her stomach. "How did this happen, Mann?"

Uncle Sam slapped Mann on his back. "Okay, Rambo, tell them or we'll never get any peace."

Neeta shot her husband a look that translated to, *Wait till I get you alone and box your ears.*

Mann's grin threatened to split his grape lips. "You should've been there, Uncle Sam. It was just your kind of scuffle—fast, ugly and extremely satisfying. Just like the good old days."

Uncle Sam sighed nostalgically, clearly remembering

those days. Apparently, Uncle Sam used to have quite a reputation for campus brawls when he was in college.

"Don't encourage him, Mann," warned Neeta Vaidya.

"Sorry," he said, not sounding sorry in the least. "Where were we? Oh yeah. Aryan called me on Thursday night—or was it Friday already?—and asked me to meet him at the Malabar Hill Police Station."

Alisha's mouth fell open.

"We went there to find that bastard Kumar."

That shocked a "What?" out of her.

"I've never seen him like that, Leesha. He was crazy. Not a mad crazy, but close. He wanted to find Ramesh Kumar and 'break every bone in his body.' Aryan's words, verbatim."

Alisha's brain fried. She couldn't believe what she was hearing.

Mann swept his eyes over her face. "Looking at you, I completely understand his mood now. We found out Kumar was at the police station being questioned. But when we got there he'd already posted bail. So, we bribed the *hawaldaar* on duty to give us his home address."

"You didn't," Alisha whispered, horrified by what they'd done.

"We did. We went, we saw, we beat him to a bloody pulp and we put the fear of Satan into him. He's not going to be a problem anymore."

"Can't believe I missed it," Uncle Sam grumbled.

"This is horrible." Alisha felt sick. Why did testosterone-filled men make everything worse?

"It's kind of sweet, actually," Diya said, shooting Mann a flirty wink which he returned.

"Stop that," Alisha snapped. "Mann, you can't go around taking the law into your own hands. The man was in jail, paying for what he'd done."

"No, he wasn't. He was at home watching TV."

"Because he was out on bail!" No one wanted Asshole Kumar to pay more than she, but it had to happen legally. Didn't Aryan know what she thought of vigilantism?

"Are you sure he is in London?" Bharati Vaidya asked the testosterone-dunked idiots in the room.

"He's in London. I spoke to him this afternoon," Mann clarified.

That aggravated Alisha no end. So, he was talking to *some* people, was he? She came to a sudden decision. "All right, Aunty*ji*. I'll come to London with you."

How dare he make her feel like this and disappear? She was going to London, she'd find him and kill him. She'd show him what happened to people who broke the law. She'd show him what happened to twenty-five-year-old boys who ran away and ghosted their girlfriends. But for now, she just wanted to go home and throw up.

But the Vaidyas didn't let her escape. They made her stay for the party. They made her laugh and forget her troubles. They made her feel like she was a part of their family.

CHAPTER 18

Finnegan's Flask hadn't changed a whit in three years.

Aryan sipped his third Guinness of the night and looked about the pub. The high-beamed ceiling, the brown rexine upholstery that covered the chairs and barstools and banquettes, the scarred wooden barrels that served as tables around the room—everything was exactly the same.

Even the people looked the same. He recognized a few weathered faces, but the rest of the young merrymakers were students or tourists. Just as he'd been, once.

Then there was Finnegan himself. Owner and barkeep of the local hotspot, he towered over most of the men in the room—hell, most men in the world—at six feet eight inches. He stood behind the well-stocked bar, mixing drinks, serving patrons and keeping a jaundiced eye on the troublemakers. He had the Eye of Sauron, a symbol of power and fear to all young turds—or so Aryan had believed back in college. And when the Eye failed, the Voice thundered its a warning. Finn's Irish drawl boomed over the cacophony, cracking a joke, or shouting at some fool caught in the act of doing something foolish.

Aryan wondered what Finn would do if he let himself go and did something foolish. Pick him up with one giant hand and flick him out on his bum, most likely. The Irishman suffered no fools. And though Aryan had done several troublesome things over the last few days, it was all in the past now.

He'd left it all behind in Mumbai. He didn't want to talk to anyone from there. Except Mann, and of course he communicated with his office every few hours and his home staff once a day. It wasn't possible to vanish off the face of the earth, no matter how much one wished it. He didn't dare call Mamu in case Neeta Mami or Nanu were about. Mann was their go-between.

Aryan munched on a basket of fish and chips, washing it down with the Guinness. He tapped a foot in time with the fast gig the live band was playing. The accordion player was a hoot, the lead singer inexhaustible. Half the pub dancing was up and dancing or stomping their feet like him where they sat. Aryan swiveled his bar stool around to enjoy the show.

He was in a happy place, surrounded by happy people. Why shake things up and start talking to other people? Nope, that would be unwise. Although, he wouldn't mind hearing from certain people. Like the property owners of the Bengaluru housing colony project. It would be ideal if they hired him in the next day or two and work began immediately. He could fly straight to Bengaluru and avoid Mumbai altogether.

There was no need for him to remain in London anymore. They'd brought the old man home from the hospital this afternoon after the doctors had pronounced him stable and on the mend. All the old man needed was rest and loads of therapy to get back on his feet.

Aryan couldn't believe Nanu and Uncle Sam had lied to him. The old man had never been in mortal danger. He'd suffered a thrombotic stroke, but because of the prompt actions of Margaret, the severity of the stroke had been contained. His father had collapsed during a board meeting, and Margaret had been to catch him. Margaret was always there to catch his father.

He tipped his glass up and drank deep. Beer tasted so much better at Finn's. Dry and stout, just as he liked it.

The only remaining side effect of the stroke—and here the doctors had become vague and noncommittal when asked if it was curable—was the speech dysarthria. The muscles in the old man's throat, cheeks, jaw and vocal cords, that assisted movement or specific function, had been partially paralyzed. His father had to stay off solid foods, breathing was an effort for him and he couldn't talk at all presently. He managed a slurred word or two, but nothing lucid.

The old man was understandably frustrated, but there was nothing Aryan could do except show up three times a day for a sympathy visit. The intensive restorative therapy would begin tomorrow and hopefully they'd see some improvement soon. The speech therapist certainly thought so. "It will take time and patience, but we'll get him capable of speech again. Mind you, not a hundred percent ever, but better," he'd warned at the end.

Margaret was a rock. She wouldn't allow the old man to break down or feel sorry for himself. It seemed she was the right woman for him, after all.

She had everything under control at home and at work. It really didn't matter if Aryan was there or not. The old man was on the mend. He was well tended. He was well loved. There was nothing, absolutely nothing that Aryan could provide that the old man didn't already have.

He was redundant here as well.

Aryan drained his beer and rotated the seat toward the bar, signaling Finn for a refill.

"That's four pints now, boyo. Ye sure yer want another?"

Aryan grinned as Finn's brogue washed over his dulled senses. He'd once asked Finn why he had an Irish accent if he'd never lived in Ireland. *Ireland's in my blood, in my bones, lad. And if it's not in my voice, granny will belt me arse, well and deserved.* Finn had such pride in his family, for his roots.

"I'm not driving, if that's what yer after," Aryan tried to imitate the Irishman.

"Sensible lad. You always were. Not like some of these gee-eyed gobshites." Finn scowled at a young man on the verge of up-chucking the contents of his stomach. Knowing Finn, he'd be more upset at the wasted beer than the mess he'd have to clean up. Luckily, the boy's friends rushed him out of the pub before he threw up.

"Haven't seen the likes of ye in a while." Finn eyed Aryan up and down as he held a clean, dry glass at a forty-five degree angle below the tap and began pouring the draught into it until it was three-quarters full. He set the glass aside.

"Haven't been back in a while." No one poured a Guinness quite like Finn. Mesmerized, Aryan watched the draught darken in color. After a minute, Finn slowly filled the glass to the top, and Aryan's pint was ready, complete with the creamy white head.

"Where's yer better half, then?"

In Mumbai, Aryan thought instinctively. But that's not who Finn meant.

The better half Finn was asking after was Harry Colt, Aryan's college roommate and current host. Ary-and-Harry. Finn had addressed them as one entity because they'd been joined at the hip through their three years at Kingston University. They'd had some bloody great times at

Finnegan's Flask, it being so perfectly located near their lodgings. Harry was the *better half* since he was friendlier and more or less unflappable—still was—while Aryan had always been temperamental. *Little seems to have changed, boyo.*

"Still at work. Our boy's become an overachiever. He eats, drinks and sleeps at the damn paper," Aryan said. Which was why Aryan wasn't in any rush to go back to Harry's place. He didn't need to be in an empty apartment, staring off into space thinking of "people."

"Oh yeah? Where's he at now?"

Aryan told Finn all about Harry's work and his spacious, converted loft in the lively neighborhood of Angel Islington that was packed with trendy restaurants, clubs and theatres. Aryan approved of Harry's ritzy new digs. His previous two flats had been abysmal and utterly devoid of light. This one had two skylights and a fully functioning bathroom. Progress in the right direction.

"What brings you hereabouts, then? Feelin' nostalgic, eh? Ya miss old Finn, do ya?"

If only it were that simple. "Visiting the Pater, Finn. He lives about twenty minutes west of here, in Weybridge. I thought I'd give ye a holler before heading back into town."

"That's grand of ye. You always were a good lad." Finn gave a toothy grin, then moved away to service the other boozers hanging about the bar, demanding their drinks.

Was he good? Aryan stared at the black-red liquid swirling in circles. What the hell was he doing in London? *You don't want to go there, boyo. You don't want to start thinkin' again.*

Aryan nodded into his glass. No thinking. No feeling. No going home. He drained the glass and set it down. If everything was a no-no, what the fuck was a yes-yes? The music changed again, and the lively Irish folk songs were replaced by long, crooning ballads.

It was definitely time to go. If he sat there listening to sentimental crap—even good crap—he'd do something stupid, like drunk-dial Sunshine.

He groaned. *Stop thinking about her, ye goddamn fool! And no names. She's just* people.

Okay, he thought, sliding off the barstool. Time to call a cab and mosey on home. No, no mosey on over to Harry's. Which was home, of sorts, wasn't it? Right. It was time to go.

Aryan pulled out his iPhone to order an taxi and a barrage of notifications popped up on his home screen. The sheer number of them made him blink. He ignored them all except for the text from Mann. His mouth dropped open as he read the message.

Head's up. Auntyji and Alisha are en route to London.

What in buggering hell? He snapped his mouth shut and four pints of super fine Guinness sloshed in his belly, making him queasy. Why couldn't they leave him alone? That's all he wanted, to be left alone and be allowed to drown in beer in peace.

That meddling son of rooster. It had to be Mamu's doing. Uncle Sam was a dead man.

Sunshine was coming to London.

As it sank in, Aryan's lovely beer buzz died an abrupt death.

WHAT WAS it about Aryan Chawla that made her do rash and foolish things?

Alisha was meticulous and organized. She was a rational person who preferred to make cerebral decisions. She was not impulsive or emotion-driven, and yet, here she was, doing something completely alien to her nature once again. Because of him.

Alisha removed her sky blue cardigan and tied it around

her waist, coming to stand by the baggage claim belt where Auntyji's luggage would be spewed out first apropos first class travel. That had been a first for her, traveling in decadence. Not that she'd reaped the benefit. She'd been too angry and worried to fall asleep on the plush bed or to enjoy the meals served with real cutlery and not plastic.

It wasn't her first trip to London though, and her UK visa had still been valid, thank heavens. She had cousins and friends scattered all over the greater London area. Some she knew well enough to impose on should the need arise. She'd already e-mailed them about her short visit, just in case.

Alisha looked about the terminal. As usual, Heathrow was drenched in trench coats and umbrellas, and not one of them sported by Aryan.

"Find out from Sameer who is picking us up," Bharati Aunty called out from where Alisha had made her sit while she collected the luggage. Aryan was supposed to meet them at Baggage Claim and take them to—Goodness! She didn't even know where. She hadn't thought that far when she'd jumped aboard the flight with her roll-on.

Alisha texted Uncle Sam and promptly got a reply that make her heart skip a beat.

"Mann got hold of Aryan. He'll pick us up." Her phone vibrated with a second text. "And if he can't, someone called Chester will." *Can't or won't?*

"Chester runs a private car company that we've used for years," Auntyji explained, looking pleased by the alternative arrangement.

Alisha wasn't. If Aryan didn't come to fetch them, she'd take the next flight home.

And then, he was right in front of her in a military green bomber jacket and no umbrella.

There she was!

Once again, the ridiculous line popped into Aryan's head

when he saw Sunshine after nearly four days. Her neatly braided hair left her face naked, exposed. Still bruised. Not as bad as the other night, not as swollen, but there was a faint bluish tinge on her jaw and under one chocolate eye. He couldn't look away even though he wanted to, his black-and-blue knuckles throbbing as he fisted his hands.

She stared right back, probably shocked by his scruffly appearance. He hadn't shaved in three days. He hadn't even showered today. He'd barely managed to wake up this morning after his semi-inebriated night. He'd hastily brushed his teeth, doused any lingering body odor in cologne, then he'd nearly burned his gullet downing a mug of steaming hot coffee. Harry, all spryly dressed and ready for work as a journalist for a local newspaper had thoroughly enjoyed the morning theatrics.

"How life changes when the ladies are involved, eh?" he'd commented.

Aryan hadn't bothered replying and had dashed out of the flat to pick up his awaiting entourage.

He greeted his grandmother with a hug, a kiss and an apology for missing her birthday. *Keep your mouth shut this time*, he ordered himself. Don't say or do anything stupid. He gave Alisha a peck on her cheek, inhaling her glorious scent, then he stepped back to help with the luggage.

"That's it?" he asked after they'd plucked Nanu's full-sized Hartsman off the belt.

"Yup," Alisha replied. "That's all I brought." She gestured toward the black roll-on next to Nanu. It was the same one she'd brought to the farmhouse. So, she wasn't staying long.

He wanted to tell her how sorry he was. He wanted to take her in his arms. But he didn't trust himself not to shake her, so he picked up their luggage and said, "Let's get going then."

His coldness hurt. He hadn't hugged her, hadn't even smiled at her. He didn't want her there.

Well, too bad. Her return flight was booked for the end of the week, that gave him three days to grovel and grow up.

Outside the terminal, the sky was a horrid dark grey in color. Just like Aryan's mood.

A black SUV waited for them at the curb. With his eyes, Aryan asked her to help his grandmother get settled in the car while he loaded their bags in the trunk. Alisha climbed in beside Auntyji and promptly started sneezing. The interior of the car was drowning in Aryan's cologne. Was this his idea of revenge? Death by deodorant.

"Weybridge, Chester," he told the driver after climbing into the front passenger seat.

"Very good, Mr. Chawla. Good morning, Mrs. Vaidya. Lovely to see you again. Hope your flight was good?"

"It was, Chester. How are you? And your lovely family?"

"All thriving, Mrs. Vaidya. Thank you for asking." Chester was a tall, wiry old man with a gold tooth and a diamond stud in his ear. A clean-shaven pirate in a charcoal grey suit.

"Alisha *beta*, this is Chester. No one knows London better than him," Auntyji said.

Chester greeted her with more enthusiasm than Aryan. "Hello, Miss. First time in London?"

"Oh no. I've been to London before." Alisha said, shivering. Sliding her arms into her cardigan, she buttoned it up to her throat.

Chester and Auntyji kept up a steady dialogue during the drive, involving Alisha in it from time to time. If nothing else, they discussed the weather. "Rain and more rain for the coming days," Chester said cheerfully.

Aryan remained studiously glum.

"Where are we going?" Alisha asked when they didn't get

on the highway going east toward London, but rather on the one going south toward Surrey.

"Raj's house, *beta*."

"Oh? How far is it from London? Will I be able to get around easily?" She didn't intend to be stranded somewhere with no way out.

"It's not far, *beta*. And Chester will take you wherever you want to go. He'll be with us on the whole trip. Won't you, Chester?"

"Of course, Ma'am. Where do you want to go, Miss?"

"I may visit some friends and cousins. Unless you have plans for us." Alisha caught Aryan's eye in the rearview mirror, and the storm brewing in them.

"No plans. Suit yourself." He shifted and she couldn't see his face anymore.

Anger she could handle. But this wasn't anger. Mortification made her cheeks burn. She shouldn't have come. He truly didn't want her there.

Morning had barely broken and it already felt like the end of a hellishly long day.

CHAPTER 19

The Chawla estate sat atop an area called St. George's Hill in Surrey, some forty-odd minutes outside of London proper.

Alisha goggled at the L-shaped brick structure in front of her and smiled ruefully. While Bharati Aunty and Chester had kept referring to "the estate" during their car conversation, and Alisha knew the dictionary definition of an estate, she hadn't realized just how large the property would be. Exactly what did Rajaram Chawla do for a living, she wanted to know. The sprawling manor house nestled in the middle of such lush, verdant land made a breathtaking first impression.

"Quite a view," Aunty*ji* commented, looking around just like Alisha was.

It had stopped raining but the sky was overcast and the air nippy. Still, she would happily go on a walking tour of the place and its surroundings. "It's beautiful."

"I didn't expect it to be quite so grand." The wistfulness in the older woman's tone was unmistakable. But how could that be?

"Surely, you've come here before?" Alisha asked.

"No, *beta*. It wasn't their home, you see. Raj bought it after my daughter left us."

Whoa. That was…sad. Alisha stole a glance at the living, breathing thundercloud beside them.

With growing irritation, Aryan listened to his nanu and Alisha admire the old man's manor house. The architect in him agreed with them, appreciating the fine lines and classical beauty of the structure, while the son balked at the idea of going in.

He hadn't stepped foot on the estate in over ten years. Not since the first summer he'd spent in London, two years after his mother's death. He'd been all of fifteen, full of righteous anger and hate. But his heart had still trusted, still foolishly hoped. Then they'd told him about the baby, crushing even that small glimmer of sunshine he'd held on to. He'd never come back.

That summer was in the past. He'd grown up since then. He was no longer an overemotional lad craving attention.

"Let's go inside before you freeze," he said watching both women huddle into themselves and shiver despite their sweaters and coats. "Need a hand, Chester?" He nodded at the bags in the trunk.

Chester shook his shaggy head. "You go on in, Mr. Chawla. I've got them."

"I won't be long," Aryan added softly.

A traditional white portico framed the main doors of the house. Gravel crunched beneath his boots as he walked towards it while the ladies thanked Chester and Nanu asked him to come back later in the afternoon so she could go visit her sister in Brent Park. Aryan's nostrils flared. What was it about women and socializing? Couldn't they stay put in one place? Did they have to go haring about, sticking their noses in other people's business? He pressed the doorbell a little harder than was necessary.

"Your sister lives in Brent Park, Aunty*ji*? May I come with you? I have a cousin who lives in that area, I can meet up with her," Alisha said as they began walking toward the house.

"Of course, you can come, *beta*."

"Alisha's going out with me, Nanu," Aryan cut in, putting a stop to the social visit agendas.

"Oh? We're talking now?"

Alisha wanted to aim a roundhouse kick at Aryan's head for making her crazy, blowing hot one minute and cold the next. She was about to shout at him when the front doors flew open and a petite woman with shoulder-length red hair and bright blue eyes greeted them with an enormous smile. She wore a white crocheted top, jeans and dark brown boots, and looked to be around forty years old.

"Mrs. V, at last! Raj is so looking forward to spending time with you," she said, hugging Aunty*ji* with giddy enthusiasm. She stepped back, ushering them in. "Come in. Please, come in."

"Margaret, you haven't changed a bit. Still so bubbly and beautiful." Bharati Vaidya took Margaret's hands in hers and sighed in sympathy. "How is he, Margaret? How are you?"

Margaret gave a one-shouldered shrug. "Good. Better." She slanted a quick, sideways glance at Aryan. "Happy that his son's come home."

Aryan was already coiled tight in tension and he stiffened even more at Margaret's words.

Studiously ignoring the escalating tension, Aunty*ji* said, "Margaret, this is Alisha. Alisha, meet Margaret, Raj's wife."

Alisha had already guessed who the woman might be but Aryan's reaction to his stepmother froze the smile on her face. His black eyes went bitterly cold at the introduction.

The wheels in Alisha's brain churned. Margaret was his stepmother. He didn't like her because she was the woman who'd replaced his mother, replaced *him* in his father's life.

She wanted to smack her forehead for being so stupid. She'd made a huge blunder by coming to London. She should've listened to Neeta, the only person who'd been against this jaunt. She should've waited for Aryan in Mumbai.

"I'm delighted to meet you, Alisha. I've heard such lovely things about you." Margaret pumped her hand heartily.

"Uh, I'm so sorry to show up unannounced. I hope I haven't caused you too much trouble."

"Of course not. Any friend of Aryan's is welcome here. Come, Mrs. V. Alisha. I'll show you to your rooms. We've prepared your old room upstairs too, Aryan."

"Why? I'm not staying," he said rudely. "I'm going to run up and check on him before I leave."

Who was this cold, unforgiving man, Alisha wondered? He wasn't Aryan. He wasn't her Aryan.

"Where are you staying?" she asked.

"At a friend's. I'll see you later." He walked away from her then. He didn't even look back as he climbed up the broad stairs with the gleaming wooden banisters. He didn't ask her to go with him.

Alisha's stomach hollowed. *Just leave,* her brain told her. *Wait. Give him a chance to explain,* her foolish heart pleaded.

Slowly, she followed Margaret towards the guest rooms. "I'll take you to meet Raj after his therapy. That'll give you a chance to settled in. Is that fine?"

"Of course," Aunty*ji* said, sounding tired and sad and everything Alisha was feeling.

"He's been great, Mrs. V." Margaret felt the need to reassure them. "He stayed with Raj all day and night at the hospital. Now, he comes to see him every day. Not for long, mind you, and he won't stay with us. But that's okay considering he hasn't visited us for over ten years."

"It's a step forward, true," Bharati Aunty said. "But I'd hoped for something different. Temper, maybe. His anger is easier to deal with than his silence. He's closed himself off." She turned sorrowful eyes on Alisha. "I'm so sorry for dragging you into this, *beta*. I had hoped," she paused, shook her head. "I didn't think."

Alisha hugged Aryan's sweet grandmother. "You couldn't have known, Aunty*ji*. And don't apologize for his behavior. He's a grown man. He has to learn how to deal with life like a grown up."

Margaret smiled slowly. "Exactly. I've been telling Raj the same thing. If you treat him like a fifteen-year-old boy, he'll behave like one, won't he?"

"He's not going to give in. I know him. He has learned to bury his feelings. To bottle up everything and pretend all is well. I have a hand in it. I should have been more open about Sandhya. I should have forced him to visit his father even if he didn't want to."

"Hush, Mrs, V. We all did what we thought was best for him, and maybe we made mistakes, but we have a chance to make it right, and we will." She opened a white lacquered door with beautiful cornices. "Here we are, Mrs. V, have a rest. I'll send in some tea and sandwiches for you. And in two hours, I'll come back and help you unpack. And then we'll go and see Raj. How does that sound?"

"It sounds wonderful, Margaret." She patted Margaret's cheek and went into her room. Her bag was already inside.

"I wish you'd call me Maggie, Mrs. V."

Bharati Aunty laughed for the first time since her birthday party. "And I've told you that Maggie is the name of an instant noodle brand in India. I'm not calling you that."

"That again?" Margaret said, smiling, and began to close the door.

Aunty*ji* stopped her by placing a hand on her shoulder. "Thank you. I know how difficult he makes things for you."

Margaret shook her head. "There's no need. He's Raj's son and Sandy's. I have to love him." She smiled wryly. "Though, I confess, I'm running out of patience. With both of them," she added and looked up at the ceiling.

"We all are," agreed Aunty*ji* with another deep sigh. "Will you send scones with the tea?"

"Classic cream. I haven't forgotten your favorite, Mrs.V." Margaret closed the door and turned to Alisha with an effervescent smile. "Let me show you to your room. And I hope you'll call me Maggie. All my friends do."

TWO HOURS LATER, after a lovely hot shower and a proper English tea complete with scones, hot biscuits and orange marmalade, Alisha lay in bed contemplating her options.

Leave or stay?

She'd politely declined Maggie's invitation to visit Rajaram Chawla. She wasn't stepping over that line without Aryan. If or when he deigned to talk to her, he'd take her himself.

Alisha tried to go boneless, a meditative technique she'd picked up online. She focused on the shades of soothing blue around her. Her room was lovely. Vaguely cluttered but spacious with lacquered antique-looking furniture. It had an old-fashioned feel to it just like the rest of the house.

Whatever Aryan's father did for a living, he was obviously very good at it.

So, here's what she knew about Raj Chawla. He was rich. He was sick. He was estranged from his son. He was

Maggie's husband. And he was somehow responsible for his first wife's death?

Alisha frowned. He'd had an affair during his marriage, Aryan had told her that. With Maggie? Probably. It would explain Aryan's animosity toward the woman. But it didn't explain why Bharati Aunty was so chummy with her. Who would be that friendly with the woman responsible for her daughter's marital problems and possibly death? It didn't make any sense.

Also, if Aryan's mother had caught her husband cheating, why not just divorce him? It wasn't as if the Vaidyas or the Chawlas couldn't afford a divorce as so many middle and lower income couples couldn't. Sandhya could've made her husband's life a living hell by demanding an exorbitant alimony and child support. But that's not what had happened. Because she'd died before actually filing for divorce? Or had she died during, like Alisha's *achan*? How had she died? Heart attack? A disease? A broken heart? In an accident? Alisha had so many questions and a pitiful supply of answers.

That aside, she understood secrets. Her own family had once been mired in them. Would Aryan find the courage to tell her the good, the bad and the ugly things about his family? She hoped so.

Riches didn't inoculate a person against unhappiness, did it? His family had everything—grand houses to live in, beautiful cars to enjoy, great careers to take pride in, but it wasn't enough, was it? Because the core was broken, the heart had been shattered.

Her own heart had suffered such devastation once. But she'd survived it. They all had—her mother, her brother and herself. Her father would've also come to terms with it if his health hadn't succumbed to his excessive drinking first.

MT had been their savior. She'd been there for her

mother through it all. Her maternal aunts and uncles hadn't let them down, either. That kind of unconditional support had meant everything to them and slowly but surely her family had healed. There were some cracks and holes left, of course there were, but nothing insurmountable.

Alisha rollled to her side. It was raining again, she noticed with a yawn. She should take a power nap before Aryan got there. She definitely needed the fortification to deal with him. He was a very stubborn man.

But then, so was she.

BHARATI AUNTY WOKE her up when it was time for dinner. Pale twilight filtered into the guest room through partially open drapes. It was still cloudy but it had stopped raining.

"I slept the whole afternoon away?" Alisha scooted off the bed and stretched. Her stomach growled, reminding her that she'd missed lunch.

"I did too. I woke up an hour ago." Aunty*ji* had changed into a light green *salwar* suit and she held her purse in her hand.

"Are you going to visit your sister? Is Aryan here?" He was meant to come back with Chester.

"No, *beta*. He's not here. He came back in the afternoon but since we were both sleeping, he left. He told Margaret to tell you that he'd see you tomorrow," she said quietly.

Alisha sat down on the bed. He'd...left without waking her up? He wasn't even coming back today? He truly didn't want to see her.

"Come, *beta*. Let's have something to eat and then we'll go and see my sister and her family. Or you can visit your cousin. Come."

Alisha shook her head. Nothing was happening like it was

supposed to. "You go ahead, Aunty*ji*. I'll probably go back to sleep."

Bharati Aunty sat down on the bed, her face creased with worry. "I don't know what is going on anymore. I don't know why he is behaving like this, Alisha."

"It'll be fine, Aunty*ji*. Go visit your sister. He'll come here tomorrow and we'll talk to him. Set him straight." Alisha strove for an upbeat tone but she declined to have dinner with the family. She couldn't bear to be around people tonight. She didn't have it in her to pretend everything was fine when they'd be looking at her in pity.

After Bharati Aunty left the room, she filled the clawfoot tub with steaming water, threw in several pinches of mineral salts that promised the ultimate in relaxation and sound sleep. She huddled in the water for a good long time, letting her tears run down her face and her snot down her nose. She cried until her skin turned into a prune and the water turned cold. Still, she stayed in the water. Then finally, anger exploded within her like a blast of nuclear power.

She got out of the tub, rage sparking her eyes. She grabbed a fluffy white towel and wrapped herself in it. How bloody dare he do this to her again and again?

She cursed him then. "I want every strand of shiny hair on his stupid head to fall out. Let him go bald. Let his lying, grinning teeth rot and his breath stink. Let his manicured, Scrabble-playing fingers fall off in a gangrenous heap on the bamboo floor of his farmhouse. No, not the floor. Let them fall on top of his precious drawing board contaminating his eco-conscious designs."

"Wow. That felt good," she said to her ramrod stiff reflection in the vanity mirror.

She looked demented. Huge, haunted eyes, swollen red. Chest heaving. Skin flushed and marked with fading bruises and travel shadows.

Her anger fizzled out abruptly. She had two days left before she flew back to Mumbai. She could change her reservation and leave immediately but she wouldn't. She'd play this game through to the end.

And bludgeon Aryan Save-the-Planet Chawla into a bloody pulp along the way.

MEANWHILE, Aryan and Harry bonded over whiskey at a pub close to Harry's place in Angel Islington. Being a Monday night, there were a total of five men in the pub, counting the two of them and the barman.

"You should have waited, mate," Harry said unnecessarily.

"I did wait." Aryan had knocked twice, let himself into Alisha's room, then had stared at her gorgeous, sleeping face for twenty minutes.

"How do you still not know anything about women?" Blond-haired, blue-eyed Harry considered himself a consummate ladies' man.

Aryan stuffed a potato chip in his mouth even though he wasn't hungry. He didn't want to discuss his failings or lack of manners. He should have woken her up, explained. He could've joined her in bed and made her laugh and hiccup until the past no longer mattered. He could've done a lot of things. But he hadn't. The deed was done and there was no point in feeling guilty about it. Only, he was feeling guilty.

"You are so fried, mate, just like a potato. She'll be plotting your demise now. I'll be sure to shed a tear or two at your cremation."

"She can fry me all she wants. It won't change the outcome." He had to let her go. He'd thought about it long and hard, and it was the only way to keep her from heartache and misery. He wasn't fit to be in a relationship. He might never be.

Aryan tossed back the Scotch in one gulp, hissing as liquid fire shot down from his gullet to his stomach.

"You've turned into a sad little fellow, mate."

"Bugger off." Aryan curved his hands around his glass as the barman refilled it.

"You used to be fun. Moody, yes. But, all in all, a lot of fun." Harry eyed him over his glass, then took a sip. "I suppose I'm on suicide watch tonight?"

Aryan stared at his friend, wondering if he'd heard right.

Harry burst out laughing. "Your face! You should see your face."

"That wasn't remotely funny," Aryan said stiffly.

"Of course, it was. Come on, man. It was a joke," Harry said when Aryan stood up and thrust his arms into his dark brown leather jacket.

"My mother isn't fodder for your sick sense of humor." Aryan threw twenty pounds on the table and stalked out of the pub. Harry had gone too far.

Harry jogged up next to him on the street. "You know I didn't mean your mother. I was being a dickhead, all right?"

Aryan didn't slow down. He'd pack up his things and check into a hotel. How could Harry joke about it? Some things were sacred. Never to be spoken of. Never to be thought of even. He stumbled on a jutting cobblestone on the street, nearly falling on his face. Harry caught his arm before he fell.

"Jesus. You're a complete mess, mate. Do you want to talk about it?"

With him? Fuck, no. Aryan kept walking, a bit more carefully now.

"You need to talk to someone, Aryan. A therapist."

"Fuck, no." Never again would he subject himself to that worthless torture.

The street was busy even though it was after-dinner

hours and cold. They passed a group of smokers hanging out outside a quaint little bistro that served amazing apple pie. Aryan could smell it in the air.

"Do you recall the psych major I dated during second year?" Harry asked out of the blue.

"Vaguely." Still irritated with his friend, Aryan tried to bring the girl's face to mind. Pretty brunette. "Why?"

"Do you remember her saying that your relationship with your mother defines all your adult relationships with women?"

"I'm pretty sure she didn't mean me specifically, but was quoting Freud there." Aryan shoved his cold fingers into his jacket pockets.

"Anyhow. Do you suppose it's true?"

"I don't give a fig one way or another. If it is true, won't I be doing Alisha a favor by breaking up with her?"

"That's not what I mean. You should talk to a professional about your mother, Aryan."

He'd had two years of therapy after she'd died. It hadn't helped then, why would it work now?

Aryan glanced at his friend. "Wasn't she the one who claimed that the size of a bloke's brain was inversely proportional to the size of his pecker? After which she started calling you Big Dick?"

"That was after I'd dumped her for the redhead." Harry chuckled. He hadn't chuckled then, Aryan recalled, he'd been livid. "I wonder what happened to her?"

Aryan shrugged. "She's probably driving her patients insane instead of saving their sanity."

Harry laughed. "Not the brunette. The redhead. She was a media and communications major, like me."

Aryan didn't bother replying. He was just thankful that Harry's disordered and disjointed mind had jumped onto the next topic. They crossed the street and turned the corner into turn into a narrow lane lined with row houses on both sides. Harry's loft was in the house at the end of the lane.

"I don't suppose I'll get to meet Alisha if you're going to break things off tomorrow."

Aryan inhaled sharply. "I'm going to tell her everything. We'll see after that."

"So, you're not breaking things off."

"I won't have to. Knowing Alisha, she'll dump me." By some miracle, she wasn't angry about the way he'd manhandled her when she was hurt. Or, was she? Had she only come after him to break things off in person?

It would be for the best, if she did. A bit of heartache for them now rather than years later. Alisha would never abide a weak man for the long haul.

Aryan waited for Harry to unlock the door of his house.

Sleep, that's all he needed now. Sleep and tomorrow would dawn soon enough.

CHAPTER 20

$\mathcal{A}$lisha woke up ravenous the next morning.

Late morning, she corrected after opening the windows to blink at the bright sun breaking past the rows of trees bordering the back of the estate. No rain. No clouds even. The neighbour's kids were taking advantage of the good weather too, she noted as girlish shrieks and happy energy suffused the air.

Yawning, Alisha went into the bathroom and got ready. After a quick shower, she dressed up a white ruffle-front shirt and jeans, put on a beige cardigan over the shirt, and slipped her feet into a pair of black pumps.

Then she went to find food before something happened to make her lose her appetite again. She found the house-keeper, Mrs. Gibbs, wiping washed breakfast plates and stacking them on the granite countertop in the kitchen. Alisha had met the jolly woman briefly the previous day when she'd brought the tea tray into her room.

"Good morning, Miss. It's a lovely day today," Mrs. Gibbs greeted with a smile.

"Has everyone finished breakfast?" Alisha hoped so. She wasn't sure she was ready to face the Chawlas pre-chai.

"Not everyone. Mrs. V is still sleeping. Mrs. Maggie and Mr. C are with the doctor, and will have breakfast after. The young ladies only just finished. Shall I set a place for you in the breakfast room?"

Too many C's and V's and who were the young ladies? Too many riddles on an empty stomach.

"I'd love some breakfast, thank you." While Mrs. Gibbs made up a tray, Alisha inquired about Aryan. "Did he come by last night or this morning?"

"No, Miss."

Dejected, Alisha followed the housekeeper into the breakfast room and began demolishing a basket of toasts, half a croissant and a cup of fruit parfait. Mrs. Gibbs gave her company, hovering about, filling and refilling her teacup. "That's the best chai I've had," Alisha had groaned in pleasure with her first sip.

"Mr. C likes it just so," Mrs. Gibbs replied, pinkening with pleasure.

Once her belly was no longer growling, Alisha decided to go for a walk around the property. She was through skulking about in her room and twiddling her thumbs, waiting for the jackass to show up. She asked Mrs. Gibbs to point her in the direction of the backyard and set off on her jaunt, using the time to think and call Diya.

A detailed venting to her bestie helped her untangle the jumble in mind. Aryan wanted to break things off. It was ridiculously clear in the light of day. Diya begged her not to jump to conclusions but Alisha didn't think she was. There was no other explanation for his behavior.

She followed a brick path that led from a sun-soaked stone patio to the pool house and through a pretty garden behind the manor house. She paused along the way, clicking photos of the vista and a variety of newly-bloomed flowers. Day lilies in varied colors, gladioli, white and yellow daisies, clusters of forget-me-nots. The sweet, intoxicating scent of lily of the valley permeated the air with magic.

Gently, she touched the tiny, pastel blue forget-me-nots that probably had a silly, romantic story attached to its name. Something mushy like a warrior riding off into battle in times long past, worried he may never return, offers flowers to his sweetheart on bended knee, wailing, "Oh my love, forget me not!" Alisha was positive something to that effect would pop up in a Google search. The world was full of tragic little love stories, wasn't it? She shouldn't feel personally targeted.

She marched up a carved wooden bridge, stood at its summit and looked down at the brook tinkling below. The water created a symphony as it jumped over pebbles and stones, gurgled its way into a koi pond filled with fat colorful fish. Alisha's heart lifted in joy. A beautiful garden for a beautiful home. Then a fat grey bunny dashed out of a hydrangea bush, gamboled over the bridge and stopped short a few feet away. It went up on its hind legs, wrinkling its nose, thoroughly enchanting her. Alisha took a dozen photos before the rabbit hopped off across the lawn.

Alisha ran after it, much like Alice in Wonderland had, and only slowed down when the green grass beneath her feet turned bright pink. It had to be Astroturf. Fake grass. Krish's college had had a field laid out in green Astroturf.

In the center of the circular patch of pink, a gigantic beech tree rose like an oversized mushroom. Stone benches had been set up along the perimeter of the pink grass. Winded from her rabbit stalking, Alisha plunked down on one of the benches to catch her breath, then gasped when she saw the belly of the tree. Rather what its abundant foliage was hiding from view.

A white and pink metal stairway spiraled upwards into the strong branches, stopping midway up the tree on a pink and blue landing. It was clearly a gateway to an elaborate tree house. A tree house fit for a Disney Princess.

The multi-level structure was painted in cotton candy colors with the windows and doors done in stark white. White picket fences circled all the landing areas turning them into balconies, and for protection.

This was what Aryan was building at the farmhouse. Only that tree house was for boys.

Alisha closed her eyes and groaned as her ears picked up the girlish chatter coming from above. *Young ladies.* It finally clicked who Mrs. Gibbs had been referring to. And the children she'd heard from her bedroom window. Maggie's kids?

Aryan's sisters.

Alisha buried her face in her hands, wondering what the hell she'd gotten herself involved in.

"Oh, hello," a girlish voice spoke from above.

Alisha squared her shoulders and looked up, smiling at the child looking down from one of the fenced balconies. Young lady was right, she looked about ten or eleven, at most. Her dark hair was pulled back in a thick, bouncy ponytail.

Alisha waved weakly. "Hello. What an absolutely pretty tree house you have there."

The girl tilted her head in such a familiar way that Alisha's heart ached. There was no doubt in her mind now that this was Aryan's half-sister. The way she tilted her head and postured in a blend of charm, curiosity and arrogance— it was classic Aryan.

"Are you sick?" the girl's brows furrowed.

"No. Why?" Alisha stood up.

"You were groaning like you have a stomachache." The girl started coming down the stairs.

Every movement she made reminded Alisha of Aryan. The same lazy gait, the same straight shoulders, the same intense black eyes. As she came lower, Alisha noticed the braces on her teeth and a black T-shirt with a red arrow pointing towards her heart with *Justin Beiber* and *One less Lonely Girl* written on it in pink and silver glitter.

"Nina, who is that?" A second girl appreared on the balcony, wearing a frilly green dress and matching hat.

Alisha couldn't help but grin at the proper English miss up in the tree house.

"I'm Nina and that's Cassie. She talks a lot. You must be Alisha."

"Yes, I am," Alisha replied.

Nina continued to watch her through Aryan's eyes. It was unsettling, to say the least. She even frowned like Aryan. The two siblings must resemble their father.

How funny genetics were. Aryan, at first glance, looked exactly like Uncle Sam, proving that his maternal genes were stong. But after meeting Nina, Alisha knew his father had bestowed an equal amount of hereditary inheritance on him.

Cassie came down too, dragging a tiny little princess in a fluffy pink tutu by her pudgy hand. Both of them glittered from head to toe. Alisha sat down on the bench again so she'd be eyelevel with the younger ladies. Both Cassie and the little one had their mother's gorgeous red hair.

"Hello. I'm Alisha and I'm staying with you for a couple of days." She didn't want them getting scared since she was a stranger.

"This is Millie. She's two. She doesn't talk much," Cassie said, taking a page out of her older sister's book for intro-ductions. She was a beautiful child with big blue eyes and a rosebud mouth. "You talk funny."

Alisha supposed she sounded funny to them with her

non-British accent. "I live in India. This is the way we talk there."

Cassie looked at Nina for confirmation. Nina even shrugged like Aryan. But, it was a gesture of approval because Cassie gave Alisha a beatific, gap-toothed smile. "We're having a tea party. Would you like some tea?"

"I'd love some tea."

Millie the ballerina climbed up on the bench to sit next to Alisha. She held up a white stuffed bunny for inspection.

"That's a very pretty bunny. I saw a grey one just now. It led me to your tree house."

"We see lots of wabbits," Cassie said.

Clearly, they weren't as enchanted as Alisha was. Of course, not. Look at where they lived and played every day.

"I don't see rabbits where I live," she said, making a sad face.

Nina was watching her closely. She was the odd sister out with her black hair, black eyes and lean body frame. Cassie, who must be all of five, and Millie were both chubby little things with fair skin and lots of freckles. The two also seemed to have been blessed with their mother's sunny disposition.

"We didn't go to school today," Cassie confided in a grave whisper. "We had a holiday yesterday and today and the weekend. So we had four days of holiday." She held up four chubby fingers.

"Wow!" Alisha tried to look appropriately awed.

"It was a bank holiday yesterday, Cass. So it's just today that we skipped school," Nina corrected.

Alisha was starting to like the dark-haired young girl more and more. It seemed Nina liked things precise and clear, just like she did.

"Do you want to see the tree house?" Nina asked out of the blue.

"I'd love to," Alisha replied, mindful of the honor Nina had bestowed.

Nina's lips kicked up in a small smile—not as wicked as her brother's, but it had promise—and the four of them went up to have some imaginary tea.

"THERE YOU ARE!" Maggie beamed up from the pink ground.

"I've been enjoying tea with your girls," Alisha said, waving back. "They've stuffed me full of such delicious goodies that I may burst. I may have to waddle for the rest of the day." Loud girlish giggles followed her words.

"It was fake, Alisha!" Cassie shrieked gleefully at the thought of fooling an adult.

"Has the doctor gone, Mama?" Nina asked.

Maggie smiled at her eldest with pride and tenderness. "Yes, lovey. And Papa's asking for his girls. Come on. Let's go see him before he falls asleep."

Nina and Cassie rushed down. Alisha followed, holding baby Millie's hand as she jumped down each step. She felt relaxed and refreshed. She'd forgotten how much fun make-believe could be.

"They're wonderful, Maggie," she said, sincerely.

"Thank you." Maggie picked up Millie and settled her on her hip and the baby buried her face in her neck. "Will you join us? Raj asked about you. He wants to meet you. If it's okay with you, that is."

Alisha felt weird again. But how could she refuse for a second time? She was a guest in the man's house, for heaven's sake. "Of course, I'll come."

They set off for the house, and Maggie began to describe the physiotherapy session. "It was better than yesterday. But it's a painful process and hard on him because he can't artic- ulate with words anymore. He can only gesture. It's frustrating for both of us and I hope to heaven things get better soon."

"It will," Alisha said automatically. She realized Maggie was probably just venting.

Nina and Cassie had run ahead of them and had disappeared into the house. Millie had fallen asleep in her mother's arms, her chubby fist going lax. Maggie, with her mom reflexes, caught the rabbit before it hit the ground and adjusted her sleeping daughter into a more comfortable position.

"Nina has taken Raj's infirmity badly. She's not usually so reserved, or well behaved. She's never seen her father sick. And this thing about his muteness...she's scared he'll never talk again." Maggie's face was white with strain. "So am I."

"You're doing everything right. He's getting the best help and treatment. He'll be fine," Alisha said, her heart going out to the family. Dealing with sickness was hard. It took a toll not only on the patient but his family too.

"She idolizes him, you know." Maggie stopped below a trellis brimming with red vine roses. It was the entrance to the courtyard that led into the house. "Nina adores Aryan."

Alisha's stomach hollowed at the sad, stark words.

"She's been raised on stories about him. That's how Raj pacifies his heart, by telling Nina all about her brother. She thinks the world of him, and he hates her." Maggie closed her eyes briefly, and when she opened them, she looked determined. "Alisha, I know I shouldn't impose on you, but I've run out of options. Would you talk to him? Make him understand? Please, help us. Help him."

"Maggie, I don't know." She knew nothing besides the bits and pieces she'd sown together from the conversations she'd overheard. "Even if he does confide in me, I can't tell him what to do."

And that was the crux of it. Whatever had happened in

the past, Aryan obviously had strong feelings about it. She couldn't just butt in and start dictating his behavior.

"He's as inflexible as his father. But he's wrong about happened. You can tell him that, at least. And to talk to his father about it?" Maggie laughed bitterly then. "Well, that's not going to happen now, is it? Raj is beyond conversation for the next year or so. And Aryan will never discuss his parents with me."

Alisha squeezed Maggie's hand in sympathy. "I'll talk to him." That's all she could promise.

"Thank you." Maggie tried to smile. "Shall we go meet my husband, then?"

Alisha nodded, wondering again what the hell was going on in this family and what had possessed her to come to London.

CHAPTER 21

*A*ryan parked the black Audi TT Roadster in front of the Georgian manor house and took his time getting out of the car. The sun was high in a nearly cloudless sky and the birds were chirping in the trees.

Get on with it, mate. The sooner you go in, the sooner you can get out.

He'd thought a drive would calm his stress levels, and so he'd borrowed Harry's gas-guzzler to attain the state. Sometimes one had to compromise one's principles for the greater good and ignore the twinges in the the gut.

Stop dithering, fool. Check on the old man. Check on Nanu. Talk to Alisha. Be quick, be brief, be brutal. Then leave. Aryan rang the doorbell.

He'd dressed carefully. Plain white shirt. Light blue jeans. He'd shaved and brushed his hair neatly. And he was an idiot if he thought looking presentable and clean would make things easier.

Mrs. Gibbs opened the door with a wide smile. She was always happy to see him. He apologized for his tardiness, then pumped her for information while exchanging pleasantries.

"Are the guests around?" He felt ridiculous calling them guests, and didn't feel any relief when she nodded. He'd run up and say hello to the old man, then he'd find Alisha and put an end to it.

"Go on up, then. Mr. C is waiting for you. Will you be staying for lunch?"

"I don't think so, Mrs. Gibbs. Coffee would be appreciated though," Aryan said, climbing the stairs two at a time. He was jittery. Should he be drinking coffee? He didn't know how things would go. Alisha was unpredictable, at best.

He heard the girlish chatter when he reached the first floor landing. Shit! The girls were home. What the hell were they doing home on Tuesday? Aryan tried his best to avoid them. Especially Nina, who looked at him with some sort of expectation. It made him uncomfortable and feel like a jerk.

He entered the old man's bedroom already wary, and when his eyes took in the happy family montage, his nerves reached breaking point.

The old man was propped up in bed, smiling lopsidedly at his wife who stood at the foot of the bed, talking and gesturing wildly. Nina was laughing. Another shock. He'd never seen the girl laugh before. Cassie sat next to Nanu on the window settee—both of them captivated by Margaret too. Even the damn visiting nurse was smiling at Margaret in benevolence. While Alisha—and here he had to pause because his brain stuttered and exploded—sat on a chair right next to his father, her arms wrapped around the baby while her chin rested on top of the sleeping red head.

Aryan stared at them all. How dare they? How dare they be this happy, this fucking carefree, when he hadn't slept in days? When he'd suffered and burned and choked on guilt.

He felt sick. Disgusted by them. With himself. And especially with her—his Sunshine.

Fury simmered inside him as he watched a travesty of a happy family.

And, as usual, he was out of the picture frame completely.

SETTLING MILLIE AGAINST HER CHEST, Alisha chuckled while Maggie entertained them about a funny episode that had happened at the head office of the Chawla Hospitality Group last week.

She finally knew what Aryan's father did for a living. He was an hotelier. He owned three boutique hotels in London and one in Edinburgh and was in the process of adding a fifth one to his mini empire. Maggie worked alongside her husband, and since his illness, she'd been shouldering double the responsibilities. Their marriage was the result of a work romance, Alisha fit another piece of the puzzle together.

Even sickly, Rajaram Chawla was everything she'd expected him to be and more.

Tall, broad and dignified, he wasn't classically handsome —not like Aryan and Uncle Sam—but he was striking, none-theless, with salt-and-pepper hair and pitch-black eyes. Sharp, steady eyes that shone with a ruthless intelligence had measured her worth the moment they were introduced. Alisha had been assessed and approved in a matter of minutes. She'd returned the favor, and his smile.

What was it about those bold, piercing eyes he'd bequeathed to his eldest two children that appealed to her so much? Eyes that were now twinkling with unabashed affection at his wife.

Aryan resembled his father, it was clear. His personality, his vitality and charisma were because of this man. So were Nina's.

Alisha slanted a gaze toward the giggling girl and froze when her peripheral vision caught a movement in the doorway. Aryan! Her heart leaped in welcome and she would've leaped out of her chair but for the baby in her arms. But why was he standing there like that? Looking at her so unpleasantly? By then, everyone had noticed him and the room fell inexplicably silent.

Was this how it was every time he came over? Everyone freezing and wearing matching looks of terror? Alisha shuddered inwardly.

"Oh look! It's that man, again." Cassie pointed at Aryan.

Alisha felt a fresh dose of horror melt her heart. Cassie didn't even know that Aryan was her brother?

"A family gathering. How nice," Aryan said tonelessly and yet sarcasm dripped from his tongue.

He didn't come into the room, not even when his father smiled and beckoned him closer. He deliberately highlighted the fact that he considered himself apart from the family.

"How was the therapy session today?" he asked, shoving his hands into his pockets.

"Better than yesterday," Raj Uncle mouthed the words because his left cheek and jaw were stiff due to the stroke and didn't allow for any facial movement.

"That's good," Aryan said and turned to his grandmother. "How's Choti Masi and her brood?"

"They are fine. They asked about you. You should go see them," she said pointedly.

He grunted in answer, then looked at Maggie and nodded in lieu of a greeting. She responded in kind.

Alisha wanted to scream at the cold exchange. What was wrong with them? Even Maggie, who was always animated and chatty, had frozen into a wax doll.

Against her better judgment, she decided to intervene. The Chawlas needed help and who better to force them to make reparations than a divorce lawyer? She specialized in broken relationships. And due to her own past, she was more than qualified to help this family.

"Hi, Aryan *bhaiya*. I did a project on wind turbines. Wanna see?" The hope on Nina's face as she walked to her brother, broke Alisha's heart.

"Not now." He dismissed her without even looking at her.

Nina faltered only briefly. "Then when? I got an A for it."

Maggie glared at her husband, clearly expecting him to control his children. Raj Chawla didn't arbitrate, he just looked defeated.

Alisha shook her head when he still didn't reply. Aryan was behaving like a child. And she could literally hear Nina's heart smashing into a million pieces.

Still, the brave little girl tried again. "I can run into my room and get it now."

"I said no. Do you understand what that means?" Wow. He managed not only to shatter his sister's heart but also stomp on it cruelly.

"Aryan," Bharati Aunty said sharply. "It won't kill you to see her project."

Finally, someone who could put a stop to this nonsense.

He didn't acknowledge the scolding, didn't apologize either. He turned his mean gaze on Alisha. She raised her brows in challenge. What did he expect from her? Validation for his misplaced anger and unkind behavior? If so, he was out of luck. She was a lawyer. She believed in punishing crimes, not rewarding them. Above all, she advocated justice.

"It's pretty good. You should see it," she said, although she had no clue whether it was or not.

His eyes flashed hot with betrayal. In his mind, she'd sided against him by standing up for Nina. But she *was* on his side. If he'd just stop and think about it, he'd see the truth.

Without another word, Aryan spun on his heel and

walked out of the room. She was beyond shocked at his conduct. But from what she understood, it was normal for him.

Carefully, she handed a sleeping Millie to her mother, and jumped up from her perch.

"I should go after him." She flapped her hands, hurting for all of them. "I agree with you, Maggie. He can't go on like this."

Then, Alisha sprinted after the foolish man who'd stolen her peace of mind along with her heart.

MEN WERE SILLY CREATURES. No, that wasn't true. Why charge the entire gender of the crime? This man was so silly.

Alisha rushed out of the house, looked about and spotted a sleek black car rolling forward, and with a heartfelt appeal to the Goddess above, leaped in front of it like a Bollywood stuntwoman. The car squealed to a stop, gravel flying, just in time to save her right foot from getting squished under its tire.

She opened the door and released her mad. "What is wrong with you, you lunatic?"

Black eyes glared at her. "Get in or get out," he said in a brutally calm voice.

She got in, and as soon as she shut the door, the car lurched forward.

"Wait!" She raised a hand up like a stop sign.

Aryan pressed the brakes hard, and Alisha was pitched forward because she wasn't wearing a seat belt. Aryan's arm shot out across her chest and saved her face from slamming into the dashboard.

"What now?" He sounded beyond irritated.

"I need my purse. My phone…" her voice trailed off when he blasted her with another aggravated look.

"You won't need them."

But she never went anywhere without her phone or her purse.

"Fine. Just so you know, I don't have any means of getting back if you decide to chuck me out of the car when we argue." She strapped on the seat belt.

"Don't tempt me," he muttered and steered the car down the driveaway.

Alisha narrowed her eyes. He'd made a Caveman joke. Not a hootingly funny one, still, it was a joke. He also seemed considerably less on edge than he'd been at the house.

"You really hate it in there, don't you?"

He didn't answer.

"We have to talk, Aryan. You have to tell me about your mom. I want to understand."

"I'm taking you to a place where we can talk without interruptions." He pushed a button on the dash and instrumental jazz flowed from the speakers.

"Where are we going? To Harry's flat?" Oh, she hoped so. She wanted to meet Harry Colt, whom she'd spoken to on the phone several times over the past months.

"No."

"Whose car is this? Harry's?"

"Yes."

"Is it a hybrid?"

Aryan's forehead creased. "No."

"Aren't you worried about messing up your carbon footprint?" From the vicious glance he shot her, Alisha decided to zip up the humor for the day. She settled into the bucket seat and let him drive them to wherever it was he wished to take her.

An hour and a nap later, Aryan slowed the car to a crawl, clearly searching for street parking.

They were driving down a busy road tightly packed

buildings on either side. And since the sun was out and beaming, most of London seemed to be on the streets, basking in its light.

"Where are we? I mean, what part of London?" she asked.

"St. John's Wood."

Alisha's patience was running thin. She'd initiated several icebreakers in the past hour—Diya's L'Oreal contract, her mother's impending holiday in Kashmir with MT, her brother's views on American politics, Brexit, SRK's new movie. To all of the above, he'd responded in grunts, snorts and one-word answers. All things considered, at least he was replying, even if in piggish tongue.

"What's in St. John's Wood?"

"You'll see."

"What will I see?"

He ignored her again. She thought about removing the jacket he'd given her and unbuttoning her shirt—he'd never be able to ignore her then. But it would probably give her bronchitis. As she'd left her sweater on the chair in Raj Uncle's room, Aryan had given her his leather bomber jacket to wear, leaving him in a plaid shirt and jeans.

After circling the same three streets for twenty minutes, he pulled into a newly vacated parking spot on Violet Hill road. There were rows of townhouses fused together on both sides of the street in typical London fashion. It was a residential neighborhood. There were only a few shops lining the street.

"Come on." Aryan grabbed her hand when they both got out of the car.

A jolt went through her when he touched her. Her heart fluttered and pitter-pattered as they crossed the street and walked through a wrought iron gate leading to a white, five-story building. The pathway was decorated with red and yellow flowers and leafy plants on either side.

A couple pushing a pram with twin boys came out of the building as they went in. The young mother thanked Aryan for holding the door open for them. Aryan chatted with the building concierge about some package while Alisha looked about the elegant lobby with its paneled walls, crystal chandeliers, and dark brown leather seating.

"Ms. Madden left a package for me," Aryan said. He was still holding her hand.

"I'll need to see some ID before I give it to you, Mr. Chawla."

Aryan showed the doorman his driver's permit who then handed over a manila envelope. Aryan pulled out a parking permit. "I'll go put this on the dashboard."

When Aryan bounded back in, he strode straight for the elevator. "Let's go."

He didn't hold her hand again. "Where are we going?" She couldn't tell what was going on in his head. His face gave nothing away.

"One more minute and I'll answer all your questions."

"Are you breaking up with me?" That's all she wanted to know. Well, that wasn't strictly true, but it was the most important question she wanted answered.

Aryan didn't know whether to laugh or sigh. Sunshine never did what was expected. She always managed to surprise him. She also read him like an open book.

He rolled the grills of the old-fashioned elevator open and gestured for her to get in. She swanned inside like a diva. He hoped she accepted his decision and leave it at that. He didn't want to argue with her. He could hardly understand what was wrong himself, so how could he explain it to her? He only knew that the tsunami that had started in Mumbai five days ago had only become worse.

London always affected him adversely. It was his purgatory.

Oddly, it was home too. He was tied to London for better or worse. That's what he wanted to show her. He hadn't planned on bringing Alisha here. He'd intended to have the talk in his father's home. Where, if she broke down or tried to murder him, there would be people around who'd come running to help. But those plans had blown up in his face because of his family and—Jesus, he'd been an absolute jerk to Nina.

He'd left in anger and shame. Then Alisha had come running out of the house and literally thrown herself on the car. And it had come to him in a flash what he should do.

$\mathcal{A}$ryan ushered Alisha out of the elevator on the fifth and top floor of the building. There were two penthouse flats on the floor. He walked to the one that reeked of neglect even in the hallway. He fished out the keys from the envelope and unlocked the door. It creaked and groaned as he shoved it open.

He didn't go in. His heart was trying to beat its way out of his rib cage as he looked inside the flat that had been his home for the first thirteen years of his life. He came to check on it every year, yet he always reacted as if a knife had slashed open his gut.

"Are we apartment hunting?" Alisha joked as she slid past him and walked into the foyer. "Did a client hire you to design it? It's in horrible shape. Yuck." She wrinkled her nose at a massive cobweb clinging to the ceiling with an enormous spider hanging from it. "You'd never guess that a beautiful, well-maintained building would have a crappy apartment like this in it."

She was right. The flat was in abysmal shape. The paint had faded and peeled years ago. The hardwood floors, though sound, were layered with grime and dust. Dirty windows obstructed the natural light that would've light up the apartment on a sunny day like this. And there were absolutely no light fixtures anywhere.

The architect in him shuddered at the wanton waste of a good space. No wonder Alisha thought he was there to do a job.

Two years ago, he'd hosted an impromptu party at the flat for his college mates. But one look at the disaster zone, and they'd taken the party elsewhere. The next day, Aryan had brought a floor lamp to the flat. He switched it on. It still worked.

The living room looked like the set in a WWII movie—cold and abandoned. But if he closed his eyes, he still could picture exactly how it had once been. The striped silk sofa set against the left wall where they'd played cards or Scrabble or watched TV. His father smoking in the balcony in the evenings, teasing his mother. Mum shushing them when they made fun of her beloved Bollywood movies by crying or laughing in the wrong scenes. The day he'd chipped the coffee table playing cricket with Dad.

Aryan walked further into the flat, slipping the keys into his pocket. He didn't know what to do with his hands, so he curled them by his side.

"This is where I grew up," he said baldly.

Alisha was ducking under another massive cobweb and did a double take at his confession. "Where you…what? This is *your* flat?"

He shuddered out a breath. "Yes."

"Why does it look like this?" She looked about wildly at the vacuum of space.

"My father gave it to me when I turned eighteen. He wanted to sell it. I wouldn't let him, so he gave it to me."

Chocolate brown eyes assessed what he'd said and what

he wasn't saying. He was an architect. Why would he neglect a prime piece of property, one that used to be his home, unless there was a diabolical reason.

"Tell me why, Aryan."

"I want to show you something." On wobbly legs, he started down the corridor on the left of the living room that lead to the bedrooms. He didn't check to see if she followed because there was no doubt she would.

He opened the master bedroom—more creaking—and walked in. It was in the same rundown state as the rest of the house; peeling walls, grimy, bare windows, musty odor, dirty floors. He unlocked the French doors that opened to the terrace, and put his full body weight in to open them, letting in the sweet, fresh, sunny air.

The terrace was in a slightly better condition than the flat, though it needed masonry patch-ups and a power wash as a start.

"What a beautiful terrace." Sunshine turned in a slow circle, taking in the various views of London rooftops and parks.

There was a pergola in one corner that used to be covered with Japanese wisteria, but no longer. It used to have seating beneath it too. Running along a wall next to it was a built-in kitchen and a fire pit where they'd had barbeques. The tree house had been the last addition to the terrace, and the first thing Aryan had pulled down.

Aryan's chest clawed for air. Maybe coming to the flat wasn't a good idea after all.

"I can see most of London from here. Oh look, there's a pretty little courtyard and garden below. Is it a part of this building?"

Aryan whipped about to face Alisha and staggered back when he saw her braced against the northeast ledge of the terrace, looking down the building.

It was beyond coincidence that she was standing in the exact spot of his nightmares.

He had to tell her everything. He went up behind her. His heart hammering as he glanced over her shoulder at the pretty courtyard that showed no signs of horror anymore.

Look away. Just breathe.

He placed his hands on either side of Alisha, caging her in. She stiffened, for a moment, then relaxed completely, leaning against his chest.

So trusting. He didn't deserve her. He never had.

"Let me tell you a story," he whispered into her ear. "But you can't interrupt. No questions until I finish. And you can't turn around. Can you do that for me?"

She went motionless within the cage of his arms, only her head nodded slowly.

"Good." He drew in a shaky breath and began his tale. "The story begins on a Sunday morning in October. A lovely day much like today—bright, a bit nippy, ordinary. I was thirteen—no Alisha, please don't turn around. I can't do this if you do."

He tightened his arms around her to prevent her from moving, then he spoke fast, without stopping.

"I was a typical teenager. A tad more spoiled than the average lad because I was an only child. I had an attitude a mile wide and opinions on everything. My immigrant parents were the bane of my existance. Everything they did or said embarrassed me—their accents, our culture, the smelly food Mum prepared at home. Especially my mum. The poor woman could never please me, no matter how hard she tried. She was timid, and I had no respect for her tears. Anyway, that weekend we fought again. I wanted to spend it with my friend at his house and she refused to permit it. The old man was in Edinburgh on business and Mum didn't want to be alone. I resented that I had to babysit her all weekend. So, pissed off, I locked myself in my room from Friday night, and when I had to speak to her, I was rude and mean."

If he'd only been a little less selfish, just a little more aware.

"By Sunday morning, she'd had enough of my obnoxious behavior. She fed me a huge breakfast." He could almost smell the fried fish out here, and the hot chocolate and the three waffles he'd consumed ungraciously. "She told me to get ready, said that if I didn't get out of her sight for a bit, she'd go crazy," Aryan paused, let the spasm of hurt pass. He could hardly see in front of him, his eyes had blurred.

"She called my friend's Mum and fixed it. She dropped me to their house, hugged me hard, and said she'd pick me up later in the evening. Not too late because I had school the next day. It was the last time I saw her alive."

Alisha struggled to turn around, but he didn't let her go. He had to finish.

"She had on jeans and an emerald green shirt with mother of pearl buttons on it. It was autumn, chilly, she'd put on a short suede parka, dark brown in color. I remember it so clearly. I remember her hair too. She'd had it up in a ponytail, tied with a green band. And she smelled of fried fish."

That's how he'd always remember her. A young, pretty woman, a mum who was thoroughly annoyed with her teenage son.

"I don't remember what I'd worn. Isn't that funny? I think I wore the same clothes for two days until my grandmother came here and made me take a bath."

"Aryan," Alisha whispered, rubbing her cheek against his. She was trembling as hard as he was.

"Let me finish, please," he said hoarsely. A mountain of guilt threatened to crush him. Delibrately, he looked down at the patch of pavestones and green, absorbing the pain. "My mother committed suicide. She jumped from this terrace, from this very spot we stand on, that Sunday afternoon after she dropped me off at my friend's house."

There! He'd told her. He could let her go now.

Aryan released her and the chill Alisha felt on her back was nothing compared to the chill she felt in her bones. Goosebumps spread all across her body at his story.

Suicide? In all her creative scenarios about his mother's demise, she'd never once imagined suicide. She tried to picture it, couldn't. What made a young woman stand on top of a wall and contemplate death after frying fish for her hungry child? What had happened so suddenly? What made a person choose to end her life like that?

Alisha braced her hands on the thick, rough wall and looked down. Five floors below, two old women knitted on a stone bench, sharing their stories and troubles. Horror filled her as Aryan's story finally began to sink in. His mother had jumped from this terrace. From *this* spot.

Jerking back was reflex. Her heart raced and so did her overactive imagination. For a second, she'd felt a ghostly hand at her back, but whether it wanted to shove her over or pull her back was anybody's guess. Alisha swung around and glared at Aryan. It was entirely his fault. How dare he tell her the truth in such a fashion?

But he wasn't even looking at her. His eyes were tightly shut, and his hands were fisted by his thighs. He was breathing deliberately like he was practicing *pranayama* yoga. Enraged and scared by what he'd told her, what she felt about it, Alisha raised her hands to shove at Aryan. But her hands froze in midair when he opened his eyes abruptly and fixed them on hers.

He hurt so much that she felt it in her own heart. There was such guilt and misery inside him. His face was leached of color as if all his blood had been drained out. Alisha closed the distance between them and cupped his cheeks with her hands. His skin was cold, clammy.

"I'm so sorry for what you went through." She didn't know what else to say, didn't know what he needed from her. So, she wrapped her arms around him and tried to squeeze all her sorrow and her strength into him.

His heart was beating in a crazy rhythm, fast one moment and barely ticking the next. Whatever was going on in his mind couldn't be good. She had to shake him out of it.

She stepped back and slapped his arm. Shock widened his eyes and she hit him again. He swayed when she shoved at his shoulder. Normally, she wouldn't be able to budge him if she threw her whole body weight at him. He blocked her hands before she could hit him for a third time. He grinned. She shook her fists and cursed at him. He doubled over and started howling with laughter.

She looked down at his bent form. Good. There were two ways to release tension—crying or laughing hysterically. She often laughed hysterically too.

A few manic minutes later, he straightened up with a groan. Tears rolled down his eyes as he shook his finger at her. "I knew you'd react in some wonky way."

"Wonky stories deserve wonky reactions." But enough fooling around. "Why didn't you tell me before? Why did you tell me now with all the drama?"

"It seemed like the thing to do," he said, somber again.

She cupped his face in her hands, wiping his tears with her thumbs. "Why did you let me think nonsensical things about…everything? Why didn't you tell me about your father and Maggie…about your sisters? Why?"

He placed his hands on top of her wrists. "I don't know. I tried to, many times. But it was never the right time or the right place or the right mood."

Alisha shook her head at his excuses. "You're a hypocrite.

What did you tell me that day? That *I* have boundaries and I had set limits on our relationship? That I don't let people in? What did you do, Aryan?" She moved away from him and walked to the other side of the terrace—no more looking down at the courtyard. She stared blankly at a row of brownstones on the opposite side of the street.

He hadn't trusted her at all.

The sun was high and there was no breeze. She should've felt warm in the leather jacket, and yet she was cold. He came to stand beside her.

"Why?" she wondered aloud. "Why would she do it? Give up like that?" It made no sense.

"I don't know. Maybe it was everything, all of us. My father, Margaret and me. I wasn't the best behaved boy," he said the last part shamefully.

"It still doesn't make any sense. She could've left your father, divorced him. And you? That's just nonsense. Are you saying that every mother who has a teenager is a candidate for self-harm?" Alisha frowned. "No, there was another reason. Was she manic depressive?"

Aryan gave her a sharp look. "Nanu thinks she was depressed. She wanted another child but they never managed to conceive after having me. She took it as a personal failure and it messed her up. And then she found out about Margaret."

That made slightly more sense. "So her hormones were out of whack because of the fertility treatments?"

"I don't know, Alisha. Maybe so, or maybe not."

"Why don't you ask your father and be sure? Why do you let it eat at you?" His face hardened at her prodding, leaving her incredulous. "Don't you want to know the truth?"

"I know the truth. She's dead. I have no interest in listening to his excuses." His hand slashed in front of him, cutting the air in half.

"What excuses, Aryan? Your father wasn't even in London when it happened. You're making it sound as if he was directly responsible."

"Wasn't he?" he cried bitterly. "If he had just kept his pants zipped or even been discreet about it, she wouldn't have known. She wouldn't have been upset."

"How do you know he didn't? How do you know what she knew or didn't know? In fact, how do you know anything if you haven't talked about it?" Her impression of Raj Chawla wasn't that of a marital cheater. If he'd been unhappy in his marriage, he wouldn't have stayed.

"Less than a year after my mother's death, he got married to Margaret. That's how I know. Not even a full goddamned year had passed," he said, his voice harsh.

Alisha didn't think it proved anything. What did Aryan expect his father to do? Mourn his dead wife forever? For all intents and purposes, she'd left him when she decided to plunge down from the parapet.

Goodness, what was she thinking? Why couldn't she dredge up an ounce of sympathy for Sandhya Chawla? Why was she judging the woman harshly?

"Aryan, isn't that jumping to conclusions?" She winced at her poor choice of words but, oh well. "Margaret and he could have become close after. They worked together, didn't they?"

"Not just that, Sunshine. He sent me away to India. I didn't come back to London for two years after...the incident. When I finally did come back, everything had changed. They lived in a new house. They had a new life. They were even going to have a new baby. There was no room in it for me."

Her heart ached for the boy he'd been. She wanted to touch him, comfort him. But he stood there untouchable, unreachable. He'd closed himself to her, to all feeling.

She knew, first hand, how fragile teenage boys could be. Her brother had been a crazy person after their *achan*'s death, hiding his pain behind a brusque anger and bad behavior. Krish had been a monster to her and Diya. She understood Aryan better than he gave her credit for.

However, he wasn't a scared, lonely little boy anymore and he needed to see that.

"I can't be with you, Alisha."

She'd been expecting him to say something of the sort but it still slayed her to hear it.

His black eyes met hers wretchedly. "I didn't expect you, hadn't planned for you. I have nothing to offer you but heartache."

"I hadn't planned for you either, Aryan. I didn't even want to meet you, but you pestered and cajoled and challenged me until I relented. You made me fall in love with you." And now he was rescinding his love because he was scared.

He sucked in a deep, deep breath as if he were inhaling her words. It was the first time she'd used the L word. He reached for her, but let his hand drop. Coward.

"Sunshine… I don't regret it and I hope you won't either. I…just need you to understand where I come from."

"We're not so different, Aryan. I've had an equally traumatic childhood, remember. I understand that certain experiences leave their mark on you." She held his gaze, daring him to look away. He wasn't the only one with tattoos of hurt around his heart.

"Thank you for understanding."

"I do understand," she repeated. "But it doesn't mean I'll excuse your tantrum." He'd hate her for sure now.

Shock flashed across his gorgeous face for a second before it turned to stone. "I beg your pardon."

She launched her attack. "No, you may not be pardoned. The way you treat your father, your stepmother—my God, the way you behaved with Nina today is inexcusable. You were horrible to her. She's just a little kid, Aryan. I'm amazed they even let you in the house. If it was me, I'd have stabbed you by now."

"They stabbed me in the back first," he roared like a wounded boar. Then as if he couldn't decide what to do—throw her over the ledge or himself—he stalked off into the apartment, leaving her alone on the terrace. Maybe not alone. There was a slim possibility of a ghost keeping her company.

Alisha ran behind her crazy lover. "Now you're exaggerating."

"What the hell do you want from me, Alisha?"

She reached out and grabbed the back of his shirt. He didn't stop and she stumbled, nearly crashing into him. "Stop. Please?"

He pivoted, furious. "Whose side are you on? I thought you understood."

"I understand that bad stuff happened. I understand you think your mother was wronged. I get that you feel *you* were wronged. I also know you have to get over it. You can't hold on to this grudge." She touched his heart, it pounded beneath her palm like a jungle drum. "It's hurting you, don't you see? It's hurting everyone. You have to stop this thing…this cold war with your father. You'll never have any peace until you do," she paused, giving him a chance to respond. He didn't. "I've been through it with my parents, Aryan. So I'm speaking from experience when I say that you need to forgive yours. You need to forgive yourself too. What happened wasn't their fault anymore than it was yours. It wasn't anyone's fault. There was nothing your father or you could have done differently to prevent what happened."

Life happened. You couldn't avoid it if you tried. Just look where one Scrabble game had brought her.

Death happened too. A natural death left change in its wake, an unnatural one left devastation.

"Will you promise me that you'll talk to your father?"

Aryan ran a frustrated hand over his head. "I can't, Alisha. I won't."

God, he was so stubborn. "I never took you for a coward. What are you afraid of? That you might be wrong? That you might be right? At least you'll know."

He was looking at her, but not seeing her. He was a thousand miles away, mired in memory.

"Let her go, Aryan. Let your mother go." And that's all the advice she was going to give him. It was up to him whether to heed it or discard it now. "She can't possibly be happy hovering about in this ghastly, spider-infested flat."

And that brought him back to the present with a thud.

"You did not just say that." He stared at her aghast.

She tilted her head to the side as if pondering some great curiosity. "Be honest. You keep this flat as a shrine for your mother, right? Like a temple, a mausoleum. You don't stay here when you're in London. You don't rent it out. Yet, you can't let it go. Why?"

Aryan pressed the heels of his hands over his eyes. Either she'd managed to amuse him or he was about to start bawling. He removed his hands, black eyes glittering as his lips began to twitch. "I'd say it's more like a courthouse."

Every single person she knew had told her she had a peculiar sense of humor. Now she'd found a man who not only matched her irreverence wit for wit, but encouraged it. Was it any wonder she loved him so wildly?

"Why a courthouse?"

"Imagine my mother as the final authority, if you will."

"The final authority on what?" She quirked an eyebrow.

He lifted his shoulders, dropped them. "I bring girls to the flat so she gets to approve. You know, dutiful son and all."

"What happens if she doesn't approve?" Would he say it? Would he joke about that?

"They get pitched over the... Fuck! What the hell am I saying?"

Alas, he didn't finish the sentence. But they did reach a sort of truce after that.

Two days later, Alisha walked out of the Mumbai airport and handed her roll-on to Diya's driver, Raju.

"Thanks for picking me up, Dee," she said, and climbed into the back seat of Diya's silver Honda CRV. She was oozing perspiration out of every pore, so she stuck her face in front of the car's air-conditioning blast. "I don't understand it. I missed Mumbai's heat and humidity while I was away—I hated the cold in London, yet, I long for it now."

"The grass being greener and all that jazz," Diya philosophised with a delicate yawn. It was past midnight in Mumbai but her BFF had insisted on coming to pick her up, even though Alisha would've taken a taxi home.

She slipped off her shoes and got comfortable for the ride home. "Actually, the grass was pink. Just your color, Dee."

"Pink?"

Alisha told Diya all about the Chawlas. "They're wonderful, Dee, warm and easygoing. You know how sweet Auntyji and Neeta are, Aryan's stepmother is the same. Only more vivacious."

"I can't believe what's been going on with that guy," Diya said, astonishment rubbing her sleep away. "There are no rumors circulating about him. And he's not exactly inconspicuous in this city, is he?"

Alisha got what Diya was implying. A Page 3 God was excellent fodder for the rumor mills. It was hard to believe that the seasoned Mumbai gossips hadn't unearthed his London life yet. "It's an old story. Maybe gossip has an expiration date."

"Then what happened?" Diya asked and Alisha shrugged.

"Nothing much after the melodramatic flat episode."

"I can't believe you compared his mother to the *Exorcist*." Diya looked at her in awe.

"Not *Exorcist*," Alisha protested. "More like *Casper*, the friendly ghost." A shudder ran through her when she remembered the ghostly hand at her back. Just imagination, nothing else.

"Whatever. And he was okay with it? He even joked about it?" Diya shook her head. "So weird. You both completely deserve each other."

Alisha smiled. "We do, don't we?"

"So, *are* you still together?"

"I have no idea." Alisha sighed. "We didn't talk about it after. But he behaved as if we were still together when we spent the rest of the day sightseeing around London. He held my hand when we strolled through Hyde Park and at Oxford Street..."

"Wait!" Diya interrupted. "You walked? You *strolled*?"

Alisha supposed it was shocking. "For a couple of hours, then my feet protested loudly. And since I wasn't dressed for anything fancy, we took a taxi to Piccadilly and met Harry Colt for dinner at an authentic Italian restaurant. Amusing chap. You'll like him. The pizzas were yummy too. If we're ever in London together, we'll go there."

"Never mind the pizzas, and we'll get back to Handsome Harry later, but right now, go on with the story."

"My mouth is watering thinking of pizza. Let's stop somewhere and grab a bite. I'm famished. I haven't eaten properly in three days."

"You just said you had pizza last night!"

"Two nights ago. Fine, I guess I can wait another fifteen minutes to eat," Alisha said grumpily.

"Did you do any shopping on Oxford?" Diya asked excitedly.

Sustenance was to be ignored but not shopping?

"I worry about your priorities, Dee. And no, I didn't go there to shop."

"The travesty! How can you go to London, stroll on Oxford Street and not be tempted?"

Alisha narrowed her eyes. "Aryan asked me the same thing and gave me the exact same look. What is it with the two of you and shopping? And do you want to hear the rest of the story or not?"

Besides, how was she supposed to have shopped without her purse even if she'd been so inclined? It had seemed unethical to spend Aryan's money with the way things stood between them. She'd amused him when she said as much when he tried to buy her an expensive coat because he needed his jacket back. She'd chosen a cheap, touristy sweat-shirt off a street vendor instead. He hadn't been too happy about that.

Diya would've had no qualms shopping up a storm in a similar situation. She would've bankrupted the man and left him standing at the cross-section of Oxford and Regent, pockets inside out. But that was only because Diya loved to shop. She wasn't a greedy person or an unethical one.

Alisha chuckled as she remembered how playful he'd

been, running around the trees at Hyde Park, trying to cheer them both up.

Diya watched her wide-eyed. "Why are you so cheerful? Why are you okay with all of this? Did Asshole Kumar knock you on the head harder than we thought?"

Alisha heaved a sigh. "Because I know what he's going through. I went through the same thing, Dee. You were there, holding my hand throught it when my parents split up and Appa died. Have I ever thanked you for it?" Alisha kissed her BFF's cheek in gratitude. "Aryan doesn't need a girlfriend harassing him right now. He needs a friend." He needed counseling.

"Let me get this straight. You're okay with the... ambiguous status of your relationship?"

"For now, yes."

"For how long? It's been a dozen years since his mother died. What makes you think he'll come to terms with it in the next few weeks or months?" Diya's frown deepened. "You took years to sort it out. You may not even have sorted everything out. And have you forgotten Krish? Your brother has major issues still, and he's thirty-three!"

"He's ready to move on. Don't ask me how I know it, but I do." Alisha wondered if she was only seeing what she wanted to. "Either way, I can't sort out his life for him. He has to do it himself. If he wants me, if he wants us, then he'll find a way back."

"Did you tell him that?"

Alisha nodded. "When he dropped me back to his father's house. It's funny in a sad way how his whole demeanor changes when he comes near the estate. It's like he erects a wall around himself so no one can get in. More importantly, so he can't get out."

The wall was crumbling. She could see it. Could he?

"When he dropped me off and again refused to come in, I

told him I'd be there if he needed to talk to a friend. But we didn't stand a chance as a couple with the way things stood." Alisha scrubbed her face with her hands, suddenly tired. "He's so afraid of his feelings, Dee. He's afraid to trust his own heart. And if he can't trust himself, how can he trust me?"

Diya squeezed her hand.

"He's exposed a side of me I never knew existed. He taught me that life can be exquisite if it's shared with the right person. I know now it doesn't have to be just my way or only his way. I won't lose my soul if I give in sometimes. He loves me as I am, Dee. He's never tried to change me. So how can I push him to change?" Alisha shook her head. She didn't even want to. "That's what went wrong with my parents. They never understood each other or compromised together. They didn't care for each other enough to share their lives, their burdens or their laughter."

Her parents had never loved each other. If they had then they would've moved forward together instead of hindering each other's progress by blame.

A deep peace settled within her heart, and hope like a brilliant butterfly began to flutter around it. Aryan would come back to her. He had to.

"I'm so proud of you, Leesha." Diya dabbed at her watery eyes. "You do know you're expecting a miracle from a man?"

Alisha wiped her own eyes, nodding.

"They're not exactly equipped to deal with life's vicissi-tudes." *Vicissitudes?* Just what had Diya been reading lately? "You've kind of stepped in for his mother. Poor lost child doesn't know whether he's coming or going so nudge him along in the right direction."

Perhaps Diya was a bit mean. "Rubbish! I've said my piece, now it's up to him. Aunty*ji* and Maggie can nudge him or poke him to speed up his vicissitude. I'm done with it. And let's change the subject before I get a headache."

"Fine. Tell me all about Harry Colt. Is he handsome?"

Alisha laughed and told Diya all about Handsome Harry.

TWO WEEKS LATER, Aryan knew three things beyond the shadow of a doubt.

One, that thinking was overrated. Two, talking to his father was easier said than done. Three, Harry was an ass.

Actually, number three wasn't exactly an eye-opener. Harry had always been ass-like.

Aryan dipped the three-inch brush into a can of steel blue paint and applied it to the primed wall. He exchanged the brush for a roller and smoothed it into an even finish. Music blared hard and heavy as he worked, his hips and feet keeping rhythm, while a team of workers scuttled about the flat behind him.

Harry thought Alisha looked like Jessica Alba—she didn't, but try convincing the ass otherwise. He hadn't stopped extolling her physical, mental and spiritual perfections since their dinner date.

For the first two days after Alisha's departure from his life, all he'd done was think, think, think, and feel sorry for himself. He'd pondered over life in general. He'd stressed about his life in particular. He'd wallowed in every terrible memory he'd buried so deep that it was shocking he'd managed to dredge it up at all. All that soul searching hadn't really helped. And point number one had been born: thinking was overrated.

So he'd stopped thinking and started doing.

Lights, camera, action. He bought half a dozen floor lamps, three bags full of cleaning supplies, basic art supplies, borrowed Harry's SLR camera, rolled up his sleeves and got to work.

He'd cleaned, scrubbed and oiled the Violet Hill flat until not a cobweb or squeaky hinge remained. He set up a lamp in every room and vanquished all ghostly and ghastly shadows. He spent an entire day sitting cross-legged in the middle of the clean living room, surrounded by the digital prints of the rooms, complete with measurements, doing what he did best —designing spaces to visual perfection.

Aryan dipped the brush into the paint and once again applied a thick coat on the wall.

He'd do this for his mother. He needed to do it for himself.

Mum would approve of his new plans for the apartment.

The old décor had been French Country—silk upholstery with fleur-de-lis prints, lace edged curtains, furniture made of finely carved wood and crystal chandeliers in every room. Back then, he'd thought the chandelier in his room had been too girly. He'd even tried to break it by flinging his tennis balls at it. Now he knew better.

Aryan jerked as a cold hand touched the middle of his bare back. The roller fell to the floor, splattering blue paint on the drop cloth and lower wall.

Swearing a murderous blue streak, Aryan swung around ready to blast the idiot who'd crept up on him. He gaped at Uncle Sam who'd leaped several feet back to keep from getting hit with paint, yelping his own invectives. "Did you just drop out of the sky?"

"Careful with that thing." Uncle Sam pointed at the brush dripping paint. "So, you finally decided to stop neglecting it?" He shrugged out of the wet trench coat and looked about for a place to dry it.

Aryan pointed the paint brush at the coat rack in the foyer. "What are you doing in London?"

"When are you coming home?" Uncle Sam countered, sweeping his eyes all over the living room which was still a mess, but a different kind of mess.

"This is my home too, Mamu," Aryan said softly. It had been, once upon a time.

Uncle Sam looked at him in surprise, then stared thoughtfully.

Aryan shrugged. "I've started something here. I need to finish it." He needed answers and so far he had none.

The design plans on top of the plastic table caught his uncle's eye and he bent to look at them. Aryan had tried to blend his memories of the past with his signature contemporary style.

"How did you find a contractor so fast?" asked Uncle Sam as a fleet of workers hauled in the new kitchen cabinets. The kitchen would be done in lacquered white and stainless steel.

"I called some friends from Kingston as well as KLC."

After earning his degree in architecture from Kingston College, Aryan had enrolled in a year-long program at the KLC School of Interior Design for an additional diploma in eco-conscious design. He was in touch with several of his colleagues from both schools. One of them had recommended the contractor.

"How long do you think all this is going to take?" Uncle Sam looked around the flat again.

He wasn't only talking about the renovation and they both knew it.

"I don't know. A few weeks? A month?" It all depended on if he ever found the courage to confront his father. Right now that seemed like an impossibility.

"Come with me." Without waiting for a response, Uncle Sam started striding through the flat, though he paused to poke his head into every room, nodding and grunting at the improvements. "I'm glad you're renovating this place."

"It needed to be done."

Aryan followed his uncle out onto the terrace. The sight of it no longer revolted him. Spending the last two weeks in this flat, night and day, had taken care of any inconvenient jolts and memories from twelve years ago. The chill he felt now was only because he didn't have a shirt on and it was drizzling.

Uncle Sam headed straight for the spot from where his mother had jumped. "I went to meet your father before coming here. He's doing well," he said, looking down.

Aryan slid his hands into the pockets of his cargo shorts. He wasn't ready to have this conversation.

"He mentioned you haven't been to see him in ten days."

Aryan shrugged. "As you said, he's doing well and I have my hands full here."

Uncle Sam pinched the bridge of his nose with two fingers. He looked tired and Aryan felt a twinge of guilt. Of course Mamu was tired. The man was juggling a pregnant wife, two small daughters, Nanu and a double load of work. All of Aryan's projects in Mumbai would need supervision too. And they'd just got the green light from Bengaluru.

Fuck. He didn't have much time left. "I'm trying to work as fast as I can."

"Try harder, son." Uncle Sam sighed. "What is it that you want? What does all this mean?"

Aryan looked up at the gloomy, rain-filled sky. "Do you think I obsess about saving the planet—saving Mother Earth —because I couldn't save my mother?"

Uncle Sam didn't answer, only stared, making Aryan feel like a fool.

"I've been thinking a lot about everything. There's this giant knot of confusion inside me and I have no clue how to unravel it."

"We are all there for you, you know that. Why have you

stepped back from all of us? You haven't spoken to Raj. You barely acknowledge Maggie. You're not talking to Ma or me." Uncle Sam frowned. "What about Alisha? I hope you told her the truth."

"Of course I told her. I didn't have a choice since you sent her here," Aryan said, resenting his uncle for bringing her up, reminding him of what he'd lost. She had no place in his life now.

"What's the problem then?"

"I don't know! All I know is that I want to be left the hell alone."

"You are alone, you fool. You wanted space, we've given you space. But it isn't working, is it?"

Aryan opened his mouth to deny it, but he couldn't.

"Are you in touch with Alisha?" Uncle Sam asked point blank.

"No."

"Why not?"

"We're not together anymore. She deserves better than me. She deserves someone who won't burden her with problems."

"I see." Uncle Sam crossed his arms across his chest. "Closing yourself off from the people who love you isn't going to protect you from pain or loss. Trust yourself, son. Trust your heart. Trust us."

Uncle Sam's words fell like punches on his gut. "I trust you and Nanu."

"Do you? Do you think I haven't noticed that you've been distancing yourself from me? Maybe you're not even aware that you're doing it. You changed when I got married. You pulled back more when Lara was born. And after Ria you moved out of our home—your home completely."

Aryan wanted to scream in denial. "That's nonsense, Mamu. That's not why I moved out." *That's not what happened.*

"I know you better than you think, son." Uncle Sam's eyes glittered with unshed tears. He grazed a hand along the top of the brick wall. "I hate my sister for what she's done to you, to our family. She didn't just take her own life, she took yours away too."

Aryan recoiled at that. "Uncle Sam—"

"Just shut up and listen. She was your mother. You will always love her. But dying doesn't make her right and your father wrong. Dying just makes her dead. But your father is alive and he loves you. Aryan, can't you see how much he loves you? Don't push him away, son. Don't leave it so late that you regret your father too."

Aryan squeezed his eyes shut. Jesus. *Jesus!* He didn't want to cry. But it hurt, damn it. It hurt.

Uncle Sam squeezed his shoulder. "I'm taking Ma back with me on the evening flight. Will you be all right in London on your own?"

Aryan nodded jerkily.

"Come home soon, *beta*. We all miss you."

Aryan nodded again. He couldn't speak. His throat was swollen with emotion.

Uncle Sam hugged him hard, then he took a deep breath and blew it out. "Come on, let's finish painting the room. We rarely get our hands dirty in Mumbai."

They went in right before the sky burst open and wept in fury and shame.

CHAPTER 24

One step at a time, Aryan climbed the stairs that led to his father's bedroom. Mrs. Gibbs had let him in, informing him that Mr. C was with the physiotherapist, Dr. Chadwick. His father's restorative therapy alternated between speech and physical.

Two weeks had gone by since his talk with Uncle Sam. At first, he'd been shell-shocked by his uncle's candor, then he'd been furious and now he was just tired.

Tired of being angry all the time, tired of being alone, tired of holding on to guilt and shame and damned tired of holding onto a grudge.

The renovation was nearly complete. Next week, the furniture would be delivered and there would be nothing, no excuse left to hide behind.

He slid the Audi's keys into his jeans's pocket. He'd borrowed the car again, damning the planet. But it felt good to get out and get dressed in clean clothes. He'd gone so far as to buy a brand new shirt in his father's favorite color and from his favorite shop for the long overdue visit.

When had he started referring to the old man as his father?

Aryan knocked on the door of the master suite, then opened it. He stilled as soon as he heard Margaret's angry cry.

"You can't just give up. You have to try harder. They told us it would take time and effort and courage. Damn you. Nobody promised a miracle."

What the hell was going on? Aryan hesistated by the door, wondering if he should intrude.

"Mrs. Chawla is right. Therapy is painful and it might seem like its going nowhere, but it does help. Enough for today, Mr. Chawla. Rest. You'll see improvement soon," the therapist assured.

"No...never. Don't...come...back." His father's words were slurred and raspy but loud enough to be heard and mostly discernable.

Aryan closed his eyes as relief flooded through him. He hadn't truly believed his father would talk again.

There was a bit of a palaver then as Maggie and his father argued and bickered about who had ownership of the old man's body and fate.

"Dr. Chadwick will come back. Apologize to him, Raj."

"That's not necessary, Mrs. Chawla. Let him rest today. I'll see you the day after."

There was a rustle of movement and the doctor came out of the room. He smiled when he saw Aryan and explained what had happened.

"Temper tantrums are expected. Patients run out of patience at some point." Dr. Chadwick grinned at the wordplay. "We have to keep pushing, gently. I'm actually more worried about Mrs. Chawla. She seems close to a nervous breakdown."

Who Margaret? Maggie?

Aryan shook the doctor's hand and walked him to the stairs. He was still frowning as he approached the bedroom again. Maggie was still talking, still pleading.

"I'm tired, Raj. I can't keep doing this all day long. I can't handle the office and the kids and you. It's too much. It's just too much. You could make it easier and go over the designs for the new hotel, but you won't. You know I hate dealing with that egotistical maniac of a designer. Why won't you let me arrange a meeting here? There's nothing wrong with your judgment or your pointing skills. And everyone already knows about the speech issue. But you won't do it." A pause, then, "I can't do everything. I can't be in five places at once. I need help, Raj. I need you, damn it."

When it seemed like she'd start crying again, Aryan went in.

His father lay on his side, staring out of the open window, pointedly ignoring his wife. Maggie's face was a beetroot red and wet. She looked dazed when she saw him. His father grunted but otherwise didn't move.

"What's wrong?" Aryan asked, looking from one mad face to the other.

Maggie hesitated for a second, then flung her arm out dramatically. "He's decided he wants to be a vegetable for the rest of his life."

Okay, a bit extreme. Aryan pulled a chair and sat in front of the old man. "What's this about not doing the physiotherapy anymore?" The old man shrugged. "I know you can talk. I heard you from the door."

Rajaram Chawla snapped his eyes to Aryan's face. Once upon a time that powerful temper would've made Aryan pee in his pants. He'd grown up since then.

"If...you...heard." His father shrugged again and the paisley quilt slipped off his shoulder.

Aryan rearranged the quilt. "Therapy isn't optional, Dad. You have to do it."

He knew he'd stunned them both—all three of them— with his use of *Dad.* He'd not called the old man that in twelve years. Maggie burst into tears and ran out of the room. His father's face crumpled too and he groped for Aryan's hand. Aryan took the hand that had guided him, protected him, punished him when needed. He held the hand that had hugged him and patted his head in praise nearly every day for thirteen years. Tears welled up in his eyes as he remembered all that they'd been to each other.

"I'm sorry, Dad. For everything." To hell with what had happened in the past. It was way past time to move forward.

His father struggled to sit up, refusing to release Aryan's hand. The old man had quite a steely grip for a sick person. Aryan helped him up.

"No...sorry," his father said hoarsely.

"Don't talk. Get better first, then we'll talk as much as you like," Aryan promised.

His father nodded, smiling lopsidedly, then he bent his head to his son's shoulder and started to cry.

Aryan wept too. He wept for his father. He wept for his lost childhood. He wept for the wasted years of both their lives. But most of all, he wept for the beautiful young woman who'd chosen death over them.

UNCLE SAM and Alisha were both right. It was fear that had frozen his heart. A preemptive rejection would save him from heartache later on—or some such rubbish, he'd believed.

He went in search of Maggie after his father fell asleep. He'd made the old man very happy today and it felt good. It felt right. He needed to make things right with Maggie too.

He found her in a pretty courtyard to the back of the manor. It had been added after the summer he'd spent there because he didn't remember it. May was coming to an end and the gardens were in full bloom. The sky was spotless and the sun bright. The air smelled of freshly mown grass and wet earth.

Maggie squinted up at him as he neared. Sunflowers bloomed tall in the two stone urns that flanked her bench. The yellow of her silk shirt was an exact match to the flowers. Now, if she had black boots on her feet instead of brown ones, she'd make a perfect hallmark picture.

He settled himself on the sun-warmed bench and slanted a look at his stepmother. She was a petite woman, beautiful no doubt, but short. His mother had been tall. Like Alisha.

Her eyes were red and puffy and her face still mottled with color. He couldn't see any freckles though. He remembered her freckles.

"You're missing some freckles."

She stared at him in confusion, then her blue eyes lit up and two fat tears slipped down her cheeks. "Lemon juice applications for fifteen minutes every other day."

"That's all it takes?" Who'd have thought?

"That's all it takes." She gave him a wobbly grin.

Aryan didn't know how to begin making reparations. It wasn't easy coming up with the right words but as he'd told his father, it wasn't an option anymore.

Maggie beat him to the punch. "Thank you for what you said to him inside."

"It was time. He's still a stubborn old man, that hasn't changed." Aryan shook his head, grinning.

Maggie wiped her face clean of tears. "He's bloody mulish. There are only two ways to deal with him, either sit on him until he relents or start crying so he gives in out of sheer desperation."

Aryan laughed. "And it works?"

"Of course, it works," she said, then looked at him slyly. "Does it work on you?"

"I'm not stubborn."

"Ha! You're his son and Sandy's. Stubbornness is in your blood, mate."

Sandy. Aryan felt an electric shock go through him. He'd forgotten that his mother's friends had called her Sandy. He'd forgotten that Maggie and his mother had been friends. Best friends.

"Why, Maggie? Why did it happen?"

Maggie didn't even pretend to misunderstand. "You understand that most of it is just speculation and that no one can really know why Sandy did what she did. I think she stopped taking her medication, her antidepressants. She'd been on them for years, since her father's passing and the last miscarriage. She wanted another baby. It became an obsession. She refused to accept failure. That's when," she stopped talking abruptly and looked away.

Aryan braced himself for the sordid truth. "That's when Dad and you—"

"No," she cut him off, looking back in horror. "There was never anything between us until later."

That was not the confession he'd been expecting. "What do you mean?"

"Sandy was my friend, I'd never poach. I might have had a bit of a crush on Raj—me and most of the women in the office—but there was never anything between us besides mutual respect and friendship. Your parents had a good marriage. A bit rocky because of the infertility issue, but they loved each other. Your father was happy with the way things were. He didn't think it was a big deal that they couldn't have more children. They had you, why would they want more?"

Maggie smiled then. "And you were certainly a handful. But Sandy couldn't let it go."

Aryan stood up and started pacing. "What are you saying? That she stopped taking her medication because she wanted to have another baby?"

"I think so. She never told anyone she'd stopped taking it. Not your father. Not her doctor. Not any of us. And she made Raj promise not to tell her family about the depression, so they didn't even know she was on medication."

"Nanu knew." She knew and she blamed herself.

"I don't think so, honey. She hid it pretty well."

"Why would she do that?" Had another child been that important to her?

"No one can know for certain why, honey."

"And Dad? How could he not suspect?"

"We were in Edinburgh, finalizing the purchase of the property that is The Chawla now. He had no clue, trust me. Sandy was fine when we left. She'd been really happy the last few months. When the police called, he went berserk. We flew back. Raj went to the police station and I came to get you."

Aryan remembered complaining to Maggie about his mother that night. How mean Mum was and how irresponsible that she'd forgotten to pick him up. Later, his father had come into his room and told him what had happened. It didn't sink in for minutes, hours maybe. Days. He kept thinking it was a prank—a nasty little prank.

"Raj is a strong man. Some call him hardhearted and ruthless, but I saw him splinter into madness when Sandy died." Maggie sighed. "He blamed himself, naturally. He'd been too busy with work. He hadn't spent enough time at home. He shouldn't have argued about the fertility treatments."

It seemed Uncle Sam was right in that too. Everyone

blamed themselves for what happened to his mother when she was the only one responsible for her actions. She'd sealed her fate the day she'd decided to quit taking her antidepressants.

"Then you went away to live with Mrs. V and your father became even more remote. He had no one left, you see. His parents were no more and he's an only child like you."

The desolate image of his father didn't tie in with Aryan's memory of that time. *What about me? I was there,* he wanted to shout at her like he'd wanted to shout at his father all those years ago. Why had he been sent away? Why hadn't he refused Nanu?

"He lost interest in everything. Even work didn't matter anymore. I couldn't stand by and let him throw away his life, throw away everything he'd built, because that's what he was doing." Maggie raised her head defiantly, her heart in her face and said, "So, I seduced him."

Aryan cleared his throat. He had not expected that. "I see."

"I'm not ashamed of my actions and I do not regret them. Yes, I took advantage of a grieving man, but I had to shake him out of his stupor." Maggie stood up, her nose and ears robin red.

Someone had made her feel that what she'd done was wrong. He hoped it hadn't been him. "That was clever. Nothing shakes up a man more than a determined woman."

"Exactly." Maggie grinned even as tears filled her eyes. "So we started having an affair."

Aryan groaned, "TMI, Maggie. I don't need the details." Jesus. The image of his father in the throes of a wild affair was now imprinted in his mind forever.

"Well, you asked. And you know how conservative your father is."

"If you say so."

She fluttered her hands impatiently. "In his private life,"

she clarified. "Having an affair was not an option, not for him. It was marriage or nothing."

And when all this was going on, had any of them thought about a thirteen-year-old boy who'd just lost his mother?

Aryan looked at his vibrant stepmother, proud, daring in a way his mother hadn't been, and let the last of his hurt melt away. "I'm glad you were there for him, Maggie. I'm glad he found love again."

"But we weren't there for you, Aryan. Will you ever forgive us for that?" She started sobbing in earnest then, covering her face with trembling hands as her whole body shook.

Helpless like any man facing a wailing woman, he drew Maggie into his arms. "Hey! What's this now? There's nothing to forgive, yeah? It's over. It's in the past. Besides, I should be begging for your forgiveness. Come on. Stop this."

He drew her back to the bench and made her sit, offering the corner of his navy blue shirt to use as a tissue since such things weren't within reach in sunny courtyards. She refused his gallantry and made do with the sleeve of her own silk shirt, now badly blotched.

"I should've spoken to you then," she said in a husky voice. "Explained things better. Once we got married, I should've insisted you come back to us."

"I was horrible to you. And I wouldn't have come." That much was true.

Maggie took a deep, shaky breath. "But you were a child and you were hurting. By the time we got married and sorted out the business mess, a year had passed. Raj would come to Mumbai every month to see you, do you remember? I started visiting too. But it was clear you didn't want me there. And you didn't want to be here, either."

"I'm sorry for that. And for the things I said, Maggie."

"No. Don't be. I'm not telling you all this for an apology. I want you to know, and believe when I tell you that your father…that it was never him. He didn't send you away. And it wasn't Mrs. V's doing, either. Everyone wanted to do what was best for you. That's all. So when we saw how happy you were in Mumbai, we thought it best that you remain there."

None of them had bothered to ask him what he wanted. If they had? But he wasn't going to think about what-ifs anymore.

"I was happy. London wouldn't have been right for me then. Too many memories. Being with Nanu and Uncle Sam was for the best. Uncle Sam wouldn't let me brood about things. He kept me so busy I rarely had time to breathe. And Nanu? I don't think even Mum could've loved me more. If I'd lived here," Aryan broke off and shook his head. "How would you have handled two ill-tempered stubborn asses alone?"

"Don't let me off so easily," she said sniffling.

"Maggie, it's over. It's done. No more guilt and no more regrets for any of us." And that's how he wanted it.

Fresh tears spilled down her cheeks. "No regrets. We certainly can't regret the man you've become. And that's on Mrs. V and Sam."

Aryan's heart swelled at the compliment. He owed his life to Nanu and Mamu, he was who he was because of them. But he owed something to his parents too.

He decided to shock Maggie's socks off. "I heard you say something about designs for the new hotel? I can take a look if you want. Take it off your hands."

She looked appropriately stunned for a minute and then she flung herself into his arms, shrieking loud enough to burst an eardrum. "You're the best!"

Aryan laughed and hugged her back. He was beginning to feel like Father Christmas.

"What's going on?" Nina stood behind them, arms

akimbo, in jeans and a black T-shirt. Didn't the girl wear any other color?

He greeted her with a smile and a, "Hey." She didn't smile back.

Maggie rose and went to Nina, but she was so overwhelmed with emotions that tears were rolling down her cheeks even as she hugged her daughter.

"What did you say to her?" Nina rounded on Aryan, tiny hands fisting.

"No! Oh, Nina, no. It's not what you think," Maggie said but Nina wasn't listening.

"You always make people cry. Asshole." She kicked him in the shin, hard.

Aryan winced at the sudden stab of pain running up his leg. "Jesus, kid."

"Nina! What are you doing?" Maggie reached for her daughter, but Nina slipped away and ran around the bench.

"Why do you come here? No one likes you. No one wants you here. Why don't you go back to Mumbai and die!"

Maggie's shocked, "Nina!" had no effect either. She tried to intervene again but Aryan shook his head. He'd hurt Nina too many times, she had a right to her anger. He went to her, ready to apologize but she kicked him again in the same spot and then ran off. "I hate you," she shouted over her shoulder.

"Oh dear." Maggie gaped after her daughter.

Aryan grinned. "I used to sport that look, right?" Angry, antagonistic, rebellious...*hurt*.

Maggie's lips twitched. "It does seem to be a family trait." In utter helplessness, she watched her daughter vanish into the back garden. "I should go after her. I need to explain."

Aryan took a deep breath and whooshed it out. "Let me go. I have a lot to make up to her."

Maggie's lips wobbled.

"Jesus. Don't start crying again."

"I won't. I promise."

Aryan started jogging towards the...what the hell was that? Pink grass?

"Did you mean it about working with the designer?" Maggie called after him.

He turned and nodded, then turned back and kept jogging.

"I'll be going to the office bright and early tomorrow. I'll see you there at nine?" she yelled.

Aryan gave a thumbs-up above his head without bothering to turn around. He was definitely filling Santa's shoes today and he was going to reach for the bloody happiness hat-trick.

CHAPTER 25

Alisha stifled a yawn and flipped the channel back to NDTV where another Indian politician was being accused of violent and predatory sexual practices. Watching gruesome news in bed had become her favorite pass time since sleep had become her enemy after returning from London three months ago.

Worry kept her up all night and sleep deprivation made her impossible to deal with during the day. Diya had warned her that if she didn't find some "sunshine" soon, someone was going to stab her. Alisha strongly suspected the "someone" was Diya.

Murderous intentions were on everyone's mind lately. She had her own set of stabbing, strangling and slashing scenarios playing and replaying in her head. She couldn't wait to get her hands on a certain someone with a British accent and act them all out—one by one, all together, repeatedly, and forever.

Aryan Rajaram Chawla was going to wish he'd never been born.

That is, if she ever got her hands on him again. The

bastard hadn't called her in three months—not a word, not a Scrabble game, not even a damned text message.

There went her sleep again. Alisha curled up under her blanket. This too had become part of the nightly ritual. She got herself worked up and the yawns vanished. Sleep should've come easily tonight. She'd had back-to-back meetings all day. She'd had no time to breathe or eat, much less think. She'd come home dog tired, and not even Vallima's magic head massage, her favorite comfort food of *idlis* and *mendu vadas*, followed by a long, hot bath had helped. She should've been in a coma by now and she wasn't. Damn that Wordfreak.

Her iPhone beeped, signaling a text message.

Are you awake, Miss Havisham?

Alisha didn't bother replying. Diya had started calling her Miss Havisham to fan the flames. She wasn't turning into the tragic bride of *Great Expectations*. First of all, she wasn't a bride mourning for a dead fiancé. Secondly, she was wearing a beige tank top and brown pajama bottoms, the absolute antithesis of bridal wear. Thirdly, she had a time limit on waiting for Aryan to grow up and that time limit was soon reaching its zenith. Fourthly… Her phone beeped again and Alisha had to stop herself from hurling it across the room. If Diya had sent her another mean little comment, she'd—

Fancy a game of Scrabble, Sunshine?

Alisha blinked. Checked and double checked the phone number. It wasn't Diya playing a joke. She sat up straight, her heart instantly blooming. "He's back, he's back, he's back," she sang.

Vivek, I love you! She texted back with an evil smile.

Don't be mean.

Three months, Aryan. You owe me three months.

Alisha switched on the bedside lamp. If they were going

to play games, it was going to be a long night. And she didn't care if she didn't sleep a wink.

I see mathematics is not your strong suit. It's been two and a half months.

Fine, you owe me two and a half months.

**blinking in confusion* You told me not to bother coming back until I had my head screwed on straight.*

A smile burst on her lips. *Is it screwed on straight now?*

Yes.

I'm very happy to read that.

Then as if her fingers had a will of their own they typed, *I missed you so bloody much, Wordfreak.*

Open the door, Sunshine.

Alisha frowned at her bedroom door. Was it a metaphor for something she wasn't getting?

What door?

Open your door!

Alisha sprang up from the bed. "Are you outside my room?"

"Yes," Aryan's wonderful, husky voice wafted in.

"How? I didn't hear the doorbell." She was utterly shocked and thoroughly elated. She wouldn't have to languish like Miss Havisham.

She rushed to the door, pausing briefly at the filigree-framed mirror. There was no way she was opening the door without checking her beauty quotient. Vanity had a time and a place and this was it.

"Vallima let me in. I called her this afternoon and explained the situation."

"Since when does she listen to you? What situation? And why the hell didn't you call me?" She brushed her hair. She felt electrified, like her whole body had powered up after months of being in energy conservation mode.

"Open the door, Sunshine. Are you going to make me wait for two and a half months?"

"Didn't I wait? Can't you wait for two and a half minutes?" She applied lip gloss and pinched her cheeks for color. There was no time for full make-up. Besides, it would look bizarre.

She opened the door.

There she was!

His Sunshine. His Alisha. All his. Only his.

She looked lovely—soft, mellow, radiant. A dazzling smile bowed her lush lips. Her hair cascaded around her heart-shaped face and fell over one bonny shoulder, covering her arm and breast. His eyes travelled to her other breast. She wore no bra. Aryan's mouth watered. Her tank top was made of washed cotton and exposed three tantalizing inches of her bare waist. He wanted to press his thumb against her navel, make her gasp. Later, he'd do that later.

She'd lost weight. Her hips were narrower, her legs seemed longer. Her toenails were the color of the inside of a peach. He loved peaches.

Inch by inch, his eyes coasted back up her body, until finally, they anchored on her face.

Chocolate brown eyes, drank him in. Like him, she was counting, cataloguing the changes two and a half months had wrought—the beard, the darker tan, the calluses on his palms.

Superficial changes were simple, visible. His hidden heart had undergone the biggest transformation. He no longer balked at the enormity of his feelings for her. He was no longer scared of losing himself in her. He welcomed the tsunami of emotions only she inspired and rejoiced in them.

She cupped his cheek and rubbed, his thick stubble making a rasping sound. He hadn't shaved in weeks. He'd been in an almighty hurry to get back to Mumbai from the farmhouse where he'd spent the last three weeks supervising the installation of seventy-five new roofs in the village.

Then he couldn't wait anymore. He grabbed her shoulders and crushed her to him. He was never letting her go. Not unless she said it.

"Never again. I refuse to miss you this badly ever again." She started crying.

"Shh. Sweetheart, hush. I'm here now," he murmured over and over, rocking them both.

"What...took you...so long?" she hiccupped against his shoulder.

He boosted her up, her legs and arms locking around him, and walked into her bedroom. It always smelled of apples and sunshine in there. He loved her room. He sat on the purple armchair and they adjusted to each other until she was curled up on his lap, her head pillowed on his shoulder. His right hand and her left interlaced.

"Long or short version?" he asked.

"Do you...*hic*...have anywhere...to go?"

Smiling, he ran his hand down her spine. He had nowhere to go anytime soon. He'd fulfilled all his obligations and completed most of the pressing tasks, work-wise, before coming to her.

"How is your father?"

"Doing well. He's back to his old bossy self. He's getting out of the house now."

She pressed a kiss to his neck. "And his speech?"

"Not great, but better."

"That's good." She toyed with the topmost button on his Polo, slid it open. "What about you? I mean the two of you?"

"We're also better. Splendid, in fact," he confessed, smiling against her forehead. Splendid enough that they were on their way to becoming the father-son team they'd been so many years ago.

He told her all that had happened in London after she left.

"I'm glad you worked it out. I'm happy for you…all of you."

Alisha drew back to look at Aryan. No more stormy eyes. Or the storm brewing in the obsidian depths wasn't one of anguish.

"Turns out I've been wrong about many things. I wasted a dozen years angry about the wrong things," he admitted ruefully.

"Men are foolish. Proven fact," she said. She wasn't one to *there-there* pat someone. Nor was she the type to spout nonsense like, "Life is nothing but a learning curve," even if it was.

"What made you think they were having an affair in the first place? Obviously no one else in your family thought that."

Aryan sighed against her cheek. "It was my grandmother's friend who put the idea in my head. One day, I came back from school and Nanu had some women over for tea. I overheard one of them ask after Maggie and my dad, and even as young as I was, I recognized the nasty, innuendo-filled way she asked it. I felt sick, wondering if it could be true. And because I was already angry, that's where I lay the blame." He remembered eavesdropping from the hallway, his back against the wall, his fist jammed into his mouth to keep from crying. He'd been mean to Nanu for days after until Mamu had boxed his ears.

"If you had cried out or asked her, she would've set you straight."

"Nanu didn't correct her friend. So I thought it must be true if she wasn't denying it or chucking the nasty woman out of the house for speaking filthy lies. But, now that I think about it, I never laid eyes on the woman again. Obviously,

Nanu boycotted her from the kitty parties." Aryan shook his head. "It was all a stupid mistake. There we were—the lot of us—with Nanu refusing to talk about Mum at all, my father messed up and in as much need of handling as I'd been, and me wondering what the hell I'd done wrong to be punished like that."

Alisha touched her forehead to Aryan's. "Promise me you'll always talk to me and not jump to conclusions. I don't want weird misunderstandings between us, ever. I have no patience for them."

Aryan smacked a kiss on her lips to seal the deal. "If you promise the same, Sunshine."

"Don't worry about me. I'm not one to bottle things up. Don't you know how much I love picking things apart? What about Nina? And Cassie and Millie?" She hoped he'd worked things out with his sisters too.

Aryan grinned and spread his arms out wide. "They think I am the handsomest, sexiest, most wonderful brother in the whole universe."

"They do not think you're sexy."

Aryan bit her earlobe. "Do you have to argue about everything?"

"I pointed out a fact. But yes, in the interest of truth, I would argue about everything."

He slanted a wicked, half-lidded look at her. "Bet you think I'm the handsomest, sexiest, most wonderful lover in the known universe?" The lower half of their bodies had been thrumming for a while.

Alisha pretended to ponder the question. "I used to. Two and a half months ago." The guy was just too cocky sometimes. He needed humbling.

He rotated his hips beneath her, making her crazy. "And now, Sunshine?"

She shrugged, but he clearly didn't believe her. And why

would he? Hadn't she welcomed him back with open arms and was even now perched on his lap like an infatuated puppy? She should've kicked his butt for making her wait and worry for months. She decided to zap some of his arrogance out, just so he wouldn't take her for granted.

"I don't think moving in together will work for us," she said, clenching her jaw tightly closed so she wouldn't start laughing and hiccupping.

His heart missed a beat. Hell, Aryan stopped breathing altogether. He'd left it too late. He should've come straight to her. He shouldn't have spent so much time on the limestone roofs he'd promised to install before the monsoons.

"I thought we agreed to move in together. Are you playing with me?"

"Playing with you? You mean getting back at you for behaving like a demented Neanderthal and rubbing my arms raw? Or for when you broke things off in London because you couldn't 'handle relationships?'" Her eyebrows shot up reproachfully.

Aryan swallowed. "I've apologized for all of it and I'll keep saying sorry until you believe me. I thought my feelings were my weakness. I thought if I rejected feeling everything, I'd be safe. Remain sane. I didn't believe I was strong enough to handle what I feel for you, Sunshine."

Alisha was dying to laugh. But not yet. She was having too much fun at his expense.

"You hurt me badly, Aryan. I have to think about this. I need some time to reevaluate…us." Someone give her a damned Filmfare award, she thought. She was giving the performance of a lifetime.

"Reevaluate us," he repeated slowly. "What does that mean? Are you reconsidering us entirely or just the moving in together?" *Moving in? Why don't you just ask her to marry you, you blethering idiot.* No, he couldn't do that now. He knew what her answer would be given the current conversation.

Alisha stood up and pretended to think hard, creating the proper melodramatic atmosphere. "Well, I was thinking that moving in is too," she paused, wrinkling her nose in distaste.

"Too what?"

"Easy." She stood above him, looking down into the black pools of his eyes. She'd fallen for his eyes first. Well, no, she'd fallen for his brain first, his amorphous, beautiful brain which lay somewhere behind his gorgeous eyes.

"I think we should get married. Make it all legal and binding and duly notarized and stamped and signed, complete with a prenuptial agreement which includes several children," she said in a rush.

She'd gobsmacked him. *Applause. Applause.*

"But what about your aversion to marriage? And the inevitability of divorce?"

Alisha flapped her hand in the air and took her seat on Aryan's lap again. "Aryan, if we've survived the last three months, I think we have a good shot at surviving forever."

His shoulders shook with mirth at her prim comment. "Very true, Sunshine."

"So? Will you marry me?" She wrapped her arms around him. "Will you be mine forever?"

"You had to steal my thunder, right? I suppose you'll go around telling everyone, including our grandkids, about how their Nanu popped the question to their Nana?" He kissed her tenderly. Thoroughly. God, he'd missed her.

"You know my feministic moves so well, Wordfreak," she said, between hungry kisses.

"I love you, Worddiva, Sunshine, Alisha. And yes, I will be honored to marry you. I'd love to be yours forever." He bent his head to her mouth again, and paused at the last minute, "On one condition."

Laughter tickled his throat when her chocolate brown eyes narrowed in suspicion. He couldn't let her have all the fun now, could he?

"What?"

"That our firstborn be named Scrabble."

EPILOGUE

That September...

Aryan Rajaram Chawla stood in front of a full-length floor mirror and admired the cut of his yellow and gold *sherwani*. The sudden blast of a *shehnai* made him peek out of the window at the bustle and movement going on below.

Uncle Sam stood in the courtyard, his arm around his very pregnant wife. They were talking to the wedding coordinators who'd promised Aryan the wedding Alisha had never wanted in her life.

He was getting married to his Sunshine today in his father's backyard. How was that for a twist in the game? Just a year ago, the mere thought of the Geargian manor would've brought on hives or a psychotic breakdown, and now it would be the backdrop for the biggest moment of his life.

Travelling was difficult for Dad, so the wedding had to be in London. Having the ceremony at the manor had been Alisha's idea. She seemed to have a thing for the pink grass.

Aryan smiled as he thought of his Sunshine. Then heaved a massive sigh.

They were fighting, again.

It was the pre-nup that had set her off this morning. He refused to sign the contract and she was adamant that he do so before the ceremony.

"It's for your protection, you stupid man. You have the obscenely fat bank account," she'd yelled at him in front of both their families at breakfast. Dad and Uncle Sam had nearly fallen off their chairs, they'd laughed so hard.

"Sunshine, the only way we're ever separating is when I'm dead," he'd said and had calmly continued to eat his eggs.

She'd been speechless for about a second. "Stupid, silly man, that's just sappy nonsense."

It was the absolute truth.

A knock at the door brought him back to the present. "Come in," he said and resumed putting the final touches on his outfit.

Krish Menon strode in. Aryan liked Sunshine's brother a lot. Tall and wiry, the older man had his mother's broad and severe face. But the austerity belied a wicked sense of humor.

"Ready to take on my *sahodari*?" he asked. A Malayalam term for sister, Aryan had recently found out.

The man looked decidedly uncomfortable in his white-gold *sherwani* and red turban. Like his sister, Krish Menon didn't care much for haute couture.

"You have my back, right man?" Aryan clapped Krish on the shoulder.

"Brother of the bride. She has dibs. The sacred bonds of *raksha bandhan* and all. You know what I mean, *aliyan*, since you have three of your own."

Krish had taken to calling him *aliyan*, which meant brother-in-law in their mother tongue.

"If you're ready, the turban guy wants to come in and fix your turban. Harry and Mann are getting theirs done right now. And we have to head down in forty-five minutes. Nervous?" Krish asked.

"Not at all," Aryan answered truthfully. He was getting impatient. "How is she?"

"Beautiful. But no, she's not nervous either. She's too angry to be nervous. It's pissing her off that you won't sign the pre-nup."

Aryan picked up his Patek Phillipe watch—a wedding gift from Nanu—and put it on, adjusting the cuffs of the linen short he wore under his *sherwani* around it. Besides the watch, Nanu had insisted he wear a pearl and ruby necklace for the occasion. He felt a bit silly for wearing jewelry but had to admit it contrasted well with the golden yellow hues of his outfit. He'd foregone his cologne as he already smelled strongly of henna. He'd had Alisha's name tattooed on his right palm yesterday.

He looked at his near brother-in-law in the mirror. "What would you do?"

"I'm more practical than romantic. I'd sign," Krish replied.

"She can't always get her way."

"And you choose to teach her that lesson today?" Krish laughed.

Then both men turned as another knock sounded at the door.

Diya poked her head in and grinned at Aryan, but froze when she saw Krish. Krish's face took on a similar deer-in-headlights expression. Aryan kept his face carefully blank as he watched the two of them. Alisha had told him they had a weird love-hate history and this confirmed it.

Diya sashayed into the room. Oh, his new brother-in-law was in trouble now.

"Hello gorgeous." Aryan pulled Diya in for a hug and kissed both her cheeks.

"I do look gorgeous. You like this hair? It's big, right? And Leesha's hairdo is brilliant. It made me weep. Our irritated bride looks ah-mazing. I'm so jealous," Diya pouted prettily.

Aryan tapped her on the nose. "Your turn will come soon. Mann should be proposing soon." It was a huge lie but to see Krish scowl was worth the sin.

"Really? I'm positively giddy with excitement." Playing her part, Diya fanned herself with an envelope as if overcome with nerves. "Oh, this is for you" She thrust the envelope in his hands. "Leesha said to read it NOW. Yes, with capital letters. Okay, boys, I'm off to greet the guests with Uncle Sam and Neeta. Wish you the best, Aryan. I know you'll be madly happy as will my BFF. Oh God! I can't cry yet, my make-up isn't waterproof." She hugged him hard and ran out of the room, taking her sparkling energy with her.

Krish cleared his throat. "I'll, uh, leave you to read that," he said and rushed out after Diya.

Aryan laughed. Another one bites the dust. Then his grin faded as he turned over the envelope in his hands. If it contained the stupid pre-nup, he was going to burn the damn thing.

It didn't. Aryan pulled out a card and started laughing when he turned it over.

A naked, dimple-faced baby boy sat in the middle of a checkered board, red lips puckered. Piles and piles of Scrabble tiles tumbled around him. A thinking cloud next to his head read, *I'm Scrabbulous!*

His bride-to-be had written only four words inside. All caps.

IT'S YOUR MOVE, WORDFREAK!

~

**Sign up for Falguni Kothari's newsletter and download
Scrabbulous Impressions,
a prequel scene to *It's Your Move Wordfreak!* here:
falgunikothari.com/newsletter**

ACKNOWLEDGMENTS

A roaring thank you to the Pillars of my Earth, my sounding boards, Trupti, Sejal, Usha, Lisa and Sharon. I wouldn't have had the courage to seek publication of this story if not for you.

To Mrs. Onden, immense gratitude for introducing me to the wonderland of words in fourth grade. You saw a storyteller in me even when I didn't.

This book was first published by Rupa Publications, India, and I will always be grateful to them for taking a chance on a debut author.

Lastly, Dear Readers, thank you for joining me on my storytelling adventures and for all the lovely messages you send to my inbox. I love hearing from you.

Love and hugs, always.
Falguni

ABOUT THE AUTHOR

Falguni Kothari is a *USA Today* bestselling author of "messy love stories" and kick-ass fantasy tales that are a "good choice for women's fiction book groups." Her novels are all flavored by her South Asian heritage and expat experiences, and delve into common, yet unconventional, themes of marriage, romance, friendship, family and parenthood. Her books have been reviewed and praised in a number of podcasts and publications, including *The New York Times Book Review*, starred reviews in *Booklist* and *Shelf Awareness*, *Popsugar*, *Woman's World* magazine and *The Times of India*. Her essays and short stories have been published in *Femina* (India), *Better Homes and Gardens*, *Book Riot* and *Writer's Digest*.

She is also an award-winning Indian Classical, Latin and Ballroom dancer, practices karaoke in her downtime, is an empty-nester, and loathes flying and deadlines.

Find her online at www.FalguniKothari.com where you can sign up for her newsletter for the latest updates and two free short stories.

www.ingramcontent.com/pod-product-compliance
Lightning Source LLC
Chambersburg PA
CBHW051636180726

48284CB00006B/1749